Under a
Greek
Sky

Under a Greek Sky

Francesca Catlow

LAKE UNION

PUBLISHING

Text copyright © 2025 by Francesca Catlow
All rights reserved.

Published by Lake Union Publishing, Seattle

www.apub.com

Amazon, the Amazon logo, and Lake Union Publishing are trademarks of Amazon.com, Inc., or its affiliates.

EU Product Safety contact:
Amazon Publishing, Amazon Media EU S.à r.l.
38, avenue John F. Kennedy, L-1855 Luxembourg
amazonpublishing-gpsr@amazon.com

ISBN-13: 9781662526299
eISBN: 9781662526282

Cover design by Emma Rogers
Cover image: © f9photos / Alamy Stock Photo; © freedomnaruk © vovan
© Kriengsuk Prasroetsun © nunawwoofy © Zigres © Anneleven Stock
© Svetlana Ryajentseva © ForestDigital © Nature Peaceful / Shutterstock

Printed in the United States of America

I dedicate this book to anyone who has ever rated or reviewed one of my books. Good or bad, you've been a bigger part of my journey than you could ever understand. Thank you for changing my life for the better.

Prologue

I feel like a used-up butterfly, with tatty edges.

If I had wings, they would be battered beyond repair, with frayed tips leaving dust on everything they touched, but at least I'd be able to fly away.

As it is, I don't have wings, I have family problems.

I guess I really thought, for a moment there, that I *did* have wings. I really believed I *could* fly and that I *could* have it all.

What goes up must come down. After today, I feel like I've crashed down and hit my head on concrete. My eyes burn and the skin underneath them feels raw.

My heart feels scorched with the pain only a child can feel, even though I'm fully grown. It's as though I've lost my footing on a ledge. I was momentarily suspended before suddenly dropping, falling, making my stomach lurch and churn.

Nothing makes sense now.

My grounding has gone, and my belief system has run away. I wonder if this is how other people feel when they find out their parents aren't together anymore. Or is it reserved for those of us who truly believed their parents were perfect, right up until the point we were told they're not?

Maybe some people feel relief, maybe even joy. There's part of me that's felt paralysed with shock since this morning.

My key slides in our door and all I want is to curl up next to Jonah and for him to tell me he loves me, and that my parents love me, and that I'm not losing anyone. His hand on my knee or his arm around my shoulders. That will be enough to keep the tears from starting up again.

What I really need is for him to tell me that they'll both be at our wedding and that they won't fight or cause a scene.

If Dad wants to bring this woman he's off with, I have no idea what I'll do. I can't even handle the idea of him being with someone other than Mum, let alone him bringing someone else to our wedding.

Would she be in all the photos? What does she even look like?

I don't want her there, whoever she is, and if he can't handle that, then I don't want him at the wedding either.

The house is dark as I slip in through the barely open door. A muddle of shapes and shadows. I quickly close it behind me, the way I always do.

'I'm home,' I call into the abyss.

It's never normally this dark. Normally there's a lamp, the TV, something.

I slide my hand over the smooth surface of the wall, searching for the light switch.

The only message I've had from Jonah today was a quick *I love you, be safe xx* and nothing more. I didn't want to tell him about my dreadful day via text. A day that should've been spent looking at dresses, instead spent finding out that one of my parents is out of the country with someone else and the other wants to leave England for good.

I stand in the dark for a moment to catch my breath. Thoughts drag their heels around my mind. How can any of this be real?

I hit the switch, making the bulb burst into life with a click, leaving me squinting.

A gasp fills the hall.

My gasp.

My shock.

Everything's been turned over.

I dash about calling for Jonah, with no answer. I trip over a broken vase that's shattered over the floor.

It doesn't slow me down. When he isn't in the living room, I skid along and up the stairs to our bedroom. Fear explodes in my chest like TNT.

Everything of value is gone.

The TV, my laptop . . . Jonah.

The bed looks much the same as when I left. The same crumpled mess, but he isn't there, filling it. His messy hair isn't peeping above the sheets.

But it's not empty.

An envelope rests there on my pillow, with *Lorena* written on the front.

Chapter One

'We can't stay here. No way.' Serena spins to gawp at us. Her mouth wide and her eyes bulging, exaggerated by the thick layers of mascara.

'Don't be a princess, Serena.' Mum moves around the space as though it's full of furniture instead of echoing with every step.

I want to agree with Mum. I want to tell my sister she's exaggerating, and that she really *is* being a princess, as usual . . . but I can't. Not that I'll side with Serena either, Mum doesn't need that right now, but I don't think she's being a princess. Not this time.

This house isn't what I expected when Mum invited us to live in Corfu, where she grew up. Even when she said we could fix up an old beach house her parents left her in their will years ago, this isn't how I thought it would be.

In my imagination, we would be jetting off to something from a postcard. Those ones where all the buildings are crisp white with bright-blue doors, and pretty pink flowers line them, or olive trees sprout up here and there. That's what the beach house would look like, but maybe a little overgrown, waiting for us to turn up and show it some affection. That maybe some shutters would need screwing in a little tighter and weeds would need to be pulled up and then we would be living in luxury by the sea.

It was meant to be sunsets and fresh fish for dinner, lying back and healing in the sun.

This is nothing like how I thought it would be. The beach house is half finished and falling apart from being left for so long. The door into the kitchen is sagging and the floor is so filthy it looks as though half the beach has been dragged in.

It has a roof. A structure. Walls. That's an advantage over the places that have the rebar sticking out at all angles. That's something to be positive about, I suppose.

But then, if it was all perfect here, surely Mum would have brought us to Corfu years ago. With her parents gone, she always made out like there was nothing here for us. Until now, that is. Now she needs change.

'Seriously, Mum, you said we would have this place liveable in no time. If this is where you were living when you were last here, no wonder you never came back . . .' Serena's voice trails off as she slowly spins in the centre of the expanse.

'This is not where I lived.'

'Where then?' Serena stops spinning to address my mum again, her arms crossing over her chest. 'I still can't get over you inheriting a place by the beach and never mentioning it before.'

'It didn't matter before—'

'And now it does?' I cut in.

'*Now* is the right time. We needed a place to stay, and here it is.'

It's tempting to point out that we could've stayed at home in England, but I can understand why she's decided to run away instead, rather than face Dad. Mum continues, 'It'll be fine. We will find people to help. I know it. Tomorrow, I will take you to meet some people.' Mum takes a few steps and runs her finger through a thick layer of grime on a windowsill, then adds under her breath, 'I'm sure they will help us.'

Mum lets out a deep breath and mumbles as she rubs away the dirt between her fingers.

Mum and Serena have discarded their bags and suitcases, their eyes flicking from one empty corner to the next, leaving me gripping the handle of my cases by the door. I'm not sure I'm able to move yet. Even though there's nothing here, it's all too much to take in.

The entrance must also be the living room, as there's a chimney breast to the left of the room and it's a reasonably good size too.

No one's even bothered to shut the front door. Outside, our front garden is made up of wiry grasses that look like lightning strikes where they've been scorched by the sun. The grass looks how I feel. Dried up in its prime.

It's not just my soul that feels that way; my lips feel dry from the plane. My skin feels tight, like it's trying to shrink and squish me down. It felt that way before the plane. It's felt that way for days.

I need to move again, standing still is the worst. It leaves me feeling open to my own thoughts.

'Where shall I put my cases? Upstairs?' I tip my head towards the wooden steps trailing up the right-hand wall.

'Yes, Lorena *mou*. The bedrooms are upstairs, let's hope it's better up there.' Mum shoots me a smile, but it doesn't carry up to her eyes.

The wheels of my cases rattle along the worn wooden floor and the grit of sand and dirt. I struggle for a moment, trying to take both cases up the stairs simultaneously as my mum and sister move into the next room, away from the expanse of the open entrance.

Everything I own now fits into four large suitcases.

Two are here with me, and two I left in England, stuffed with childhood things and some photos that I don't want to look at.

That's all I could bear to hold on to from my old life. The life that took years to build and moments to pull apart.

With Jonah in the wind, everything we had purchased together, or anything that remotely reminded me of him, or anything he had even touched, I didn't want to see again. So I did a car boot sale to cleanse myself of our life together.

Not that he left anything of value when he disappeared.

I managed to scrape back two hundred pounds of the thousands he took from our joint account. It wasn't even enough to cover the taxi to the airport or the flight out here.

I leave one case behind and heave the other one beside me, grinding and banging on each step as I go. As soon as I get to the landing, my heart plummets all over again.

Up here is no better than downstairs. Nothing's been finished. The landing's filled with unpainted doors and plasterboard walls and the floor is more sand than wood.

I swing open the first door. Behind it there's a room with a loo and a sink. That'll be fun to tell Mum and Serena, there's not even a shower or a bath yet.

A toolbox with tools scattered about decorates the floor. It reminds me of Pompeii, where everyone stopped what they were doing and ran away from the clouds of ash. Someone was working here, then everything stopped. It all ended.

My grandfather, I guess. It must be his old toolbox that was left here. It must have been him hard at work, only to leave and pass away before he got to finish what he was doing. All Mum told me was that he died peacefully.

It feels odd to step into the world of someone I've never met and see a dusty snapshot of their past. It's like seeing a ghost but without feeling afraid, only a little resentful that they won't talk back.

Abandoning my own case, I twist the tap. The piping moans but, to my relief, water coughs out.

I turn it back off with a squeak before briefly touching the tools, feeling the weight of a spanner in my hand.

My grandfather held this in his hand. It's the closest I've ever been to him.

I wish I could've met him. At least it's nice to be in the place where he spent his life. I've always assumed it was too painful for Mum to come to Corfu with no one left here for her, no parents to greet her on arrival. It's the one thing I could understand. But now, with Dad off with someone else, I can understand wanting to come home to start all over again.

I place the spanner back in the toolbox, along with the other items that have been accumulating dust for the past few decades. I don't want them to upset Mum further when she's doing so well to hold her head up.

In my whole life she's barely ever spoken of her parents. I've never tried too hard to push the matter and I've only ever seen one photograph of them. One where they're both laughing, arms wrapped around each other. Mum told me it was from Easter when she was a young girl.

Leaving the room slightly neater than it was when I found it, I investigate the first of the three bedrooms, the one next to the bathroom. There's no bed, but it's cleaner than the hall and it looks more finished too, with all the walls already plastered.

It's stuffy though, with the shutters open but the window shut. I lean in to peer out towards the road and over to a sweeping villa that looks ready for a romantic getaway. It's all white, with pink flowers. Just the sort of place I was hoping Jonah and me would go to on our honeymoon.

I push the thought of what was meant to be to the back of my mind and close the door to the room behind me.

The air in there is so hot it feels like it's burning my nostrils with every inhale, making my lungs want to collapse. To step back on to the landing is a relief by comparison.

The room opposite is bigger and has space for an en suite but not even a sink inside yet. The shutters are closed, making it cooler than the first room. I slip out and make my way to the last room, back towards the staircase.

I walk in, and I see it, what I've longed to see.

There in the third room, I feel like Goldilocks: this is my *just right*.

It's not as big as the second bedroom, or as finished as the first, but none of this is what matters or what catches the breath in my chest.

A view out across the rolling white-gold sand and the glittering azure. It's the first thing to really lift me in days.

A few weeks ago I was filled to the brim with excitement, saying goodbye to all my lovely colleagues to start my own company, only to have it all snatched away by the one person I trusted the most.

Everything has been grey from that moment to this.

Somehow, this view manages to remind me the world is a big open expanse and I'm only a small part of it. I'm just a grain of sand rubbing shoulders with everyone else.

I have to have this view.

'Shotgun,' I holler over my shoulder.

There's no going back now. I can't let the past week be what defines the rest of my life. Jilted and robbed before even making it to the altar.

No.

I have to find a way back to something of my own, and it starts here, with this room.

Chapter Two

Somewhere below me, Serena yells something back to my declaration of *shotgun* with underlying irritation. She knows I'd only bother calling out if it was something special.

And it is. It really, truly is.

Golden sand stretches not far below my window, out towards the undulating turquoise cloth that is the sea. The sun throws glitter down on to the cloth, forcing me to squint, even though I want to keep my eyes wide open to take all of it in.

Stepping forward, I press my hand to the glass as though I might be able to touch it, and all the grains of sand would run through my fingers.

For the first time since opening that dreadful letter from Jonah, my heart manages to pull itself out of the dark hole it's been living in as I peek out into the shimmering allure of the sea.

'Great. So I'm guessing Mama gets the big room, you get the view, and what do I get? The bathroom?' Serena huffs somewhere behind me.

I don't even turn to look at her. I've seen this exhale a thousand times before. It's scorched into my mind from all the times she's believed I've somehow got something she hasn't. The pout of her bottom lip and her fingers digging into her hips. If she added in stamping her foot, she'd still look three years old each time she does it.

A niggling part of me wants to say, *yes, all that's left is the bathroom.*

Instead, I tell her the truth.

'There is no bathroom. Not up here, anyway.'

Her feet pad across the rooms until she abruptly stops.

I guess she's found the room with only a toilet and sink.

'Mum!' Serena screams from the top of the stairs. 'Where the hell are we going to wash? There's no bath or shower!'

'The sea,' I call back to her.

I bite back a rare smile at the thought of making steam puff from Serena's ears.

'Lorena, that's not funny,' she growls, before thumping back down the stairs.

I shouldn't be so hard on her. She's actually been amazing with everything that's happened. After initially throwing her toys out of the pram about Mum and Dad's break-up, she put them back neater than they were before, knowing we needed her. Quietly storing away her thoughts until the next outburst. That's just her way. It's been the same since she really *did* throw things out of her pram. As soon as she could talk and walk, she wanted to sort out her own problems, crying, *I can do it myself.* She likes to be the boss of everyone around her while she's there too.

It doesn't bother me. We might not be all that much alike, but I know no matter what, I can always count on her to hold me up when my legs give way, and she can always count on me to do the same for her.

I turn my back on the view that bubbles with life and face my empty reality.

We need mattresses, even inflatable ones. Anything. There's no way I'm sleeping on dirty floorboards.

My rough lips rub together and I close my eyes in thought.

I don't have a choice.

I don't have the money for a hotel, or to buy anything new. I'll have to rely on whatever Mum and Serena suggest. I've worked so hard for years to be left with nothing, relying on the generosity of my mum.

I shouldn't be here.

It's a Saturday. I should be trying on wedding dresses all day. Twirling around until they splay out, stepping up on a pedestal to show off the train, giggling over glasses of champagne.

It wasn't meant to be.

Nothing I'd planned was meant to be.

A horrid gummy feeling makes my insides feel like they're sticking together. They've felt this way on and off since it happened. Since I found out everything in my life was a lie.

'Stop it, Lorena.' Even though Serena's voice has lost its edge, I still jump hearing it back in my room. I didn't hear her creeping up the stairs. She doesn't sound harsh or mean in the way she's been talking about the house or about me getting the view . . . It's the opposite.

It's like her voice has transformed into a soothing blanket on a cold day, there to offer me something I don't have. Something I don't know if I'm capable of having anymore.

'I know.' I open my eyes and wish I hadn't. 'I wasn't *trying* to think about him.'

Her dark-green eyes are filled with sorrow, and I hate knowing my pain is part of the reason for it. I know I'm only part. But even being a percentage hurts. She's my little sister, I should be protecting her, not the other way around.

Dad is a big reason for her overreaction and sensitivity. She was always closer to him, and I've always been closer to Mum. She's barely spoken to him since he left for Mexico with some

13

other woman, leaving Mum to tell us about it. Not only could she always wrap Dad around her little finger, but they shared in things together, things Mum and I just weren't interested in like watching tennis or talking about sports cars. I'm pretty sure Serena only really likes them for the way they look, but she learnt a lot about them to connect with Dad, and now he's gone without so much as a phone call.

Even when life all seems to be planned out, with engagements and family dinners, I control nothing. I don't really know anyone, not even my own mum and dad. Not even about where I'll be living. Nothing is how I imagined it would be, and everyone's been hiding something. Mum has been hiding this house from us and she certainly didn't lead me to think it would be anything like this when she did decide we were suddenly allowed to know about the place. She won't even talk about what's more than one step ahead of us.

Up until recently I guess I've seen my life a little like an equation, with one step logically leading to the next; the problem is, I was never given all the data. I've never been in possession of all the facts. Since Jonah left, I have no idea where the next step will take me.

'I've got an idea.' Serena steps towards me, stretching her arms out to pull me into her shoulder. 'I could blow out your hair, and style it for you, then we could find a nice place to eat. The whole village is packed with tavernas.'

She tugs at the longer strands of my chestnut hair, which reach between my shoulder blades.

'Really? So I'll wash my hair in the sea, then what? How are you going to dry it?'

'All the plugs work. Mum was right, there's only a few things to do.'

'When did you become the optimist?'

'Since I saw that face of yours sag.'

'Cheek!'

'Not *saggy*.' She squeezes me a little tighter. 'You know what I mean.'

'We don't even have beds.'

'I'll find us something, you know what I'm like. I can use my glittering charm to get us anything we need.'

I groan as she squeezes me tighter than before, knowing that she's probably right. When she puts her mind to it, there's not much she can't do.

'It's going to be OK,' she coos as she rests her head on my shoulder. 'Everything happens for a reason.'

'It's good to see you two getting along.' Mum leans on the door-frame, folding her arms as she observes us.

Serena releases me and twists to face her.

The light in the room is starting to glow red and orange. It's not enough to cast a glow on Mum's complexion, though. She still looks a little grey around the edges.

She's lost weight she didn't need to lose, and her skin reminds me of delicate cream tissue paper. I'd always seen her as the queen of olive skin, but now . . . now she's more like a ghost that haunts my mum than her usual self.

Together, the three of us are propping each other up.

I'm glad that triangles are the strongest shape. We need all the strength we can get.

'We need to go out, get drinks.' Mum tucks a strand of black hair that's escaped from her claw clip behind her ear.

'We were going to get ready—' Serena begins.

'No. We need to get out of here and drink until we don't mind sleeping on those sun loungers out there.' Mum points towards the window before placing her hands firmly on her hips.

I've never seen my mum like this. She exits without another word, leaving Serena and I giving each other sidelong glances.

Chapter Three

Mum walks two steps ahead of us, studying everything in the same way a baby looks at the world. As though she's never seen anything quite like it before.

We pass taverna after taverna. Some with chic cocktail lists and elegant furnishings, others that look like they might have been unchanged for years. The warm evening air is filled with the scent of fresh herbs and ovens crammed with native delights.

Each taverna brims with tables circled by happy people of all ages, here to enjoy their holidays. I can't even begin to relate to their smiles. And from the look I catch on my mum's face as she turns to gawp at yet another taverna as though she's lived in a cave her whole life, she can't relate to them either.

'Didn't you say you grew up round here or something? Where's good to go?' Serena crosses her toned arms and leans forward, upping her pace to catch Mum's eye as we march.

'I did spend many days here by the beach, but then . . .' She lifts her arms only for them to slap back down by her sides. 'It looked nothing like this. I hardly recognise any of it. I left here in the late nineties, it was less than half this size. I remember when there was a donkey living in a field over there and the road here was made of dust and sand, not tarmac.'

Mum looks mildly distraught, riddled with confusion.

'Where did you go back then?' I do my best to use a soothing tone, because Mum looks one step away from screaming.

Mum stops in the road like a rock forcing a river to move round it, and a few family groups have to move further into the road to carry on towards their chosen eateries.

She brings up a finger as though it's a light bulb of thought. 'The Waves. It has to still be here.' She turns on her heels and heads back the way we came.

Serena glances at me and shrugs as we both do our best to keep up.

Even Serena, who always has something to say about everything, has found times to be quiet in response to Mum lately. Neither of us quite know how to behave or where we fit in the world.

Serena was all too happy to drop all of nothing and come to Corfu. She's a virtual assistant, so all she was giving up was a room in a house where she was renting. I still appreciate her being here with us, even if it was an easy decision for her.

At fourteen, she announced that she wanted to be a virtual assistant, because all she really wanted to do was be free. Serena is also a small-scale influencer on TikTok, posting videos of her travels and her luxury lifestyle. It gets her some free stuff and sometimes strangers gift her money just for being her.

Up until I quit my job as a cosmetic scientist, she was also kept in the know about what luxury cosmetic brands were launching next. Not now though. Now, I have nothing to offer anyone.

Jobless and homeless, relying on my mum to put a roof over my head, albeit a slightly shabby one. At least the location is beautiful with the endless places to eat, a scattering of interesting-looking shops and golden sands. I suppose that's what's important: location, location, location.

'Do you think we should ask where she's going?' Serena's ponytail whips my ear as she leans in close to me.

17

'We already know where we're going.'

'Do we?' Her top lips curls over her whisper.

'Yeah. *The Waves*.' I point to a white sign with blue writing swirled on it, directing us towards the sea and, I guess, a taverna called 'The Waves' or '*Ta Kymata*', according to the sign.

The road slopes down to the beach, increasing our speed with each step. This is the same view as I have from my window, down to the strip of golden sand and the blazing red setting sun beyond.

Where the road turns to beach, there's a taverna that kisses the edge of the sand with its terrace. No wonder it's called The Waves – there are only a few rows of sunbeds and parasols then a stone's throw to the throb of the sea.

A young man welcomes us and Mum goes straight into Greek, asking for a table for three and a carafe of white wine. When she speaks English, she's lost most of her accent, making it surprising to those who don't know her when she speaks Greek so fluently.

God, I wish I could do that.

I can understand what my mum says, but it's harder when I listen to anyone else. It's like my brain stops working properly for everyone but her. Like everyone else is going a little bit too quickly. Maybe that's it. Maybe if they all slowed down, I'd be able to take it in. I can answer Mum in English but it's as though the Greek part of me is always listening, locked away deep in my brain, tied up and gagged, so I'm unable to answer anyone with my Greek tongue.

It's unsurprising, I suppose, as Mum spent my whole life hiding all this from me, that my Greek half hides away too. A flicker of anger burns in my chest. I do my best not to throw fuel on the fire. It's not Mum's fault I'm emotional right now.

Losing her parents really must've hurt. I need to remember that.

Grief does strange things to people. Maybe it paralysed her, breaking her so deeply it took Dad leaving to push her back into the warm arms of Corfu. I should try to give her space to open up to us. Now we're here, hopefully we'll find out more about her life when she was young.

We settle at a square table with a paper cloth showcasing a map of Corfu. Mum traces the lines of the island with her finger. She hasn't said she's missed being here, but how could she not? I've only taken a minibus full of suitcases and a short stroll since arriving and I can imagine it would be a wonderful place to grow up. One I don't think I'd want to leave.

One more step and I'd be on the sand. I'm tempted to kick off my flip-flops and take that step. To let it engulf me in its warmth. If I do it now, I might let the sand eat me up completely and stay there hidden forever.

'Why is it you two get the view and I get to look at tables and wall?' Serena pulls her chair in with an unnecessary aggression.

Mum leans in. 'Because I don't want to be seen. That young man doesn't know me.' She tilts her head sharply towards the double doors the waiter disappeared through. 'Others might, and I'm not ready for a big conversation with anyone yet. I need to see . . . someone tomorrow. I need to talk to someone else first.'

Serena's lips loosen out of their golden pout. I have no idea how she does it, how she can go from off the plane to as appealing as a glazed doughnut in seconds, but she manages it every time. I've always enjoyed cosmetics, but I could never do a turnaround as quickly as she can.

The waiter comes back with menus, quickly followed by the carafe of wine Mum ordered on the way in and three glasses.

'Who do you need to talk to?' Serena interjects without looking away from her phone as she takes a selfie with parasols and the setting sun as her backdrop.

I watch Mum from behind my menu. It's the perfect shield.

Mum's eyes flick over the menu before she slaps it down to the table, snatching up a breath.

'You have an uncle. Spiros. I need to speak to your Uncle Spiros. It's only fair he is the first to know we are here. I have wanted to tell you both about him but . . . it's been hard to find the right time. The right words. But, well, now you know.'

Serena lowers her phone and gawps from me to Mum.

It feels as though the air has been snatched from my lungs and my fingers have gone numb. I'd always believed my mum to be an only child. She's never said anything that's led me to believe otherwise.

'You have a brother?' I lean towards her and press my menu down next to hers.

'Yes.'

'Here?' Serena adds, pointing at the table.

'Yes.'

'In Corfu?' I join in.

'Lorena, you're meant to be the sensible one.' Mum shakes her head. 'Of course here, this is where we were born.'

'Hey,' Serena squawks, 'I'm the only one here with a job, why am I not the sensible one?' She looks genuinely hurt, even though I'm the one with the chemistry degree and it's not my fault I have nothing left after working hard all these years. I didn't choose to get robbed.

'I suppose it would be good for you both to know some things before you meet him tomorrow—'

'Like why you two never talk? And why we had no idea of his existence? Does he even know about us?' Serena exchanges her phone for the carafe of wine, filling all our glasses almost to the brim. 'This sounds like one of those dreadful TikTok rants people do. I can't believe my life is now one of those dramatic stories.' She slouches back in her chair, absorbed in her wine and her own take on this drama.

'What on earth are you talking about?' Mum shakes her head.

'You know? Those videos where people tell big stories about the crazy things in their lives. People love to share this sort of thing.' Serena keeps both eyebrows up, waiting for Mum to acknowledge her understanding.

She doesn't; instead, she screws her face up with irritation. 'It's not *your* story, it was never about you, Serena. Not everything is. We had a falling-out, that is all you need to know. I left when I was younger than both of you to live in England, you know that. Spiros has a life here. He looked after our parents until recently and I've seen online he does tours of our . . . his,' she corrects, 'olive groves now. He inherited the olive trees, and I was gifted the land by the beach. It's tradition. The boys are given the money, and girls the worthless land by the sea.' Mum's mouth slides into a half-smile as she turns her face towards the sea. The fading light glints off her sunglasses.

It's not always the case anymore, that the olives are the more lucrative land. Not since the boom in tourism. I'm sure the irony isn't lost on any of the wealthy women who run businesses by the beach.

'He was always the good boy. I was the young one . . . the rebel.'

I glance at Serena, tilting her head, now taking an interest in Mum's reverie of memories.

'Spiros likes to work hard and laugh loud.' Mum lets out a deep exhale and removes her glasses, carefully folding and placing them on top of her closed menu. 'He'll be good at these tours, he was always good at entertaining people, telling them a tale. Let's hope he welcomes us tomorrow. I've booked us all on to one of the tours, tomorrow at nine. So, don't go drinking too much wine.'

'I thought you said we should drink until we can sleep on those loungers,' Serena huffs.

'Recently,' I mumble as I mull over Mum's words. 'He was looking after your parents, our grandparents, *up until recently*? I thought they passed away before I was born?'

Mum looks out to sea and her fingers tap and twitch on the table before she looks down at her lap.

'I suppose that is what I've led you both to believe, isn't it. Well . . . no. They passed away only a few years ago now.'

'We had grandparents here we could've known and you didn't bother to tell us?' Serena's voice is dripping with incredulity, expressing exactly how I feel. 'Seems like Spiros isn't the only one good at telling a tale, is he, Mum?'

'I had my reasons, Serena, ones you can't understand. Tomorrow you will meet Spiros and you will hopefully gain an uncle.'

'Wait, hold on.' I begin to shake my head, as though the action might shake loose my thoughts. 'Spiros? As in the boy you told us stories about when we were growing up? That kid in the stories was your brother? So I guess the little girl was you? The one you called Mou?'

Her lips press together as though she's making sure her lipstick has been evenly spread. 'Mou means me or mine, remember.'

All our bedtime stories would begin with *There once was a little boy named Spiros and a little girl named Mou . . .* They would go on unbelievable adventures and have crazy antics, from getting stuck high up in olive trees to trying to captain a homemade raft out to sea.

'Yes. All those tales of running through the olive groves together were true. They were things we used to do as children. It was my way of sharing my childhood with you.'

'True!' The word bursts from my lips.

Yesterday, these stories were as real as dragons. I can't believe all her tales were rooted in reality. That the characters have lives that have carried on after the stories ended.

'You're Mou?' I breathe. 'What about when someone gave Spiros a giant bullet they found left from the war? Was that true? Did he really take it apart and blow up a gate?'

'Yes. We used to get ourselves into all sorts of trouble when we were kids.'

The idea that Spiros and his little friend Mou were actually Mum and her brother is somehow inconceivable. All of this is inconceivable.

'I can't believe those children in my head are real. Does he know we're coming?' I glance between my mum and my sister.

Mum shakes her head. 'No, no. I put it under my first name only. I don't think even he will suspect from just *Thalia* after all these years with no contact.'

I can't imagine not speaking to Serena for a week; even when she gets on my last nerve, she's still my little sister. Our shared past binds us together, compressing us into something no one else can truly be a part of. The way the pressure of time turns sediment into stone.

What happened here that was so bad, Mum felt she should lie to us all our lives? I thought it was bad enough not telling us about the house she inherited, but this? My whole life, my whole upbringing, has been riddled with lies. Lately, everything seems like it's a creeping ivy of fiction, trying to pull me apart. First Dad and his cheating, then Jonah, now this.

'Tomorrow,' Mum continues, as though she hasn't just dropped bombs on us, 'you will meet him and you can make up your own minds about him.'

For a moment, we all sit in a bubble of silence that's filled with the chatter of strangers around us and the sea's gentle hum.

'I know this must be a surprise to you both—'

'You don't say,' Serena interrupts.

'—but I had a whole life before you were born and it's impossible as a parent to pass on every detail. I want us to move forward now, not stare into a past that will never change and can only be seen by the distorted memories of ageing minds.' Mum raises her glass and, with a shaky hand, I lift mine too. 'To new beginnings.' Our glasses clink together. Mum drinks deeply into her glass.

I can feel Serena's wide green eyes on me as I sip the cooling white wine.

We have an uncle we don't even know. For some reason, Mum has been hiding him from us all our lives. Maybe because he might tell us the real reason she left here. If she didn't leave because her parents passed away, which is what I had always been led to believe, then why didn't she visit them?

I have to find out the reason why.

I haven't felt this spark since I decided I was going to create a cosmetics line to nourish skin with chemically simple ingredients and find a new way to do things. Solving mysteries in make-up is one thing, but this equation is about my family, my heritage.

I have to know the truth.

Chapter Four

'Does he speak English?' Serena muses before slurping back a frappé in her takeaway cup. She seems to have brought the most random things with her to Corfu, including a pink glittery container for her morning drink.

Luckily, Serena being Serena, she had also packed three thick yoga mats, as she read there was someone teaching yoga in our village and she thought we should all join in. It gave us all something to sleep on last night instead of damp sun loungers, at least.

As we trail behind Mum, I roll my shoulders to pull out the knots from sleeping on the floor.

'Of course he speaks English. How else would he be doing these tours? Greeks don't need olive grove tours. Bored tourists need tours.' I can't see Mum's eyes behind her sunglasses, or even her face as she moves away, but I know she's rolling them.

'Or people who actually like to better themselves and learn something as they see the world,' I pipe in as one of my shoulders clicks.

My neck feels as though it belongs to someone else, and my right hip feels as though an elephant fell asleep on it. I guess I must be the elephant.

Mum clicks her tongue. 'Perhaps.'

We left our car in a dusty lay-by. Mum hired it from God knows where. A bright-red Suzuki Jimny.

Mum doesn't look dressed to traipse in and out of olive trees. But, as usual, she's managed to capture the perfect smart-casual look, in tailored black shorts and a floaty white blouse.

I had no idea what to wear to meet an uncle I know nothing about, while taking a tour around an olive grove. It's hard enough to imagine there's all that much to even say about olives in the first place. They grow, they get picked and they get squished into oil.

Unless they're going to get into *my* levels of science, which I would love, but I can't imagine it would be possible for a tour aimed at people on their holidays. I don't imagine many would find the molecular structure of olive oil half as interesting as I do.

'Do I look OK? You two always look so put together. I'd be happier back home with my lab coat on.'

As soon as the word *home* slips out of my mouth, it feels like a needle has just pierced the membrane of my heart, popping it like a balloon.

I don't have a home – or, if I do, it's a yoga mat in an empty shell by the sea.

'You look great, polka dots are always cute.'

'Thanks.'

I run my hands along the hips of my wide-leg cotton trousers. It's already much too hot for trousers. I wish I'd gone with shorts, like Serena and Mum. At least I had enough sense to tie my hair back into a ponytail to keep the weight of it off my shoulders.

It's a steep incline, the sort that makes calves like mine burn. I'm from the flattest region in England; even a slight incline sets off my shins.

'How much further?' I look out across the cascade of olive trees at the side of the road, poorly hidden behind shrubs and bushes.

Their dark-green leaves always look to me as though they've been left out in a frost on their underside. There's something elegant and majestic about the way their trunks wind, and the silvery underbelly of the leaves looks like a crown.

I can't believe I've spent my whole life without this part of me to hand. All of this was part of my mum, part of me, and I've never seen it until now.

I can almost imagine her as a little girl, playing tag between the trees, getting under people's feet while they worked, or collecting olives to throw at each other in battle, the way she said she and Spiros did in the stories I thought were fictional until last night.

We should've been here as kids on holiday, getting in everyone's way. Last night, Mum wouldn't say a word more on the matter, claiming the past is in the past and at least now we're here and we get to meet our uncle.

I was awake half the night regurgitating all the lies people have been telling me my whole life. From Jonah to Mum to Dad, then to the more obscure as I drifted in and out of sleep. Everything from a friend I had in primary school telling me her real dad was a spy, to an ex-colleague who said they posted me something a day before but when it arrived it had an order note from the day they told the lie.

I need a clear mind. This is the only time I can make a first impression on an uncle who doesn't know I even exist. Mum says he's a good storyteller. I'm not sure if that's a compliment right now.

'How many other people will be on this tour?' Serena carefully touches her top lip to blot away any gathered sweat.

'None. I booked all the places.' Mum turns to face us. With great ceremony, she sweeps her left arm towards an opening in the hedgerow. 'We are here.'

Serena steps through first. The last time I saw her walk this cautiously was when she had to cross a broken bridge over a narrow ditch back home.

'*Kalimera*, welcome, are you all arrived?' A man's voice bubbles with joy somewhere outside of view.

Serena hesitates, clearing her throat as she steps to one side. She always has words – normally, anyway – but her silence speaks volumes. I wonder if her stomach is churning the way mine is.

'I guess so.' Finding my voice, I glance at her and step to the other side to see a stocky man with tightly cropped slate-grey hair barrelling towards us with open palms.

Serena and I both look back to Mum as she steps forward, waiting for her to confirm that this is our uncle, that this is Spiros.

The man's trainers skid on the dirt track as he comes to a stop. The smile drops to the ground, leaving his eyes hiding under his eyebrows.

'Thalia?'

It's like we no longer exist, like we are curtains in a theatre, and now the show has started, we've suddenly become invisible.

'*Nai.*' Mum slips so naturally into Greek, like she's never spoken English before. Even though her English is so good, she has no more than a beautiful lilt of Greek that pops out a little on occasional words.

Sentences and paragraphs rush between them like a river cascading to prevent them taking another step towards each other, while we stand like guards at a gate, listening but not understanding the nuances.

'Translation, please?' Serena's voice is like the smashing of a dam, and everything runs away as we all turn and look at her. 'You're both speaking way too quickly.'

Mum looks at us like she'd forgotten we were even here to start with.

'Spiros, these are my daughters, Lorena and Serena.'

It doesn't matter that Mum's pulling her shoulders back, or keeping her chin up, I can see how much stress this is causing her. She's breathing at twice a normal rate, and she's too still, too calm.

Mum loves to talk with her hands, although less since Dad left. Everything about her is less since he left. It's going to be hard to forgive him for that.

Spiros clutches his heart, crumpling his *Spiros Olive Tours* T-shirt under his heavy hand.

'Two nieces. I could never have imagined—'

'*Kalimera*, welcome,' another man's voice calls from down the slope.

There's a crumbling stone outbuilding that can't be more than one or two rooms in size. A man sheltering his eyes from the sun walks towards us. From here, he's all beard and muscle.

'I did not know the party was here.' He stops and places his hands on his hips. 'Perhaps not all here.'

'Spiros, do you have a son?' A quiver hits Mum's vocal cords like a guitar string being struck.

'I do,' Spiros chuckles, turning to the young man now at his side, 'but this is not him. This is Christos. Eleni's cousin's son. Christos, this is my sister, Thalia, and her two daughters, Serena and Lorena.'

We both giggle and wave our fingers between us, stating in unison, 'The other way around.'

'I'm sorry, sorry, please forgive me my mistake. This is Lorena and Serena.'

'It is nice to meet you all, I did not know Spiros had a sister.' Christos wrinkles his nose as he looks down at the man by his side.

Christos steps forward and shakes my mum's hand, then takes mine. His rough fingers meet with mine and a gentle smile forms under his beard as his dark eyes look me over. He has the hands of someone who uses them for a living. They're strong, yet he doesn't grip me the way some men do, like they want to crush each finger together to prove their strength. He has found the perfect balance.

Serena lingers when she shakes his hand, putting her left hand on top of his. 'It's so nice to meet you,' she adds with a weighted look at the ground before meeting his eye again.

I can't blame her. If I was even remotely interested in looking at men again in the foreseeable future, he would definitely be worth a closer inspection. At a guess, he does all the heavy lifting around here and Spiros does the directing.

Even squinting in the sun and glittering with sweat like a morning dew, Christos's face looks as strong as his legs. Powerful and sculpted, with a well-kept beard and short hair that's wavy and messy on top. It looks styled but not overdone. As though he's taken a little product and rubbed it in with a rough hand and left it that way.

'I cannot believe you are here. We have so much to talk about. Unless you are only here for the tour? The booking says fifteen of you?' Spiros sways to look around us, as though we might be hiding twelve more people behind the bush and out on the road.

'I was afraid if you knew it was me . . . you might not want to see us, with how I left things . . .'

Spiros's forehead falls into deep lines as he steps towards my mum, cupping her face in his hands. His eyes reflect the sun as droplets ready themselves to water the olives.

'You are my sister, even when you are fool, and when I am fool, I still love you.' He kisses her cheeks, and she laughs into a cry before the embrace.

Christos leans a little closer to them, clearly not wanting to interrupt but still opening his mouth with something to say. 'How about I take your girls for a short tour of the groves while you two start your talking? Yes?'

A few mumbles and a sniff of yes, and Serena and I are silently following a tall, dark, handsome stranger into an olive grove.

I haven't seen Serena this giddy since she purchased her first Louis Vuitton handbag.

Chapter Five

'I am a little lost.' Christos stops between olive trees to sway on his heels, strumming his fingers on his hips as he grips them.

'And there was me thinking you were a tour guide. How can you give a tour if you don't know where you're going?' Serena's eyeballs will start to ache if she looks seductively down and up one more time.

'No, no. I feel, how is it you say? On the back of your foot. I thought we were having a big easy tour coming and now Spiros has left me with his nieces.' He turns and begins to walk slowly again. 'He has never told me about you before. When was the last time you saw your uncle?'

'Never.'

Christos spins to look at me, his finger pointing back towards where we left our mum.

'Never?' His finger turns on me. 'You have never met Spiros? But he is all about family.'

My shoulders rise and fall under his weighted gaze.

Serena steps a little closer to Christos. 'I don't think our mum has spoken to him since before we were born. She didn't even tell us he existed until yesterday.' Her top teeth dig into her bottom lip and her eyes are as wide and bright as the cenotes of Mexico.

My nose wrinkles at the thought of Mexico and what Dad might be getting up to there with his girlfriend, Megan. They'll be back in a few days and that's when Dad'll find out what Mum's done in his wake. Upping and leaving him with as little as she could.

A shiver rolls over my spine, making the accumulating sweat on my lower back run cold. She didn't even leave him a note like Jonah left me . . . but then it was Dad who left her, and not the other way around.

'What would you like me to do with you?'

Serena's left eyebrow arches and I know it's time for me to step in before she says something I don't want to hear.

'How do you mean?' I fold my arms over my chest.

'Would you like me to give the tour of the groves? Or we could sit at the table where the olives and food will be served. Or, where they would have been . . . will they be served now?'

How would we know? We know as much as him.

We exchange shrugs and Serena quickly decides we should take a walk through the groves because she *would just love* to see where Mum and Spiros would run around as kids.

I hang back, unable to suffer through Serena's flirtation with the tall and rugged Christos. It's only been a matter of days since everything with Jonah and the thought of anything that could remotely lead to love is sickening right now.

A particular olive tree catches my eye. It has not one but two thick swirling trunks with deep crevices and knots. They're each as thick as a large man-sized thigh. Stopping to admire this natural work of art, I run my fingers over the undulating surface and rest in the cool cocoon of its shade. It's like two bodies have combined forever in a beautiful cascade of nature.

'She's over two thousand years old. Spiros says she is magic, enchanted.'

My entire body contracts at the sound of Christos's voice so close behind me. I hadn't even realised they'd stopped, let alone turned around and moved closer to me.

'She's gorgeous,' Serena says from somewhere a bit further away.

Christos places his hand not far from mine on the cracked bark.

'Some people say very old trees stop giving olives, but she is still our best producer each year. The younger trees have nothing on her.'

'Is that part of the tour?' I tilt my head to look up at him, but he's still studying the tree.

'It is, but usually we guide people to them. I've never been guided to her by someone else. Not that I often give the tours. I help with big groups. Like this one.' He looks down at me and his face lifts into a half-smile.

We begin moving again to join Serena, our feet crunching over the dry earth in time with one another.

It must only be about three weeks since Jonah and I were walking through woodland together. It was a Sunday and we thought it would be nice to go for a walk and have a pub lunch. Everything was as it always was, laughing and joking, hands glued together. Each step in time. Or, at least, I thought we were.

How could he be like *that* one minute and be a completely different person when I'm not around? How could he tell me he loves me, sip wine in a pub garden on a Sunday and talk about what we would name hypothetical kids and dogs, then take everything from me?

My heart begins to pound and my jaw locks. The overwhelming burning sensation that comes when I let in thoughts of Jonah begins to consume me, making my skin prickle.

I can't burst into tears right now.

Mum doesn't need that. I don't need that.

We shared enough tears back in England before she decided, over too many bottles of wine, to start again in Corfu. She said she was leaving England because she couldn't stand to be in the same country as Dad when he got back from Mexico. That it was time *to heal old wounds.* I remember her saying that so vividly, because the 'old' part didn't make sense to me. I rationalised with her and Dad's relationship being old. But now . . . now I think perhaps the wounds she was slurring about weren't just those to do with Dad.

Then hours later I'd lost everything too, so my only options were to make a home in Corfu or to beg friends to let me sleep on their sofas until I could find another job. Staying at our old family home waiting for Dad and his new girlfriend to come back was never an option. Ever.

'Would you like me to tell you about how we harvest our olives? We have two different methods. One is traditional, with our hands and some tools we hold, the other is by machine. Or you could satisfy me and tell me *why now*? Why now come to Corfu? Why after all this time without being here?'

'I'm more than happy to satisfy you, Christos.' He really did line himself up for that one. Serena's golden highlighter is almost like glass as her cheekbones lift higher on her face. 'My dad's gone off with some woman from work and Mum decided to claim her inheritance by the sea. Simple really.'

'Serena.' I grit my teeth and narrow my eyes at her. If Christos wasn't between us, I'd probably knock into her for good measure.

'What?' She narrows her eyes on me. 'It's all true.'

'Yes, but it's not our truth to tell.'

'It was not my place to ask. I am sorry. Here.' Christos quickens his pace and bends down to pick up something that looks like a very small garden rake.

Without Christos between us, Serena presses her elbow into my ribs as she eyes him and his tight shorts.

'Will you stop?' I say under my breath.

'Never.' She almost skips towards him, her voice full of glee at her new plaything.

I can't believe this is my broken life.

'This is what is used to get the olives from the trees with our hands. We do all these trees here' – he motions the rake in a circle around him – 'by hands. It stops the trees getting damaged, but it is hard work. This is mostly my work. I am the one to break my back, but that's good. I like it this way.'

'Lorena, Serena!' Mum's voice carries between the trees.

She and Spiros are heading our way like they're on a mission. I guess today's olive tour has been cut short.

That, or it's really about to begin.

Chapter Six

'I cannot believe we have two nieces.' Eleni grips both of our hands with hers across the wide olive-wood table. 'I wish our boy was here for you to meet. He lives in Athens, big high-flyer. You're both so beautiful, like your mama, *nai*?'

Spiros rang his wife, our Aunt Eleni, to meet us in the olive groves. She's only just arrived, but already she's kissed us about fifty times and filled the paths with her light and brightened Spiros's round face too.

She's got spiky dyed-red hair and the remains of over-plucked eyebrows, but what stands out above it all is her welcoming smile.

'We are so happy you are here. You tell us anything you need, and we will help you.' Eleni nods towards Spiros, who returns her nod.

'Funny you should say that—' Serena sits up tall, with a grin.

Mum quickly cuts her off with a rumbling roll of her name, 'Serena.' It almost growls from next to Eleni.

'What?' Serena's hands slump down on to the table. 'We don't have beds, and I for one can't sleep on a yoga mat *again*. I'm happy to pay, but if someone could help us get some beds to our place, that would be amazing.' Her perfectly manicured nude-tone nails exaggerate her gesture of touching her heart.

If I'm honest, I'm surprised she's waited this long to bring it up. She's not one to wait around for someone else to get things done.

'Thalia? What is this? You have no beds? Where are you staying that has no beds?' Eleni's sparse eyebrows drop as she addresses Mum.

'The beach house.'

Eleni rattles off words in Greek, desperately looking from Mum to her husband across the table.

She turns back to English without a pause. 'You must stay with us.'

'Thank you, Eleni, but no. We're going to spend time together fixing the place up.' Mum's lips slip into a small smile.

'Then you must take beds from our spare rooms. That is two, both are double size. The other room is an office now, with no beds.'

'I have a spare bed.' Christos has a low rumbling voice that manages to be soft yet carries well enough to catch us all off guard. I can feel him in my chest. 'It is only a small one. For one person.'

'I don't mind. I want to be single.' My voice is sharper than intended, almost brittle. I do my best to soften it. 'Thank you. That's very kind.'

Christos presses his lips together like he wants to laugh. 'I will bring it for you in my van. Where is this beach house?'

'No, no, you can't do this for us.' Mum slices her hands in dismissal.

'Then I am doing it for Spiros and Eleni. They have been good to me for many years. No one uses the bed, you can have it. It is my welcome gift.'

Eleni stretches to the head of the table to pinch Christos's cheek, like he's a child. 'You're a good boy.'

'If you say so, Eleni. I will be good now and open the wine for the tour. Unless you are now going to be showing everyone around, Spiros?'

Eleni laughs. 'Bring the food too, we will need something to soak it up.'

I glance at my wrist to check the time, only to remember I sold my watch at the car boot sale too. I got five pounds for a two-hundred-pound watch, but it was a quick sale, and it's meant I don't have to look at time ticking away without Jonah.

'I'll help you.' I slip my leg over the bench and stand to follow Christos.

Serena's shoulders sag. She's probably disappointed she didn't think to help him. Eleni starts asking questions about Serena and what she does for a living, preventing her from jumping up to join us.

I'm glad. I wanted to take a breath and clear my thoughts by helping Christos; I have no interest in sharing the painful details of my life right now with people I've just met. And unlike Serena, I have no interest in any handsome Greek men either. It doesn't matter how big their biceps are or how dark their tan might be, I'm in my new man-hating phase. Hating is too strong, I don't want to hate people for existing, I just don't want them near me filling my head with lies and betrayal, the way Jonah and Dad did.

Overall, I think I'm handling it all rather well. If handling it is ignoring it and focusing on Mum's pain and this new start in Corfu, then I'm doing great. Better than great. Better than Jonah, I'm sure . . . wherever he is.

'It's down here, thank you for lending your hand.' Christos points towards the outbuilding close to where today started. 'Eleni home-makes the food, I put it out when the timing it right and carry things here and there, answer some questions when we have bigger groups. I do anything that is needed.'

'Then do the heavy lifting in harvest?'

'Exactly.' Christos nods as we trot towards the building over the undulating earth, from its soft inclines to steeper sways.

'How did you get into this business then? With Eleni and Spiros?'

Christos bows his head with a heavy breath. 'Like I said, they have been good to me many times. I want to help them. It is good to be useful and I have no great ambitions for life.'

Taking two steps up, I follow him into the cooler air of the pale white and grey stone building. The walls are thick, and Christos has to dip low to get in the door. He's at least a head and shoulders taller than Spiros, but that's not saying much. It's not like Spiros is a giant, making Christos monstrous, but he is tall.

There's only one window and it's the size of my laptop on its side, keeping the room cool and shaded from the heat of the sun.

It's set up to be a shop. Beautifully decorated olive oil cans are stacked in front of me, on a table that's pushed against the back wall. To the side are jars of olives next to bars of sweet-smelling soaps in all different colours. Everything looks smart and clean and well thought out.

A large fridge hums in the right corner. Christos opens a cupboard next to it and pulls out a blue-painted wooden tray that's seen better years, and a white one that's in no better shape. Placing them next to the cans of oils, he swings open the fridge and begins to load them up.

'What do you do?' Christos asks as he places wine glasses carefully on one tray.

'Nothing.'

'I hear that pays well.'

A smile crosses my lips and lingers there for a moment as I watch him out of the corner of my eye. Christos carries on with his work as though he was being completely serious. I'm not used to such a dry way of being playful. I guess I've got used to Jonah, with loud jokes and big smiles.

'Not as well as my last job. I was a cosmetic scientist until about a month or so ago. I quit my job to create my own line of products. Skincare, make-up . . .' I pick up a purple soap from the table and hold it to my nose, hoping the olive oil and lavender combination will soothe my nerves.

Why did he have to ask a question that leads down this dark rabbit hole? I guess all things in my life have led to Jonah for quite some time. He's not *the one that got away*, but the one who ran away with all my savings and ruined my hope of starting my own business any time soon.

That's what happens when you live with someone and slip on an engagement ring, only to find out it *isn't* a big fat diamond in a Tiffany box, it's actually a cubic zirconia fake in Tiffany's clothing. Which is exactly what happened to me when I tried to get some money back for the ring Jonah got me. It seems the Tiffany box he'd purchased to put the ring in was worth more than the ring itself.

'That does not sound like nothing.'

'Yeah, well . . . it didn't happen. I, erm . . . I guess I didn't have as much money saved as I thought I had. So now I'm doing nothing until I work out what I *am* doing.'

I put down the soap and do my best to push out a smile. There's a good chance it's more of a grimace.

Christos squints at me for a moment, as though shielding his eyes from something I've said, before his face relaxes again.

'Life can take us in many directions. I find it best to follow behind, because it doesn't matter what you do, you can't change it, and you cannot control it. Here—' Christos lifts the tray with the glasses and one of the wine bottles. 'You take this one.'

'Wise words.' My fingers briefly skim the back of his rough hand as I take the tray.

'When you make all the mistakes, all you have left is wise. So I must be very wise. Although, I can't imagine how you do not know how much savings you have before you quit a job.' He shakes his head. I guess that's why he was squinting at me.

With that, Christos picks up the tray, filled with stuffed vine leaves, olives, bread, more wine and a can of olive oil, and turns to leave like it's nothing.

'Me too,' I mutter under my breath before following behind.

Although, I wonder how many mistakes you can make with no ambition working on an olive grove? Surely not as many as me.

It doesn't matter. Serena can tell me when she eventually finds out. I have enough of my own problems and family mysteries to deal with.

Chapter Seven

'When did Christos say he'd get here with the beds?' Serena paces the empty room, filling it with an echoing clap from her flip-flops. I can hear her as I plod back down the stairs.

She's asked this question about twenty times so far. Mum and I have both repeated *this afternoon* so many times we've stopped answering her.

'Please stop pacing. You're giving me a headache.' Mum fans herself with a blue and gold fan she got at one of the gift shops in the village.

'Are you sure that's not because you had too much wine with your olives this morning?' Serena stops. She's changed out of her shorts and put on an incredible white minidress. She's even redone her make-up, ready for Christos's arrival.

'I'm going to the beach. I can't stand the pacing or the heat anymore. Call me if I'm needed.'

They both blow me kisses and tell me to enjoy myself.

I'm not entirely sure it's a good idea, going off to the beach alone. This will be the first time, other than to sleep, that I've been properly alone for more than ten minutes.

My dreams are often filled with Jonah and what he did to me. The sign-off on his letter, *I'm sorry, please forgive me.*

Never.

I could never forgive him for taking everything I had and pulling it apart, limb by limb.

As I step out of the door, I pull my shades down from my head and over my eyes. If I can't find anything else to think about, I don't want people to see my eyes clouding up.

Not that they'll be looking at me. It's not like I intend to parade up and down the beach in one of those cheeky bum bikinis in a neon pink. All I want to do is find a nice spot to lay down my towel and have a little nap while getting a tan.

Perhaps now is the time to teach myself to meditate or something. Or at least start to think how I'm going to make money and pay for things instead of expecting Mum to fund everything.

I've been writing down what I owe her in my phone. From flights to food. At least I'll be able to help with manual labour, I guess that's a job in itself. It'll be good to feel useful when we start work on the house. Not that any of us actually know where to start or have the skill set for anything more than painting walls.

Serena said she would pay for Wi-Fi right away, because she'll need it to get back to her virtual assistant work soon. It's only me who can't contribute something.

Just before the road slips into the sand, I take off my sandals, letting my feet slide into the warmth of the golden floor. I only take another three steps before hopping about to put my shoes back on. The sand is scorching. With only a couple of steps, I feel as though I've burnt the undersides of my feet.

I can't believe I didn't think that through. It must be about three in the afternoon, the sand has all day under the blazing heat to get to boiling point.

With my sandals firmly back on, I march on to get close to the sea where it might be cooler, kicking up clouds of what feels like hot ash as I go.

Moving around the sun loungers and parasols, some with people huddled in the shade and others arranged like sunflowers to follow the light, I find a stretch of beach next to a boat hire place where people are sitting on towels instead of loungers.

The air is filled with laughter and salt in equal measure. It's the perfect place to cleanse and heal wounds.

I find my spot, not far from an empty beach tent and a snoozing couple holding hands.

That was Jonah and me, once upon a time.

Back before his letter, apologising for taking all the money out of our joint account, back before I knew his life was stacked precariously on a house of lying cards and I was sitting there on the top, waiting to fall.

I thought I had already fallen.

Fallen in love.

But can you love a lie? It's like being in love with a fictional character in a film or in a book. Only, I truly believed I was there in the narrative because he forgot to tell me it was all fiction.

His letter said he loved me. But it also said he had to leave because he owed too much money. He said he was doing it to *keep me safe*.

If he had really loved me, we could've solved it together. He wouldn't have left me stranded and alone with nothing. We could've found a way. Instead, I was left with a house he'd emptied of things he could sell and a note full of lies.

I'll never know if that's why he took all my savings and jewellery. To *keep me safe*. It could just be another lie. Maybe he had decided he'd had enough of me, and it was kinder to say it was for my own good that he took my money and left. That it was his problem, not mine.

But it was my problem, because it's not like there would be any point reporting someone with a key taking things that could legitimately be theirs to take, even though I paid for most of it.

He told me his parents had died when he was little; I wonder now if that was true. Maybe he robbed them too. Maybe his name isn't even Jonah.

Now I'm being silly, I've seen his passport and his driving licence. That was his name on there, I don't think he would've forged that. Even if he never worked where he said or did half the things he claimed.

Years of lies and I ate them up.

I shake my head and lie down on my towel. A delightful breeze strips away some of the heat and begins the process of covering my wounds in salt.

Removing my sunglasses to avoid getting a strange tan line, I do my best to let in the light through closed eyes. That hot tingle on my skin. An almost fizzing sensation.

My first real bout of sunshine this year. Something it feels like I've lived without for so long. England was rainy when I left, the pathetic fallacy to mirror my heartache. I hated it.

I feel like I've been living in grey forever while telling myself I was in the sunshine.

Now, with my eyes shut and sunglasses off, all I can see is the pink-red tinge of my own eyelids and the lines of my veins running through them. My life in motion.

The blue sky and the golden sun go unseen, but are deeply felt.

The heat is more comforting than having another human pressed over me. People can't bring comfort anymore. They bring the fear of gut-wrenching pain.

The sun touches every bare part of my skin and fills it with vitamin D. Helping me and nourishing me. Hopefully making me whole again.

I have to look after myself, though; the sun will burn me quicker than Jonah did.

I'm not really safe anywhere. Even Mum, who I've always been so close to, has been lying to me since birth.

I'm doing my best to stay calm about her hidden past and meeting family members she only told us about in fictional settings, because I know she's in pain too. Dad didn't even tell her about his affair, or that he was taking someone else to Mexico. She only found out because he was so careless about it all, she saw an email.

I've always told Mum and Serena everything. I'm the glue that holds the two of them together sometimes.

A big part of me wants to ask a thousand questions about my grandparents and Spiros, but I'm just not up to it. Not yet. I'm too afraid she'll lie to me about it all anyway, or hide things from me.

After the past week, I doubt I'll ever be able to trust anyone ever again.

Chapter Eight

After a swim in the sea to refresh me, I wash my hair under one of the showers on the beach.

It's good to feel clean again, even if I am trailing sand back to the house with each and every step.

As I turn into the patch of dried grass that will eventually be a front garden and driveway, I'm met with a blue van, its door thrown open, with a single mattress and bits of bed-frame still inside.

I was secretly hoping I'd avoid seeing more of Serena's outrageous flirtation, but I guess this is round two for the day. She's been single for about three or four months after a six-month relationship with someone I hated from day one. He was more interested in the mirror than anyone else. Serena might come off that way, but I know there's more to her than that. Underneath it all, there's a lot of kindness and love, and she's smarter than she likes to let on, getting mostly As at school.

Christos fills our doorway as he stoops to make his way towards the van.

'*Yassou*, hello.' He nods as he carries on to the van.

'Hiya, do you need a hand?'

He looks me over for a second as he wrinkles his nose.

'Do you have a hand?'

I look down at my arms, one with my towel wrapped around it and the other with my beach bag.

'I can put this down—?'

'No, no, it's fine. Serena has been *more* than helpful.' I can't read his tone. Whether he's annoyed at her overt attention or thinks it's sweet and funny.

I suppose that's no surprise, I couldn't tell that my soon-to-be husband was going to rob me blind, or that my mum had been hiding family from us, so why do I think I can pick up the vocal nuances of a complete stranger?

'I have put the other two beds together, now only yours. It is the easiest. It won't take long.'

He picks up parts of the metal frame and takes them in with the ease of carrying shopping bags.

I follow on behind him.

'Good, you're home. Get dressed, we are taking Christos for dinner to a place named Cicala. He has a friend working there and we are treating him for all his hard work. Your sister is getting ready.' Mum rolls her eyes before she moves towards the rooms that have a half-finished kitchen and dining room.

I'm stuck behind Christos halfway up the stairs when I realise the state I've left my room in from looking for my bikini and towel. I was so fed up with Serena's pacing sending me round the bend that I threw everything about in a hurry to escape.

'Can I get past you? Please?' I begin edging from side to side as though I'll eventually manage to find space on the stairs to squeeze past him.

'Not really.'

I have no choice but to stay behind him at a snail's pace, as there's no room to pass until we get to my door.

'Hold on, let me get in there first, it's a mess.'

As I stumble about trying to pick up clothes, the contents of my beach bag spill out and it looks worse than ever. I end up kicking it all into the corner. When I look up, Christos has gone and left the bits of frame in the hall and disappeared back down the stairs.

With him gone, I quickly look through my clothes and grab a simple black dress and clean underwear and make my way to the bathroom to change.

'You can't wear that,' Serena hisses out of her bedroom door, 'look!' She's wearing something almost identical to what I'm holding.

'*Really?*' My head drops back, and I note the mosquito watching us from the ceiling. 'Fine, I'll get something else.'

'He has a friend, you know? He's a waiter or something in this taverna we're going to. Maybe he's cute.' Her voice wiggles about more than her eyebrows.

'So what if he is? I'd rather be dead than date.' I turn back towards my room to be faced with Christos at the top of the stairs with more bed-frame. Our eyes lock and there's a subtle lowering of one eyebrow.

I do my best to smile politely, as though I haven't said anything at all, then nip back into my room to grab the first dress I see, because ultimately, it doesn't matter.

Once I'm dressed, Mum demands I put more make-up on and take care of myself, clucking around me, looking after me in the only way she can right now. Doing her best to force me to be the girl I was before my bones were ripped away from my body.

While Serena clucks round Christos upstairs, I do my best to brighten my face for my mum. I know she's doing the same for us, doing her hair and make-up and plastering on smiles for most of the day. We all need a bit of normality, and I guess me wearing make-up is part of that for her. Not that I bother with foundation or anything like that, it's too hot, it would slide right off.

I've loved cosmetics since I was a child. Every weekend, I'd ask Mum whether we could do face masks and then whether I could do her make-up. Then at school, I excelled in science, so it made sense to bring together my two passions.

I used to love to put make-up on Serena too. When she was only just able to sit up, Mum went to the loo and by the time she came back I'd got her lipstick out of her bag and circled it around Serena's mouth. She was giggling and gurgling and happy for my attention. Mum wasn't so happy about it.

Mum always says it's my fault Serena's as into make-up and fashion as she is, that I brought her up to love cosmetics.

I moved more towards the science, and she became endlessly able to make any make-up trend work. I still love it, but I like to keep things clean and simple now. People don't realise how the chemicals put into cosmetics can build up in their systems and cause potential damage. It's one of the reasons I wanted to make my own brand. I've spent so much time creating products that are magnificent on one level and atrocious on another. My shift has been towards care, both for the outer layers of skin and what it does after it's absorbed.

I had it all worked out.

Until I didn't.

The more time I spend with Serena, watching her layer on mask after mask of foundation, the more I want to see the real her underneath. The beautiful kid who had confidence without the thick fake lashes and the exacting eyebrows. I hate that she feels she has to hide behind a wall of make-up. I want to find a way to nourish people, instead of helping them to lie about their faces. It would be nice for us all to find beauty and confidence in the truth, and just enhance who we are, rather than everyone trying to lie about it all the time.

'We're ready!' Serena announces as she and Christos come down the stairs.

'You all look very lovely, and I look . . .' Christos looks down at his loose-fitting T-shirt and fitted shorts. They might be the same shorts from the morning, but the T-shirt is different. It isn't the work logo one that matched Spiros's.

'Don't be silly.' Serena places her hand on his bicep as she reaches the bottom of the stairs. 'You look endlessly handsome.'

Christos's head rises and falls. 'Thank you, that is too kind. Follow me, I will show you the way.'

As everyone files towards the front door, I close my eyes and snatch a breath.

I really hope tonight doesn't get more awkward. I'm not sure I can handle it.

On the other hand, we need to stay out late enough for our house to cool down, and that might mean drinking more than is sensible.

Chapter Nine

Alec, Christos's friend, is gorgeous . . . on the inside, I'm sure.

On the outside, he's as old as my dad and with half as much hair.

That's not really fair. For his age, he is trim and has a good bone structure and a gentle manner, but is thankfully not someone Serena will try to push on me. He's also someone Mum sort of knew when she was growing up.

'How do you know Alec?' Mum undoes her claw clip, letting her thick black curls fall heavy on her shoulders.

She pretends she doesn't dye her hair, but I know she does. She looks good for fifty-two. People often think she's our older sister, not our mum. To which she promptly tells them not to be ridiculous.

I can only hope to look half as good as her when I'm in my fifties.

'He used to help me with the olive harvest. It's heavy work, so now he sticks to lifting plates and menus. We got on well. He puts up with me. This is his first year working at Cicala, though.'

Alec comes back to our table with a tray full of drinks, placing down three frozen daiquiris and one pint of Mythos.

'You're not having cocktails, Christos?' Alec grins as he places down the pint. 'You surprise me.'

'Not today, my friend.'

'Perhaps another day.' Alec taps him on the shoulder, maintaining the smile on his face and adding laughter to it.

'I can't believe you work here.' Mum rests her chin on her fingertips. 'Are you still with Maria? When I left, you two seemed very happy together.'

'We marry, yes. Err, there are two girls, my girls. Zoey and Cora.'

I get the feeling Alec's English is best suited to taking orders of food. He switches to Greek to finish his sentence.

Mum's face crumples and Alec presses his lips together before shrugging.

'*Yamas*, to your happy return.' His face pulls into a shallow smile before he turns back towards the bar with his tray.

'What did he say?' I lean forward to sip from the straw sticking out of the bright-red drink.

'His wife passed away a few years ago. His girls are a similar age to you two. That's what he told me.' Mum absent-mindedly runs a finger along the rim of her glass.

'I'm sorry to hear that.'

'Me too,' Serena adds.

There's an awkward silence that falls over our table. Death isn't a great conversation starter when you don't know one of your party all that well.

I clear my throat and pull my shoulders back, readying myself to change the subject.

'So, Christos, you said Spiros and Eleni have helped you through the years? I'd love to know more about my uncle through someone who knows him. What have they done to help you that was so great?'

'He gave me a job, a purpose. They helped me to get my house and give me much guidance.' Christos begins drinking deeply into his pint, as though that's the end of it.

He didn't really tell me anything new about my uncle.

I bite my cheeks and sit back in my chair. Disappointment nibbles at me like my teeth on my cheeks.

'Yes, my brother is a good man. Thank you for bringing the beds from their house. It is a shame they couldn't be free to meet us here tonight. We must share another meal together soon. I would like to host . . . as soon as we've fixed the house.' Mum slumps back into the white wooden chair. Now it's only Serena sitting to attention.

'Yes, I was thinking about this, there is a man, Anton. He is the biggest man in Greece.' This comment brings a little light to Christos's face. 'When he was young, he fixes houses and then he sold them or rents them to people. He has more money and time than he knows what to do with, so he likes to help people. He does jobs here and there, but I'm thinking, this is what he used to do. Fixing houses is how he made his money. It might be good to ask for his help. I don't know him very well, but Alec knows everyone, you should ask him for a number.'

'Thank you, Christos, what would we do without you? No wonder my brother speaks so highly of you.' Mum sits tall again, like a balloon being pumped up.

Running his fingers through his beard, Christos shakes off the compliment.

'Please, excuse me.'

Serena tilts her head to watch Christos's every move as he walks to the bar.

'Do you really think this Anton in the biggest man in Greece? Like, maybe a world record holder?' she muses.

The image of a man so tall he can't fit through the doors in our house shoots through my mind.

'I doubt it, surely if you're that tall it would be hard to be a handyman. Although it would be helpful to pick all the olives off the top of the tree.' I raise my eyebrows at Serena, and we share a moment of childish laughter.

I take a deep sip of my sweet strawberry drink before replacing the glass on the table.

'Do you think Christos is a little . . . evasive?'

Mum jumps in to his defence. 'Not at all. He seems like a helpful young man, he even offered an idea to help us. What has he done that's evasive?'

My shoulders rise and fall as I shift on my seat. 'I don't know. He didn't really tell me anything new or interesting about Spiros. I was hoping for a bit more information about who he is and the good things he has supposedly done.'

'Helping someone get a house and a job isn't good enough for you?' Mum presses her lips together to punctuate her sentence.

'Yeah, I'm probably being silly. I think all the lies and hiding from Jonah have made me feel like everyone's hiding something.'

I open and close my mouth, locking my teeth together. I don't like to add that it's also probably because she's been hiding Spiros from me this whole time too.

'I'm sorry, Lorena, my love, I know you've had a lot to deal with. It's not just Jonah who has had a part to play in that.'

Mum stops as Christos comes back with a small rectangle of paper. 'This is the number. Alec will tell him you will call.'

Mum takes the paper and slips it into her bag on the back of her chair.

'You're a good boy, Christos. And what of you, do you have a girlfriend waiting for you at home?'

'No.'

There's something about the way Christos says *no*. Like he's a gun and the answer was there in his mouth, ready to shoot out. Even Mum visibly reacts, recoiling just a touch.

Maybe he's desperate for Serena to know he's single. Why else would he be so keen to tell us he hasn't got a girlfriend? The whole idea makes me want to cringe, but I do my best to hold it in.

Christos clears his throat. 'I'm glad to hear you will all be coming back to take the olive tour soon, properly this time. Especially you, Lorena. I think it will be interesting for the girl who *does nothing*. It might make you think about *something*.'

I look from one of his dark eyes to the other, trying to figure out what's really going on behind them.

When I can't, I raise my glass and say, 'I guess I'll drink to that.'

'*Yamas.*' We all clink glasses as Alec appears with our plates.

He briefly chats away to Mum in Greek.

I'm intrigued as to Christos's meaning, but I'm not in the mood to make a big deal out of it or pretend that I care. I'm still functioning with a hollow void where my stomach should be, and it's impossible to care about very much at all.

I drink enough of the sweet daiquiri to give myself brain freeze. The throbbing numbness hits me between the eyes in the same way the whole day has. A blinding pain that's still not enough for everyone to hide all their deception behind.

I guess at least today I've been allowed to peek behind a door in Mum's life that I didn't even know existed before. I guess it's a start.

Chapter Ten

Four daiquiris and two shots later, Christos is long gone and we're wandering back down to our new Corfu home.

'I cannot take this anymore!' As soon as we're in the door, Mum tugs off her flowing dress and marches through the house in her underwear, waving her hands by her face. She continues to throw open the double doors that lead to the back garden.

It's almost midnight and outside the heat has died down to something bearable, but inside . . . the house is still hot.

Serena's hysterical laugh echoes around the rooms. 'I need to pee.' She doubles over before almost crawling towards the stairs.

I stumble after Mum, one foot hardly wanting to move around the other.

There are four very old and fragile-looking white plastic chairs and Mum has dared to sit on one. So far, we've all been avoiding them. She pulls her knees to her chest, and in the starlight she looks like a child gazing up at the night sky.

'Your father flies home from Mexico tomorrow. Back to the big empty home with a for-sale sign at the front.'

'You've put the house up for sale?' I blink hard, doing my best to find the last of my sobriety somewhere way down in my consciousness. 'Already? Before he's even home?'

She makes a small noise, which I think is in place of a yes. A hum of agreement.

I knew Mum had put almost everything in storage. Some things went to the car boot with me, but she paid some people to pack up the last thirty or so years of marriage and hide it away in a storage unit.

I knew she wanted to put it up for sale, but I thought she would at least speak to Dad first. She obviously wants her own slice of revenge.

I helped her do it. We both did, Serena and I, and they helped me clear through my mess too. What was left of it after Jonah took everything of value.

Three years versus thirty.

Over and over again Mum has said not to compare, that we have both had loss and betrayal and we both deserve better. She's never once made me feel like her loss is bigger than mine.

'And how are you, my angel? Has it helped your heart to be here in the sun?'

'Yeah. It's good to be away from the reminders of him. Here, it's like a blank canvas at least.'

'Or a blank sky.' She raises her arm, swooping it over her head. 'You will look back on all of this one day with different eyes. Nothing stays the same. Nothing, nothing, nothing . . . But that's OK. It's all footsteps in the sand. Footsteps to your destiny.'

'It's the same for you too, you know. Dad was a stepping stone to me and Serena, and now you're on the path to something else. Something better.'

I hope it's true, but something inside me twists at the thought of believing anyone at face value anymore. 'I can't believe I went for all those years without seeing my parents when I could have.' Mum's voice falls so low, I wonder whether she's talking to me, whether she's even meaning to talk out loud. 'I was a fool. Even after they passed, I never really believed it. In my head they were here, living. I was such a fool.'

'Why didn't you come back?' My voice reflects hers, as soft as the breeze.

'Because I was a fool.'

'How did you even know when they'd passed away?'

'Spiros . . . I don't know how he found the address, but he wrote me a letter. I was such a fool to never reply. I was frightened. Are you ever frightened, Lorena?'

'All the time.'

Mum's hand reaches to mine as we both look up at the stars and their own mystery.

'What are you two whispering about?' Serena cuts in. 'If it's heartbreak, I've told you both, you're banned. Sad men times are over.'

I look back at my little sister. She didn't know any of this about Mum's past either, and she has always been Daddy's little princess. This has to be hard for her too.

I reach my other hand out towards her and she takes it. We all look up at the stars in the thrum of the cicada song. All I can think about is whether Mum will ever tell me the whole story – and if she doesn't, can we ever have the same close relationship again?

Chapter Eleven

'So, you tell me' – Spiros claps his hands – 'what do you buy your olive oil in? Come on, back home, what is it in?' He scans everyone.

It's not just me, Mum and Serena. There are around fifteen or more people on today's tour, all eager to learn.

'Hands up, who is buying in plastic?' A few put their hands up. 'Glass? Who has the pretty glass ones with the fancy bottles?' A few more hands go up and people whisper in each other's ears, looking from one to the next. 'And what crazy person buys their oil in a big ugly metal can?'

Two people put their hands up and a rumble of laughter rolls around them.

'You are the winners!' Spiros throws his arms up. 'Plastic, I am very sorry, this is not even oil from the olive. Glass, you start with good oil and the sun has destroyed it through the glass, but in the ugly can' – Spiros presses his hand to his heart – 'you get the beautiful oil.'

'You're kidding me? My mega expensive oil is, what? Gone off or something?' A bloke in an expensive-looking polo shirt looks at his wife and back to Spiros in disgust.

'At least yours is oil. God knows what I've been buying.' A woman with big teeth and a loud voice laughs from the other side of the group.

'I will explain.' Spiros pulls up his shorts an inch and rests his foot on the stump of a tree, leaning in for effect. 'In the plastic, it is what is left over from the olives. It is the middle, yes? The stone, the by-product. It is the lowest-grade oil, and sometimes mixed with a different oil for taste. But not so good for you.' He punctuates his words with his hands, speaking slowly and firmly.

This part of the tour means a lot to him, I can tell.

He's doing his best to make it feel dramatic. 'The plastic bottles, it is as you say, a con. It is bad oil, left in a bottle that will make it even worse in the sun.' He moves towards the table behind him and opens a jar. 'Pass this around, you smell it.'

When the jar arrives in my hands, I close my eyes and take a deep whiff. There's a staleness to it. It still smells like olive oil, but not the best I've had.

'Now this one, a good oil, extra virgin, none of the waste products, but left out in light, in the glass bottle.' He waves his hand in the direction of the sun.

He passes around the next jar, and it smells like a normal olive oil to me. The same as I have in the cupboard at home. Smelling this one, I realise the other one was a little off.

'Now you taste my oil. Follow me.'

He leads us through and towards the table where we sat for lunch only yesterday.

Each place along the table has a fresh white place mat, and perfectly placed in the centre is a blue glass with a saucer on top of it to keep any flies out.

At the head of the long sweeping table is Christos, with his hands linked behind his back. We briefly saw him at the start of the tour; he welcomed us with kisses on our cheeks before getting back to all the things that need doing behind the scenes.

'This is not your wine, or your water, no. This is your oil. If you don't listen and do as I tell you, I will know it. First, please remove the plate and hold the glass in both of your hands. Warm it like you would a brandy.'

Serena looks from me to Mum out of the corner of her eye, but Mum's already doing it. She's done this before, maybe hundreds of times. I've never seen it before. She's never told us which oil to buy, or which one was bad, but there's something about her movements that looks natural, like she knows it all.

'Take a deep smell, different, *nai*?' Spiros's cheeks bulge in a wide grin as he too takes a sniff from one of the glasses. 'Before you drink, listen carefully – remember, I said I will know if you don't listen to me. You must put it in your mouth' – he circles his finger around the glass – 'move it around your mouth and your teeth, only then you must drink. Do at least half the oil. Yes? Are you ready?' The grin doesn't want to leave him now. '*Yamas!*'

With that, we all pour olive oil directly into our mouths like it's a shot of ouzo.

As I move it about, it's not at all how I thought it would be. It's smooth and almost creamy. It's liquid oil, but it doesn't feel greasy.

Someone splutters in front of me, then two others at the end of the table begin to cough. I quickly swallow it back and feel heat rising in my throat, enough to make me wonder whether I really was gargling ouzo.

Serena does her best to stifle her own cough of surprise at the heat but doesn't quite manage it. Her cheeks blush rouge and she does her best to keep her face covered with her hand. I'd hedge a bet she doesn't want to look silly in front of Christos.

Spiros bubbles with even more laughter, and even Christos raises a smile in the depths of his beard before turning to the table behind him where a tray is laid out with wine glasses.

'It burns? Yes?' Spiros places down his blue oil glass. 'You have never noticed before, because your oil at home, it is not so good quality and you have it with your bread and your salad. Ours is, as the English say, jam-packed with antioxidants. You notice no burning in your mouth, yes? It is just here?' He rubs his throat, exactly where the heat had slid down.

Around us some people are laughing, quietly exchanging their surprise, while Mum sniffs her oil glass again with her eyes closed. It's different this time, like she doesn't want to let go of it.

'This is how you tell a good oil. It must be extra virgin, as I tell you before, it must be kept in the right conditions – a metal can, not fancy glass. They just want a pretty bottle to make you believe it is better. No, now you know. But don't worry, when you eat with bread, no burn. So now you can try!'

Christos finishes putting wine glasses out for everyone, then turns back to the table behind Spiros. There's something under a long line of foil. He pulls it back, revealing two beautiful platters of food on thick slabs of olive wood.

He slides off the first, carefully balancing it, muscles holding taut as he pushes it along the centre of the table, followed by the next.

There are all the things we had yesterday, but now they're beautifully presented on these platters. Breads, cured meats, olives, vine leaves, cubes of feta, mini cheese pies cut into cubes, peppers and more. There's a vibrant array of colour and it's all been placed with care to look decorative before we dive in and destroy it.

Christos offers around wine and water, and of course Serena flutters her eyelashes for some wine. I don't blame her. The internet is getting connected tomorrow, and she'll have to get back to her work and her clients. She might as well have another day of holiday while she can. Before this beautiful island switches into normality.

'Are you OK, Mum?' Gently I press the top of my bare arm to hers.

'Yes, yes. I'm fine. My grandfather hated the good oil. Funny, isn't it? He always liked the oil he was brought up with from later in

63

the season, where he would dip his bread straight into a barrel. He thought this was all much too fancy.' She shakes her head. I can't recall her ever speaking of my grandparents, let alone hers. 'Are you OK? Did you like the tour? Spiros is so good, isn't he?'

I nod as I reach for some bread.

Last night, sitting on her plastic chair, she looked more defiant. There was the fragility of a child, but that same resilient strength children have. Like they could bounce out of any situation. Now, she's more brittle. Even with the musing on her grandparents, she seems more guarded. A silence has fallen over her as we've walked through the olive trees. I guess as we fill up on olives and wine, she's filling up on memories.

There's a growing sense of grief or remorse circling around her. Something.

I'm sure it's linked to what she was saying about her parents and her being a *fool*. I'm sure she's not. I just need to find out what really happened all those years ago. I don't think she would've left all this behind for no reason. I just wish she trusted us enough to share more with us.

Serena's phone begins to chime from the back pocket of her shorts, making everyone glance in our direction. She swiftly apologises as she inches it out.

Her face changes as she looks at the screen.

'Sorry, I have to take this.' She slides carefully off the bench then runs down towards the rows of trees as she takes the call.

Mum dips her head at me. 'Put some food on your sister's plate. She won't take much with Christos here, but she should eat with that wine.'

I load up both plates with treats, but it isn't long until she returns.

Her face glows red and her eyes look watery, but a smile is plastered on her face.

'Are you OK?' I lean into her, keeping my voice low.

'Yeah, yeah. Fine. I'll tell you later.' Her lips press together in an even harsher smile, before she brings her wine to her lips and guzzles it back like it's water.

'You don't seem fine.'

'Please, not now,' she hisses as Mum leans around me to see her.

'Who was on the phone?' Mum asks.

'No one, a client. I'll tell you later.'

Mum clicks her tongue. 'I understand.'

'I don't, could someone clue me in?' I look from my left to my right so sharply I'm putting my neck at risk of an injury.

Mum takes a breath as Serena buries herself in a slice of thick-cut bread.

'It was your father.'

Chapter Twelve

All I want to do is ask questions, but we all know it isn't the time.

People around us try to engage us in conversation as we make our way through the food.

It feels like the longest time. The sun moves around until it's burning my neck and all I want to do is run away again.

I haven't spoken to Dad. He doesn't know about Jonah, or that we're all here in Corfu. Not unless Serena has said more to him. I don't think she would. She thought the sun shone out of him and this has really knocked her back, even if she hasn't said it.

None of us are talking about anything enough. About how we feel and what's gone on in the past. I want to break down that wall, but I also want to hide behind it, so I don't have to keep letting in the pain Jonah and Dad have left in my heart.

I guess Dad must be home now, and has seen the empty spaces and the for-sale sign. I wonder if he thought Mum would have been there waiting for him with his slippers, after lying about his work trip. Not that he called her once. Not that he contacted any of us the whole time he was away.

Once everyone's finished enjoying the meal, Spiros and Christos lead us down to the shop.

'There is one last important part to our tour. You remember me talking about all the things we can make with oil? Well, my wife, Eleni, she makes soap by hand, and we give you a soap at the end of each tour. Please take your bag from Christos. Each soap is made with our simple olive oil, and we save the extra virgin for our cans, which you can buy, if you wish. Still, the beautiful soap, with only a few ingredients, is soothing and will keep your skin young. If you would like anything from our shop, Christos can help you.'

Christos gives me a look, a lift to his eyebrow, before he turns back towards the shop. For a moment I stand still, staring at the opening to the building where he was standing only seconds ago. I wish people were as simple as science experiments. That I could calculate each variable and come up with answers. Each person has way too many variables and thinking about what each micro-movement could mean is almost enough to give me a headache.

'I'm sure Christos just gave me some kind of weird look,' I say close to Serena's ear.

'Maybe it was something to do with what he said yesterday? About you liking the tour because it might interest you or something? Was it something about you doing nothing? What was that all about, anyway?'

'Nothing, something dumb I said when I helped him bring the food out yesterday.'

How can she not have even seen the look and have more idea than me as to its meaning? She's probably right, though; this must've been the part of the tour he thought I'd like, with my background in cosmetics and with me picking the soap up yesterday to smell it.

It's nice that they're keeping the soap simple. Working out chemical formulas for capturing youth and to keep the shelf life of products for longer has been my bread and butter for years. Constantly striving for softer skin, fewer lines, youthfulness.

But this . . . maybe this *could* be interesting. Simple, tried and tested beauty with a twist. Just like I wanted to do when I quit my job back in England. I hadn't been thinking about olive oil at the time, but this is very interesting.

Maybe Christos was right, maybe there is something here for me.

Olive oil was used in some of the cosmetics I worked on in the past, but to a lesser extent. I need to speak with my uncle and find out a little more about how they do things here.

Maybe Eleni could chat to me about it all too, as she makes the soap. It would be a great way to spend more time with her and Spiros and maybe even get their take on why Mum left all those years ago.

A few people crowd around Christos – mostly women – asking about soap and the various oils on sale and what the difference is and a multitude of other questions they could've asked Spiros but have chosen to ask him instead.

'I'm going to get some air.' Serena waves her hand in front of her face.

'I'll come with you.' Mum steps in line behind her.

I hold back, picking up soaps to smell them with a fresh perspective. Thoughts move around my mind. Could I do something to work alongside everyone here? Maybe making a moisturiser or even make-up? Ideas bounce about. I'd need a workspace and a host of other things. Including set-up money that I don't have anymore. If I wanted to make something a little more fancy, I'd need a lab too.

I put down the soap and briefly squeeze my eyes tightly shut.

I'm getting ahead of myself. How can I do these things without any money?

When the crowd thins and people start thanking Spiros just outside the shop as they head away from the olive grove, I move towards Christos as he says goodbye to the last two women and begins moving things back into place.

'It's the soap, right? That you thought I might be interested in?' I say casually as I step towards him.

'I thought, maybe. You were picking them up yesterday and you say you have nothing to do. You might be interested in the traditional soap-making. Here, I put two in your bag.' He presses his finger to his lips. 'Shh, OK? Don't tell anyone.'

There's no playful smile or flirtation that I can detect. Not what I would expect when someone is giving me something extra for free.

'Thanks, that's really kind.'

He gently shrugs as he hands me a bag before picking up two remaining bags. Walking past me, he takes them outside.

For the past twenty-four hours, Christos has stayed pretty level, even in the face of Serena's flirtation. He hasn't really given anything back that's more than polite interest.

There's something about him, a shadow to Spiros's light. Not in a bad way, but he isn't like Eleni or Spiros, who easily break into grins and clap their hands together when they're happy. He's been welcoming and kind, but, no matter what Mum says, I'm positive there's something about him that's held back, even when he's making kind gestures like giving me a bed or some soap.

Christos moves towards the bench where Mum and Serena are sitting looking out at the olive trees.

Their backs are to us, but Serena is slumped forward and Mum's rubbing the space between her shoulder blades.

Christos hesitates, turning back towards me. 'Perhaps you could give these for me? I must be going. Please say goodbye for me.'

'OK, well, thanks for the soap, and the idea.'

Christos dips his chin and begins to stride towards Spiros, who's standing at the hedge talking to the last customer.

I hesitate, stuck between wanting to know what's being said and wanting to hide from it all.

Sucking in a deep breath to inflate myself ready for action, I march towards the bench.

'A gift of soap from Christos. He also says goodbye.' I pass them the bags.

They both look like a bolt of lightning has struck their faces with pain.

'What's happened?' I continue. 'What did Dad say?'

Mum's hand contracts into a ball on her leg and her jaw clenches too.

'He was really mad.' Serena's voice cracks. 'I ended up hanging up on him. I've never heard him like that before.' She sniffs and tilts her chin up to the sky. 'Don't fucking cry, don't fucking cry,' she mutters to herself.

'He has no right to make you feel like this. I will call him later, explain—' Mum begins before I cut her off.

'No you won't.' My voice hits like a drum and they both look at me under folded foreheads. 'You don't have to explain anything to him. Did he explain anything to you? I'd only been with Jonah three years' – my finger hits my chest so hard it hurts – 'and even he left a note of apology. And he had problems, and he said he still loved me. Dad . . .' My voice squeaks out as I drown in my own words. I take a slow breath, blowing it out carefully.

Against the heat, my whole body has started to tremble, as though the emotions I'm feeling are causing an earthquake inside a glacier.

'Dad doesn't deserve to be chased. Not now, not ever. You deserve better than that. If you go to him now, you lose all the power.'

I love my father. I know he didn't do this as an attack on me or my sister or even my mum. He's just another stupid man with enough charm and money to attract a woman of a certain type and a certain age. That's all. He's an idiot.

That doesn't give him the right to make everyone else around him feel like dirt because he's having a midlife crisis.

Mum stands and wraps me in her arms. It's a brief embrace as the heat of the midday sun is beginning to make its mark on us all. But it's enough to make me feel like things will one day be better than they are today and, without words, know she's grateful for my support.

'You're so strong, Lorena. I'm so proud of you,' she confirms in my ear.

I don't feel strong. I'm pleased that the façade is holding well for Mum though. Sometimes I feel like I'm being melted in the Corfu sun and all that's holding me up is the desperate need to find out the truth about things. Without that, I might fall apart.

'I just can't believe he's calling Serena about this and not you. Putting her in the middle. It's not right.'

'Maybe he did, but I left my phone back at the house.' Mum shrugs. 'And besides, maybe I've put you both in the middle too, by telling you and bringing you here.'

'It's different, he was the one off in Mexico with someone else,' Serena pipes in, still sitting on the bench.

'Did you all enjoy the tour?' Spiros moves around us. 'You look like it was not so good.' He stops in front of us, placing his hands on his thick waist.

'It was good, we all enjoyed it. There was just a phone call, nothing for you to worry about. When will we see you next?' Mum quickly stands to be by his side. 'A man is coming tomorrow to help us with the beach house. Other than that, we are free. His name is Anton Greenwood.'

'Oh yes, yes. I know him. Everyone knows you when you are so tall.' Spiros thoughtfully rubs his cheek as he smiles. 'Eleni tells me to invite you for Sunday. All day, a big celebration for your arrival home. Oh, and there is food to give you in the fridge. She made things to keep you fed.'

'That is so generous of her, tell her thank you. We can't wait for Sunday. Where do you live now?'

Spiros looks down at the ground and takes a small step back.

He clears his throat and continues to rub his cheek, a little harder. 'The old house. Mama and Baba's house.'

Mum's eyebrows strike up and fall just as fast. For a split second she tucks her lips in, like she's holding words back, before switching into a broad smile.

'Perfect. That is perfect.'

That's all she says, but I don't believe it is, however convincing her smile might be.

Chapter Thirteen

Three taps gently strike my door.

'Lorena? Can I come in?' a low voice stage-whispers.

'Sure,' I loudly whisper right back.

Serena only opens the door enough to slide inside, as though it couldn't open any further.

The only light in my room is from my phone screen. I turn on the torch light on my phone and place it on the floor, so she doesn't have to put the big light on.

The only other light is from the stars outside my open window and the tavernas not too far along the beach.

'Can I sit down?' She points at the end of my single bed, and I nod towards it.

We all went our separate ways all afternoon. Mum went for a walk and Serena went to the beach. It meant a complete avoidance of any further conversations about Dad or the past.

Even when we went out for dinner, as we still don't have a stove to heat up what Eleni made for us, Mum picked the loudest place she could, with men dancing and setting fire to things at every given opportunity. It would've been brilliantly entertaining if there hadn't been a strange cloud over us all.

Serena curls her legs underneath herself on my bed. Not my bed. Christos's bed. I'll give it back as soon as I have one of my own.

'Dad called me again.' She rubs her fingers over her forehead. 'He told me to tell Mum that he wants a divorce.'

'Why the hell can't he tell her that himself?'

'He says he's too angry at her for leaving him.'

'But he left first.'

'That's not how he sees it.'

'How?' Even though I'm trying to keep my voice calm, it comes out with so much anger it cuts through the air.

Serena's shoulders rise before dropping back down with such force it's as though her muscles were unable to hold them up for a moment longer.

'I don't know.' She bites at the corner of her mouth. 'He went on holiday and came back and she was gone. That's how he sees it. I didn't want to argue with him anymore.'

Without all her make-up on and in a baggy sleep T-shirt, she looks the same as she did at fourteen. Those ten years have slipped between us like ants disappearing through cracks in the walls.

In ten short years we've gone from two teenagers playing grown-ups to actually becoming them. I'm only two and a half years older than Serena, but that equated to being three school years above her. It seemed like such a big age gap when we were in school. I was the cool older sister that she looked up to. Or I thought I was, and she acted like I was.

Now I'm the train wreck desperately wishing I could say something to ease her pain.

When we were younger, she would come and sit on the end of my bed, exactly like she is now, only my teenage room was always awash with make-up and clothes. It was impossible to find the floor half the time. Now we're in an empty box with suitcases in one corner and a bed in the other, and all we're full of is pain. Deep, unsettling and only possible when you grow up and realise life isn't all fun and games.

All those years ago, the dramas were so much easier. Not that we thought that at the time. Worrying about boys and what to wear to parties.

She would burst into my room begging to borrow a top or curl up on my bed to tell me about her first kiss, then the first time she had sex. We've never hidden anything from each other. Even the bad stuff and the embarrassing stuff. I remember when she stole a lipstick because the woman at the make-up counter treated her like she couldn't afford it, and she told me right away. Or when I told her that I had a crush on a teacher at school. I trusted her not to tell anyone else.

She could've embarrassed me with that one so many times, but I was right to trust her.

Now we have to deal with the realisation that our parents are as flawed – or more flawed – than we are. That they're riddled with more than the cracks beginning to show on their skin, but deep ridges of imperfections too, which are declaring themselves with age and maybe the fear of ageing.

I suck in a deep breath, letting it out slowly as I shuffle down the bed until my head hits my pillow and my feet are to one side of Serena.

'You are not a messenger, Serena. Dad is a grown man. He's, what? Fifty-seven soon?'

'Fifty-eight.'

'Fifty-eight, and he can't call up the woman he's been married to for thirty years and say, *Oh hi, I'm sorry I'm a cheating bastard, can I have a divorce?* It's not up to you. Do you want me to call him and tell him to leave you out of it all?'

'What? So you become my messenger?' She attempts a laugh, but it falls flat. 'No. I said it wasn't up to me. He didn't say he was pissed off I wasn't taking his side in it all, but his tone . . .' Serena looks down at her knees and shakes her head, making her hair cascade around her face like a waterfall she can hide behind. 'He said he only had an affair because he could tell Mum didn't love him anymore, because they never did anything fun together anymore.'

I prop myself up on my elbows, as though doing so will make me hear things differently.

'Wait, what? Is he talking about the woman who for his last birthday paid for him to jump out of a plane?'

'God, you're right, I'd forgotten about that.'

'I just think he's trying to justify something that he can't, and find a way to take the heat off himself.' I pause and slump back down, knotting my fingers together over my stomach. 'Did you see Mum's face when Spiros said about living in the *old house*?'

'Yes!' Serena slaps down on her bare thighs. 'What *was* that?'

'Not a clue. But then' – I lift my arms and gesture towards the ceiling – 'what is any of this about? *Really?* We still don't know why she left or what happened with Spiros or our grandparents. Last night, she started saying she was a fool not to come back. I wish I'd been more sober so I could hold on to more of it.'

We sit with our own thoughts for a moment in the glow from the outside world that's dying one light at a time.

'I hate this.' Serena uncurls herself and slides along to lie next to me.

It's more of a squeeze than it used to be, lying next to each other. Neither of us is that big, but as teens we weren't fully formed. We had that wiry look, as though our arms were too long, but only because they didn't have enough flesh on them yet.

'Do you want to sleep in here tonight?'

'No . . . yes.' Her *yes* is tiny, like a money spider creeping in unannounced and barely seen.

I can count on one hand the number of times Serena has slept in my bed since the age of five or six.

When our grandmother on Dad's side died, when our dog died and when she watched a documentary on UFOs and it featured the infamous Rendlesham Airbase case. Seeing as Rendlesham is in our county, she was irrationally afraid she might suddenly be abducted.

Three times, and two were because she was so consumed with loss she couldn't be alone.

'That's fine, you can stay, but if we sweat so much we slip out of the bed, I'm blaming you.'

A snort of laughter and tears pounce out of her. Leaning towards her, I kiss her head.

'Get some sleep. It'll all be better in the morning.'

'You sound like Mum.'

She's right, I do. But that's all I have, the repetition of someone else's words on my lips, because right now I don't have the strength to form originality. The only slight positive in all this is that it's nice not to be the weak one for a moment. It's nice that I can help my baby sister, even if it is just in the act of lying next to her like we did as kids.

'One day,' I begin, 'we'll look back on this with laughter in our hearts.'

Another one of Mum's sayings that's been regurgitated over the years.

'I'm not sure it will. Not this time. Mum and Dad are getting a divorce and Mum doesn't even know yet.'

'I'm pretty sure she knows. She wouldn't have come back to Corfu after thirty years of avoiding the place to hide from him if she didn't think it was probably ending in divorce. I mean, come on, she's the one who put the house on the market. She's said it's over.'

'Yeah, but she never actually said the word *divorce*.'

'I don't think a word can change the actions.'

Silence shrouds us, heavier than the thick sea air that pours in my window.

It's not long before Serena's asleep. I try to stay still as I wonder if tomorrow really can be better. Instead of reliving the bone-crushing pain of our recent past.

Chapter Fourteen

'Yes, I can help you.' Anton looks at each wall in what will one day be our kitchen as he slowly turns. 'It will be easy. Easy enough.'

Mum throws her hands in the air with delight.

Easy. This is the best news we've had since getting three free beds to use.

I was sort of disappointed when Anton knocked on the door this afternoon. By the way everyone spoke about him, I was expecting someone closer to seven foot. I guess he probably is still the tallest person I know, at maybe six foot five. But whether he's five feet tall or ten, to me, he is a hero.

'What will you charge?' Mum's hands clasp together so tightly her knuckles look pale. Even though the house is always quite dark, as we keep the shutters closed most of the day, her knuckles are still glowing a little.

Anton begins to meander back through the kitchen door to the sweeping living space as he talks, probably to be in the room where there's a fan whirring above our heads.

'You will need to buy all the supplies, but I can make a list of what is needed. Alec said he would help me, and he explained your situation . . . so I will do it for free, with one condition.'

Serena glances up at us with interest from the floor, where she's been sitting all morning with her laptop on her knees.

Mum and I fold our arms in perfect synchronicity. A condition? My mind races with ideas as to what it could be.

'I have two daughters, Gaia and Lily. You must do something for them. That is all I ask.'

'That's it?' I've never known anything like it.

'That's it,' he confirms. 'My family means everything to me. I don't need the money, I like to help people. But something nice for my daughters that would make them smile like your daughters will smile when this is all done. That would be nice.'

'Of course, thank you so much.' Mum's voice is breathy and her eyes begin to glaze with emotion. 'I am so grateful.'

'Well, it's not done yet. But I don't think it will take as much as you think. And you three will be put to work too. This is your house.' Anton's sharp green eyes narrow on Mum, then flick towards me and Serena.

'We want to do everything we can.' Mum beams.

'I will send you a list today. It might be worth Alec taking you to get things or helping you order things online. He's helped me in the past. Right, I best go, my wife tripped and hurt her knee, which is not so good when you have a toddler to run after.'

We run through the pleasantries of goodbye, but what Anton's really done is given us hope and light.

Apparently, after the plastering is finished upstairs, it's mostly decorating and fitting bathrooms then picking furniture. It might look ugly now, but most of the boring stuff was already in place when we got here. Well, apart from heating and cooling. But after a chat, we're going to get a wood burner for now and hope that heats the place enough in the winter, and eventually get a couple of air-conditioning units in.

'Right, I'm going out.' I march across the echoing room and pick up my handbag.

I managed to catch Spiros's elbow as we were leaving yesterday to ask if I could come back today after he's finished with the tours to talk to him about soap. He looked a little baffled but he said yes. Last night I went out and hired a quad bike. I didn't really want Serena and Mum asking a million questions. Not yet. So I left it in the car park at Cicala. I popped in for a quick juice and checked it was OK with them that I left it there.

'I'll go with you.' Mum skips a step to catch up. 'I could do with some air. Serena, what about you? Walk?'

'Actually, erm, I was hoping to go alone?' Guilt travels down my throat, catching like a lump. 'There's a couple of things I need to do, if that's OK?'

'Yes, of course.' Mum's mouth lifts into a smile but her shoulders round with deflation and the smile doesn't last long on her face. 'Have fun.'

She turns around and walks through the void, out towards the kitchen and through to the back door.

'Well, that was rude,' Serena mutters without even looking up from her laptop.

My teeth bury themselves into my cheek, just enough to bite back rising to her comment.

'See you later.' I turn towards the door and make my way out into the blinding late-morning sun.

There's a steady flow of people wandering down the road towards the beach in only bikinis and sarongs or board shorts, with bags overflowing with towels.

I'm only a few steps down the road and I'm regretting not bringing the hat I got the other day, but there's no way I'm turning back now. If Serena's fingers have left her laptop, she might start ranting at me for being mean.

It's only a short walk to Cicala. I wave at Alec and the owners before getting to the quad bike.

The independence of hiring a quad bike is strangely profound, even if I did have to use some of the money Mum gave me to do it. She didn't want me to feel like I had to keep asking for money, so she put some in my account. It wasn't much, but enough to do this for a day at least.

It's like being a kid getting pocket money again.

Feeling the power of the quad bike's engine rumbling and the wind rushing past me as I go is exactly what I need. It's time to find my own clarity again.

Although, last night solidified something to me: relationships are pointless.

I got a string of texts from my dad, so did Serena, with a strange mix of anger and begging.

I sent one back, saying it was nothing to do with me, but that – if he was interested in me – I was safe and with Mum and that I wasn't with Jonah anymore. He sent a simple *I'm sorry to hear that* and stopped messaging.

My insides nip at the thought of it all. At the actuality.

We ran from it all, and in doing so I haven't thought too much about the reality we left behind until now.

No more family Sunday dinners. No more hanging out with my mum and dad in the same room, even.

No more popping over to see them with a bottle of wine and Jonah on my arm. We all loved sharing a bottle of wine and a takeaway on a Friday night . . . how long was Dad actually cheating on Mum and she didn't know? How long had Jonah had been lying to me? From the start? Somewhere along the way? Maybe the whole time I didn't *really* know Jonah.

My dad will always be my dad, and I'll always love him, but the way he's treated Mum and the way he's been so dismissive of me and Serena has been a real eye-opener.

Mum hasn't said anything bad about him. She's only listed the facts as she has them and how she feels about them.

She could rant and scream that he's the worst man alive, but she hasn't.

I take a deeper breath of the fresh Corfu air as the quad bike glides along on the winding roads and past a cascading flow of green. The land slopes away at such an angle that the tops of thin green cones that are cypress trees are the same height as the road.

The drive up to the olive grove feels like it'll never end, because I have no idea where I'm going. Mum doesn't need satnav telling her when to turn or when we will arrive. The journey is still there, alive in her mind.

The views are enough to make my skin feel the pulse of electricity running through it again. In the far distance, the body of the sea looks as unmoving as the clear sky. Here and there, flowers erupt in shades of vibrant blue, fuchsia and sunshine yellow to distract the eyes from the millions of shades of green, until eventually it becomes one predominant shade: olive.

Leaving the quad bike where Mum left the car for the tours we've taken, I hike up to the opening in the hedge. I'm a little early, but I don't think Spiros will mind me looking around while he finishes up. I did say to bring Eleni, but I thought perhaps, if she hasn't come with him, I could go back up to the *old house* and see her.

Maybe I could find something out from them about Mum and her departure from Greece before we go there on Sunday. Maybe Spiros would be kind enough to shed some light on it all while he tells me about soap.

It's not that I don't know how to make soap. It's an easy process that can be done with only two or three ingredients. But I want to know what they do now, what they might want to do, and all the thoughts they might have on the subject of skincare and cosmetics.

Everything from how many trees they allocate towards their soaps to where they store it all.

If I'm going to make a life here, I need to start to understand what's required of me and what possibilities there are.

A beetle the size of my thumb whizzes past my head as I turn to go through the hedge, making me flinch before I catch sight of Spiros. He's walking down to the shop. I wave across at him and he diverts to come towards me, arms open in welcome.

'Lorena! What are you doing here?'

I stutter over words. 'Erm, I said I wanted to come in the afternoon and talk about soap. Remember?'

Spiros rubs his hand over his shaved head. 'Today? This is today? I thought Sunday?'

'That's OK.' I wave my hands dismissively, hoping this casual motion will hide my disappointment.

My stomach tightens. I really wanted to have a few days to think things through before telling Mum and Serena my idea, just a moment to process it myself and see if it's possible before they get excited for me and the pressure mounts to come up with ideas.

'I'm so sorry, today we have to help Eleni's mother. She is very old and very stubborn, never wanting help. We have to disguise it, you know? Help when she no looking, by cleaning when we go to the bathroom and things. Christos, though, he will help you. Come, come, I'm getting some more water, it's hotter today. It'll be hotter tomorrow too. Forty tomorrow.'

I shouldn't moan, because even staying out of the sun as much as I can during the afternoons I'm still getting a deep olive tan already, but forty degrees in a house without air con makes me feel a little ill.

'It's OK, I think I've bothered Christos enough, what with stealing his bed and all. I was really hoping to speak to Eleni too – you said she makes it all? The soap, I mean.'

'Yes, yes, but Christos, he helps with everything. Anything we know, he knows. He is like a second son to us.'

'You must be really close to his parents?'

Spiros marches along the undulations of the burnt grasses, as he silently nods. In the corner of my eye, I catch his face screwing up in thought before he can find a way to change the subject.

Chapter Fifteen

Being left alone, Christos and I walk slowly between the olive trees. The whole place is alive with the sound of chirping cicadas and bees buzz between us like we don't exist.

There's a swell of nerves in my stomach that I can't place.

I think it's knowing Serena can get a bit jealous when she likes someone. I had to hide the extra soap because I didn't want her to read something into it that isn't there, so spending time one on one with Christos, her current distraction, makes me feel a bit off balance. Plus, he isn't really the person I want to be talking to anyway.

I lick the gathering tang of salt off my top lip, and begin. 'I'm not really sure where to start.'

'If you want, I can start?' Christos suggests.

'Oh, yeah, OK, that makes sense.'

'Well, we have problems with licence, and you will need a licence if you want to have a cosmetic business. Here, with the tours, Spiros pays thousands and you don't know if it will be approved for the licence. It's every few years to be renewed. Farming licence is easy, but others' – he shrugs – 'it can be a little harder.'

'Wait, I need thousands of euros just to apply for a business licence before I can even begin?'

Christos nods and continues walking.

'Then you—'

'Well—' My head begins to shake back and forth and my fingers dig into my sides. 'Then this is all pointless, isn't it? The whole thing. I might as well give up now because I don't have any money.'

'I'm sure you can find it. If you go into business with Spiros, maybe he will help you?'

'No.' I can feel the lump forming in my throat, that clever little mechanism the body has created to force the windpipe open when all you want to do is close it. 'This was meant to be something *I* could do. I'm useless, I'm going to have to do something else in the meantime and save up, because I don't have anything. I'm sorry to waste your time like this.'

Turning away from Christos, I begin to jog down a slope in a direction I've never been where the olive tree branches knit together above my head and the world becomes a cooler and wilder place. A place I might manage to hide in.

My feet skid beneath me as the slope extends.

'Lorena, wait.' Christos's feet pad in step behind me.

I abruptly skip to a halt, covering my face with my hands as tears run cold along my burning cheeks.

I'm overwhelmed with emotions I've been keeping in and this is the worst possible time to let them out.

'I'm so sorry,' I mutter behind my hands as my shoulders judder. 'I'm not usually like this. I never normally cry.'

'Crying can be good. Needed.' Gently, Christos rubs my upper back. 'Come on. Let me get you a glass of wine.'

Laughter splutters with snot and tears behind my hands.

'And a tissue?'

'And a . . . err . . . napkin. We have many napkins.'

Keeping my hands over my face, I follow Christos back through the roots of the trees. That's all I see anyway as my lungs jerk out each breath in disjointed spasms.

Embarrassment kicks me so hard that, between sniffs and splutters, all I can say is sorry.

Over and over, *I'm sorry.*

Christos takes me into the shop and places a fold-out chair for me to sit on. Grabbing a handful of dark-blue napkins, he pushes them in my direction.

I proceed to blow my nose and scrub my cheeks with them.

Christos kneels, sitting his weight back on his heels in front of me.

'You've got some' – he grimaces as he peels something off my chin – 'napkin.'

'I'm so sorry.'

'You have to stop saying *sorry*. You cried, it's human to cry. Do you say sorry when you laugh?'

'It depends why I'm laughing.'

A smile forms behind his beard and a gentle squint touches his eyes in amusement.

'All right, well, maybe you *should* be sorry you are crying then, if the reason is crying *at* someone the way you might laugh *at* them.'

'Can you cry at someone else's expense?'

'No, I think not. It is not the same.' He chuckles. 'Now, why are you crying? Because it is too much money? It's possible, do you have something saved for this new adventure?'

Tears slip over my cheeks without control.

'No, I . . . I was robbed. They took everything I had. It's why I'm here. All I have is what my mum gives me. I'd quit my job before . . . I was going to start my own business in the UK but then . . .' Each word feels like trawling through the thickest mud. 'All my savings, anything of value . . . gone.'

Christos strokes his fingers through his beard and turns his head to look out of the door and into the burst of sunlight streaming in.

'I will give you the money.'

'What?' I splutter.

'Usually I give most of my money to charity, at Easter, but I save some, in case someone I care for needs it. You have it. Better you than a bank.'

My mouth hangs open at the man kneeling in front of me. The man I've sort of known for two days and who's offering me money.

'What . . . Why?' I look from one of his perfect almond-shaped eyes to the other, searching for sense.

'I have no use for money, you can have it. It would be nice to see you start your dreams.'

This isn't the first time I've had a man down on one knee proposing something to me that's too good to be true.

The image resurfaces of Jonah taking my hand and telling me he'd love me forever and the tears of joy that overwhelmed me back then, when I thought I was being handed my future . . . when all I was being given was a lie.

'Have you eaten?'

I shake my head. 'No.'

Christos stands, heads towards the fridge and pours out two wine glasses of water, instead of the wine he promised.

Did I hallucinate his proposal of money? I feel like I've slipped and hit my head and now I'm in a dream or imagining things.

He pulls out a bowl and fills it with olives before throwing some cured meat on a small plate and putting the dishes out in front of the soaps.

'Drink water. The crying will dehydrate you.' He holds the wine glass in my direction.

'Thanks.'

I begin to sip, the ice-cold water refreshing me in the heat. He was probably right not to give me wine.

Christos half sits on the table display, watching me.

'I can't take your money.'

Christos shrugs. 'It is there if you want it. I can give you ten thousand euro, at most.'

I hold his gaze, locking us together as seconds slip by.

'You're a strange man, you know that? Or is it just a Greek thing? Because that Anton is helping us out for basically nothing too.'

'We have a similar ethos, but no. Not all Greeks. Many have to work hard for a living and spend it on family and would maybe give you time but not all would be able to give money. No two people on this world are the same. I have nothing to spend my money on and Anton has more than he can spend.'

Placing down his glass, he holds out the olive bowl towards me. I gladly take one. It's past lunch and the crying has taken it out of me. As I remove the flesh, I'm left with the stone. Christos throws his outside and I follow suit, discarding it out of the door.

'Even if you have nothing to spend it on right now, surely you will one day?' This man is crazy, trying to throw money at me. 'You'll meet someone, fall in love and have a million handsome children.'

Christos shakes his head. 'No. I'm not interested in that. Not *any* of it. I haven't dated a woman in many, many years.'

'Serena will be disappointed.' My fingers rush to my lips but they're not fast enough. I press against my mouth and squeeze my eyes shut.

'It's OK, I noticed the flirting. The man in the moon, he noticed and told me.'

'She's not subtle when she wants something.'

Christos tilts his head to the side and turns down his mouth. 'Sadly, she will not be getting this *thing*. I have never had a relationship, and I will not start now.'

'Never?'

'Nope.'

'Not *any* kind of . . . relationship?' I do my best to project all the thoughts in my head without saying them, hoping he understands my meaning. Just because he doesn't want a wife doesn't mean he doesn't have one-night stands, I guess.

'No. I don't have women in my life. Other than Eleni, but she is family.'

He tosses an olive in his mouth and passes me the bowl to take another for myself.

'Wow. Lucky.'

Laughter resonates out of his chest.

'You are the first person to say that, *lucky*. All the women I meet they say they are sorry for me or want to take me home and show me love. *Lucky*.' He tosses another olive in the air, catching it in his mouth with ease.

'I bet your parents are disappointed.'

Saying Eleni is the only woman in his life has got me wondering about his parents, that and Spiros screwing up his face when I mentioned them earlier. He didn't say they had passed away, he nodded in agreement that they were close . . . but his face seemed to say something else. Maybe they *were* close once, but they've since passed away?

Christos pauses, with another olive ready to be launched into the air.

He lowers his eyeline, rolling the small purple olive between his fingers.

'I wouldn't know.' It flies into the air for him to catch in his mouth. 'Eat more, drink more, then we talk business.' I want to question him more, but it's clear he doesn't want to talk about his parents, dead or alive. Also, I need him to know I can't take money from him.

'But I don't want your money.'

'It is your choice, but it's there if you change your mind. You are here now, we might as well talk about the fact, otherwise Spiros will ask what I taught you, and when you say nothing' – Christos rolls his eyes – 'I will be in trouble.'

'OK, we can talk about it, but we can't do it.'

Christos stops chewing and raises an eyebrow in my direction.

'That's not what I meant.'

His other eyebrow shoots up, joining the first as he begins to chuckle quietly. 'Yes, I know we can't *do it*, I already told *you* that.'

Laughter spills out of me as freely as the breeze rustling the leaves outside. I guess that answers that then, he doesn't even have one-night stands or anything.

It's good to laugh and to let in the light through the cracks. I might not be able to make all my own dreams come true today, but the kindness of a stranger who's fast becoming a friend lifts me over the tears. Even if I couldn't bring myself to tell him the full heart-destroying story that brought me to a river of tears and to my penniless state.

Today feels like the first day of something positive. I've made a friend.

Chapter Sixteen

'I have something to tell you, and you're not going to like any of it, but please don't shoot the messenger.' I grip Serena's shoulders, ready to tell her the bad news about Christos not dating and I'm pretty sure not doing anything at all with women other than perhaps offering them huge amounts of money for no apparent reason.

'I have great news.' Mum bursts into the house. 'Tomorrow, Anton and Alec are going to come and start all the plastering upstairs, a wood burner will be delivered tomorrow also, and next week kitchen tiles, a dishwasher and a host of other things. And' – she thrusts her hands into her handbag and pulls out a fistful of paint swatches – 'we have these to look at.'

Her skin looks bright and tanned, healthy. I've almost got used to seeing her with a grey air about her; this makes a delightful change.

'This is great, Mum, but Lorena was about to give me some bad news and I literally can't function until she tells me what it is.'

I step back. 'OK, well . . .' I pace the room, trying to find the right words, to lay the groundwork without creating any hurt. 'I went to the olive grove today, because Christos gave me this idea about natural soaps and selling natural olive oil cosmetics. Only, Spiros couldn't talk to me about it in the end, so I got talking to Christos—'

'And now you're in love and dating. I wanted you to get over Jonah and be happy, but did you *have* to sleep with Christos? You know I like him.' She begins her own pacing and arm waving. 'I knew I should've called shotgun.'

'Serena!' I can't help but laugh at her outburst. 'That's not it. It's not at all it. I didn't sleep with him, I don't think he sleeps with anyone, and he told me he doesn't *do* relationships, that's all.'

'Hold on.' Mum puts one hand up to stop me. 'I am more interested in these olive oil cosmetics you will be making than the sexual habits of Christos.'

'Eww, Mum, never say sexual habits again.' Serena's face contorts.

Mum doesn't even react; she keeps her eyes on me, waiting for a response.

'Sadly, I won't be making any. The set-up fees alone are outside of my non-existent budget. I'm thinking of seeing if one of the hotels needs a cleaner or a taverna needs a waitress so I can earn enough to make it happen. It might take a few years, but that's what you get when you fall in love with a thief, I guess.' A catch strikes my vocal cords in a way I didn't expect.

'No, your father will pay for it. I want a divorce – he has agreed, and we will get half the money for the house and we will gift you both some money.' Mum squeezes my arm. 'Until then, learn everything you can in the same way you were going to before. Who will buy the products, where will you sell them. I'm sure Spiros can make space on his table, and you have the beautiful Natur Aura shop up the road from us who might be interested? It will work out.'

'You've spoken to Dad?' Serena tucks a loose strand of hair behind her ear, as though it might make her hear better, before she folds her arms over her chest.

'Yes. It's not your concern. You have your relationship with him, and I have mine. The two have no connection.'

'No connection?' Serena's fluffed-up eyebrows shoot up. '*No connection?* We are made from both of you, you both brought us up, everything about both of you connects to the other.'

'Not anymore, Serena. The past leads to the future, it doesn't own it.'

'No, of course it doesn't, but—'

'Serena, today is a good day. A day where the sun has decided to bring us good fortune and all things can begin afresh tomorrow. We all have a lot of hard work to do, please, I beg of you, no ranting today.'

'I wasn't ranting, I was asking.'

Mum purses her lips and keeps them closed. She knows as well as I do that sometimes it's best not to engage. If you don't argue, then Serena can't argue back. It's hard to argue with a blank face.

It's my turn to do what I do best and keep the peace in this triangle by changing the subject.

'I'm sorry again about Christos and his no dating or, as Mum put it so beautifully, no sexual habits rule. He told me he has literally *never* had a girlfriend.'

'That's OK,' Serena breathes as she turns back to her laptop waiting on the floor. 'I love a challenge.'

'I'm serious, he basically said he doesn't *do it*.' I recall our playful conversation, but how he clearly said he already told me he doesn't *do it*.

She winks before turning away.

Mum mouths, 'Thank you,' and squeezes my arm again.

'Dad messaged me too, by the way,' Serena says as she slides down the wall to sit back on the floor. 'He told me to tell you he wanted a divorce.'

'It was wrong of him to involve you.'

'I know.' Serena pauses, looking down at her laptop on the floor next to her leg. 'What if he wanted to come out here and visit us? Me and Lorena, I mean. He knows where we are now. This is where you met, right? He was on holiday with his friends when you fell in love?'

Mum's weight shifts from one foot to the other.

'It was something like that,' Mum agrees.

'What if he turns up? What then?' Serena tilts her head.

I hadn't thought about that. Although I doubt he would, based on everything so far. He hasn't bothered messaging *me* much, because he knows I won't pander to him the way Serena will.

'He won't. He swore he would never come back here.'

'So did you, didn't you?'

Serena has a valid point. Her knees flop out and she leans forward, waiting for Mum's rebuttal.

Although Mum has never explicitly said she swore she would never come back to Corfu, the fact she hasn't returned until now makes me think Serena's pulling at the thread that I've wanted to but haven't had enough energy for.

Mum's chest rises and falls before she turns away. 'I will take you for dinner at sunset. I've booked Cicala again so we can speak to Alec. Be ready.'

For a moment we're both completely still as Mum creaks her way up the wooden staircase. It's like we're children again and we've been given orders and we know that she'll take away our toys if we don't follow them.

As soon as she's out of sight, Serena rolls her eyes and flops back.

'Do you think Christos will be there tonight?' she begins.

'I doubt it. I don't think he's very social. I'm going outside. See you in a bit.'

Serena grunts a response as she turns back to her laptop.

Heading to the back garden, I let myself be consumed once again by the hum of life. Not just the white noise of cicadas now, but the chatter from the beach beyond the reeds and bushes at the bottom of the gardens. In the shade of next door's tree, I sit on one of the sad plastic chairs and let the heat melt my thoughts.

What I would do to burn away my past and to remove the pain and the residue of love I still have for Jonah. That's the thing though. The receptors for pain and pleasure are so close in the brain, and it's the same for love and hate. They're intimately linked, almost coiled together.

I don't know how to unpick the past from the present. Or if I'll ever be able to. I wonder if Mum feels the same. It definitely seems like she's here to try and unpick her past from her present. I just wish I knew how.

I wonder if Christos's past is anything to do with his strange attitudes to the present and the future. I know why I never want to date again, why I think the life of a spinster is a good one. Historically, it *was* a good thing, a desirable thing. A name for a woman who could make money from spinning yarn and so not need a husband to support her. That's not to say she was well off either, but she didn't *have* to marry. Christos has money, clearly, so he doesn't have to marry either. Sadly, in that respect, I'm a lot worse off than a spinster right now, but I'm sure I'll scrape my way to spinster status eventually.

I close my eyes and tilt my head back so the sun pours down on my face.

There, in among the red glow, I can see Christos in my mind's eye. I think he could be a good friend if he wasn't such an enigma. It's hard to fully trust someone when it's so obvious they're holding things back. At least he's kindly trying to offer me money, instead of taking my hard-earned life away.

I should've told Serena that I'll be seeing him again so he can show me some of the things they use to make the soap, and to discuss more about my business idea.

I'm sure I would've, if the subject of Dad hadn't been brought up.

Chapter Seventeen

'OK, so, I have a question,' I begin.

'Do you have anything that is *not* a question?' Christos doesn't flinch or laugh or raise an eyebrow. I'm starting to think he's almost always serious.

'Yes, but not today. Do you ever use extra-virgin food-grade olive oil in your soap?'

'No.'

'Why not?'

'It would be a waste.'

I roll my eyes and slump back on to the dry itchy grass, tucking my hands behind my head.

Lying under the olive trees is the only way to spend the sweltering heat of this afternoon. In a swimming pool or in the sea would be good too, but this helps my mind in a different way. I need this sort of focused distraction, and I can't imagine Christos hanging out at the beach for a chat. He looks too well suited to sitting among trees.

'The benefits for the skin are so much greater, and you can charge as much for a skincare product as two or three cans of olive oil. Maybe more. I've got some simple ideas . . . and some fancy lab-based ones too. But to begin with, honey to soothe along with high-grade olive oil to plump skin with all those healthy fats, as well as locking in the moisture. I just need to decide how to stop it from being too greasy without putting too many additives in it.'

I look over at him, waiting for some kind of response or acknowledgement.

Instead, he stays still, staring into the distance through the trees.

'What do you think?'

'I was thinking what trees Spiros might be able to give you for this. Your ideas are yours. You do not need me for them. I am here to listen, not to talk.'

I roll on to my side to see him better. Light from the sun sprinkles over us through the leaves of the trees, making his tan look even more golden than usual.

'What would you normally be doing right now? You work all morning in the summer. Then what? What are your hobbies, who are your friends? I hate to think I'm keeping you from them.'

'Does it matter?' he breathes.

'Yes, to me it does. What would you be doing?'

'Gardening, cleaning, sleeping. Probably sleeping.' Christos joins me in lying back, putting his hands behind his head.

Through the leaves over our heads, the wisp of a solitary cloud hangs in the sky without a breeze to move it along. That perfect bright blue, like nothing I've seen anywhere but here. I still can't decide which I prefer, the night sky bursting with the glitter of stars, the scalded reds of sunset or the blinding blues of day.

It's nothing like England, that's for sure. I know for a fact it's raining there right now.

Wednesday . . . in England I would've had a spin class in the morning and then spent the day working on the new products, maybe some business meetings lined up, then Jonah would've arrived home at five thirty on the dot and we'd have cooked together. Probably something simple, like pasta, because who can really be bothered on a Wednesday to cook anything complex?

Then we would've snuggled on the sofa to binge-watch the latest TV show. It was always Friday nights he was out late.

'Most girls don't lie on the ground. They would moan about the insects and the grass.'

Christos's voice slices up my thoughts and I'm grateful for someone to pull me out of the loop in my head, someone who won't ask what painful thoughts are there.

'I might have a few months ago . . . I've stopped caring.'

'After you were robbed?'

Or maybe not, maybe he can pull at those painful strings too.

'Yeah.'

'Did they ever catch who did it?'

'No.'

How could they, when I never reported him? He had access to everything. I was stupid enough to think joint accounts were safe when you're getting married. We'd only changed it over a couple of weeks beforehand.

It all lined up afterwards, of course, him getting a bee in his bonnet about bringing together our assets. He gave a bunch of reasons that all seemed to make sense – I guess because I wanted them to make sense.

'I'm sorry, I hope they do.'

A bumblebee hums around my head, looking for some nectar.

Every last living thing on this planet is looking for something. There are no exceptions to this rule.

Whether it's the next meal, love, solace, a holiday . . . we might not know it or realise it or ever even think about it, but we're all on the hunt for something. Jonah was hunting for my money.

I wonder what my mum is hunting for.

'What are you looking for, Christos?'

'I don't think I understand.'

'We're all looking for something. Right now, I'm looking for a way to make my new business idea work. A way to move on from . . . disappointment.'

I don't add the heartbreak part. It seems unnecessary for someone I've known half a week and have already ugly-cried in front of.

Poor man is probably only here talking to me out of pity as it is.

'Peace.'

'Is that a hint that I should leave you alone? I don't think you'll find peace with me here.'

'I won't find it, with or without you. But, since you are asking, peace is the answer.'

Maybe that's something we're all looking for, but it's mostly reserved for post-mortem. Rest in peace, or they passed away peacefully, or they looked so peaceful. They all make me think of sleep or death.

Maybe it's best to live without any peace, to mess it all up and spend time working it all out again and again.

'It's peaceful here,' I offer.

'It is, yes, but peaceful is not the same as peace. Now, when are you talking to Spiros about all of this? I was thinking Sunday. I have been invited to join you all. I think they want to set me up with your sister. If I am helping you, you need to help me with distraction. I would rather not disappoint *another* girl.'

'Wow . . . that didn't sound at all big-headed.'

'I want to keep my peace, nothing else.'

I sit up and look down at Christos; his arms are thick with muscle. He's broad, but without the added weight of anything outside of the practical. He has muscles because he uses them, even if they are appealing enough to make it likely that many girls *have* been heartbroken by his proclamation of never being with any of them.

He isn't fazed by being called big-headed, either. Under his impressive beard and his strong bones, he stays the same. That same solid rock that only rarely glimmers into a smile.

'Are you going to help me?' His dark eyes lock on to mine.

'If you agree to be my sounding board, once a week at least, then yeah, I'll keep Serena from being too much, as much as humanly possible.'

Removing his right hand from behind his head, he stretches his long arm towards me, extending it for a handshake. 'Deal.'

Our hands entwine and firmly grip together, like seaweed tangling into one. A warmth creeps up through my arm at the intimacy of our secret.

'Deal.'

Chapter Eighteen

Spiros and Eleni's house sits in pride of place at the top of a slope. It's a sweeping stone building that looks more like a mansion than a house.

'This was my home as a child. It's where Spiros and I grew up,' Mum says softly as she studies the building like it's the face of an old friend.

'Wow.' Serena slides her sunglasses down her nose to take it all in.

Spiros got all this, and Mum was gifted the rundown beach house by the sea.

Even though, thanks to tourism, her place does have a high value, I still think Mum must've pissed off her parents to only get *that* compared to *this*.

We step up towards the house, where palm trees have been perfectly placed in among the stones, and head to the front door.

Before we even get there, Eleni throws open the impressive white door, her arms spread as she approaches us. She's wearing an elegant orange and red patterned chiffon cover-up with enormous arm holes that make it slip down her shoulders as she comes towards us.

'Thalia, Lorena, Serena! Welcome, welcome. We are so glad to have you here at last.'

She kisses our cheeks, her face refreshingly cool. When she reaches Mum, she launches into Greek as we pile into the house. It's mostly to welcome her and to tell her she hopes she will feel welcome, and to feel at home again. I think, anyway.

The air inside is as crisp and cool as Eleni's cheek. It's perfectly monitored with air conditioning. Everything is painted white, and the floor tiles are white too.

It's not what I expected. I can't really picture what I expected now. Something more rustic, I guess, with slightly worn rugs and busy ornaments. This looks plush and elegant. I guess Eleni and Spiros look like . . . people who might have more simple taste. Who work hard but . . . I don't know. I didn't expect them to be the type of people to bother about appearances. Whereas this . . . I do my best to close my mouth because I can feel Mum's glare from the corner of my eye as she wants to tell me to stop.

'I like what you've done with it. It's beautiful,' Mum says in English.

'Efcharistó. We have been cleaning it up ready to host some events. The work, it's almost finished now. Spiros has his tours, I want parties.' Her hands splay out and she bubbles with laughter.

'Our son, Giórgos, lives in Athens with his girlfriend selling our oils across the world but I can be organising events for clients here. I want my boy back home again. I'm hoping this will bring him home to Corfu after his big adventures.' She winks at us as though this is a secret she's trusting us to keep.

The doorbell chimes with a tune so elegant, it takes me a moment to realise what it is.

'That must be Christos! It is so hard to get him out to dinner sometimes. We always try to get him here. I hate him being all on his own every night. I'm so happy he says yes to dinner today.' She squeezes Serena's arm as she passes her. 'Not that I gave him a choice.'

Eleni saunters back the way she came, her linen trousers grazing the floor as she goes.

Serena's beaming grin and tight shoulders catch my eye. That little passing squeeze from Eleni has probably given her a whole new layer of confidence in her chances of getting a date with Christos.

Alarm bells in my head are clearer than their doorbell; it's time to change the subject.

Mum edges in front of us into a large open living room with a television the size of a window in one corner and windows the size of doors lining a wall, with French doors in the middle.

All the furniture looks heavy, and good quality.

'I can't believe you grew up here. It's beautiful.' I keep watch of Mum from the corner of my eye as her finger slides along the back of a leather armchair.

'We were very lucky.'

'I can't even begin to understand why you wouldn't come back. What happened that was so bad—'

'Look, here comes Spiros.' She interrupts me before I can even begin probing for answers.

The doors to outside open and Spiros bursts through to welcome us with kissed cheeks. He speaks softly in Greek to Mum, but I don't catch what he says.

Her chin dips and she lifts her lips into a smile that wilts faster than it was raised.

Christos and Eleni quickly join us with more *kalispera*s and kisses.

'I have big surprise for you all. Please, follow me.' Spiros grins with a twinkle in his eye as he looks over at his wife, who's mirroring his contentment.

It's all I can do not to gasp as we walk out of the door. My heart skips with the view. The building extends out to a white brick balcony that's edged with clear Perspex, giving the impression you could so easily fall off the edge.

Serena and I move in sync towards it, to take everything in.

We're so high up, we have an unobstructed view of the world below. The hum of life from here is like all the birds, cicadas and creatures are singing to the clouds and the gods, and we are lucky to be a part of it.

To top it off, there's the sunset, slinking its way down in the sky like a cat slinking along, vanishing into the trees around us.

Tears sting in my eyes as I'm overwhelmed by the beauty of the world around me. All the ugliness of humanity that's been clouding me lately falls away. It dissolves into the trees because we're so small. I'm so small, and this . . . this is vast. The world, the universe, I'm like a grain of sand.

The olive trees don't have such problems. They link routes and relish in community. They cover themselves in tiny white flowers and fruit and spread their seeds without caring.

I need to be like that. I need to be an olive tree.

'This is not the big surprise, the view is always here.' Eleni presses one hand on my back to move me along carefully.

'Lorena, Serena, this way,' Mum calls across from the top of a staircase that leads down towards the bottom of the view.

Everyone else has begun to move down stone steps to the side of the house. Turning, I admire the large arches that line the walls, four impressive curves of stone sheltering the swathe of glass doors and windows.

'Eleni, your home is so beautiful.'

'You're very kind, Lorena.'

Dragging my eyes away from the all-consuming scenery, I take in the scene that's playing out instead. Serena's head's craning because she's so close to Christos's elbow as she takes each step, it's the only way she can see his face.

His eyes catch mine. Not a muscle moves on his face, but I've spent enough time with him now to read the silent plea for help being sent my way. Our deal pricks my skin, along with the last of the sun.

Marching to keep up, I carefully but quickly move down the curl of steps to a completely different terrace. This one leads out to an infinity swimming pool, and to my left a pergola with a table, similar to the one at the olive groves. It's huge, comfortably seating twenty guests. It fits snugly there and is already laid with a cream and gold table runner, Greek clay wine glasses in cream and matt gold cutlery. Tea lights in short golden bowls line the centre at intervals and inviting fairy lights weave in and out of the pergola.

There, sliding out of seats at the table, are two men and a woman.

'Wow, this place is so romantic. Don't you think, Christos?' Serena coos up at him, before even noticing the people coming towards us.

Before he can answer, I jump right in. 'It really is beautiful. Did you have this swimming pool when you were kids?'

Mum blows out, vibrating her lips, and Spiros bursts with laughter.

'No, no. This is all Eleni ready for her parties. But yes, big romance. A place for engagement party or anniversary. Which brings me to . . .' Spiros turns to the three people moving towards us.

They all look to be in their late twenties or early thirties, smartly dressed, but not too formal. The girl looks particularly elegant in a long floating dress that moves like a butterfly's wings, dancing in the breeze.

'This is our son, Giórgos, his business partner, Petros, and his now fiancée, Aliki! Welcome to their engagement party!'

This is met by gasps of joy and congratulations.

From not knowing I have an uncle to gaining a cousin in the very same week feels like I've been living in a box up until now, not knowing about the life outside of it. How could Mum keep all this family from us? I can't understand it.

'Giórgos—' Spiros falls into Greek. 'Come, meet your Aunt Thalia.'

Mum holds his face and tells him in Greek how much he looks just like his father when he was young. Tears glitter as the dying sun makes it look like King Midas himself has touched her eyes.

She then turns to Aliki and congratulates her and tells her how beautiful she looks.

Giórgos's business partner comes to shake hands with Christos, who he has obviously met before. Christos is quick to introduce us while Mum hogs the attention of the newly engaged couple, holding their hands.

Petros is clean-shaven and well put together, with an expensive watch and smart woven loafers.

'It is nice to meet you both, and with such happy news to share in.' Petros almost bows his head to the happy couple.

Mum turns to us, still holding the couple's hands and thrusting them towards us in introductions.

We all bounce off each other with excitement at this revelation of good news.

With each joyous move, a thorn digs deeper into the side of my stomach. Each smile makes my face ache and each platitude is another that rings in my ears. This is what I heard when Jonah and I got engaged.

It's not to say that it doesn't feel like an infection, spreading inside of me at the thought that I too should have a fiancé on my arm, showing him off to family and watching their faces light up in the sweet clarity of joy for someone else. Joy for me.

I should pity Aliki and Giórgos. They're yet to learn the pain that comes with falling in love and trusting someone who shouldn't be trusted. Mum and I, we know that one now. We know the truth that comes with blind love.

I press my lips together in a hard smile to try to push down the hot negativity that burns the back of my throat as I congratulate them once more and say how happy I am for these people who are strangers, but shouldn't be.

Two minutes ago, they *were* strangers; now they're family. I want to embrace that, not ruin it with my own experiences. I want to befriend them – they probably know more about my mum's upbringing than I do.

A man appears at my elbow with a tray of pale-lemon cocktails sprinkled with points of golden dots. He's smartly dressed in a white T-shirt and fitted navy shorts.

For a moment I'm unsure whether this is another cousin I don't know about.

'This is our first try with the party staff. This is "*The Dirty Olive*". It uses some of our oil-infused gin that will be coming to the shop next summer. Aliki's idea.' Eleni grins as she takes a glass. 'We have an order for a place in London already.'

We all follow suit and take a glass. Pausing for a moment to inspect the small golden dots floating on top of the fine white foam, I'd guess they're also olive oil, there for decoration.

The drinks look very appealing and I'm interested to taste my first olive-oil cocktail.

'To family.' Spiros raises his glass. 'We are so happy to have you all home. And to the happiness of the couple, Giórgos and Aliki! *Yamas!*'

We all raise our glasses towards the sky, careful not to spill any before taking our first sips.

It's sweet and fruity with a smooth kick that glides down nicely. It reminds me of the burn from the oil the other day as it slides down and warms me. I'd certainly have another, or order one at a bar.

'You are all welcome to stay tonight, or we have taxis that will get you if you prefer. No driving, we need the full celebration tonight, yes.' Eleni gives a nod to someone who must be high above and music begins from the undergrowth. It's Greek music, as though a live band are playing in the distance, but it's actually hidden speakers all around us.

'This is amazing, Eleni, thank you so much for everything.' I mean it. Even with the pain of someone else's engagement thrust into the limelight, it's good to have something else to focus on outside of myself. New people and new family could help me to grow and heal. Maybe I can try to feel happy for them without the fear of loss digging its heels in.

Christos steps to be close to me, I can feel his calm presence looming at my side.

Mum and Spiros begin chatting in Greek and Serena is all over the glamorous newly engaged couple.

Christos's voice vibrates in my chest as he leans in and says, 'We need to talk.' I nod and follow behind him as he breaks away from the group.

'If you want help, you have to help me.' Christos takes a deep sip of his cocktail. 'She squeezed my arm.' He indicates the bicep peeking out from under his pale-green shirt.

'It is a nice bicep. Nice shirt too.'

'It was a gift.'

'From a previous lover?'

'Stop, I told you, no girlfriends. It was from Spiros and Eleni.'

'Do you seriously not have *any* other friends?'

'Not unless I can help it. I told you. I like my peace, this is all.' Christos glances over my shoulder. 'Please do not let her sit with me over dinner, or I will leave and not help you again.' He narrows his eyes on me. Or perhaps he's squinting as the sun lowers and a shard of golden light hits him across his eyes, making them glint with burnt amber flecks. 'I'm sure Eleni will try to put us together, they think if I can fall in love I will be happy . . .'

'How about I ask for us to sit near Eleni? She seems to be the driving force behind all the new ideas here. And look, if Serena is touching you inappropriately or making you feel that uncomfortable, you have to tell her. She won't be doing it on purpose. She just thinks she's impossible to resist.'

'I don't really care, I just don't want to hurt her feelings . . . or Eleni. But you are right, Eleni will do anything to bring her son home. This' – he scans the perfectly placed pots and the sweeping pool – 'it is not for her. It is to bring a new toy for Aliki and Giórgos to play with.'

'Tell me what you really think.'

Christos's face screws up and the fingers of his left hand scratch into his thick black beard.

'I did.'

'No, I mean . . . it was sarcasm.'

He grunts before taking another sip of his dwindling cocktail.

'Here she comes,' he says behind the glass, as though Serena is someone to fear deeply.

I quickly turn back to him. 'Look, I don't want her to get paranoid. I'll leave you two alone now, but I'll sort the table plan with Eleni. She's just a person. A really nice, albeit over-enthusiastic one.' I sip the last of my drink and he does the same. 'Just be nice to my sister, OK? She might be coming on strong, but she's a good kid. I promise.' I take a step away before turning back to him. 'And if she touches you again, and you don't like it, tell her to stop, otherwise how will she know?' I look back at her as she gets stopped by Eleni, her eyes still locked on us. 'If you had a little sister, you'd understand. Trust me.'

Christos's jaw and shoulders tense and his nostrils flare as he looks into the bottom of his empty glass.

'Fine. I can play nice.'

As the sun disappears and more fairy lights burst into life, I go off to meddle.

I catch sight of my mum and Spiros talking on the other side of the swimming pool. Their faces look like they've been touched by the hands of grief. I desperately want to demand they tell me exactly what they're talking about, but I know that would only end in my mum shutting down completely.

I wonder if they're talking about missing their parents. I don't know what I'd have done without my mum's support. She's so loving, there's no way she could've been a bad daughter.

Once I'm done reorganising Eleni's seating plan, maybe I can get everyone drunk enough on these cocktails to find out the true story about why she left.

Chapter Nineteen

Our wine cups refill by magic as we relax with olive-themed entrées at the table.

I do my best to soak the alcohol up with bread, but I can already feel a warmth in my chest that the night can't completely account for.

At least I've managed to persuade Eleni to rearrange the table. She had wanted to put Serena and Christos together. I'm pretty sure there was a set-up planned, but she seemed pleased by my interest in him and his in me, even if I did slightly ruin her perfect boy-girl table pattern.

Little does she know that he feels safe in the knowledge that his good looks have no effect on me. Jonah was my vaccine and I'm immune to men now.

The only disappointment for me tonight is being so far from Spiros and unable to penetrate the conversations between my mum and him. I would give anything to find out more about her past. She always used to say generic things about having a lovely childhood, idyllic. It's only now I realise how broad her brush-strokes were about the way she grew up. I'd never spent enough time asking questions; I guess I always imagined there wasn't much to tell. Until recently.

Christos is to my left, with Petros on my right, followed by Serena and Mum. Eleni is opposite Christos, and although she is trying to take the whole table into conversation, it's obvious she's glowing at having her only son sitting next to her with his new fiancée on the other side of him.

So far, talk of face cream or natural lipsticks seems pretty far off, and now I'm stuck with the quiet drinking of Christos on one side and the chatter of Petros and Serena on the other, when all I really want to know is what Mum is saying to Spiros at the end of the table. Is it general chat? Are they talking about the past? At this rate, I might never find out.

Christos lets out a deep exhale before excusing himself from the table between courses. No one bats an eyelid.

'Lorena, how long are you in Corfu? We aren't here long, a few weeks, but we will be back very soon. We want to get married here.' Aliki brushes her long curls off her shoulder as she leans on one elbow to project her voice in my direction.

Her English is very good, but there is a strange American accent muddled into her Greek, like she learnt from watching too many films as a kid.

'I guess I live here now. At least, if I can find my way. It's actually something I'd like to discuss with Eleni.'

Eleni's ears prick up and she pulls her eyes off her son for long enough to show her interest.

I wish Christos hadn't left the table. I need him to help me formulate my ideas with his practical knowledge of what might actually be possible with the olive trees they have.

'Well, I was a cosmetic scientist, back in England, and I really wanted to start my own brand. I had a, erm . . .' A lump forms in my throat because I don't want to admit what happened. They might be family on paper but they're still strangers, and I'm not ready to spill my entire embarrassing life to everyone. '. . . a run of bad luck, and I need to start again. After looking at the beautiful soaps you make, I was inspired. What about a line of extra-virgin olive oil and honey balms in beautiful packaging? Then perhaps creams and make-up, if they're successful? I need to sort something with—'

'Lorena was telling me she had all the fees ready for the business application forms. What she needs to know is, can you spare her idea some extra-virgin oils?' Christos's leg kicks into mine as he slides on to the long bench next to me. My mouth hangs open ready to correct him, but I don't get the chance.

'It sounds like a great idea. All natural is best.' Aliki leans across Giórgos to grin at her soon-to-be mother-in-law. 'It is a shame we cannot have the organic certificate yet, even though there are very few chemicals used here.'

'Aliki, is this a product you could be interested in working on? Aliki and Giórgos met in Athens while working on products. She is a designer. She designs our . . .' Eleni clicks her fingers by her temples.

'Labels, Mama. She designs the bottles and labels.' Giórgos's shoulders pull back and he kisses Aliki's forehead.

'*Nai, nai!* Thank you, labels! Those cocktails, they make my English, *poof!*' Her eyes roll to the sky before she laughs.

'I do like this idea, Eleni. I think it ties in nicely with the brand we are building here.' Aliki nods and her chin dips as she looks at me straight in the eye. '*If* you can come up with the right products and you get the government approval, then we can talk.'

Christos's elbow presses softly against me. My heart is pounding so hard I can feel it in my head.

I never said I would accept his money, but I guess now he's forcing me into it. At least I know that Mum said she'll be able to help me out in the future, if I need it.

◆ ◆ ◆

'Do you remember when Baba said he would build us a pool if we picked all the olives one year, knowing it was impossible?' Spiros rumbles with laughter.

'No!' Mum leans forward in the dark, her face golden in the glow of the fairy lights.

Away from the pool, through a maze-like hedge that's been neatly cut, there's a circle of squishy chairs around a fire pit. It's not lit. It's much too hot for that, even past eleven at night. Instead, it's filled with more fairy lights.

The air hangs with the scent of the mint that's planted all around us to keep mosquitos at bay.

It doesn't completely stop them coming over now and then, but I'm sure there are fewer than there would be otherwise.

A bat swoops over our heads, helping to keep down the population of such things too. It picks them off one by one while we act like bait to bring the insects in for it to snatch up.

'You were too little,' Spiros muses. 'I was maybe, eight? We thought if we worked hard we could do it. That was back when we waited for the olives to fall in nets and scraped them from the ground. Not like now.'

'Can you tell us anything else about our grandparents?' I gently probe.

'I can.' Giórgos folds one leg up to rest his ankle on his knee as he sits back in his chair.

'Our *yiayia* was kind, and always smelt of sweet baklava. It is my favourite, so she would always make it for me. Our *pappoús* had bees. I would help him collecting the honey and she would use it to make the baklava. Our *pappoús* . . .' Giórgos sighs and swirls his wine in the glass. 'He could be grumpy, but he was happy with the bees or smoking and playing *távli* with his friends. When I was little, Pappoús would walk me around the olives and tell me it would all be mine when I was grown and Yiayia would tell me to do what I wanted, but to never leave my mother without saying goodbye and the promise of a return. I always took this very seriously.'

Over the constant cloak of the cicadas, silence falls like settling dust between us in the dark.

My mum looks like a statue made from marble. Her features locked into place.

Was this an intentional dig at her? Did *she* leave without even a goodbye? There was obviously no promise of a return. Or if there was, she broke it. I can't imagine how my grandparents must have felt.

'Please excuse me.' Mum steadily moves from her seat and glides away from our fairy circle.

For a moment, I hesitate, suddenly unsure of myself, then my feet and hands take over dragging myself up and out of the chair to chase after my mum.

'Lorena, wait.' Spiros's voice calls after me, but my feet keep moving quicker to keep up with her. Looking around the shadows on the terrace, she seems to have disappeared.

A shadow moves towards the stairs and I do my best to catch up with her.

'Mum,' I call after her, but she doesn't stop. 'Mum!'

As I reach the bottom of the stone steps she's already at the top, and I do my best to take them two at a time in my cloudy haze and inappropriate footwear.

I run to keep up, calling until she stops at the glass doors, pressing her forehead against it. Her shoulders tremble and her curls dance under the weight of crying.

'What did I do?' she mutters to herself in Greek.

'Mum, I know you must have had a good reason to leave. You can't punish yourself for the past.'

116

'If you or your sister were as stupid as me, I would feel like I had failed. My heart would be broken. That's how she felt. Broken. He's right. I left without a goodbye. Not even a goodbye.'

'Why?' Her head begins to shake as footsteps clatter up the stairs behind us. 'Please don't keep shutting me out.'

Mum turns and takes my face in her hands.

'I'm not trying to shut you out. I'm trying to protect you.'

Protect me? In what way do I need protecting?

'I can't believe you two left me down there in that awkward mint cloud,' Serena hisses as she reaches us. 'Spiros is berating Giórgos in Greek, Eleni's telling him not to be too harsh on him. Christos looks like he wants the ground to swallow him up and Aliki and Petros look bloody confused. What the hell was that even about? I mean, I know it was aimed at you, but what's with the low blow?'

'It doesn't matter why.' Mum presses her ring fingers into the corner of her eyes to hold in tears. 'I deserved it. I should go, you two stay, please. I will see you back at the house.'

'No.' I cross my arms over my chest. 'You can't leave without saying goodbye. That will just make it worse. You have to face them. You can't keep running away.'

Mum's head hangs down, turning her face into a mass of hair. With a snatched breath, she holds her head back up and pushes the hair from her face.

'How did you get so wise, Lorena?'

'I've got you to look up to.'

A smile briefly streaks across her face like the magic of a shooting star, before she walks past us both and back the way we came.

Serena and I exchange wide-eyed looks; it seems we're getting accustomed again to these silent conversations. We used to have so many when we were growing up. We share in a shrug before following on behind her, silently.

Scenarios run through my mind like microfilms. From huge fights to forgiving hugs. I don't have the courage to ask what Mum might say to anyone when she gets back there. As we approach, the sound of voices pulses like the beating of rain. Some hard, some soft, all a mass of confusion.

'Giórgos,' Mum begins, breaking the rain of voices, 'I think my mother makes a good point. She always did. I have missed her every day since I left, but we all have our reasons to leave. I'm sure you have reasons to leave for Athens, you are lucky to have such supportive parents. We all have different relationships with each other, no two are the same, and however much we try to understand what someone else has been through, we never can. It doesn't matter how similar we are, we can never be the same. You are my nephew, and I would love to get to know you, but I understand if you don't feel the same.'

'No, no, I'm sorry I offended you, Thalia. It wasn't my intention. I wasn't thinking. I was only thinking about things they both used to say and do. I'm so sorry I hurt you.'

'No, you didn't. I hurt myself.'

Chapter Twenty

Mum's clap splits the air like a thunderclap right after lightning has hit my skull. 'Right, girls, today paint and then we can lay floors.'

'Fuck's sake, Mum, don't do that. My head is pounding after those cocktails and the wine last night.' Serena rubs her forehead and slides down the living-room wall to the concrete floor.

Mum's jaw clenches at Serena's language and her fingers twitch, but she doesn't berate her for it.

Serena's laptop is quietly playing some sitcom I've never seen before. The overwhelming sound is the canned laughter every now and then.

'Don't you think we should talk about last night?' I grip my takeaway iced coffee; my fingernails strum down it like the droplets of condensation.

'What is there to say? It was lovely to meet my nephew, it was a delicious meal. Each course better than the last. I liked their modern take on traditional food. The mini moussaka was very fun. I would never have thought of that.'

'Mum, I meant—'

'I know what you meant, Lorena. Do I push you to talk to me about how you're spending your afternoons? Or about how you feel about Jonah, or every single thing you got up to at university? Or am I here for you when you need me?'

Guilt makes my ribcage suddenly feel a little bit too small. Mum has never pushed me to talk to her, but she's always been clear that she's available to me. I've always told her about my life because I wanted to.

'You're right. But I've always told you about my life because I thought we were close. I wanted to tell you things.'

Mum's head tilts to one side and there's a moment before her lips part to softly reassure me. 'We are close. Please, Lorena, don't push this. They say knowledge is power, but my love, once you know things, you can't unknow them. Please, think about that.'

I nod as I try to digest what she's telling me. Although she's right and I can't take knowledge out of my head, it's not enough to stop me wanting to know why she's withheld family from us.

But for now, I'll mull on it, as she's asked me to. I've had a gutful of unpleasant secrets repeating on me lately as it is; maybe I'll leave it alone, for now at least.

'OK, I'll think about it. So what do we need to do today?'

'Wait a second, I thought Alec and Anton were going to do it.' Serena presses her cool drink to her head.

'They will be working upstairs, so let's make a start on the painting down here. We don't want them to think we're lazy. We need to wash the walls first, they're filthy. Grab a sponge and I'll fill the bucket.'

By the front door, there's the beginnings of our supplies that Alec and Mum ordered. Everything from pots of paint to rollers and laminate flooring. There're even some basic tools, because even though Anton is fully kitted out, Mum said we need some of our own – *just in case*.

Mum disappears into the kitchen with the bucket as Serena shuts her laptop. I scoop up a sponge and throw it in her direction.

We begin scrubbing down the walls. Alec kindly left us with a stepladder, which has also proven to be very helpful. He must've been a very good friend to Mum when she was growing up. As I press the sponge into the wall and swirl it in big circles, it whirls around my head that Alec *must* know things too. Maybe he's not the only one. When we arrived, she was worried about people recognising her – perhaps those people know why she left?

With the walls clean and drying quickly in the heat, Mum opens the plastic box filled with tools. Picking out a flat-head screwdriver, she begins to prise open the first pot of paint.

We all agreed on painting the wall behind the wood burner in a rich taupe, and all the other walls cream. Eventually, we want a taupe sofa and burnt-orange cushions.

The lid of the paint clicks off with ease and Mum lets the paint ripple into the tray.

With satisfying sweeps, we begin painting the wall. There's something therapeutic about it. Silently being with others at work, fixing something.

'Oh shit, I dripped on the floor.' I jump back, looking for something to clean it up with.

'Lorena, we will be laying flooring over this concrete mess, don't worry about a drip of paint,' Mum reassures me.

I shake my head in soft laughter. 'Oh yeah. I might not be as hung-over as Serena, but I do think I left my brain at Spiros and Eleni's place.' A thought bumps into my head, and it's one I don't want to ignore after the conversation in the fairy garden. 'I know you don't want to talk about *why* you left, but can you tell us something about growing up here? I know you used to tell us stories about the olive groves and playing games with Spiros, but . . . I don't know. Did you have a boyfriend before Dad?'

'Of course. I had many boyfriends before your dad. But that's all they were. Boys.' Mum's rhythm of painting slows and her head rests down towards her shoulder.

'Anyone you might want to see again now we're here?' Serena begins to unwrap a new roller to join in with painting and the conversation.

'I'm sure they're all married and happy – anyway, I'm not interested. I am interested in these products you want to make, Lorena. I saw Aliki take interest, but I couldn't catch what was being said.'

'Yeah, I just want to start with some balms, creams, and maybe move on to natural make-up. Really high-grade extra-virgin olive oil instead of the usual lower-grade stuff that's used.'

'I want to support you. Maybe I could start talking to people I used to know and see who would be interested in stock next year? If you can show demand, maybe Eleni and Spiros will be able to give you more oil away from their other endeavours.'

'Thanks, Mum. That'd be great.'

'It's good to feel useful.' She sighs as she tiptoes as high as she can to paint the wall.

'Wait, whoa, what's that meant to mean?' Serena waves her roller, slopping paint across the floor without even noticing. '*Feel useful?* Like you haven't been holding us together our whole lives? As though you've never worked? I remember when Dad had a tantrum and quit his job and you had to work nights in Sainsbury's for a while. You've always held down everything for all of us. What do *you* want to do, Mum? Like, you're in your early fifties, that's barely middle-aged nowadays. This time should be about you. Dad's off being a—'

'All right, all right. Point well made, Serena,' Mum interrupts with a laugh in her voice.

We all turn back to painting the wall in a row. Slowly filling the mottled white with an elegant sheen of taupe.

My arm already burns with the continued motion. I let it drop to my side and turn to face my mum and sister.

'She's right, Mum, what do you want to do? I don't suppose it'll be that long until this place will be finished, then you'll be a free woman. What next? Do you think you'll stay here forever? If you do, what will you do all day? How will you pay the bills?'

Mum rubs her wrist over her forehead to avoiding getting paint on her face.

'I think I would like to sell things too. Pottery, art . . . I was good at those things when I was younger. I haven't had as much time for it, what with running the home and organising events for your father's company. Now, you're both right, I think it *is* my time.'

'Good,' Serena says with force as her roller slaps into the paint tray. 'Now can we go back to talking about your old boyfriends? That sounds like a fun convo if you ask me.' Her eyes widen and laughter ripples over us.

It's been a long time since we've spent so much time just as us three. When Serena turned twenty-one, I paid for us all to go to a spa for a weekend as a birthday treat. We all drank wine and had massages in a beautiful woodland setting. That was a few years ago now and that's the last time I can think of. In fact, it's one of the only times I can think of, other than shopping trips when we were teens.

Sometimes it can be hard to find the time to slot together, however much we want to; things just crop up and work takes up more than half the week.

Come to think of it, Mum had been asking for a while to get us three together. I wonder if it's because she was feeling isolated, knowing Dad was probably off with someone else. She must've felt so alone.

I'm so glad Serena and I agreed to be here for her in Corfu. I just wish I knew how long it was all going to last. Mum seems determined to stay, but I can only stay if I can make money doing a job I love. If I can't, I'll be heading back to England to interview for jobs there.

Not yet though. The thought of being away from Mum and Serena is too much right now. I feel like a chick standing on the edge of a nest, not wanting to jump. I'm not sure when my wings will be strong enough.

'There was one boy, when I was only just a teen and he was a couple of years older. He used to leave me gifts at the front door and my father didn't approve at all—'

Three sharp knocks strike the door, putting a halt to Mum telling us about past loves. She swings the door open to Alec, who pulls her in for a bear hug. She wriggles and laughs, worrying she'll get paint on him.

'Yes, yes. I'm here in my best clothes to work,' he says in Greek. 'My God, it's so hot in here. It's so hot, even the cicadas would burst in here!'

'Did you just say something about hot cicadas?' I chuckle as I kiss Alec's cheek in welcome.

'Lorena, you speak Greek?' He narrows his eyes on me with new interest.

'No, no! I don't *speak* Greek, but I understand a lot. Mum has always used both languages with us. Sometimes I don't even notice when she goes into Greek to talk to us. As long as she doesn't speak too quickly, I can keep up.'

'While you live here, you will learn to speak!' Alec gently taps my shoulder.

Mum shows Alec upstairs as they chat and laugh together. It's nice that she has a friend here that is outside of us. I hope Serena finds some more friends too. I'm not ready for her to leave.

Chapter Twenty-One

'What is all this?' Christos runs his finger over my forearm, making goosebumps rise from my spine and over my entire body. He doesn't shy away from touching me, as though it's the most natural thing in the world to run his fingers over my skin.

'Paint. We're painting the downstairs while the upstairs is being plastered.'

'I thought you were ill.' Christos leans on the olive grove's shop wall.

'Thanks.' I roll my eyes.

We send a last wave in Spiros's direction as he disappears out of sight.

'How was your mum when you got home?'

We begin to walk and talk now Spiros has left us to our afternoon.

'Forget that, why the hell did you lie about me having the money for the business forms?'

'I asked first. You have to answer to me.' Christos slides his hands into his pockets like he could stand there all day waiting for an answer about my mum. The sunlight catches in his eyes, making them glint mischievously.

I'm sure he could wait forever. From everything I've seen, he really doesn't have anyone checking in on him other than my aunt and uncle. No one else he'll tell me about anyway.

Closing my eyes, I tilt my head back to feel the heat from the sun and to see the blotchy red of my eyelids connecting me to my own energy running along my veins. It's a desperate attempt to keep calm in the face of everyone avoiding my questions lately.

'Mum's OK.' I look back at him and decide to play my own game. 'She wants to take Giórgos and Aliki and everyone out for a meal tomorrow night. I think Alec is booking us in at Cicala again. I'm sure I can get you an invite? I know how much you'd love that, being so social. Maybe I could sit you next to my sister? I'm sure she'd hate it, but I know how much you'd love it . . .'

Christos begins to meander away from me, down the slope and into the loving arms of the olive trees that cast cooling shade for us to relax in.

'That is enough, thank you. I am busy. I am always busy.'

'Really? Doing what?'

'With my peace.' He takes a deep breath and lowers his head, slowing a little. 'I did promise Alec I would come in for a drink after his shift tomorrow. Now I know why he asks me. I was tricked.'

'Yay!' I mock-jump up and down, tugging on his short sleeve. 'Serena will be so pleased. Should I message her now, or should I let it be a surprise?'

'I can cancel him.'

'No, don't. I'm only kidding.'

'Instead of *kidding*, let's talk about these.'

Christos bends down and picks up an olive off the ground, rolling it between his fingers.

'You need to think of the cost of the product.' He passes the olive to me, and I begin to roll it in my hands the way he did. 'There is extra virgin with machine and extra virgin by hand.'

'OK, so from what I remember, when you use the machines, you can only take a crop every other year or something, right?'

Christos nods.

I remember on the tour hearing how it can strip the tree of leaves and everything and stop them flowering, whereas the rake they use by hand isn't so damaging, but takes a lot more time and effort.

'We . . . we only use some trees this year, others next year with machine.'

'Right, so you rotate them?'

'Yes, rotate.'

'One litre of hand-picked extra-virgin olive oil is perhaps fifteen euro before you even start anything else. Spiros owns the oil press, and many other farms pay to use it. It saves us much money but was a big investment for him.'

I contemplate the costs, how much time it might take to make simple batches of products, then more complicated cosmetics. How much it might cost to run a small lab. I'd need to hire a place, because I can't run it out of my bedroom. Then I'll need to pay back my loan to Christos. Even if that's with Mum's money, I'd then need to pay her back.

'Wait, you little ratbag! You distracted me and never answered my question about lying about money.'

'What did you call me?' Christos steps to face me, placing his hand on his broad chest like he's holding himself back. It's almost impossible for him to hide the smile, even behind his beard.

'Ratbag. You're a ratbag. Like a bag of rats.'

Laughter touches his chest and his throat until the low vibration of it fills the air between the olive trees. I've never heard him laugh before.

My cheeks begin to pinch into a smile of my own. It's good to laugh at something so simple, and to hear someone's glowing laughter fill the air because of me.

Spending time with Christos is refreshing. I'm glad he'll be at Cicala tonight.

My phone buzzes in the back pocket of my denim short-shorts.

It's probably my dad. He was messaging me last night, attempting to find a new normality that doesn't involve Mum. We've never messaged much before. Mum's always organised get-togethers and all the details of our family life. Now he has to find his own place, one that she didn't organise for him.

I look at the screen to find a text from an unknown number.

I still love you. I can't stop thinking about you. I'm sorry.

Laughter drains out of me, along with all the blood in my head.

'I cannot believe I offer you money, and you call me a rat bag.' Christos says 'rat bag' like they're two very separate words that live miles apart.

I can't focus on it. On him.

Spots scatter across my eyelids as if my phone screen is as bright at the sun and it's left a mark on my retinas.

'I have to go,' I mutter as I step back.

'Wait? What? You insult me and now you leave?'

He's still laughing, but I'm not joking.

I take one step backwards, catching my foot on a root and almost tripping. I grab the nearest tree as Christos lunges forward and steadies me under my elbow.

'What is wrong? What is on your phone that is so bad?'

'Nothing. I'll see you tomorrow night? After dinner. Bye.'

I turn and begin to run.

'Lorena, wait, you look pale! Wait.'

I don't wait. I can't wait.

My lungs feel as though they're about to collapse under the weight of a new crushing gravity.

There's only one person who would've sent that. It has to be him. It has to be Jonah.

Chapter Twenty-Two

My heart won't stop beating in my head. It's not meant to be up there, hammering.

I thought maybe looking at the sea might calm me down. I couldn't keep going anymore on the quad bike. I was beginning to feel hot sick burn in my throat, and my hands were trembling so much I had to pull over.

I have no idea where I am. A quiet track in the middle of trees and dusty roads. Luckily one with a lay-by.

From up here, everything seems both huge and small. I have to stay on the quad bike. There's no way I can stand. Not yet.

Pushing my face into my hands, I let out an involuntary screech of frustration.

How can I let him make me feel this way?

I know he had problems, a big mental health problem, and I desperately want to feel sorry for him, and if he had spoken to me before leaving a letter and got help, instead of stealing from me and lying, then sure, I could feel sorry for him. I would've stood by him to the end. That's what you do when you agree to marry someone.

We would've found a way.

This message on my phone is making my skin itch and my hands shake.

I hate him.

How many stages of grief are there? Is hate one of them? I think it's meant to be anger, but this feels like hate channelling its way through my bones and carving out ugly new avenues through my body.

How could I have put my life in his hands? He says he loves me, still loves me, but he never did. How could you love someone and take everything they've worked so hard for? I shared everything with him. He knew what I had set money aside for, knew how much it was going to cost me to rent a lab and to buy materials. He knew I was taking a risk and he told me he would support me, help me.

The thought of it now, the words we shared knotted up in our duvet or walking hand in hand through the park, makes me want to pull my hair out from the roots. He tied my hands behind my back and threw me off the ledge when I was most vulnerable. I can still hear his reassuring voice in my head telling me that quitting my job was the right choice, all while telling me the joint bank account was right too.

He must've been laughing his head off at me. This is probably a game to him, messaging now. How could it be anything but that? He says he loves me, and I used to believe him. At least he's made me realise there's no point believing anyone. There's no point.

I have to focus to stop my hands from shaking or I'll be here all day.

A hornet whizzes past my head, making me flinch, and a new shot of adrenaline ties my arteries into knots.

I look as far into the distance as I can, at the blue sea merging with the sky, then the olive trees below, and concentrate on my breathing as tears stream uncontrollably down my cheeks until they drip off my chin and pool on my chest.

Poor Christos, I left him confused and laughing at the word *ratbag*. He's been so kind to me and I ditched him. He's not a ratbag at all. He's a little odd, but I don't think he's a ratbag. But I've been wrong before.

I'll have to buy him a drink tomorrow night to say sorry.

Right now, I want to go back to the house and get into bed and never leave. The thought of ever going out for drinks again has been swallowed back up into obscurity.

Gritting my teeth as hard as I can, and with my fists like rocks at my sides, my whole body squeezes with frustration and another growl bursts out of me.

Never again.

Never will I let a man do this to me ever again.

◆ ◆ ◆

'Give it here.' Serena snatches the phone out of my hand and Mum peers over her shoulder with an open mouth.

After only a glance at the words, Serena surrenders the phone to Mum. 'I can't believe this. I cannot believe this. What does he think? Does he think that you'll come running back after all he's done? After all the damage he's caused?'

Serena looks filthier than when I left her. Paint flecks all over her hands and face, her hair flopping about in a messy bun as she stomps around the room.

'If I ever see him, I'll—'

'When are you ever going to see him hanging out in Corfu?' I exhale.

Mum's brought in the white chairs from outside and I flop down on to one of them.

She holds the phone with an outstretched arm. She swears she doesn't need glasses, but soon her arms will be too short for her to read anything.

'Will you reply?' Mum looks up, still squinting.

'Of course she won't, don't be insane, Mum. What are you even thinking?'

Mum narrows her eyes away from me and on to my sister. 'I didn't ask you, Serena.'

Even if I did want to reply, I have no idea what to say. Would there really be any point in ranting and raving about the pain he put me through? Or that he could've told me about it, and I would've helped him?

'Lorena?' Mum bobs down beside the chair and rests her hot hand on my knee. My skin must be cooler from rushing back here on the quad bike because her hand feels like fire.

'I don't know. No. Serena's right, he doesn't deserve a reply.'

'You should change your number.' Serena presses her lips together before adding, 'And block that one he messaged from.' She nods towards my phone.

I look around the room for the first time. 'I was only gone for a couple of hours and you've already finished the cream walls too. I take it the men have gone for the day?'

Mum squeezes my knee and a reassuring smile crosses her lips.

I know they're gone, because there's no van outside the house anymore. But it's always good to check that no one else is about before having a full-blown crying meltdown. I don't feel like explaining myself to anyone right now.

'Yes, and they have finished plastering two rooms, now only two more to go up there. Once that is done, Alec will fit the flooring for us.'

'I thought we were doing it?'

Mum stands, her knees clicking loudly back into place.

'He offered to help when he left. I wouldn't want to offend him. I know he has more time now he is alone. I can understand. His daughters live in the south now, and in the summer they're very busy.'

'You have us, all day every day.' I do my best to force my broken face into a smile.

She reciprocates, but I can see the cracks that go deeper than any line at the corner of her eye. The ones that Dad caused when he shattered the fabric of our family.

'I'm going to go have a look,' I say as I begin to stand.

'I'll come with you.' Serena looks around to find a place to abandon the cutting-in brush she's been using for the edges.

'No, no. It's fine. I'm just having a quick look.'

Creaking away up the stairs, I can feel a rattling in my chest where this message has so deeply shaken me that I don't feel quite right on my knees.

The hall looks smooth, ready to receive a new colour once it's dry. Glancing into my room, I can see it still needs to be done.

I catch sight of the view from my window. Instead of moving down the corridor to find out whose room will be the first to be painted, I sit on my bed and look out at the people on the beach.

They look like toys from here. Toys acting out lives instead of living them. What looks to be a dad and daughter play tennis on the beach.

I've never played tennis with my dad.

He would be the one to take us to the cinema when Mum had things to do at home. Or Mum would swing open the games cupboard and let us pick the game for us all to play with him as she cooked dinner.

I search my mind for things we did together, just me and him. I can't think of a single thing that was *just for us*. Not one.

How can I have lost something I never had? I can't imagine finding something *just for us* now I live on an island a million miles away from him.

Two faint knocks at my open door are still enough to spring my shoulders up to my ears and for my hand to clutch my chest.

'Mum, you made me jump.'

'I'm sorry, my love, I didn't mean to startle you. I just wanted to check on you and tell you something. But I've forgotten what I wanted to tell you while I was here checking on you.' Mum rubs her head. 'Sometimes I think stairs are a portal to suck the life out of my short-term memory.' She exhales as she takes a seat next to me on the bed. 'Sometimes I wish they would select some of the long-term memories instead.'

For a moment, we both gaze into the distance. I wonder what Mum sees when she looks out of the window. Is she looking at the beach and the sea, or the people? Is she wondering about their lives and their relationships or admiring the ripples in the sea and the way they leave young children convinced that magic has to be real?

'The sand near the sea can sometimes feel like sticky wet mud.'

Peeling my eyes away from the girl and the man playing tennis, who I think are laughing at how bad they are, I let my gaze come to rest on my mum, squinting at the window as she continues.

'We think of sand as dry, slipping through our fingers and counting down time. A place to lie and hear the soothing coo of the sea. Then there's this gooey mess. That place between the beach and the sea that sucks us in and bogs us down. Do you know what I mean?'

'It is sticky.'

'Yes, but it's a part of life. We have to go through the sticky mess to get to the bright turquoise sea where we can let the salt heal our wounds and the water cool our skin. Each footprint down to the beach, whether it's through the warmth of the golden grains or that sludge at the edge, is a part of your story. It's a part of what gets you to where you need to be to soothe your soul. You'll get there, one step at a time. Even if sometimes you get a little stuck, you'll get there.'

I rest my head on my mum's shoulder, the way I always have. I used to watch telly like this sometimes, as a pre-teen, until my neck would ache.

'You too, you know. You'll get there too. We all will.'

Mum rests her head on top of mine and we look out of the window, only now I'm not watching the people and wondering what they might be doing with their lives. I'm thinking about how to get myself back to the sea.

Chapter Twenty-Three

The eight of us sit around a large circular table at Cicala next to one of the protruding trees with their crooked trunks that seem to burst through the middle of the restaurant. It looks so real, but it's fake. It has to be, otherwise it would create such a mess on their beautiful, elegant furniture.

There's semicircular seating curving around one half of the table and four chairs on the other side. Petros, Giórgos, Aliki and Serena are on the comfy-looking seat together, and I'm on a chair with the other grown-ups.

Mum and Serena both look particularly beautiful tonight, Mum in a simple bronze-tone wraparound dress with matching eyeshadow, and Serena in a stunning shade of teal and lime that I think only she could get away with. Anyone else might look overdone. Not her. She looks like a beacon on a dark night.

Mum said I look good. After a lot of wobbles and tears last night and this morning, I think my face is a little too puffy around the edges to *look good*. Maybe just good enough. I do like my dress though. It's my plain fitted black one I wanted to wear the other night, but Serena wouldn't let me. Mum gave me one of her beautiful chiffon wraps to wear over it, but so far it's been too hot to do more than leave it on the back of the chair.

So far, the night seems to be going well. The fish here is fabulous and freshly caught. We all had different things, lobster, sea bass and some fish that I had no idea what it was. We've all been chatting about the wedding, olives, sharing simple stories that don't come with a disaster attached, and all of it's been slipping down with frozen strawberry daiquiris and porn star martinis.

Every time I think about the message from Jonah, I take another sip or order a fresh drink to keep my mind away from him. To keep my mind as far away from logical thoughts as I can get.

Serena has been on very good behaviour too, only asking once when Christos might get here, and she hasn't asked since just before the starter arrived. Which is impressive, as we've just finished dessert.

Not that I had dessert. I finished another cocktail while everyone else had another course.

'Please excuse me.' I slip out of my chair to nip to the bathroom.

'Wait, I'll come with you.' Serena shuffles along and slips out after me. Her heels clip on the floor until she's close enough to catch my elbow. 'Did you hear what Petros was saying?'

'Nope. I was drinking. Anything good?'

'Kinda, yeah. He was saying maybe I could do some assistant work for their company and how impressed he was with how I'd set up my own business and living my best life, blah blah blah.' She throws her hair over one shoulder and grins.

'Good. You deserve everything. You're so pretty.'

We push open the door to the loos together.

'God, I love these toilets. They're perfect for a selfie.' Serena pouts as she catches sight of herself in the mirror.

It is an attractive room, with smoked-glass doors and big mirrors on the walls.

'I like them because they're clean.' I close the cubicle door, leaving Serena reapplying lipstick.

'Do you think Christos isn't coming tonight? I thought you said he was going to be here to see Alec?' Serena carries on talking.

'Yeah, at the end of Alec's shift, I think. You need to give up on him. He doesn't date, or anything like dating. He likes to be alone. He's a big fat waste of time.'

'I like a challenge,' she calls over my flushing toilet.

As I move around the door she's leaning on one of the sinks, waiting for me.

'Don't you need a wee?'

'No. I just wanted to look in the mirror. What if my lipstick had faded?'

'Then I guess the world would end, or someone might scream at the fear of seeing your natural lip colour.' I catch sight of my own smirk in the mirror as I move soap around my hands and rinse it away.

'Just because you don't care anymore, doesn't mean we're all like that.'

All my muscles stop moving. Each and every one stops apart from my heart, which pumps blood at a dizzying rate.

'I didn't mean it like that. You're beautiful, I was just—'

'No.' I look at my own mouth in the mirror. I had made an effort tonight. An understated effort, but I still put on products that I like, the mask to make everyone recognise the *old me*. 'I know what you meant. I don't wear obvious lip liner or fake eyelashes, so I'm not trying hard enough. Maybe that's why Jonah *really* left me? Right? Because surely all I want is to catch some stupid guy anyway, so my worth is only worth what some random bloke puts on me. Or you, what worth *you* put on me, maybe?'

'Stop it. This is because he texted you. I know it was a shitty thing of him to do, but please, don't take it out on me.'

She's probably right, but that just makes it worse. I'm the idiot coiled around past mistakes and ready to make fresh ones because that's all I'm good for now, to be the punchline in a bad joke. The sort no one laughs at, the sort that makes everyone cringe.

It's too late. My mind swells with angry words.

'No, no. This isn't about him. It must be *so* hard to be confident all the time, wear tight clothes and fuck about from country to country doing everyone else's admin without a care in the world.'

'That's enough, Lorena.' Serena's eyes glitter in the light.

'Because I've hurt your feelings? I didn't think that was possible. It's not like I said you've put your lipstick on wrong.'

'You can be such a bitch when you're drunk.'

I shrug, because I'm bored with this now. Bored by her judgement, my own judgement, and the fact I'm not happy enough with me to really be able to not care what she thinks. I do care and I hate that she's probably right, I probably am overreacting because my insides still haven't recovered from Jonah's stupid text.

It pisses me off that her opinion *does* matter to me and she knows me too well.

Serena's eyes form cat-like slits of anger before she turns and leaves.

I wish I didn't care.

I take a step towards the door and notice the gold tube discarded next to the sink. Picking it up, I click off the lid and look at the colour of the lipstick.

It's a brand I told Serena to use. An expensive one that has been doing great things to help lock moisture into lips.

My lips do look a little pale. I've probably left all traces of lipstick on the rim of the thousand cocktails I've had.

Carefully, I put my finger on the lipstick and press it into my lips to bring a subtle blush of colour.

Clicking the lid back on, I grip the small golden tube. This thing I told my sister to buy. My little sister who listens to me.

I was too harsh, but she was an idiot too.

Closing my eyes, I can feel a gentle sway, as though I'm standing in the sea and the waves are jostling me.

I'm glad I'm a little numb. Maybe a lot numb. I need numb.

Pulling my shoulders back, I take one last look in the mirror. I need to keep my head up and not project the lack of self-worth I've had lately on to my sister.

I might be drunk, but even I can see that's a shitty thing to do.

Making my way back to the table, I clock Christos and, surprisingly, Serena isn't sitting at the bar with him. She's back next to Petros. He nods and I do the same.

'Lorena, everyone is leaving.' Mum intercepts me before I get to Christos. 'Aliki and Giórgos have to be up early tomorrow. Come and say goodbye.'

I begin doing the rounds of goodbyes and cheek-kissing, then get to my mum.

'I'm going to stay and have a last drink with Christos.' I turn to Serena. 'Here, you left this in the bathroom.' I hold out her lipstick.

'Do you *really* think you should be having another drink?' She sucks in her cheeks and snatches the lipstick out of my hand.

I hate that because I'm having problems right now, my little sister genuinely believes she has the right to comment on my actions like this. Whether or not she thinks she's somehow helping, she's not.

'You're only jealous because Christos actually talks to me,' I whisper as I kiss her cheek.

As I pull away, her nostrils flare and she turns to leave with everyone else.

Mum looks from her to me. 'What's happened?'

141

'Nothing. She'll be fine in the morning. She's just being a cow. Thinking she has the right to comment on me and try and boss me about. She's arrogant and self-obsessed, it's insane. The usual. That's all. You know how she gets.'

Mum steps closer to me and places her hands on my shoulders. 'Be gentle on her. Arrogance is born from insecurity. You're not the only one in pain, my love, and your sister might not always get it right, but she loves you.' Her eyes narrow on me and she pauses. 'Be safe, and enjoy your drink.'

She taps my nose lightly with her index finger, the way she would when I was a child, then leaves a last kiss on my cheek and walks away.

A molten rock in my throat threatens to choke me. I smile and wave a last goodbye to everyone as they take a few steps into the road. I shouldn't have been so hard on Serena.

She keeps her back to me, locking her interest on Petros instead.

I want to blame Jonah for this, for making me so tangled and drunk and bitter. But only I have control of my actions, and even if his actions were the ones that pushed me down a cliff, it's up to me to deal with hitting the bottom.

And maybe that's what today is. It's hitting the bottom.

My phone buzzes from the table where I've left it.

I pick it up, and there on the screen is another message from an unknown number.

Chapter Twenty-Four

'What are you doing?' Even with a rumble of laughter in his voice, Christos's words cut through me.

I look up as though I'm seeing him for the first time, as though I've been suspended in ice for centuries and I'm only now able to see the world around me again.

My phone presses against my chest to hide the screen from my view. I'm too afraid to open the message. Not now. Right now, I have to ignore it.

'Nothing.' I do my best to rebound into a smile.

'Nothing? Are you not going with everyone else?'

'No, I thought I'd crash your night with Alec and have another drink. I felt bad for running off the other day.'

I slip my phone along my bum cheek and drop it on the floor. For a moment, I'd forgotten I was wearing a dress. My attempt to slip the phone into an imaginary pocket didn't work.

It bounces along the floor.

'What are you doing?' Christos fizzes with laughter before knocking back his drink and pushing it towards Alec at the bar.

I crouch down to pick up my phone, doing my best to keep the hem of my fitted dress in check. As I stand, I stumble forward, catching my hand on the back of Christos's bar stool.

'I was putting my phone in my pocket, but I don't have a pocket. Haven't you ever done that? No, I bet not. Boys always have pockets. You know that's sexism, right? That we can't have pockets. Like, pockets are a luxury for us. It's so messed up.'

Alec returns to the bar as I hop on to a stool next to Christos.

'I am not sure you understand sexism.' He shakes his head.

'You have to be kidding me?'

'With that look, I am kidding. That look nearly knocked me from my chair.'

'Lorena, you are joining us? This is good, although I am very afraid your man, he's already been drinking.' Alec raises an eyebrow towards Christos before continuing, 'What are you drinking?'

'I'll have what he's having.' I dip my head to Christos.

His hair is a little messier than usual, and although his good looks shine through, there are shadows under his eyes tonight that haven't been there before and his beard doesn't look quite so perfectly kept.

Alec picks up Christos's empty glass and begins to move behind the bar.

'So you've been drinking. All on your own, or have you been out with friends?'

'I said before, I have no friends.'

'All on your own then? How did you get here? How will you get home? Where do you actually live anyway? I've been assuming you live near the olive grove, but I don't think I've actually asked.'

Christos begins to rub his head. 'That was too many questions.'

'Here is vodka on the rocks.' Alec dusts his hands over his sides. 'Enjoy. I must . . .' He points to a table that needs clearing.

'Neat vodka? Really? What the hell happened to you that you enjoy sitting around drinking neat nail polish remover?'

'Who says I enjoy it?'

I study him as he sips the clear liquid in his glass. It could so easily be mistaken for water as it touches his smooth lips. He looks into the bottom of the glass, quietly swirling it, making the ice rattle like a wind chime.

The urge to pee again begins to seep into my thoughts before I can even bring myself to take a sip. It's right there next to the background noise of the text message I can't bring myself to open.

I hop down from the stool as smoothly as I can manage in the swaying room.

'I need the loo.'

'I'll come with you.'

'I didn't realise you were a woman.'

'What?'

'I thought it was only women who did that? Went off to the loo in pairs.'

'I just need to go.'

I let out a sarcastic hum as I press my finger to his chest, doing my best to eye him suspiciously before making my way to the toilets.

It feels strange heading over to the loo with a guy, but I like that they're all in together, only separate cubicles. It seems more family-friendly somehow. When I was a kid, sometimes my dad would take us swimming if Mum was busy. I hated that he would have to get changed somewhere else. It was a lot of pressure to be in charge of Serena even for a minute.

As soon as I close the cubicle door behind me, I feel the urge to make conversation so he can't hear me. To talk my way through this. I begin to hop a little from one foot to the other

– I've had too many big cocktails too quickly and now they're all catching up on me.

'So how come you're drinking so much? Do you always drink so much?' I call through the cubicle wall.

I want to be finished before him, because all the doors are thick frosted glass and I really don't want him to even see the blurry outline of me hovering over the seat if he happens to look in the mirror. I don't think it's that clear, but just in case.

'No.' Great, he's doing his best to be rubbish at conversation, the way he so often does. 'Are *you* always so drunk?'

'Sometimes, but I have my reasons.'

The unread message on my phone races back through my mind.

I don't want to read it now. If I read it now, I'll reply now and I know I really shouldn't reply.

'I have reasons too.'

His toilet flushes and I'm quick to do the same, leaving the cubicle at the same time as him.

'But it's not like you have girl problems. You don't have a girlfriend.'

'That doesn't always stop me having girl problems.' As Christos lathers up his hands, he eyes me in the mirror, a smile tugging at the corners of his lips as he looks me over.

'I'm not a problem. You don't sleep with people, so you don't get all those romantic problems other people have to put up with, like broken hearts and stuff.'

Christos begins to wipe his hands slowly down his sides to dry them as he turns to face me. I can feel the heat of his eyes as his eyebrows descend over them.

'What? I *do* sleep with women, I just don't date them. Did you think I was some priest?'

'No, I just . . .' My words fall away. I keep focused on washing my hands to the sound of Christos's rumbling laughter. 'I was sure you said you didn't have sex. I asked you if you did *anything* . . . something like that and you said . . .' In the mirror, I can see my cheeks have a rouge glow as I try to recall the conversation and how insane I am to seriously think he could look like *that* and manage to avoid having sex, when women probably line up for his attention.

He stops laughing and leans an inch closer to me as his tongue briefly wets his lips. 'Of course I have sex. I am not dead. Not yet.'

My pulse rushes the alcohol around my body even faster than before and the room spins a little more as I try to focus on Christos leaving the room, laughing to himself.

I begin to dry my hands under the dryer with a whole new fascination and confusion.

I've been a complete idiot assuming he just wasn't interested in people or physical connections in that way, when all this time it wasn't at all what I thought. He's just into a modest bachelor life, or something like that.

My fingers dig into the sink to settle the rolling sensation rippling through my body.

Standing tall, I smooth my hands over my hair, catching the soft tendrils that like to frizz in the heat, before calmly making my way back to the bar.

'Where's Alec?' I slide myself back up on to the stool, pressing my hands into the wooden bar to hold myself steady.

'Finishing his shift.'

The ice in my glass has melted in the short time I was gone, and I'm left with a watered-down vodka that really needs a cranberry juice or something. I sniff at it. The harsh smell really does remind me of nail polish remover. I place it back down, pushing it an inch or so away from my hands.

Ambient music plays around us, and the last table is vocal, really vocal. Booming with laughter and probably all more drunk than me.

'So you'll have sex with a girl, but you won't get married, right?' I begin.

'Why do you care?'

'I don't.'

Christos leans in, placing his hand on the back of my stool, stopping only a few inches from my face. 'Good.'

I can smell the alcohol on his breath, muddling with my own. He might even be more drunk than me. Behind it, there's the darker scent of his aftershave and it's slightly dizzying, more than before.

He pulls away as the group begins to leave, calling *kalinichta* over their shoulders to the owners, tucked away around the corner at the front of the restaurant taking a well-deserved moment of rest, while Alec starts to clear away the debris from their table.

'What's with you tonight?' I tilt my head at Christos.

'Nothing. Bad day.'

'Is it because I ran away from you before? It was nothing to do with you, I promise. I actually wanted to say sorry about skipping out on you when it was me who pushed to see you in the first place.'

'No. It is nothing to do with you.'

'What then?'

'I am here.' Alec slaps his hands down on the bar. 'Lorena, you want something . . . else?'

'Porn star martini for the road, please.'

'Vodka, thanks.' Christos pushes his empty glass back across the bar.

I push my watered-down drink in his direction. 'You can have mine.'

Alec lets out a breath hard through his nose, but he bites his tongue and sets to work picking up syrup glasses for my drink.

'Alec, do you know what was so bad about Christos's day that he's determined to destroy his liver?'

148

I shoot them both a playful little smirk, but neither of them rises to it. Instead, Alec watches Christos out of the corner of his eye.

'I cannot say.' Alec slides a fresh vodka towards Christos.

Picking up my abandoned vodka, Christos pours it into the fresh one and, instead of sipping at the drink, he necks it in one then slowly pushes the glass back to Alec.

My cocktail glass, filled almost to the brim with its sticky pale-orange liquid, gets placed in front of me, followed by a shot of fizzy wine next to it.

I haven't taken my eyes off Alec, who picks up the vodka bottle and pours out more into Christos's empty glass.

Watching this exchange is enough to stop me spinning so much. I can't believe Alec would let someone get so drunk; surely he has some responsibility? They're friends too, he's one of Christos's only friends, or so I'm led to believe.

'You can't keep drinking like that?'

'It is the last,' Alec confirms to me.

'And why not? Putting it in a fancy glass with sugar will not change it, only the perceptions.' Christos gently flicks the side of my shot glass with a ting. 'And you mix your spirits and your wines. Much, much worse.'

I pour the shot of wine into the glass, almost spilling it, and take a deep sip of the sweet liquid. At least mine is enjoyable and doesn't burn on the way down. There's no way he could enjoy that paint stripper.

Christos begins to talk to Alec in Greek. It's slow and steady enough for me to understand. 'Don't tell her anything, OK? I don't need all the bullshit of sad eyes—'

'She understand Greek, yes?' Alec cuts in.

Christos inches round on his chair to face me. 'You understand me?'

I nod my head.

149

'Then why don't we talk in Greek?' he continues in Greek.

'Because I don't *speak* Greek, I only understand it. Mostly.' I sway my hand from side to side along with my head, leaving my vision lacking focus again.

He shakes his head and rolls off a bunch of words I'm pretty sure are swear words. As Mum never uses those around us, I don't understand them.

I shrug it off.

This bloke is the perfect distraction from my own insanity and the weird text message waiting to be read, because there's definitely way more going on here than he's telling me.

He basically said as much to Alec – or at least, I think he did. I think he was telling him not to tell me something.

My brain is too fuzzy to hold on to anything. Alcohol is leaving me feeling like my skin and head are made of cotton wool.

A high-pitched whistling cuts through the air and over the music, like I've suddenly been struck with tinnitus.

Alec pulls his phone out of his pocket and mutters something before disappearing to the right of the bar, in the direction of the kitchen.

'What are you hiding?' I lean in towards Christos. 'I know you said you're hiding things from me. Things you don't want me to know.'

He doesn't answer, and keeps his eyes locked on the glass he's slowly shifting round in a circle.

'Did you accidently have sex with a girl and now she wants a relationship?' I lean in even closer, so close I can smell a note of tobacco on his clothes. 'Or have you fallen in love with olive oil and that's why you don't date?'

'What?'

This catches him off guard enough to get him to look at me.

Alec comes back and says in Greek, 'Sorry to break the party, that was my eldest daughter. She's locked herself out and I have a key. And I am taking you home.' Alec shrugs and scratches the back of his head.

'Fine. I am ready for this day to be over now.'

As Christos goes to step off the stool, he shoves it backwards and somehow twists and falls to the ground.

'Oh my God! Are you OK?' My hand covers my mouth in surprise.

I look down at him, splatted on the floor, and it's hard to rein in the erupting giggles from behind my hand.

I want to help him up, but if I get off my stool I'll stand on him. He begins to prop himself up on his hands and twist about to get up, only to stumble forward, catching himself on the table I'd been sitting at with my family.

Alec jogs around the bar and I manage to slide safely off my stool.

'I'm fine, I'm fine,' Christos insists.

'Do you want some help?' I do my best to focus my eyes on Alec.

'I do not need help,' Christos snaps.

'I wasn't talking to you.'

Alec nods at me behind Christos's back and we each take an arm to manoeuvre him to Alec's car. We stumble down Cicala's ramp and straight into the road. It's late enough that there aren't too many cars, but a kid on an electric scooter speeds past us as fast as he can through the village. He's only holding it with one hand and isn't wearing a helmet. Even through my blurred alcohol goggles, I could still see there was no way that child was a day over fourteen.

'They are idiots, they have no idea. It's so fragile, so fragile. Isn't it fragile?' Christos rambles on as we all do our best to walk in the right direction.

'Who?' I shouldn't question ramblings, but it's impossible not to.

'That stupid kid with no helmet. They're fools.'

It's a two-person job to get him in the car. As Alec moves to the other side of the vehicle, I pull the seat belt around Christos, clicking it in place. I glance up, our faces only a breath away from each other.

'You're very beautiful. I hate that.' Christos's lips slide into a lopsided smile.

'Why would you—'

Alec opens the driver's side door and drops into the car, making it shake.

'I'm coming with you. You're going to need help getting him out.'

Before Alec can argue, I've slammed Christos's door and put myself in the back seat. The look in Christos's eyes in the dim car light was enough to make my heart race and confusion drown me.

I'm not ready to go home yet. When I go home, I'll have to read the message on my phone, and no amount of alcohol is going to make that bearable. Looking after Christos, finding out what's behind that lopsided smile, that's a perfect distraction.

Chapter Twenty-Five

'I'm staying. Can you message my mum and let her know? Tell her he needed looking after. If you message, she'll know it's serious.' I plant my hands on my hips and do my best not to sway.

Christos has perked up and is searching his kitchen cupboards for leftover alcohol.

His place is clean and simple. Empty.

No photos, no decorations, no ornaments. Nothing.

All the walls are white, all the furniture is pine or oak, all with a natural polished finish. The only thing of note, as I try to sober up, is the man in the middle of it, moving cereal boxes from one place to the next.

'Lorena, I can't leave you here.' Alec talks to me in Greek as he runs his hands over his face and paces back and forth. He stops and studies Christos. 'Not with him like . . . this.'

'You don't have time to take me back. I'm fine. There's a spare room, I remember him saying. Just go. I'll look after him. I don't want him to pass out all alone.'

Whatever happened to him today must have been dreadful. It's hard to imagine having no relationships and still ending a day this broken. Fine if it was every day, from being lonely, but this is one random day. A really bad one, by the looks.

I do my very best to look and sound sensible. Trustworthy. Which I am, and I am slowly sobering up. If I looked as deranged from booze as Christos does, I hope I wouldn't be left on my own. When Alec does leave, I might make a bowl of cereal or find some bread for toast. Toast would be so good right now. I haven't seen any bread in the alcohol search though, not that I've been paying that much attention.

'You should not be worrying. He has these days, once, twice a year. He will be fine. It's normal.'

'And if he's not fine?'

Alec hesitates, his eyes drifting between me and Christos.

'OK, yes. I will tell your mother. Do you want me to get you later? Or the morning?'

'It's OK, I have nowhere to be. When this one sobers up, he can take me home.'

Alec's hand lands heavy on my shoulder. 'Good luck. *Kalinichta. Kalinichta*, Christos.'

He leaves via the kitchen door, the one we came in through. I don't even really know where I am, or what this village is called. This was probably a bad idea.

I'm pretty sure Christos isn't a psychopath, although he does say some odd things at times.

'A-ha!' He holds up a bottle in triumph. 'Fuck, it's empty. *Po re malaka*,' he grumbles.

I shake my head. 'Do you want some cereal instead?'

'No, thanks.'

I pull my phone out to look at the time, and there's the message from the unknown number. Only this time my phone unlocks as I align it to my face, and I can see some of the message through blurred eyes. *This will be the last time . . .*

154

I don't want to know.

I place it on the kitchen table and pull out a chair, flopping down on to it. Before standing straight up again to open cupboard doors, looking for a glass.

I should get us both water. Or maybe coffee, if he won't eat cereal with me.

Each cupboard is a little sadder than the last. There are only a few plates and bowls, not enough to involve having anyone over. There's a cupboard for canned goods, but again, there's only a few items lining it. Eventually, I get to the cupboard with glasses, and there are only four tall tumblers and four short ones alongside some mugs. Nothing else.

I begin pouring water and making coffee for us both. I pass him a glass of water as I continue with the coffee. There's a packet of biscuits next to the cereal. I pull them out and pass Christos two, taking two for myself.

Opening the drawer for the cutlery, it's the cleanest I've ever seen, but only because there's only four of each item. I take out a small spoon to put sugar in the coffee then place it on the countertop next to Christos.

'I've heard of minimalist, but this is insane.' My hands slap down by my sides. 'You must at least have a shit drawer. Everyone has a shit drawer.'

I lean my back against the opposite counter, shaking my head before tentatively sipping at my sweet black coffee.

'A *shit drawer*?' He pours some of the cold water from his glass into his mug then begins to drink his coffee. Placing it down again, he folds his arms over his chest from the other side of the room and leans his back against the counter there.

'Yes, a drawer that's filled with manuals for things you don't even own anymore, random napkins, straws, lost spoons, keys for things that never existed. A shit drawer.'

'No.' He takes a deep swig of the hot coffee then marches towards me as though he's suddenly stone-cold sober and I've said something crazy. 'I have this.' He pulls out a drawer that's by my hip. It's not a shit drawer, it looks perfectly organised with a few papers in it.

Christos slides it slowly shut as he leans over me, the bulk of him lingering only millimetres away.

I look up at him, my heart pounding in my chest in a way that fills me with fear as sweat begins to gather between my breasts.

'Why do you hate that I'm beautiful?'

His mouth tugs into a subtle smile, hidden under his beard. He leans in, so close to my ear I can feel the warmth of his breath on my cheek.

'Because it makes me want to do things I don't want to do.'

I look up and our eyes meet. All I've achieved with this one look of confusion is to bring our mouths closer together. I can see him in macro. Every detail of his tanned skin and the different shades of brown and black in his beard, the golden-rose of his lips.

With each breath I take, we edge closer, until I can feel my chest pressing to his and his velvety lips are so close to mine it's impossible to resist. Soft and warm, we collide. As though Christos was always there on my skin, his hands on the base of my spine, drawing me in.

Electricity fills me up and lands, like him, on the tip of my tongue, and it tastes sweet and warm like the beginning of summer. Before I completely dissolve into him, reality hits, alarm vibrating through me, and I pull myself away.

'I can't do this.'

Our voices merge, so much so that I'm not sure I spoke at all.

Was it me who said that? Was it him?

Did I pull away? Was it him?

Was it both of us?

Peeling myself away from the counter digging in my back, I move away from him, looking this way, stepping that, not knowing which way is up.

'I should go, shit, no, I can't go. I don't have a car and even if I did . . .' I shrug. 'Don't think that kiss means anything, it doesn't.'

'Good. I don't want it to. I don't have relationships, remember?'

I stop pacing and my chest heaves like I've been jogging around the room instead of pacing.

'Good,' I agree.

He takes one long look over me, from my heeled sandals to my light-brown eyes.

'Good.' The word falls slowly from his soft lips before his top teeth dig into the bottom one.

That's enough to tip me over the edge.

I step forward and wrap my fingers around his neck, pulling him to kiss me again. Suddenly desperate to taste his lips on mine one more time, to find out if it really was that good.

Our mouths open to take in as much of the other as possible, our fingers working frantically to tug clothes off like it's a race. Dragging at his shirt, I notice a tattoo creeping over his shoulder and edging down his back.

'This doesn't mean anything,' I repeat between heavy breaths as Christos's beard tickles along my neck.

'Good,' he repeats, as he pulls up my dress.

Our bodies sway this way and that as we both fight to pull in as hard as we can. Glueing ourselves closer with each planted kiss.

My fingers fumble to undo the buttons on his shirt so I can get my hands on the firm muscles underneath.

Pulling my dress over my head, I step back to prop myself on his kitchen table in only my underwear.

His mouth finds mine again and his hands move expertly over me, making me gasp. To think he hadn't been with women, or

157

didn't want to be, now seems like a laughable reality, one where I haven't lost my senses.

My skin tingles in the same way it does when I've been swimming in the sea, almost itching with a new pleasure.

Christos stops and we rest our foreheads together, our eyes meeting as I clasp my hands around the back of his neck to steady myself.

'Are you sure?'

It's a question I don't want to ask myself. I was ready to be with only Jonah for the rest of my life and now I'm here, with my legs wrapped around someone else and feeling strangely OK about it.

His fingers trace along my stomach and under my knickers at the hip, forcing all the air residing deep in my lungs to leave me.

'I'm sure.'

He pushes into me, making me cry out as he fills me.

And there it is. We've crossed the line. He's pushed himself past the line and there's no going back.

This is probably a bad idea, but my body can't stop calling out at the pleasure of it.

Chapter Twenty-Six

I squeeze my eyes tightly shut and listen carefully to the drum rhythmically pounding in my head, begging it to stop.

Images float around me, Christos's mouth pressed to mine, my legs around his waist, the weight of his body on mine on the kitchen table, then on the stairs, in the bedroom . . . It all rushes over me like I'm watching us in the third person. As though it wasn't me at all. But it was. The passionate, fearless me.

It's never been like that with anyone before. Probably because there's always been expectation in the past. Here, we've already decided it can't have a future. I don't want to be hurt again and Christos . . . I'm not really sure why he doesn't settle down. Maybe he was hurt once too.

What the hell am I going to say to Serena?

How can I look her in the eye after last night? After telling her he isn't interested in seeing anyone – not that he is interested in that, but still, he was interested in more than I thought he was.

The bed-springs moan as Christos carefully gets up off the bed. I keep my eyes closed, but I can hear each floorboard complain as he disappears out of the room. I might have to stay here forever with my eyes shut, because I have no idea what to say to him.

This enigmatic man, the complete opposite of Jonah. Jonah lied about everything, and Christos is open about hiding who he is and what he's thinking. I thought I knew everything about Jonah, his habits, his love of giant mugs of coffee, his dislike of dogs. Everything. I didn't know the *real* him though. He just showed me enough to make me believe I knew him.

That's probably true of everyone, we only see what we're shown, but some people choose to show a shadow or a lie. They find it easy to deceive everyone around them.

In Christos's case, I've been shown a sexy puzzle openly telling me he doesn't want to share the whole picture. It's the most honest anyone has been with me lately.

'I know you're awake, Lorena.' I flinch at the sound of his voice.

I was sure he was in the bathroom, or at least not in here.

Slowly, I pull the thick cotton sheet over my head.

'What are you doing?' he continues.

'Hiding?'

'Why?'

'I thought it might be less awkward this way.'

Silence can be heard over the drum in my head. If I don't say anything, he might stand there in his swollen silence forever.

I yank the cover off and sit bolt upright, shuffling myself backwards and bringing my knees up to form a ball.

'I know, we are two adults and what we did was . . .' I tilt my head towards one shoulder then the other. '. . . well, it was bloody amazing actually—'

Christos can't help but let out a small snort of satisfaction, adjusting his posture to stand a little taller against the door-frame, crossing his arms over his bare chest.

'It doesn't matter,' I snap. 'It can't happen again. I don't do relationships—'

'Good. You know, neither do I.'

'Good.'

'Good.' Christos's voice lowers and there's a shift in the way he's looking at me.

Our eyes lock and I know he must be thinking about how this all started last night, because that's what I'm thinking about. My heartbeat overtakes the pounding in my head, like a fiercer drum over the top of it.

I need to get his eyes off me before last night starts all over again.

'What does that tattoo mean?' I glance at his shoulder. 'It's Greek? Right?'

Christos stretches his arm across his chest to reach around his shoulder and touch the black lines on his skin. The tattoo itself isn't just the Greek symbols and letters, there are swirls and lines around them too.

His fingers slide back down and he shrugs. 'It's hard to read something on your back.'

'Are you kidding?'

'No. Should I get a pen and write on your back? You can see . . . well, that is the point. You can't see.'

I shake my head and puff air through my nose. He really doesn't want to share anything with anyone. I shouldn't let it get to me, it's good, it proves what I've been learning – people hide themselves and I'm better off keeping to myself.

'I need to get ready, can you take me home?' I begin standing up, wrapping the sheet around me to hide myself. The air in the bedroom is crisp from air con and the sheets smell masculine, of him. I smell of him.

'I can, but we need to talk. And not just about tattoos and sex, although I can happily talk about that too . . . but first we need to talk business.'

'Fine. Make me a coffee and we can talk. But only about business . . . not the other stuff.'

161

I shuffle round him in the door-frame. He doesn't move out of the way, he hovers over me, watching me. I feel like a glow-worm wriggling past him while he watches with a keen interest.

My phone has been discarded outside the bathroom door. A memory flashes through me like a shot of adrenaline. I didn't want to read the message from Jonah, so I dropped it there late last night in between . . . everything.

This isn't the time to read it. I need to be dealing with today's problems. This isn't the moment to let in heartbreak. This is the time to wash off last night's make-up and work out what the hell I'm going to say to Serena when I see her.

Maybe if I tell her I had a message from Jonah, and that it made me do something crazy. It's not like I have any interest in dating Christos. Last night was just sex, nothing else. He's an extremely good-looking man, and I guess I needed a rebound, or something.

It was a bad idea. It's all a bad idea.

The girl in the mirror looks like a washed-out version of me. The slightly off-colour version, but my mascara held out well enough, only a hint of Alice Cooper. This is the first time I've noticed it's not only Mum who's looking a little gaunt from emotional trauma. My eyes look round and my hair takes up more space than my head. I need to run some straighteners over it to sort it out . . . if only I could, before heading home.

The bathroom is as boring as the kitchen. Only practical items allowed. Although, this room does have a colour. The walls are cornflower blue and the toilet seat matches the walls.

Two sharp knocks smack on the door, pulling me out of myself.

'You said coffee? *Nai?*' Christos's voice is flat. It gives nothing away.

'Yes, please. Two sugars.'

'I do not have sugar.' His feet thump down the stairs.

I want to call out telling him I know he does, because I put some in our drinks last night, but I can add it myself when I'm down there.

My phone blares out, echoing in the tiled room.

Mum. Shit.

'Hey.' I catch myself smiling in the mirror. If I smile, hopefully it'll translate in my voice. Hopefully, she'll believe everything's fine.

'*Kalimera* – is everything all right? Alec told me you were staying with Christos last night? This isn't to do with Serena, is it? Because you argued and you know she likes him?'

Of course that's what everyone will think. They'll think I slept with him out of spite, because we had a small drunken spat. It couldn't possibly be because we are two grown adults, or we accidentally let our bodies take over, or a passionate attraction that couldn't be ignored . . . No. It's because my sister pissed me off, and I'm being a bitch.

I clear my throat. I can already feel the tension prickling over me before I begin.

'Well, you know I was a little drunk.' I twist the soap dish to keep my mind away from the vision of Christos's naked body writhing over mine and my fingernails digging into the tattoo on the back of his shoulder. 'Well, he was a lot more drunk. I have no idea what had got into him. I've never seen him like that.'

'How could you have? You barely know him.'

'You know what I mean. It was a surprise, that's all. He's normally so calm, quiet. You know?'

'Appearances can be deceiving. When will you be home? I didn't want to be the one to tell Serena who you stayed out all night with, but she's already up.'

'You can tell her I stayed here, I haven't got anything to hide.'

Hopefully, bravado can pull me through this and maybe she'll believe nothing happened without me having to lie about it.

I squeeze my eyes shut; the marching band in my head is working hard to regain my attention.

'Well, I'm glad I stayed with him, anyway. Alec said he thought he needed the company.'

I'm glad Mum can't see my face and that eye-rolling is a silent activity. *Needed the company.*

I bite my cheek. Maybe we both needed the company. A distraction for bleeding hearts and uncontrollable situations.

It's true for me, anyway, and the way he was behaving, it might be true for him too.

'Mum, Christos is making me coffee and we're about to talk business. I don't know when I'll be back. When he sobers up, I guess. I'll see you later, OK?'

Mum makes a sound in the back of her throat like a disgruntled cat before saying she'll see me later and hanging up.

I stare at my phone for a moment when Mum goes, wondering about the unopened text. The little number one hanging on to the corner of the message icon box on my screen.

I can't spend the day hiding in Christos's bathroom, even if I want to.

'Coffee is ready,' booms from somewhere downstairs.

I move quickly so he doesn't begin to think I really am hiding from him.

It's awkward moving about in the bedsheet. I've bunched it around my waist so I can get downstairs and find my dress.

When I get to the stairs I begin to trot down them, holding up the material as best I can while trying to make myself sound lively and airy, even if each step feels like I've rattled something else loose from the sides of my brain.

I stop dead about four steps from the bottom, as I catch sight of one of my shoes on it, and the other one at the bottom of the stairs. My pace slows. I start to fight with the sheet so I can pick them both up, placing them neatly against the back wall of the living room.

'Here.' Christos comes in from the kitchen diner and walks to the coffee table to put it down for me.

'I'll just . . .' I point towards the kitchen diner.

He tracks me with a lift to his face as I dash past him and hunt out my dress, slipping it over my head before returning to the living room.

Nothing matches in here. I hadn't noticed last night. I had better things to concentrate on as we clawed our way through here to the stairs.

It looks like he went into a charity shop and took whatever they had, no matter the style. There's a worn floral armchair and a hard-looking red sofa with flat-looking cushions. The coffee table has a shiny dark veneer and the TV cabinet is glass with black metal legs.

I pick up the coffee. A fan is already whizzing over our heads and even in a building like this, with thick stone walls and air con in the bedroom, it's obvious it'll be another hot day in Corfu.

However much I'm gasping for a drink, there's no way I can drink a boiling-hot black coffee, not right away anyway. I only managed last night because I think I'd let the kettle cool quite a bit before pouring it.

I slump down on to the floral armchair. It's like sitting on concrete roses that puff with dust.

'Sorry, no one ever sits there.' Christos presses his full lips together in an apologetic line.

He sits on the sofa holding his mug under his nose, leaning his elbows on his knees and staring into space.

'What was with you last night?' I study him to gauge his reaction.

There isn't one. No glint in his eye, no twitch of his lips. Nothing.

'I don't know what you mean?'

'The drinking? The endless hunt for vodka?'

'Oh good, not the sex then, let's ignore this one, yes? I think that is a good idea too.'

Heat rises up through my legs, my chest, and lands at my cheeks.

'I was actually more interested in the drinking that got us there.'

'I told you, it was a bad day. It ended well though. Anyway, how about you? What bee got into your bonnet? It seems maybe it was a hornet, not the bee, after you ran away from me the other day, then all the drinks you had.'

I run my hand up and down my thigh before tucking it between my knees. If I expect him to open up to me, I guess I should give him something.

'I had a text from an ex-boyfriend. It's a long story. It threw me through a bit of a loop. I guess it made me act a little . . . irrationally.' I open my mouth to tell him more. To say we were engaged and that he hurt me, and it was the same idiot who stole my life's savings, but I don't. I close my mouth and pick the coffee up from the table.

It's so dark, it kind of reminds me of Christos's eyes in the shadows of his room late last night.

I shake my head. 'And what was so bad about your day that only a bucket of vodka would fix it?'

'The vodka did not fix it.'

'Fine. That sex with me was the only way to fix it.'

This at least brings a brief smile to his lips and a flicker of something deep in his eyes.

'Nothing can fix it. The sex was nice though. A welcome distraction.'

'*Nice?* I'm not a pair of socks with a peppy slogan.'

'OK, OK, it was more like you say earlier, *bloody amazing.*'

I can't help but press my lips, biting back a mix of sadness and regret at him only thinking it was *nice*. I do my best to hide my petty feeling behind my mug before sipping at my coffee.

'Don't look like that. Nice is good, and what I remember, it was amazing.'

'Do you not remember?' A new and different wave of guilt washes over me.

Did I accidently take advantage of him? It's easy to forget that a big strong man, who when sober knows his own mind, might be led astray and regret everything the next morning.

'I didn't take advantage of you, did I?' I narrow my eyes on him, my hand gripping my chest.

Christos begins to cough over his coffee as it catches in his throat.

'No.' His voice is raspy and as dark as the coffee. I can feel the vibration of it down to my toes. 'It was a bad day, it can't happen again, *us*, the day will happen again, but us . . .' He shakes his head. 'But, last night, I wanted us to . . .' His words disappear as he puts down his mug on the coffee table.

'Good.'

Christos looks at me out of the corner of his eye. That word seems to have a new meaning, a new connotation that wasn't there before. I'll have to stop using it.

'I need to get home, Mum's already called wondering when I'll be back.'

'When will we talk business? I have been looking at the forms for the business. It is all in Greek, of course, so you will need help.'

'Mum could help me, or Spiros and Eleni.'

'True. Then you only need my money.'

The muscles in my forehead collapse under the weight of his accusation.

'I didn't even ask for your money, you tricked me into agreeing. Not that I have agreed, I haven't.'

Christos shrugs, slapping his hands down on his legs to stand, making his way towards the stairs at the back of the room before turning to the kitchen. He comes back out with the sheet I left on a chair wrapped in his arms.

'You have it right, it is up to you. I was thinking this is what you wanted. I will shower and take you home.' He disappears up the stairs and his disembodied voice calls back down, 'You can borrow any clothes.'

'No thanks.'

There's no way I can turn up at home wearing Christos's clothes. Serena would claw my eyes out, screaming *I saw him first*.

When I was fifteen, I kissed a boy during spin the bottle. He was in my class, and she'd never even told me she had a crush on him. When I got home and told her, you would've thought I'd pulled the head off her favourite Barbie doll.

I close my eyes and rest my head back on the chair.

Today is going to be a hard day. I just pray Serena doesn't hate me by the end of it, and that Christos and I can at least remain friends. I need to find out what really happened to him yesterday. Why he was so drunk.

It'll all have to wait though. Right now, I feel more like sleeping than chopping my way through all the questions that sprout like weeds.

Chapter Twenty-Seven

'Bad night?' Anton slides a long black pipe out of his van as he raises an eyebrow in my direction.

'Something like that.' I tug at the hem of my skirt and change the subject. 'How's it coming along in there?' I nod towards the house, stepping out of his way as he manoeuvres the pipe round.

'Good, good. Soon it will be up to you three to finish. Upstairs at least.'

'We're all really grateful for your time.'

'We are.' Mum appears in the doorway. 'I'm glad you're home safe, my love.'

Christos had offered to let me shower at his. I'm already regretting saying no, as I'll have to go for a swim then shower on the beach. I exhale hard at the thought of it.

The thought of showering at his and putting these clothes back on was worse than not showering at all. At least this way I'll be able to get clean and put new clothes on straight away.

Anton squeezes past, leaving the pipe in the living room before heading back out to his van.

'Alec is already upstairs doing the last of the plastering.' Mum walks towards the kitchen, knowing full well I'll keep in step with her, even while trying to kick off my heels.

'And Serena?'

'I'm here.' She removes her head from the cupboard before carefully closing it.

Her movements are too methodical. Like a well-calculated villain instead of her usual casual slamming of doors.

'So, what happened with Christos?' She stares me down while holding a large bottle of Evian.

'Can I have some of that, please? My head is still thumping.' I point to the bottle.

She exhales hard but moves towards our small stock of glasses. 'Well?'

'*Well* nothing. He was really drunk and needed looking after and we . . .' Her eyes become as thin as blades at the word *we* on my lips. I have to change direction, there's no way I can start any sentence with *we* right now and live to get to the full stop. 'I mean, I got another text message.'

Serena stops pouring and Mum steps forward, pushing her hair behind her ears as though this will help her to capture every word I divulge.

'From Jonah?' Mum interjects.

'What did it say?' Serena slams down the bottle and folds her arms over her chest.

'I've been too afraid to open it. I used Christos as a welcome distraction. I should've dealt with my own problems but it was easier to get tangled up in his.'

At least that's true. It might be a messy metaphor for all the tangled limbs, but at least it's not a lie.

I scuff my bare foot on the dusty floor, wondering how much I should say.

'I can't believe you haven't looked at it yet. How is that even possible? You have to open it.' Serena's bright-green eyes search my face, her mouth hanging open at the end of her sentence.

My phone is waiting in my hand. Waiting with its one unread message.

I do what I should've done last night – I flick open the screen, leaning back against the kitchen wall, wishing it would suck me in.

Instead, I suck in a breath and hold it in my chest as I take in the words in the box.

> *This will be the last time you hear from me. Promise. I've missed you. I want you to know I really am sorry. I had no choice. I need to know if you forgive me? X*

'Well?' Serena edges closer.

I can't read it out, my chest burns as a juddering breath eases out of me through pursed lips. I thrust the phone in her direction and cover my face with my hands.

My back slides along the wall until my bottom hits the floor.

He needs to know if I forgive him? Why? To make it easier on him, so he can run off with my money and my blessing?

'What the hell? Seriously? What the hell? As if he has the cheek to send this.' Serena drops down next to me.

Everything from last night – our spat in the toilets, our harsh words – has melted away, because at the end of the day, Mum's right. Serena does love me, and I love her. She might piss me off sometimes, but I'd do anything for her.

'Are you going to reply?' Mum holds the phone out for me to take, Serena must've given it to her.

'I don't know. What would I even say? That all is forgiven, even though he tore down everything I'd saved for, everything I'd worked for? He said it would be the last time I'd hear from him anyway, so even if I reply, I wouldn't get anything in return. I need to forget about him. I want to help fix the house up today. The living room's really starting to look good. I'll go down to the beach, have a wash and forget all about this.' I shake the phone in my hand.

Rubbing my fingers under my eyes to catch any tears this bullshit might've shaken loose, I begin to stand. 'It's this room next, right? While the walls upstairs dry and while the men start putting the shower in? I'll get washed and we can paint in here.' I plaster on a smile and turn on my heel so I don't have to look at the pity gathering in their faces.

Jogging to the top of the stairs, Alec meets me there.

'Lorena, *kalimera*. How is Christos? Are you both going well today?'

'Yeah, he's fine.'

'You take him to bed OK?'

I'm not sure whether to laugh or cry. Surely this is a Greek vs English language phrasing, but in my head that sounds dreadful. At least I can answer honestly and still come out of it unscathed.

'Yeah, I took him to bed OK.'

I can't look him in the eye when I say it. The words are muttered and I have to pray I'm not the colour of a cherry.

'I'm just going to . . .' I point to my room.

Alec steps towards me. 'Thank you, for staying. It is hard for him' – I wish he hadn't said *hard* – 'but it is good he makes you a friend. He is needing friends.'

That's something that's glaringly missing from Christos's life. Walking into his house is like walking into a social vacuum. It's as though I was the first person around his age to set foot in there.

'What's up with Christos?' Maybe Alec can shine some light on it, I'm sure he knows something.

Alec squints at my mouth, then my eyes, in confusion.

'I mean, why was he so drunk? Why doesn't he have many friends?'

'I can't explain you it, that is for him, not me.' Alec shrugs and lowers his eyes to the floor. His lips turn down a touch and I could swear it's sadness crossing his face. 'I have to help Anton. Thank you, for Christos.'

Shutting my door behind me, I begin to peel off last night's clothes as though they've been glued to my skin.

I can still smell him on me, a deep masculine smell that lingers. It's intoxicating even now. Like danger and temptation made a scent from fire and sex and rubbed it all over him.

I'm surprised Serena didn't point it out when she snatched the phone from my hand. There's not one part of me he didn't touch and leave a sensation that I can't forget.

I slump down, naked, on my bed. How could I let this happen?

There's no way I could ever want to fall in love again. There's no way I could trust another man, not after Jonah, and definitely not a man who clearly has more baggage than an airport.

My hands skim my stomach at the memory of his mouth desperately tasting my skin.

It can't happen again, however good it was.

Chapter Twenty-Eight

I miss the sea.

It's only a matter of steps to get there. I might count them next time I walk down there. If it was a straight line from our back door to the edge of the sea, I reckon it would only be eighty or a hundred steps. Maybe less. I guess it depends how big the strides are. Eighty to a hundred of my steps, maybe.

How is it only forty minutes since I was there swimming and washing away Christos? It already feels like more, and I already need to go back and shower all over again with the effort of painting.

'Can we start sleeping during the day and doing this at night? It's too hot.' Serena wipes her brow with the back of her hand for the hundredth time.

'If the men are working, we are working. You can have a rest this afternoon, after lunch. Maybe. You two don't know a hard day's work, that's the problem.'

We both gasp and grunt disagreement, but ultimately our idea of a hard day's work has always been sitting at a desk, not screwing cupboards into walls or climbing ladders to paint ceilings. A stroll on the beach is more physical than any work we've ever done.

In reality, it's not too bad, I suppose. The cupboards were already in, but the doors had been left outside in a pile and have gone rotten over the years. Mum managed to get some new ones at a good price. We're also changing the colour from cream to white. Everything's going to be simple and sleek.

I'm on paint duty with Serena while Mum puts some of the doors on at the other side of the room, where it's all going to be tiled. It had all been prepped ready for the tiles to go on, we just need to actually tile. We didn't have to buy those as there were white tiles left in the corner of the floor, and unlike the doors, they've survived the test of time. But then they didn't have to contend with the elements.

'Did you do much physical work when you were last living in Corfu? Did you help with the olive harvest?' I glance over at Mum's red face as she pushes another door into place.

'You've heard how things have been done over the years, you took Spiros's tour. I was born in the seventies. There were still traditions we followed back then. Tourism was in its infancy. My father didn't believe it would take off the way it did. He couldn't see it being lucrative. He always made money from the trees. It was only later in life he decided to do something with this place and by then . . . it was too late. Anyway, what was the question?'

'Did you ever do any physical labour, other than giving birth to us?' Serena squints at her brush as she glides the paint around the edge of the door-frame.

'I did, actually. Traditionally, it was the job of the women to collect the olives and the men to carry them up to the mill. I used to enjoy picking, gathering, helping with the nets. When I met your father, I had been bringing oil to one of the tavernas and was meeting a friend after.' Mum stays squatting on the floor, one hand resting on the door she's put in place. Her gaze fixed on the empty cupboard.

I shoot a look towards Serena. Her nostrils flare but we keep our conversation wordless. A pattern of expressions that speak more words than could be spoken in the same slice of time.

Words flood my brain, but they're all questions I can't imagine Mum wants to answer. Questions like, how are you feeling? Do you miss Dad? She's avoided talking about him when she can. More so since he got back from Mexico.

'What are you thinking?' I venture the simplest question that bounces between my ears.

Mum jumps up like she was never still. She reminds me of those tiny toys on springs that you push into the floor, and they rebound with an unbelievable force.

Her hands clap together. 'I was thinking about what to do next. The walls are looking good now. I think I'll check on Alec and Anton.' She gives a nod as though she agrees with herself and leaves us to continue painting.

We wait all of ten seconds before we start whispering to each other.

I start, 'Have you spoken to Dad lately?'

'Sort of. He's making out like we all left him, when he was the one that left. I mean, I guess we did all leave . . .'

I can feel Serena trying to open a door, one that asks whether we were wrong to up and leave him because he had an affair. It shouldn't change our relationship with him. She's tugging at the door handle of the question, and I don't want to pull on it with her.

It's not that I don't care, I do. He's my dad, after all. That doesn't mean I'm ready to take on all of his problems along with my own, and Serena got her dramatic streak from him.

However much I want answers from him, I don't think I'm going to like anything he has to say. Right now, second-hand information from Serena will do nicely. There's no way I want to argue with him about who left who when the answer is clear. 'He left first. If he hadn't been off in another country, he would've known what was happening in his own house. I'm here because I needed a fresh start too. He's the one that barely knows what happened between me and Jonah because he hasn't bothered to ask. All he said was, *I'm sorry to hear that.* Where's the fatherly love in that? He didn't even ask if I was OK.'

'Have you asked him what happened with him and Megan? How they got together?'

'Eww, no! It's completely different anyway! Wait, why? Have you?' I twist to face her, aiming my roller in her direction.

She turns her face away from me and shrugs. She begins to study the wall as though she's looking for the next place to paint. Instead, she drops her paintbrush back in the tray and paces the room.

'I might have.'

'You know curiosity killed the cat, right? Probably because its head exploded at all the shit it found out along the way that it wished it didn't know.'

I shudder at the thought of their work romance. This proves it. If I can't even hear about it from Serena, there's no way I'm ready to hear a word of it straight from him.

I drop my roller next to her brush and my voice finds a volume edging towards normality instead of our previous whispers.

'Let me guess, she persuaded him, it wasn't his fault, they have a connection . . .'

'Outside.' She turns on her heel and I follow her out of the open door and into the pounding rays of the sun. It can't be that far off lunch now.

'We can't talk about Dad without it becoming a competition, can we? I know the way he went about things was wrong—'

'Really wrong. He gave no respect to Mum whatsoever.'

'Fine, that much is true, but that doesn't mean he doesn't love us because he fell out of love with Mum and accidently fell for someone else.'

'I know all this.' I shade my eyes against the sun.

Although drinking water and clearing my head in the sea helped a lot to dull down my headache, the sun hammering on me is enough to edge in some of the dehydration from last night.

'This isn't even a conversation. I was worrying about Mum and that random little daydream, that's all. Don't you sit around and wonder why she never came back here? I mean, look at the place.' I do a little twirl for effect, showcasing the green bushes with little flowers sprouting on them, and the clearest baby-blue sky imaginable. 'All I want to know is *why*. What the hell happened here that meant she only came back now?'

'I guess we have different priorities, Lorena. You're fixated on the past, and I want to know how the future is going to work. What about Christmas? Have you thought about Christmas?'

'No.'

'Exactly.'

'The men are done for the day.' Mum appears in the doorway like she never left. 'Anton needs to get home, Alec needs food, but I think he'll be back later. I'm going to take him out for something. Do you two want to come?'

'I'm OK, I think I need to get some sleep.'

I move towards the doorway and Serena does the same. 'I think I might get something on the beach,' she says.

'Suit yourselves. Be good.' With that, Mum turns back into the house, dusting herself off and smoothing out her hair.

'Beach nap?' Serena hesitates in the door. In her bralette and her black shorts, which only just hide her bum cheeks, she looks about ready for the beach as she is, but I guarantee she'll spend the next twenty minutes getting ready to lie down on the sand.

'Nah, I think I'll head back upstairs.'

Scooping up my phone from the kitchen counter, I follow Serena up the stairs and we part at the bedrooms.

As soon as I'm in mine, I flick open my phone screen.

This will be the last time you hear from me. Promise. I've missed you. I want you to know I really am sorry. I had no choice. I need to know if you forgive me? X

I lick my lips; they feel so smooth, and yet dry. It's like they're made of shiny plastic. Christos must've removed a few layers of skin with his beard and all the heated kissing.

There's no way I can ignore the message anymore. Pretending it's not really there when it's been sitting in the back of my mind like a tick, sucking all the life out of me, isn't working. In the sea and while painting walls I've been thinking about this, and only this. Only Mum's past could manage to pull my thoughts from Jonah and what I want to do about it.

I'm not sure I can forgive him.

Just like with Dad, there were a million ways he could've dealt with this that were better than the way he did. He didn't just break my heart, he broke my ability to trust.

Maybe Jonah only half did that. He took one of my hands and Dad took the other and they both thought it would be fun to pull until my chest ripped open. Like orcas, they've toyed with their prey. They told lies and made me believe in worlds that were never real. Worlds of trust and loyalty, where words can be said and believed.

I hate him for that.

I hate them both for that.

I'll forgive Dad, one day. I don't think he thought things through far enough as to how they would affect Mum, Serena or me. He was only thinking to the end of his cock, probably. But every action we take has an effect on someone else.

I send a message back to the unknown number.

Do *you* forgive you?

I pace the floor, only to stop to look out of the window and down towards the beach. There're fewer people today. At least, fewer people on our path to the sea. A couple walk hand in hand. It's impossible to tell their age from up here. They could be fresh and starting out, or together for half a century. They leave their footprints side by side in the sand, trailing behind them. I wonder if they've always been faithful, or whether they hide things from each other.

I can't remember hiding things from Jonah. Only gifts for his birthday or Christmas. There's nothing I can think of that would've betrayed his trust.

I take a breath. Not a light, snatched breath, but a deep and cleansing one to help fortify my soul before looking back at my phone.

An exclamation mark has appeared next to the message I sent back. It's been unable to be delivered.

Numbness pushes out from my bones as I sit back on my bed. It takes over every part of me, wrapping me in a cold sweat against the heat of Corfu.

I guess I sent it too late.

If his message is to be believed, that's it forever. I'll never know why this will be his last message. Is he changing phones again, or something more nefarious?

I'll never know.

It's like I've walked into our house to find it pulled apart all over again. I'm back there tripping over all my belongings, panic-stricken because I'm worried for Jonah. Worried he'd been attacked, when the reality was his attack on me.

Four small knocks rattle my door, making my heart skip out of my window and on to the sand.

'Yeah?' I respond to the sound.

Serena pops her head around the door. 'Can we talk?'

Every action has an effect on someone else. Something in her eyes makes me wonder how I'm affecting her.

Chapter Twenty-Nine

'Where did you sleep last night?' Serena bunches her legs together at the end of my bed.

She looks so small, like a kitten. Fragile and beautiful.

'I've told you, at Christos's house.' Anxiety balls up inside me like a cyst that's ready to burst.

'But *where* in his house?'

Everything piles on top of me and begins to press on my chest. Like an avalanche has toppled and buried me alive. I don't want to lie to my sister, I feel bad enough about arguing last night and letting the stupid texts from Jonah get in my head and needle me. But right now, it all feels like too much. I'm sick of it. Sick of all these thoughts swirling around me and clouding my judgement, clouding every part of me.

My hands gravitate to my temples and then to my eyes, kneading them as I will myself to come up with something good, not a filthy and ugly lie. I don't want to be like Dad or Jonah. I want to protect Serena.

Dad wasn't protecting Mum, and even though Jonah says he was protecting me, I don't believe him for a minute.

I can't lose her over this.

'In his spare room. Why?'

As soon as the words tumble out, I wish with my whole heart I could take them back. With her pushing me and my brain buzzing with all the thoughts I didn't want to hear, the only priority that's clear is avoiding another argument and not losing another person in my life. It's bad enough I feel like Dad isn't even interested in being a part of my life, and Mum is hiding half of hers; I couldn't make things worse with Serena. I couldn't.

But now . . . now all I want to do is take it back.

'But the bed from his spare room is here.' She taps the bed. 'We're sitting on it.' She continues to press her finger into my clean white sheets. 'Unless he has loads of rooms? But I got the impression there was only one spare.'

'Fine.' I press my fingers over my face to cover myself completely, knowing what I have to do. The thought of Christos and what happened dances past my eyes and words mumble out of my mouth from behind my hands. 'I slept with him.'

'I knew it! I knew there was a reason I could smell him on you. You smelt like a man when you got home.'

A strange mix of fear and peace rolls over me. I told the truth, now I'll have to deal with the consequence and hope Serena will be OK with it, even if she did have her eyes on him first.

'Yeah, I mean I—'

'I knew you'd slept next to him, or in his bed.' She rapidly switches to kneeling and keeps her eyes on the bed. 'I hope our argument had nothing to do with it.'

My mouth hangs open. I didn't lie, but she clearly thinks I meant it literally. That we slept. Maybe my emphasis neutralised it somehow, or maybe she only heard it the way she wanted to hear it. Or maybe she's not ready to hear the truth.

She's snatched the wind from my sails and the air right out of my lungs. My mouth feels like it's been stuffed with cotton, muffling my words as I try to think what I should say or do next. I wanted to be honest, I have been honest, so why do I still feel like I'm lying? 'No, I mean, it was a stupid argument. I'm sorry, I was drunk and being a cow. It was me. I just . . . those messages from Jonah, they've made me feel like I'm back at square one.'

I'd used Christos and his good looks to distract me. I hid my pain in the warmth of his arms and the maddening passion of his lips. I should correct her, I should come clean, but I don't want to make things worse, what good would it do? I've told the truth once; pushing the point would be spiteful, like I need her to know. It's not as though I owe her this information, it's my life, after all. And it's not like it'll happen again. It was once, that's all.

The lump is back, the one trying to force my airway open as my tear ducts want to overflow like the crashing of a waterfall.

'Hey, hey, don't let Jonah do this to you. You've got me, and Mum, and I know Dad still loves you. That hasn't changed. He's already asking when we can go back to England and see him.'

I don't like to tell her that it's not just thoughts of Jonah making me want to cry.

'Really? Dad barely sends me a message.'

'Yeah, well . . . he did ask about coming here but I told him that was a stupid idea. I do think we'll have to go and see him at some point soon.'

A tear rolls off my cheek and the salt of it touches my lips.

'Why has everything got to be like this?'

My fists ball at my sides, wishing they could claw my own eyes out, because I can't tell Serena this, and even when we hate each other, it only ever lasts hours and this wasn't done to hurt her. But now I'm holding things back.

'Why don't we go to the beach together? It's bloody boiling in this room.' She pulls at her bralette, like her boobs need more air. 'We can swim, and sleep, and tan. It'll be nice.'

I nod my head. How can I deny her?

Her hands slap her thighs and her mouth changes shape entirely, pulled into her intoxicating smile. A smile so big it could change even the darkest mood.

'Come on then, you get ready and I'll meet you downstairs.'

I nod my head again, sniffing back the idea of crying.

Get ready. Now I need to get ready to swim all over again.

The problem is, I don't feel able to prepare myself for much right now. It's as though I've lost all my skill sets and I don't know which way to go.

My phone comes alive with my message tone, and the screen next to me lights up.

My heart is in my mouth at the thought of more messages from Jonah. I scramble to pick it up, my fingers becoming as clueless as worms.

Christos's name adorns my screen, and with it comes a new rush of very different nerves.

> *I think we should talk soon. Do you want to come to my house tomorrow for dinner to talk about business?*

If I took away the part about business, this sounds like he's asking me out on a date. There's no way I want to date anyone, and particularly not Christos.

It's like my mind and body are in a sauna, and the heat is misting up my vision. I need to put a stop to this.

> *Are you free now? Serena and I are going to the beach if you want to come?*

That should be enough to let him down gently but also to show him I am still interested in working out how the hell to earn some money for myself. Or at least, how to get myself into debt with him in the hope of money somewhere down the line.

> *No. I do not go to the beach. I am free tomorrow. This is not a date, if you are worrying.*

He doesn't go to the beach? Ever? Or am I reading more into this again, like with him not dating vs not sleeping around?

I also don't want to say I was worrying, but equally, I was worrying.

> *What do you mean you 'do not go to the beach'? EVER? Lol! You must be kidding??*

Serena's feet skip past my door, I need to hurry up.

I jump off my bed and hunt through one of my suitcases for a bikini. We all need furniture for our clothes, but we've decided to paint first. It makes more sense that way.

My phone chimes as I slide on the bikini. I wrap myself in a burgundy sarong before turning to pick it up and look at the message.

> *Are you coming tomorrow?*

I hesitate over the message. Everything from his wording to the voice in my head screaming at me against that lingering marching band.

> *What time?*

◆ ◆ ◆

'Look what I got us!' Serena exclaims as she returns to the beach after telling me she was only getting us some water.

She wiggles two boxes at me. Both have images on them of smiley women holding giant inflatable sparkly doughnuts.

'You're kidding? They're just like the ones we had as kids.'

I'm not sure whether to roll my eyes or squeal with delight.

'Here.' She throws one of the boxes towards me, but I don't manage to catch it. Instead, it lands in the sand by my hip and grains fly into the air like unsettled fruit flies. 'You blow up that one, and I'll do this one.'

'Thanks, sis.'

Her hands claw at the packet, ripping the woman's cardboard face in half. I pick up my gift, flicking my nail over the corner of the sticky tape and opening the box carefully, prising out the glittery white inflatable.

Serena drops to her knees, landing on her towel in the sand, and begins heaving deep breaths and blowing hers up with complete abandon. It's like we're kids on holiday, ready to put our armbands on for the first time.

It's the first time since we arrived that I've let in the fun beach vibes of being away from England and here in Greece.

I follow suit and begin puffing air into mine.

It takes a few rests and a lot of puff to blow them up. My cheeks soon ache from pouting and my lungs begin to burn.

'Done.' Serena proudly holds the ring in front of me. 'I now know why we used to get Dad to do this shit.' Her eyes get lost in the glitter of it. As though she's looking through it at something far away. The smile on her mouth changes, shifting until it lingers on her lips but nowhere else on her face.

'I think you're right. We'll organise a trip to see him when we have the house sorted.'

She looks at me as though she'd forgotten I was there.

'I'd like that.' She sucks in one last deep breath, exhaling it with a judder as though she's been crying. 'Come on. Let's try these bad boys out!' She hops up, still on her towel, and kicks off her sandals. 'Are you ready to run? It'll be like *Baywatch* holding these, only way faster or we'll burn our feet.'

'It'll be nothing like *Baywatch*, more like . . .' I scramble to find a quippy response but can't find one in my cloudy head. 'I don't know. Just not sexy running holding these. More like people running in sumo suits.'

'Good point, maybe we should get inside and run?'

My eyebrows shoot so high I'm sure they're hiding in the cloud in my head.

'Please tell me you're kidding?' I begin kicking off my flip-flops too. 'I like the childish fun of the inflatable, but running with it like a hula-hoop surely crosses the line?'

Serena's shoulders rise and fall. 'Fine, we can hold them. Three, two, one, run!'

Then we're off, throwing up powdery grains of golden sand with each pointed toe that briefly meets the beach until we connect with the cooler sludgy stuff around the surf, then straight into the sea, giggling, splashing, jumping.

The salt of my tears kisses the salt of the sea. But these are new tears burning my cheeks. Ones from the joy of laughing at my wonderful little sister.

Chapter Thirty

'I'm surprised you answered, Sunshine.'

It takes me a moment to reply to his familiar tones. The subtle northern lilt that he got from Nanna and living in Hull when he was a kid.

I don't like to tell him I answered without even looking who it was on the line. That I was half asleep when the phone started to ring.

It feels like a year since we've spoken. In fact, the last time I spoke to Dad was probably a few days before he went swanning off to Mexico under the ruse of a business trip. I'd called to speak to Mum, to arrange our little get-together to discuss wedding dresses, and he answered the phone. Thinking back, he was distracted then, but so was I so it didn't bother me. I barely remember what was said.

Since then, it's been text messages or nothing at all.

'Hi, Dad. I'm surprised to hear from you.'

'Can't your old dad call and check up on you?'

'I mean . . . he can, he just doesn't usually.'

I shuffle back on my bed, crossing my legs like I'm waiting for a school assembly to begin.

'You disappeared to Corfu. I'm back home and missing you. It's you that left.'

'Please don't.'

'No, all right then. Megan's told me to try and see it the way you would. She's really helped me.'

I grit my teeth and manage only a single word. 'Good.'

'I'd love for you to meet her, you know? Megan, I mean. I know this is a hard time, but you girls are grown up, not little kids, and we need to accept this change. I want to be a part of your life. At least Serena talks to me . . . I'm still surprised you answered the phone.'

I don't like to tell him I'm as surprised as he is.

'How are you? Still sad about Jonah?'

'Erm . . .' I don't know how to respond. I feel like he's managing to show sympathy and at the same time be completely condescending. 'I'm getting there.'

'I feel terrible, you know, about everything.' The line begins to crackle and his words become disjointed.

'Dad, you're breaking up. Dad? Can you hear me?'

'. . . OK, later then . . . can you hear me? I'll . . . another time. Love you.'

The line goes dead. It's only now I realise how hunched over I am, with my phone pressed hard enough to my skin to leave a line across my face.

I need to talk to Serena, tell her about the call. I hop out of bed and march down the landing.

When Serena isn't in her room, I jog down the stairs to find her. 'Where's Serena? She's not in her room.'

Mum's in our favourite corner, outside in our back garden. It's where the last of the evening sun can be found as it sets over the sea. It's just about visible through the scrub and bushes. Like a lion's mane, the sun's rays reach out from burning orange to a dusty haze.

There's not a cloud to be found. I haven't seen one in days. Other than in my own head.

Mum doesn't turn to face me, she's facing the sun, her arms stretched along her thighs and her chin tilted slightly up, her eyes shaded behind sunglasses.

'She's exploring. That's all she would say.'

I pull out one of the white plastic chairs, dusting off the seat before sitting down next to my mum.

I've had a lot of sun already today; even with lotion, my cheeks have captured the red tones of the sun and sprinkled them over my tanned cheeks. Serena and I spent hours fighting waves before resting on the inflatables, letting those same waves of mother earth rock us like Mum did when we were babies.

'Everything OK, my love?' Mum stretches a little finger in my direction and briefly brushes the back of my hand with it.

'Yeah, I was just on the phone to Dad. We got cut off.'

The cicadas fill the silence, so we don't have to. They chirp and call and never worry about who slept with who, or how it might affect the emotional sanity of another cicada. Or, at least, I assume they don't.

'How is he?'

This isn't a question I was anticipating, not one I really know how to answer.

I prop my feet on my chair until my knees reach my chin, the way Serena does on my bed. There's a part of me that wants to hide from this conversation. Fear rises up like goosebumps, because I don't want to hurt her.

'He's OK, I think. There's still some residual hurt from all of us vanishing on him, but I don't think he has much right to that pain. I think he's starting to accept that.'

I don't like to tell her that he was actually being OK for a change, and was talking about how that Megan of his has helped him see things from my point of view. I can't even say her name in my head without putting on a tone, as though her name is allegedly Megan but it's yet to be proven in a court of law.

Mum leans to her left, away from me, stretching her arm towards the ground. She brings a ceramic cup to her lips. It's painted cream with olive green around the rim. The green paint has been perfectly dripped around the edges.

'That's a cool cup, where did you get it?'

Changing the subject is preferable. I hate the awkwardness of bringing Dad into conversations.

'The shop up the road, Natur Aura. I got us all different colours. They're traditional wine cups. I also got a bottle of white wine. If you want some, it's in the cupboard under the sink in the kitchen. I thought it was the coolest place. Alec came back this afternoon, he plumbed in the sink. We've ordered an oven and some other things too. So we will be able to store things and cook things at last.'

I make a little whooping sound and quietly clap my hands.

'I'll get a cup and join you, I think.' Sliding my legs down from my chair, I head back indoors.

I was hoping to speak to Serena about Dad and whether she had any ideas about keeping him at bay. After he was talking about meeting Megan, even to me, we clearly need a plan of action.

It's not that I'm saying he's wrong, at least about me and Serena being adults now, I just don't really want to deal with his affair in my face. It's bad enough that he posted a picture of them together on Instagram. It was one from Mexico, laughing in swimwear. They might as well have had their middle fingers up instead of cocktails.

I crouch down and swing open the cupboard under the sink. There are two bottles of wine pushed together and the new cups in turquoise, lime and aqua tones. I drag forward the first bottle; condensation trickles its way down the glass, making my hand damp.

There's only about a single glassful left in the bottle, and it's still chilled. I press my hand to the second, full bottle. It's still chilled too. Mum must be drinking fast to have almost demolished one bottle and for it still to be cool in this heat.

I pick up one of the beautifully hand-decorated cups and the almost dead bottle of wine, and place them on the counter. The contents fill the cup to the brim, and they're only small cups.

Carefully, I step out of the open door, sipping as I walk to avoid spilling wine on my feet.

'You're not topping me up?' Mum calls, waving her wine cup in my direction.

'I'd have to start a new bottle.'

She shrugs, turning down her mouth before twisting back towards the sunset.

I turn and make my way back to the kitchen, retrieve the bottle and bring it out with me. Placing my cup on my chair, I unscrew the top and fill Mum's cup. That makes a whole bottle of wine, in what I can only imagine is less than an hour and a half. Maybe less than an hour.

Not that I'm counting.

I'm not used to Mum drinking like this. She enjoys a large glass or two, now and then. But not this.

This is different. This would be what she might call *medicinal*.

In the first few days after finding out about Dad and Jonah, there was a lot of medicinal drinking. But never alone. We would open a bottle together, drown our sorrows together.

This might be the first time I've known my mum to drink alone.

'Before Serena left, we got into a small . . . fight. About your father.' Mum takes a sip before pushing her sunglasses further up her nose.

Even as the sun sets, sweat accumulates on my top lip and the cool wine is a welcome relief.

'What was said?'

Mum moves her head softly from side to side.

'She thinks we should invite him out here.' Her tone is incredulous, before she quickly adds, 'Not to stay in the house, and not today or tomorrow, but she thinks this could be good for you. To show you we are all still here for you.'

'For *me*?' Without getting up, I shift my chair round to face her more, instead of the sun.

This begins to explain the soft tone Dad was finding for me. Maybe Serena prepped him to be kinder to me after our time together today. Perhaps she used the insight to give Dad a conversation to smooth things over with me. She's probably given him more Jonah details too.

I know she's a daddy's girl. I know that might never change, but I'm not happy about her using our conversations to force us all into her narrative. Or worse, into his.

Mum doesn't answer, she just patiently waits to find out if this is something I would like, because she knows if it is then it's two against one, and we've always had a reasonably diplomatic house where many problems were solved with a discussion or a vote.

This is different though. Those problems weren't involving the same emotions and a broken marriage.

'Mum, you need time to heal. Right now, that's all that's important to me. I love Dad, but he went off with some woman, couldn't be bothered to tell his own kids he was breaking up the family and, yeah, we're grown-ups, but he gave zero respect to any of us.'

A warm breeze churns up the twigs and debris on the ground and a loose strand of hair dances in my eyes. The breeze brings a fresh smell of the sea. That deeply fresh something that's there in the salty taste on the tip of my tongue but almost impossible to compare to anything else I know.

As though the breeze has a flavour in its warm embrace.

I think both Mum and I need a warm embrace right now from somewhere neither of us will find it. If Mum feels anything like me, she'd take a warm embrace and check her back for a knife straight after.

'There's no way to change any of it. Not that I would, I love you girls too much to change anything. If I could go back in time, I would do it all again. Even the hours spent losing my Greek accent at his father's insistence.'

Here it is, another opening, and one where Mum has had enough to drink that I might just manage to get *something* out of her. She's talking about slices of the past; now all I need to do is prise my way in there.

'Grandad made you lose the accent? Are you serious?'

Mum hums in agreement but doesn't elaborate.

'You and Dad always seemed so happy together. I think that's what's thrown me the most.'

'It always surprises me what children don't see. I suppose we are all blind to what parents *really* are until we become them ourselves.'

'Why, what were you *really*?'

'Two people with an infatuation who woke up one day to the cold reality of staying together to prove a point.' She continues to mutter to herself, I think in Greek, but the rest is too low for me to understand.

'To prove a point? What does that mean?'

Mum's hand slaps down hard on her leg. Carefully, she lifts it and looks at the palm.

'Yes! I got it. That's one less mosquito in the world.'

'I know they're gross and spread disease, but the world still needs them. I know they want to use genetic engineering to wipe them out, but think of all the animals that eat them. Everything has a place. A purpose. Like you said about Dad, you got us kids.'

She wipes the insect off on the chair leg, slopping her wine on the ground.

Even with the sun disappearing from here, and showing up in another part of the world, it's still light enough to see the wine hit the dirt floor.

I clear my throat, trying to find ways in so she tells me things without knowing she's telling me . . . if that's actually possible. I just don't know which direction to go in; she keeps letting out riddles and I'm not sure which string to pull to get her to talk.

'I do wonder if all this is a midlife crisis. With Dad, I mean. When you met him here on holiday, all those years ago, you just said it yourself, you were infatuated, right? I mean, it's only recently that he's been an idiot. You two have always seemed *infatuated*.'

'He wasn't on holiday,' Mum says. She presses her cup to her lips and begins to sip.

'Yes, he was. With his friends, remember?'

Mum begins to laugh into her cup, before taking another, final swig.

'I didn't realise you were there?' She cocks an eyebrow in my direction behind the heavy waves of hair.

'Well, no, but . . .' I take a bigger sip of sharp white wine.

Has the alcohol gone to her head? How could he *not* have been on holiday?

'Fine, if he wasn't on holiday, then what?' A small warmth fills my chest and confidence to push her a little comes along with it. 'What was he doing here if he wasn't on holiday? He *was* here, right? You met him in Corfu?'

'Yes, yes, we met in Corfu. There are things you don't know, Lorena. Children don't need to know *everything* about their parents. We don't owe you an explanation for everything we do, you know.' Mum slides down in her chair a little, and in the pinky-purple light of dusk, she almost looks like a sulky teen with her hair pulled back and a pout on her lip. I wonder if this is how Dad remembers her from back then. 'We are people. You get to a certain age and after that you get older on the outside but you're still the same person inside, with a mirror that looks more and more like a lie each day. We have our own lives and complicated webs made and weaved over many, many years. I don't want to be trapped in mine anymore. That's what happened. That's what *really* happened. I got trapped. It's my fault. I trapped myself. I can't blame him. We all know the phrase, *you make your bed, you have to lie in it*. Well, I have done just that until he kicked me out of it. I should've got myself up and out years ago.'

When I was younger, I always wanted to be able to stop time. To freeze everyone as still as a statue and carry on living, doing whatever I wanted, and no one would know it was me eating the ice cream or playing tricks. Right now, I feel as though it's me who has been frozen in time and Mum is carrying on as though she doesn't know I can hear her.

Every muscle wants to move and can't. My brain can only hear the sound of cicadas and everything else is a flatline. That sound becomes the flatline.

Snatching a breath, I try to find words. 'Mum, I—'

'Please, don't. I've said too much. Maybe one day you'll look back and be happy you didn't waste your life with Jonah.' Mum begins to stand, stretching her arms. 'He did you a favour. Showing you who he was and setting you free. It's better that way. Better than you knowing who he was and committing to put up with him for the rest of your life.'

She bends down, wraps her fingers around my cheek and presses a kiss into the hair on the top of my head.

'I'm tired, we've worked hard today. *Kalinichta*, my love.'

I can't even close my mouth, and manage to choke out a 'goodnight' as she walks away.

I can't believe the riddles she's left me with.

I'm so sick of people hiding everything from me like I'm four and they don't want to upset me by telling me painful truths about mythical creatures, like I can't handle unicorns not being real.

Mum deserves my love and support, I don't want to hurt her, but the fact she's openly keeping things from me . . . I suppose like Christos, which is better than Jonah and Dad who both deny the truth is even out there. Mum openly tells me there's a truth that I don't know, but she also tells me I can't have it. It's the closest to the truth that there is without being given it.

I can't work out if I managed to get some answers, or just more questions. I don't know if Mum will ever truly open up to me about this or continue to hide behind the same thing everyone else does: that it's for my own good not to know things.

There's one person who might know though, and I know exactly how to get them on their own . . . hopefully.

Chapter Thirty-One

Serena takes my hand as I make my descent. I lock my eyes on the wooden plank and keep my knees slightly bent, doing my best to plant each step as the boat rocks, ushering me off at a quicker pace with the weight of my backpack pushing me forward.

I say a speedy 'thank you' to Serena and the staff who are helping people off the boat, and join everyone else at the harbour.

'This was such a lovely idea for us all.' Aliki shades her eyes with her hand as we all march along the concrete and towards the island of Erikousa. 'Thank you, Lorena, for this idea. It is nice to find balance with vacations and business.'

'I'm pleased we could all get together again. I know you've got a busy schedule while you're here,' I agree.

Aliki begins to tell Serena and me about the things they've been up to as Giórgos and Petros meander behind.

I suggested we all come across here, as none of us has been before, and find a peaceful place to discuss business matters. I had hoped to have more in my head about business before sitting down for a chat, but seeing as I really want to know what Giórgos's take on everything is with Mum and her past, I'll have to wing it. After all, they're not in Corfu that much longer before heading back to the mainland.

There's a gentle breeze laced with the smell of salt and cooking food. It's enough to make the heat bearable. The sea moves up the beach tentatively, as though the sand has to be treated with care and attention.

It's quiet here, even though quite a few people have got off the boat and there's a taverna on the beach further along. It's a lot quieter than Agios Stefanos, where we've come over from. There, all the sunbeds are filled with rows and rows of tanning bodies, rotating like planets spinning on an axis.

As we carry on along towards the beach, the atmosphere is different too. It's even more laid-back, and somehow the sea is an even clearer shade of blue. I wouldn't have thought that was possible. Agios Stefanos is only across the water, visible from this beautiful island, and yet there are differences.

'Beach bar or have a wander?' Serena pulls her beach bag higher on her shoulder before pushing her dark designer sunglasses back along her nose.

'Let's walk.' Petros nods along the road and Serena steps in time with him.

'Are you still enjoying Greek life? It must be so hard not knowing the language.' Aliki holds the edge of her wide-brimmed hat as the breeze momentarily picks up before disappearing completely.

'It can be hard, but I understand a lot and I've been using an app to try to get myself speaking Greek. It'll take time but it's worth the effort. It's nice to have a fresh start. Although I will be happy when the house is finished. We're making some good progress though. We'll be able to start painting more rooms soon and Mum's going into Corfu Town today to look at some furniture shops. It'll be nice to have some comfy chairs to sit on, instead of the old plastic ones we've got now.'

We walk along the narrow road lined with vibrant green bushes, some with fuchsia flowers emanating their sweet scent. Each step further away from the beach we go is one step further from the delights of a sea breeze, and we're melting like ice cream in the heat.

Serena pulls an ocean-blue fan with a golden trim from her bag. She wafts it in front of her face before aiming it at a taverna on a corner where the road bends. 'Shall we stop here? I need a drink.' Her cheeks puff out with her exhale.

I wonder whether I look as red as her. I feel it. I can feel droplets springing up on my skin, under my sunglasses and in the small of my back.

There's no disagreement. We settle down on mustard-coloured metal chairs in the shelter of hanging vines and begin to peruse the menu. Before even picking up his menu, Petros has the good sense to order water for the table.

After a brief look at the menu, I decide on hummus and pitta. I can't stomach anything else. I'm too hyped up to ask Giórgos questions about what he was told when he was growing up, if anything. The waitress comes and takes our orders and is soon back with fresh juices and chocolate milkshakes.

Even though the air has been cleared since the engagement meal, Giórgos's attitude towards my mum has played on my mind. Was he really innocently reminiscing, or was he getting a dig in at Mum? I need to pin him down somehow and ask questions.

After Mum went to bed last night, I knew I had to find a way to have some time with Giórgos away from her. As soon as I had the idea to invite everyone out, and, after sending a couple of messages, I realised today was the only day they were free before heading back to Athens. Which gave me very little time to think or plot ways to accidently bring up the subject of my mum, my dad and Spiros, and my grandparents.

I barely slept last night. It was too stuffy, even with the window open, and all I could do was roll around thinking up ways to unearth more information about everything Mum is hiding from me. I hate that this is making a distance between us. If I find out on my own, then she'll have to deal with it and maybe we can rebuild all the bridges that feel so wobbly right now.

'How long were you a cosmetic scientist in England?' Aliki smooths her linen shorts and looks at me with great eagerness.

All I want to do is change the subject and find out about my mum's past.

'Since qualifying at university. I was very lucky to get a good job almost right away. I'm excited to start work on these products, and for you to design beautiful packaging for them.'

'I've already been thinking. But I need to try them before I'm sure. I want to get back to Athens and make some sketches. We aren't really meant to be working too much for this trip. Only what we have already booked.' Her hand finds Giórgos's on the table and they share in the smile of people deluded and blinded by pheromones.

I can't believe I was that stupid once. I can't believe I got tricked by those stupid smells we all secrete, and the sweet smiles anyone can put on

Mum was right, I suppose I was lucky for things not to have gone any further. To not have the burden of someone else. We both learnt that the hard way.

Serena and Petros begin their own conversation; now might be my time.

Shuffling my weight on my chair, I begin, 'It's nice to come back for some family time, and to start wedding plans of course.

Giórgos, can I ask a question? It doesn't matter what the answer is, I'd just like it to be truthful.'

His thick eyebrows lower and his eyes skim from Aliki to me. 'If I can, yes.'

'When you said about not saying goodbye, did you know that's what my mum had done? Left and not said goodbye? Only, she never really talks about those times, not really. Even stories of Spiros and her as kids were told to us like they were fiction, like she made them up in her head, not things that really happened.'

My outpouring has given Giórgos time to hesitate.

'Yes. I knew she never say goodbye. My baba, he told me this was what Yiayia was talking about. Why she would cry sometimes, because your mother brought shame on our family and didn't even say goodbye. This is all I know. How hurt they were, and how they felt she had brought shame. If I can be honest . . .' He looks around, as though someone at the next table might be listening in and he's afraid they'll take note and pass on the gossip. 'I always think your mother was evil.' He sniggers at this idea. 'It was a simple, childish idea. But, to me, how could anyone be so cruel to my grandparents? I'm a man now, I know life isn't so simple as I thought it as a child . . . but . . . there was still a part of me thinking, she should know how they were hurt. I went too far. I am sorry. I should never have been so rude to her.'

'You did.' Aliki narrows her eyes on him. 'It was not your place to open your big mouth. She is here now, this is what matters.'

'I can't believe you thought our mum was evil.' Serena shakes her head. 'That's crazy.'

'It was because I could not understand, so the idea grew in my head. This monster who hurt my grandparents, my baba. I don't think this now. I didn't know any facts, only my thoughts.'

'Did our grandparents actually say anything about her being evil? Or anything else? Like how she brought shame on the family?

203

Anything at all?' Serena's leaning into the table, pausing any conversation she was having with Petros to join in with ours.

'No, I think they were hurting because they loved her and missed her. I know nothing about what happened, only the pain after. You would have to ask her . . . or my baba.'

My hummus and pitta is placed down in front of me. It has a neon-green oil drizzled all over it. The contrast is elegant and beautiful and gives me a few ideas for the cosmetic line as it moves forward. But mostly, I'm left feeling as sickly green as the swirl on my plate, knowing that the only way I get to find anything out is from Spiros, or my mum.

◆　◆　◆

As everyone else goes for a walk along the shallows, cutting through the crystal water and making miniscule silver fish dart in all directions, I consider the only other person I might be able to get some information out of.

My dad.

I scoot down to sit closer to the edge of the sea, resting my feet in the water to keep cool as I watch the gentle rocking of a paddleboard someone has left loosely tied to a boulder in the water.

He was there when she left Corfu, didn't say goodbye and didn't look back until now. Is he the reason for all the shame? Last night she said he wasn't on holiday when they met, so what the hell was he doing here? Working?

I look across the waves to see the four figures still slowly moving away from me along the shoreline. Petros pauses to pick something up and throw it into the sea. Probably a stone. Serena does the same, only right after she throws her head back in laughter.

I have five minutes, maybe ten. If they come back, I'll have to move away. I can't wait anymore.

I pull my phone from my backpack and tap on the screen to call him.

I hate that by not sharing her life with me, Mum is forcing my hand, forcing me to ask Dad. I deserve to know why all of this has been withheld from me for all these years, why I wasn't allowed to know my grandparents and my cousin.

At the same time, I don't want to let her down or go behind her back. She'll probably feel like I'm invading her privacy, forgetting her choices have directly affected me.

I have to do this. I have to call him.

As the call tone sounds in my ear, my heart begins to squeeze. I can only imagine it's trying to make itself small enough to fit in my oesophagus and rest in my mouth.

'Lorena, you never call.' There it is again, that soft buttery tone of his, like he could never ever do anything wrong.

'Hey, Dad. Can you talk for a minute?'

'Should I be worried?'

'No.' I attempt a laugh but it comes out a little shrill.

'OK, good. I have a few minutes before Megan and I go to the gym. What's up?'

The gym? I don't question it but that's almost as shocking as the affair. He used to say how he thought gyms were full of stale onion-smelling air and a breeding ground for germs and low self-esteem. I guess he's forgotten that now.

I clear my throat to give myself time to push those thoughts away. 'It's a simple question—'

'Where are you? Are you at the beach?'

'Erm, yeah, we're over at Erikousa Island.'

'Beautiful place. I could hear the sea, that's all. Anyway, shoot.'

I clear my throat again, and hear something at the other end of the line.

Dad whispers, 'Not long, it's Lorena,' as though I can't hear him whisper. I push the idea of some gym bunny, *Megan*, flicking her hair and fluttering her eyelashes at him as far out of my head as possible.

I lost Jonah, which was bad, but at least there was no one else involved. I don't stay awake wondering why it was her and not me. I hate that Dad has done that to Mum. I hate that he might've placed insecurity or a lack of worth where it doesn't belong. I hope she doesn't feel that way.

'I wondered why you were here, I mean, in Corfu, when you met Mum.'

'I was on holiday with some friends, that's all.'

'Something Mum said, it made me think there was more to it than that.'

'Something your mum said? Really? That does surprise me.'

'Yeah, last night, she had a few glasses of wine and—'

'Don't worry about that then, it's the drink talking. You know how people get when they drink. Talking rubbish about the past. Maybe she got muddled. It wasn't my first time in Corfu, maybe she meant another time.'

'It wasn't your first time? For some reason I thought it was your first time?'

Everything scrambles in my mind and the heat from the sun pressing down on my head is becoming unbearable and my phone is getting too hot to keep pressed to my face.

'OK . . .' I try again. 'Well . . . I'm sure Serena would've told you we have this cousin, Giórgos? Well, he said he thought Mum left because she brought shame on the family? I wondered if it was anything to do with you, because she came to England with you and came back without you . . .'

'Look, Lorena, I really don't see what any of this has to do with me.' His tone has shifted to something skirting irritation.

'You were there, you know the truth.'

'The truth is simple, your mum was being oppressed and she came to live in England with me. That's it. No big deal. If you hear anything different, then it's a crock of shit.'

'But what about—?'

'This is worse than when you were a kid and you had to know whether the tooth fairy was real. You find a thread and you won't stop tugging until you're done. Who cares about who else gets hurt.'

I press my lips together, thinking of the fat tears that had rolled down Serena's crimson cheeks that year. I'd have done anything to take it all back, to change it.

'Now, I really have to go. Megan's waiting. Speak later, yeah? Love you, Sunshine.'

I know if I don't say it back he'll be upset, and I don't need him sulking on top of everything else. It's not like I don't love him, but irritation has hooked itself inside me, as though I'm a fish and I'm about to be swallowed whole.

I hesitate, but ultimately I give in. 'Love you too.'

'Bye.' He hangs up the phone.

I wish I could, but I don't trust him.

I feel further from knowing the truth now than ever before.

It shouldn't bother me, but it does. It really does. He's right, when something doesn't sit right with me, I won't let it go, and it's got me in trouble more times than I can count. It's why I like science – if something doesn't make sense, pull it apart until it does. Test it, theorise it, anything to find the truth or the best path.

Technically, Mum's correct too in all this. I am her child and I don't have the right to know everything that goes on in her or Dad's life, but I have a strong suspicion that the past is haunting and lingering and casting shadows over our present, and I have to know why.

I only want to make sense of it all. I just don't want to hurt anyone in the process.

Chapter
Thirty-Two

I regret not accepting Petros's offer of a lift back to our beach house.

Serena and I thought it would be lovely to walk back from the harbour. We enjoyed the walk this morning. That was before a day of too much sun, before the sand was painfully pressing in places it shouldn't and before I had a wet bikini on.

Too late now.

Now, my calves are burning and all I want is to be back home, lying in my bed.

We do our best to march up the incline, pausing now and then to take in the expanse of the sea and look back across to the forest-green delight of Erikousa Island.

'Did I tell you I invited Christos today?' Serena says between heavy breaths.

'No.' My shoulders tense and I can feel my eyes bulge thinking about the bullet I dodged with her misunderstanding the truth.

'Yeah, do you know what he said?'

'No?'

'He said he doesn't like boats. It's strange, because when I mentioned it to Giórgos he said Christos used to have his own boat. He didn't say anything else though, only that I should ask Christos myself why he doesn't like boats anymore.'

'Maybe he gets seasick?'

'Yeah, I wondered that too, but why have your own boat then not? I'd have thought you're always seasick or never. I dunno.' She shrugs before stopping on the grassy verge, swinging her backpack off her back and pulling out her sleek white water bottle.

I hesitate over telling her that he told me he doesn't like the beach. How can he live on an island and avoid the beach and the sea? Surely it's impossible.

While Serena gulps back water, I take another look out across the subtle changes in the blues and green of the sea. The rippling lines moving towards the shore. What would make someone dislike boats and the beach and, I assume, the sea? How could anyone hate the sea?

I close my eyes and tilt my head back to the sun. Even through my eyelids, it's blinding.

Maybe I'll ask him. Maybe I'll be able to solve one mystery at least.

'Can I change the subject?' I turn my back on the sea and wait for Serena to load her bottle back into her bag.

'Yep, but only if it's equally interesting or gossipy.' As she swings her bag over her shoulder, she shoots me a cheeky grin.

'It is. It's about Mum. I would've told you sooner, but well, I don't know what I'm processing here, and last time I tried to talk about the past you were . . . kind of dismissive.'

'I like gossip, but I do think you might be sniffing at the wrong tree.'

'Barking, barking up the wrong tree.'

'Oh yeah!' Serena lets out a small snort of laughter.

I begin to tell her what Mum said, what Dad said when I called him, and point out to her what she heard with her very own ears straight from Giórgos's mouth, that Mum had brought *shame* on the family.

Serena stays pretty quiet throughout my monologue. By the time I'm done, we're off the road and walking down the slope to the beach so we can cut across to get home.

Serena pulls her bag off her back again and dumps it in the sand before pulling off her white shirt, leaving her in only a bikini and hat. She throws the hat down to join her shirt and bag.

'It's hot.' She presses her hands to her slim hips and turns away from me.

'What are you doing?' I call as she begins kicking up sand towards the sea.

'I'm too hot,' she calls over her shoulder.

I begin to strip off too, shedding my bag and my clothes before running after her. Catching her just as she's taking oversized strides into the sea. I do the same.

'Don't you have anything to say?' I demand.

Serena keeps wading in, deeper and deeper.

'Serena?'

'What?' Her voice is high as her fists crash on to the waves. 'What do you want me to say? That everything Mum and Dad ever had was shit? A lie? That our whole life was bullshit? What? That Dad is evil and Mum's heartless? All I want is things the way they were. To believe in love at first sight and that playing Monopoly at Christmas that never ends was fun for everyone. I don't want to know anything else about Mum and Dad, I can't take it anymore. It's all too much.' She drops down into the shallow water so it covers her shoulders.

Slowly, I sink in and join her.

'I'm sorry. I think worrying about Mum and Dad and family secrets has been my way of not thinking about myself and Jonah. It's been a way to keep my mind busy. To look at everyone else's flaws instead of my own. I shouldn't have put that on you.'

The tip of Serena's nose turns as pink as a rose, and I know she's fighting off tears.

'It's OK, I understand it's easier to talk about everyone else and not yourself. That's why we all love a bit of gossip. It's just, right now, with Dad being a thousand miles away and not able to see him . . . Even when I talk to him, *she's* always there, you know. *That Megan.* They practically live together in our family home. She's probably the reason it hasn't sold yet.' Serena snatches a breath. 'It doesn't matter. It's out of our control, right? Best to focus on our own lives.' She shakes her head and stands back up. 'Tell me something positive. I heard you say to Aliki that you're having a meeting with Christos tonight about filling in forms to apply for business permits and stuff. That's exciting?'

I stand and follow behind her as she edges back out of the sea, much more gracefully than the way she stormed in.

'Yeah, it is, as long as it all gets approved. Otherwise, it's a big waste of time and money for nothing.'

'Money? Has Mum lent you some? I thought she was being tight until she knew the house was sold and stuff?'

'No, I mean, not that much money. Spiros is helping out, as it'll be alongside their business, he didn't want to make a big deal out of it, you know? Because, because Mum couldn't front the money right away. I think he didn't want her to feel bad or for me to feel embarrassed, maybe? I'm not sure.' I can feel my palms begin to sweat even though they're still damp from the sea.

Serena is way more fragile at the moment than she's been letting on. Mum was right to tell me not to be too hard on her. I have to protect her. It's not like me borrowing money affects her anyway, she doesn't *need* to know. I don't want to hide things from her, but I don't want her to misinterpret his help and think there's more going on here than there really is.

'OK, well keep me updated on things with Christos, yeah?'

'I take it you still like him then?'

'He's a good-looking guy, but I'm not chasing someone who would say they don't like the sea or boats or whatever to avoid hanging out, so . . .' Serena shrugs.

We pick up our things, all of which are covered in sand again, as are our feet, and we march back towards the house.

We walk in a bubble of silence. I guess, normally, this would be the point where I'd reassure her, tell her there's some great person out there waiting just for her. Someone she'll love forever.

Not today. Not anymore. I can't tell those lies and I don't want to continue a conversation about Christos because the guilt strangles me. Silence is a much safer option.

At least it's not like I'm in love with Christos, or even want to be with him. That would make this a whole lot worse.

Even so, I want to avoid hurting Serena anymore. I've already done enough of that with my silly investigation about Mum and what really happened when she left the island. I guess Serena won't be my partner in finding out more any time soon.

At the start, I really thought she would be. I really thought she was strong enough to go along with me for the ride.

Perhaps not.

Perhaps I'm destined to be alone on all fronts. Life would be easier that way. Although, life without Serena would be as dull and as painful as living with my head in a plastic bag.

I look over at my sister, the sea water evaporating from her skin leaving snaking white lines of salt on her like tan lines. She'd hate that, if she noticed.

The big sister in me wants to hold her hand and tell her it'll all be all right. I just really want to know that it's true for myself first, that it really will be all right.

Chapter
Thirty-Three

The olive trees have voices of their own at sunset. When I close my eyes, I can hear them under the cicadas and the knocking sounds of the bats. They have their own creaks and whispers as they pass information along.

'Did you know trees talk to each other? Mushrooms too. Did you know mushrooms share more DNA with people than they do other plants?'

Christos rubs his hand over his forehead. 'How is this helpful to the forms?' He taps on his laptop screen.

Jonah stole my laptop and I didn't want to ask Serena for hers. Luckily, Christos has one and agreed to meet on neutral ground. Which means form-filling in Spiros and Eleni's olive grove, where the tours take place. I thought it was the best way to avoid recurring memories of writhing bodies slipping into my mind.

So far, it's working. Mostly.

Although, I haven't been much help with the forms. He could probably have filled them all out without me. I'm surplus to requirements, but as I'm an important person in this, he still thinks I need to know exactly what's going on, which I appreciate. And other than the occasional mosquito, it's nice to be back in the air between the trees. The cleanest air you can get, filtered and pure in the best possible way.

It's relaxing to hear the chatter of the olive grove, even if Christos is unable to appreciate it.

Something in the form has irritated him, I can tell by his jaw locking and the rolling of his eyes.

'Why are you doing this?'

I study his face. The soft roll of his beard and the wrinkle forming between his brows as he gets annoyed at the screen. Even angry, he's irritatingly rugged and good-looking.

He looks up with a pout on his lips and the memory of those very same soft lips on my skin forces me to cross my legs.

'Doing what?'

'Being so nice to me.'

'I promised myself to help people. I tell you this, that I save money to give to people who need it, to help people.'

Fine golden beams of light dance over his face as the leaves rustle above us in the gentle breeze.

I've held off asking him about beaches and boats. I'm trying to build up to it. I feel like I'm always building up to things lately. I'm always brimming with questions to badger people with. We've been here an hour already, working our way through everything.

'Why do you look at me like this?' Christos narrows his eyes on me.

I mimic him, pressing my eyebrows down.

'Like this?'

'No.' His eyes begin to roll and he gently slaps his hands down on the wooden table between us before pushing the laptop far to one side and closing it. 'I hate screens, they hurt my eyes.'

'Let's take a break then. Shall we walk?'

He grunts acceptance and begins to stand, pulling one leg out from the bench then the other. I try to do the same, but it's not as easy in my skirt and flip-flops.

Mum took most of our clothes to the laundrette and she forgot to pick them up before they shut, meaning I was left with inappropriate dressy clothes and nothing else. The best I could manage was a flippy floral miniskirt that I hate wearing because it's a little too short when I move, and a pink T-shirt that doesn't really go.

We crunch our way along the dried grass and towards the rows of trees.

'Can I ask you something?'

'Why are you asking? We both know you will say the question, like it or not.'

'True. Why don't you like beaches or going on boats? Serena asked Giórgos and he said you used to own a boat.'

'No, I used to *borrow* my father's boat. That was many years ago.'

I slow my pace, manoeuvring over the thick root of an ancient tree. With the light fading around us, I'm reluctant to go too deep into the grove and away from the floodlights back at the shop or near the table. I've never seen them on before this evening, I've only ever been here in the blaze of the day until now.

I slow my pace, ready to gently push more answers out of him. 'Oh . . . and why not now? Is it something to do with the passing of your parents?'

Christos jars to a stop. For a split second I scan the ground for a snake or something else that might stop him in his tracks, but there's nothing obvious there.

He turns to face me head-on. 'Passing of my parents?'

'Yeah, I mean, I assumed . . .'

He steps towards me, towering over me. '*You assumed?*

215

'I thought they were alive but then I assumed they must have passed away because you never talk about them and Spiros and Eleni helped you like they're your parents and . . .'

'You must never assume, Lorena.' Christos's finger presses to my chest. He steps forward, I step back. 'It can only lead to trouble. I think you like to get in trouble, asking too many questions and see what will happen.' Slowly his finger traces around my breast.

My back presses to the tangled olive tree behind me and Christos lowers his mouth to mine.

Even if I had the space to pull away, I wouldn't. I tilt my chin up towards him. My lips meet his before they get all the way to me.

His fingers gently squeeze, his thumb skimming over my T-shirt, before snaking up to my throat and into my hair.

I begin to tunnel my hand into his T-shirt sleeve to grip the curve of his muscular shoulder and his enigmatic tattoo.

I can't blame alcohol this time; even last time, I couldn't really. I'd sobered up a lot and knew exactly what I was doing.

But now, if anyone found out, we'd have no excuse.

I snatch my lips from his, twisting my face to the left.

'This can't happen again.'

'No.' He rests his forehead heavily on mine. 'But it was the only way to shut you up.'

He peels himself away from me, wipes his lips with the back of his thumb and begins to walk back the way we came.

The blood rushes back to my legs and I begin marching up the slope towards him.

'Are you kidding me?'

'No.' He stops and faces me, folding his arms over his chest and shaking his head. He looks like Zeus about to cook up a storm. 'No, I am not *kidding*. You are always pushing to know everything about everyone. My life is not for talking or gossips. It is mine. I do not need some woman coming along, thinking they can save me,

216

when it won't happen.' He turns to walk away and then casually adds, 'However good they are in bed.'

My jaw locks and my fingers tingle with an energy like no other.

'Well, I'm so sorry I cared.'

'You don't care. You just want to know everything, everything, everything.' He waves his arms to match his point. 'You will never know me.'

We march harder and faster towards the wooden table.

'What the hell happened to you to make you so closed off? I have no desire to *save* you. You're not a princess in a movie. Unless you want to throw that beard of yours off a tower for some idiot to climb? And even then, that idiot wouldn't be me.'

Christos plonks himself back down on the bench as soon as he gets there, facing out to the slope of the groves, and towards me. 'You are talking riddles now.'

I stand my ground.

I'm beyond irritated that he thinks I'm nosy or something, or that I want him in some way. I can't help caring about him as a friend. Yes, I do find it odd that someone living on a Greek island would avoid the seaside but that isn't my only motive for finding out. Unless I'm doing it again, hiding from my issues by burying my nose in someone else's. Either way, I'm not doing it to be dreadful the way he's making out.

I'm tired of everyone hiding things from me, I can't stand it from yet another person.

'I'm not talking in riddles, I'm upset. If you don't want to tell me about your life, then fine. But I told you about mine. And I thought I was pretty clear that I'm not interested in you in any romantic way. If anything, I feel insulted that you would say that when both times *you* kissed *me* first. Not the other way around.'

'One I was drunk, two I was getting you to use your mouth for something more . . . useful.'

Every muscle in my body twitches and goes hard with fury. 'You weren't that drunk when it happened.'

Christos shrugs, knowing as well as I do that although we had been drinking, neither of us was at a drunk peak anymore when we crossed the line.

'I'm starting to think you aren't who I thought you were.'

'No? Who do you think I am then?' Christos leans one elbow on the table behind him and hitches one foot up to rest it on the knee of the other leg.

'I thought you cared about other people. With all that saving money for others, being so bloody generous and helping with stupid forms. Now I think you live alone because you're such a selfish pig no one can bear to spend time with you. You trick people into thinking you're good and then you use them up, just like all men.' I can feel my emotions about Jonah spilling in.

I press my lips firmly shut and fold my arms tightly across my chest.

'This is where you are all wrong. I am just a man using his time on this planet until it is done. I just want peace, nothing else.'

'And what's that about too? You always sound so morbid. Like all you do is watch time tick by instead of enjoying it. No friends, barely any family, you don't let anyone in. Eleni has to almost force you to get-togethers.'

Christos's chest rises in a deep breath, and he closes his eyes as though he's trying to calm himself or tune me out, before releasing it through his mouth.

'If you want to put your mouth to good use again, I am happy to do the same. Anything is better than this.'

I'm completely bewildered. Frozen like a creature with one foot stuck in amber, slowly getting sucked into the golden liquid. I'm being split in two. Christos is just like amber, sucking me in with his golden skin, so alluring and in desperate need of touching, while my sanity knocks on my skull in an urgent attempt to tell me I have enough problems right now and I don't need to add Christos to the list.

'I should go.' The words circle in my throat, trying hard to shy away from being heard.

I step forward to lean across Christos to grab my bag and phone from the other side of the table. In doing so, I've put myself within touching range.

Christos tilts his mouth to my ear. 'Sure?'

His voice vibrates in my chest and I can feel it deep in my core.

For a moment I close my eyes and try to push the memory of the taste of his skin out of my mind. Salty and sweet, soft and firm.

I tilt my face down towards his and our eyes meet as my teeth dig into my cheeks in response to a fierce surge of lust.

What's one more mistake when all I do is make mistakes?

I slide down on to his lap, our lips coming together slower this time before becoming more urgent. His hands move up my skirt and mine grip his face.

As he pulls my T-shirt over my head and his hands slide into my bra, I wonder if there will ever be a day when I look back on this and think it was a good idea. Probably not.

It's too late now, as we begin to test out how sturdy yet another table is.

Chapter
Thirty-Four

Do you still want to work together?

I stare at the message on my phone, hovering it over my face. The ghoulish light fills the room before I switch the screen off and slip it under my pillow. I shift on to my side, tucking the cotton sheet between my legs and pressing my cheek to the cooler corner of the pillowcase.

I don't like to tell Christos that for the past week I've been avoiding even thinking about anything that's outside decorating the house.

On the plus side, the house is beginning to really take shape. Anton finished working on it today and Alec said he'll continue to help here and there if we need it.

Mum has invited Anton and his family out for a meal with us tomorrow so she can gift his daughters the way he requested. With or without a gift, we owe his family for all the work he's done for free. If he ever needs anything in the future, I don't think any of us would hesitate. I've never known anyone donate so much time to a project. And all because Christos and Alec said we needed help.

I guess Christos has also donated a lot of his time and money to me. Or, at least, he says he will with the money. But then apparently

I'm sleeping with him, so it's quite possible that's why he's doing those things. As far as I'm aware, no one in this house has been sleeping with Anton or Alec to get things done around the house.

It's taken weeks, and cost Mum everything she had in savings for the materials, but they've saved her thousands in labour. No *thank you* is big enough. They have both given their spare time and Mum has spent much of hers coming up with something for Anton's daughters. I think they'll like their gifts though. The younger daughter is only a toddler and the elder is around university age. I can't remember if he said she was starting soon or she started last year. I'm sure I'll find out when I meet her face to face.

The music that had been drifting in my window from a nearby taverna comes to an end. All our windows have mosquito nets on them now, making life a lot less itchy. I haven't bothered with curtains or anything yet. Serena offered to buy me some, but I declined. I owe enough money. She's started painting her room, and Mum's is almost finished. They keep asking what colour I want mine, but I'm OK with the freshly plastered look for now.

I switch to face the wall and away from the moonlight casting its silver glow. It can be soothing to be awake in the dead of night. When all the people have left the bars and restaurants and it's just me and the gentle shh of the sea, it's as peaceful as it gets.

Normally. *Normally* I like it.

Since getting Christos's message a few hours ago, I haven't been able to sleep and it's like I've been bitten by mosquitos that don't exist and my skin itches. My soul itches.

I can't take it anymore, my skin can't take the prickly heat, my brain can't handle the thoughts whizzing around it. I need to find some clarity.

Throwing my sheet off me like it was a trap and I've managed to free myself, I scramble around in the moonlight for something to put on. A loose zebra-print dress with puffy sleeves comes to hand.

It'll do. It's been too hot to wear it during the day, but right now it'll be fine to stroll along the beach in the dark.

Grabbing my phone from under my pillow, I use the screen as a torch. There's no point putting the torch light on, I don't want to wake anyone else up and have them asking what I'm doing up so late, or where I'm going and whether I'm OK.

It's been strained this week anyway.

Since realising I needed to leave things alone, like Dad said, like Serena and Mum wanted, I haven't felt like I can communicate openly with anyone. As though I'm trapped.

At least we've all been busy with the house. The kitchen looks sleek now and all we really need to make it feel homely is furniture. All the big stuff is done. Talking about the renovation and Mum and Serena looking at bedspreads has given us some safe conversations to keep life simple.

I creep down the wooden stairs in the dark. As with all wooden stairs, they creak and moan in places. With the exception of one of the bottom ones. The problem is, I can't remember which one is loud and which one is quiet. At three steps from the bottom, I hover, trying to remember, before I give up and jump the last few.

Slipping on my flip-flops, I disappear out of the door and into the night. It's still not *really* dark, even now. I don't suppose it ever gets *really* dark here in the summer. The sky is too clear and the stars and moon too glittering to be as black as the bottom of the sea.

It's only a short march along the road before turning towards the sea. We intend to clear a way through the back of our garden at some point, maybe putting up a gate so we can go straight out on to the sand, but it's not possible yet, particularly in the dark.

As soon as my feet connect with the damp midnight sand, I kick off my flip-flops and keep walking towards the water. Dotted lights hover over the sea in the distance, looking like spaceships. A person less sober might believe that's exactly what they are, but I know they're yachts moored out at sea with high masts illuminating the space around them.

A few steps away from the dark wet line left by the sea, I drop to my knees to stare out at the reflections of the stars.

We shouldn't have slept together.

Once was perhaps forgivable. The second time . . . I suppose I could blame anger? But really, I was happy to be provoked and pretend I was angry when all I really wanted was to have another taste of him.

I try to shake the thought out of my head, the childish line that we keep crossing.

If I am going to continue working with him, we need to find some sense in all this, and we probably need to stop having sex. Twice is enough.

I twist my wrist and my phone screen comes alive. Two thirty-seven in the morning. There's no way he's awake.

Flicking across the screen, I navigate back to his message.

Do you still want to work together?

Yes. Yes I do. But I need to find sense in one of my relationships, and without it I don't think I can continue with this friendship, and most certainly not into a business relationship. These things have to be built with some kind of trust, even if I am finding that pretty hard at the moment. Without it, I think I'd be better off heading back to England and applying for something simple there.

My thumbs move slowly over the screen, trying to find the right words. Typing some out and deleting them only to put some of the same ones in again and adding a bunch more before hitting send, and only then reading it back to myself.

I do want to work with you. But I can't work with someone who would do anything to stop me asking questions. No matter what the questions are. I think I need to explain some things, and you do too. I'm on the beach in Agios Stefanos, near the sea in front of our house. I'll be here for an hour. I'm leaving this up to fate . . . and you. x

Fate. It's such a stupid concept. It's easy to blame things on fate when we have no other reasoning. I must be spending too much time with Serena to come out with something like fate. She's all about fate and karma and things being meant-to-be.

I believe in science. Not God, not fate, not karma. I like hard facts. I wish I could believe in God. There is a scientific hypothesis for the possibility of a God. That he or she or they started the big bang, and they are our God. It is an interesting one, but not something I've spent enough time looking into.

I feel silly even saying 'fate' now. Tiredness must have taken over my mind and polluted it. Sleep removes toxins from the brain and clearly I haven't been having enough of it to keep mine clear.

I type out another message and send.

I don't actually believe in fate, I'm using it to make a decision I don't want to make. Sorry. x

In the dark, I roll my eyes at how I sound. He'll wake up in the morning and think I'm insane. He's probably right.

The sea breeze blows my loose hair off my puff sleeves and down my back.

I wonder what Jonah's doing, or if our paths will ever cross.

If he's even still alive.

I hang my head to face the sand beneath me instead of basking in the glory of the night sky.

We didn't have honesty. I thought we did, but we didn't. All I had was a nice story.

If I did see him again, I don't even know how I would talk to him. Whether words would spring up or evaporate in the heat of my emotions. I'd probably freeze like a deer and let him walk past me. It won't happen now I live here. That's something I can be grateful for, at least. Even if I'm too weak to even look at the texts he sent or re-read the note he left me. I read it once and tucked it away never to be read again, but to remain my reminder not to trust people with my heart.

I lie back on the sand and watch the night sky again. The odd satellite circling and the occasional flash of an aeroplane. They all look as though they're the same distance from me as the stars. As though they're all a million miles away or as close as the clouds. Maybe closer.

Jonah might be looking up at the stars too. I close my eyes and take a deep lungful of the salty air. I'm not over what happened, what he did. I'm not sure I'll ever be able to trust anyone after what he did, but at least I don't long for him anymore. Not how I did at the start. I'd swing from anger to missing our routine. I'm past missing him now.

At the start I was overwhelmed with shock and a loss so like grief it was unbearable and dark and hollow. Coming to Corfu has really helped. It's given me a distraction when I needed it the most. It's given me time to see it was a lucky escape and I'm better off without him.

It's not like I can completely stop caring or worrying or wondering. I'm sure there will always be a part of me looking into crowds or into windows and wondering whether I'll see his face. Although I still don't know how I'd feel if I saw his sharp eyes looking back at me.

Chapter Thirty-Five

'Am I here to watch you sleep?'

I open my eyes. No time has passed and yet here he is, Christos, hovering over me in the dark. A silver line, a glow, around his head like a halo cast by the moon. Squinting, I can almost make out his features as he moves closer to me.

'I wasn't asleep, I was resting my eyes.'

I dig my elbows into the sand, then my hands to sit up. I find my phone in the grit and pick it up to check the time.

Three fifty-two.

Apparently, I had fallen asleep. I can only blame the melodic rocking of the sea not far from my feet. But I won't be admitting that any time soon. To me, it feels as though I did a really slow blink.

I shake my hands through the back of my hair to set free some of the sand tickling my scalp.

'You were sleeping. I have been watching you and you didn't notice me. If you were awake, you would be hearing my feet.' Christos moves to sit to my right on the shadowy beach. 'You're lucky it was me and not someone strange.'

'I don't know. I think you're a little bit strange at least.'

'Is that all? Everyone is a little bit strange. *Nai?*'

'Yeah, I guess. To be honest, I'm surprised you're here. I thought you didn't like the beach.' A tone settles into my voice. The perfect note of sarcasm to show him I've caught him out without having to tell him. To make him know that I've noticed he's here even though he said he *never* comes here.

'I don't.'

'Or the sea.'

'I don't.'

'So why are you here?'

Christos wraps his arms around his knees and looks out across the water and the sky. It's impossible to differentiate between the two now. It's all a swirling mix of purples and blacks with bright white puncture wounds.

He slowly tilts his chin down towards the sand before releasing one of his knees, letting his leg droop and using his free hand to scrub at his beard.

'I do not know. I think maybe I like to be punished, and there is something about you that feels just like, what is the word . . . torture.'

I shift my weight, pulling my skirt over my knees. This is the first time I've felt anything close to a chill in ages.

'Excuse me?'

He exhales through his teeth. 'Nothing. I'm not awake at night, I like sleep. I'm good at sleep, but tonight, nothing. No sleep. Then I get your message, and I wonder, maybe I should come here . . .'

'I don't believe in fate.' I have to press the point. I don't want him thinking I needed him here or something soppy like I think fate has brought us together.

'You said.'

'Do you? Believe in fate?'

'No. I can't believe in anything, not for many years.'

227

'Me neither. I believe in science. I don't even believe in people anymore.' The chill rolls up my spine and along the back of my neck, as though each grain of sand has grown spindly fingers to crawl over my skin. 'Why do you *claim* to hate the beach and the sea, Christos?'

'Why are you wanting to know everything?' He turns to look at me. A dark shadow over his eyes makes them disappear completely as his forehead presses down on them.

I know what I have to do.

It's only fair, I guess.

If I expect him to open up to me so I can find trust in him for us to work together, I guess I owe him the full truth as to why I'm struggling with people holding things back from me.

'You know I said someone stole everything from me, all my money and things?'

The shadow of Christos nods.

'Yeah, well, it was my fiancé who took everything. It turns out he had racked up some gambling debts. He had a problem. An addiction. I had no idea about it. He'd hidden it from me. When he proposed, he said about this great joint bank account, and it had all these benefits . . . I stupidly trusted him, and within the same month he cleared the account and took anything of value from our house.'

The memory of my life scattered across our home, the one we had created, flashes in front of my eyes. Sheets and cushions and things that didn't make sense, thrown to the floor. Like he would do anything to find a single pound coin.

The last time I saw him he was snuggled up in our bed, then it was like he'd never even been in it. I'd been sharing my bed with a thief the whole time, not someone I loved. It was as real as falling in love with an action figure.

'It's why I never want a relationship or love or any of that shit in my life again. What's the point, when it only ends in pain? Did you know, when you lose someone and they hurt you badly, it can cause real trauma to your heart? Visible trauma from heartbreak. It has a serious, medically visible effect. I can't go through that again. I'll never trust anyone again. Not like that. And you know about my dad, of course. Well, I found that out on the very same Saturday I was robbed. Yeah . . . I'm trying to find ways to trust people again, enough to maybe go into business with them or take out a loan with them or let them fill in my forms. It's hard when you actively know they're hiding shady stuff too. It's bad enough knowing my own mother is hiding her entire past stuff from me. I'm so sick of being surrounded by lies.'

'Your fiancé took your money?'

'Yep.'

'Did you tell the police?'

'What would be the point? I willingly put the money in a joint account, it's hardly stealing. I might as well have put it straight in his hand and said *here you go, feel free to spend my life's savings by pissing it up the wall, thanks* . . . It's my fault for trusting him.'

'He sounds like a *malaka*. A fucking idiot.'

The lapping of waves by our feet fills the air and the sand caught near my follicles is beginning to itch again. Lying in the sand was a bad idea.

This was a bad idea.

Suddenly, I'm struck by homesickness for a home that no longer exists. There's nothing there to go back to. I'm completely displaced, like floating weightlessly on the thick, salty sea. I'm seaweed being pushed along with the current.

Christos shifts about and lets out a hard breath. He sounds irritated. I open my mouth to tell him I think he's being insensitive, but he manages to speak first.

'My sister, Nephele, she drowned . . . in the sea. This is why I hate it. This is why I never come here. My tattoo, it's about her. It's for her.'

Words catch in my throat.

I've been pushing him, thinking he was being ridiculous or there was some sort of insane flaw that possibly meant he wasn't trustworthy, when in reality he has his own trauma to deal with. His own pain caught in his chest.

'I'm so sorry.'

I can't find words big enough or sorry enough for pushing him and for demanding he meet me here, when all he's really done is offer to help me along and given me a physical distraction when my mind couldn't take any more.

If I lost Serena, I can't imagine being the same again. No amount of money matters when compared to life. I still have my family, even if we are a little broken right now; we will fix it all, create a new shape of ourselves. But he can't bring his sister back . . . no wonder he's always talking with the morbid slant. He clearly hasn't recovered from the loss.

'It's not your fault.' His shoulders rise and fall in the dark.

'No, I know. I just can't imagine all you've been through. If I lost Serena . . . I'm sorry I made you come here, if I'd known—'

'You did not *make me*. I'm a donkey, no one can *make* me do things. I'm only here for the torture of your company.'

I slide my hand along the damp sand and find his, slipping my thumb into his palm and my fingers over his.

'If it's torture you want, then I guess we'd best keep working together.' I snatch a shaky breath to steady myself. It's hard to believe people anymore, to truly trust their word. But I've been too hard on him. Here in the dark, I can see everything more clearly than ever.

'Friends?' My voice is small, but the word is clear over the whispers of the sea.

Christos tilts his chin down, and I think he's looking at the shape of our hands in the starlight.

'Friends.'

Chapter Thirty-Six

The first proper shower for a month. A whole month showering on the beach after swimming in the sea. At times, there's been a slight magic to a cold shower on the beach, and straight away stepping back on sand, knowing nature was clinging on and not letting go no matter what, there for the ride . . . but mostly the added exfoliation has been driving me crazy.

Tonight, stepping out on to a brand-new fluffy bath mat felt like never before. As though I were in the world's most prestigious spa, getting ready for a night of luxury.

Being this clean and fresh feels like a new beginning. A clean slate. Even last night, talking to Christos on the beach, felt like a shift into something new. As though we've stepped away from whatever that crazy, lust-driven madness was and we're finding something real. A new path to walk down.

A bit like this new path we're walking along, Mum, Serena and me. I've never gone this way in the village before. Being a stone's throw to the beach, and with tavernas and shops so close by, I guess I've never needed to explore this road.

'Have you been down here before?' I turn to Serena, assuming Mum has as she lived around here when she was growing up.

'Yeah, haven't you?'

I shake my head.

'If there was ever a question as to whether you help with the laundry, you've just answered it.' Mum rolls her eyes.

'What?' I screw my face up, thinking about the piles of laundry I've made to help separate things out.

'The laundrette is along this road.' Mum points further along and to the right.

'Oh.'

'There's also a little shop that sells wooden games and bowls and salad servers and things next to it. It's really cute. I can't believe you haven't been along here.' Serena joins in with the eye-rolling.

'Right, my beautiful girls, I believe we're here.'

To our left, a man with thick, wavy, shoulder-length hair stands under an entrance sign that reads 'Greek Secret'. He welcomes us with a smile.

Mum goes straight into Greek and he looks pleasantly surprised.

'I believe Anton Greenwood made a reservation here for seven of us. We're a little early,' she explains.

'Perfect, come this way. I'll tell Gaia you're here. My name is Yianni, can I get you a drink to start?'

We follow behind him. There's a sweeping wooden bar to the right and to the left, where we are headed, vines wind their way up and along a trellis. Unobtrusive Greek music plays from hidden speakers around the taverna.

We order some water and cocktails before Yianni disappears towards the bar.

'He's a nice-looking boy, maybe you should see if he's available instead of fussing over Christos.' Mum leans in to Serena.

'I'm not sure I can go out with a bloke who has nicer hair than I do.' She pouts her lips and leans to watch him pass our order on to the woman behind the bar. 'And I don't *fuss* over Christos.'

A young woman almost skips out of the kitchen, her dark hair pulled into a messy bun on top of her head. She scans the taverna and makes a beeline for our table.

'You must be Thalia.' She then squints her bright-green eyes between Serena and me. 'Serena' – she nods at my sister – 'and Lorena. I'm Gaia, Anton's daughter. It's nice to meet you.' She slides into a chair, a wide smile beaming over at us.

'It's nice to meet you, Gaia. I could've guessed you were Anton's daughter by those beautiful emerald eyes.' Mum smiles softly back at her. 'Where *is* your father?'

'They will probably be late. My little sister is going through a stage of dressing herself and she puts everything on backwards, then she has this big tantrum, screaming and crying when someone tells her it's on backwards.'

'How come you're here without them?' Serena presses her forearms into the table and leans forward a touch.

'I work here. My best friend, Natalia, her parents own it, her brother, Yianni, he runs the place. I came over to see Natalia before she started work. If you come back tomorrow, you can see us all singing and dancing.'

'That sounds wonderful, we might just have to do that.' Mum looks from Serena to me.

'Dad tells me you were brought up in England? Do you speak Greek?' Gaia beams at me and Serena.

'No, not really,' I shake my head, 'but I do understand a certain amount when people talk slow enough.'

'Yeah, me too,' Serena confirms.

Yianni comes back with a tray. He offloads our drinks and places down bread, olives and dips too. He narrows his eyes on Gaia. 'Make sure you share.' Then he pats her playfully on the head.

She tuts as she pops an olive in her mouth, and I do the same.

'Gaia, before I forget, can you cover for Ruby tomorrow? She has some work to do at the beach.'

'Who's Ruby?' Mum rests her chin on her fingers and looks up at Yianni. I'm sure she's only asking on behalf of Serena, who's already made her lack of interest pretty clear.

'The woman behind the bar.' He looks over at her. She doesn't notice, she's talking to a barman who's just arrived. 'That is my fiancée, Ruby.'

Mum shifts her weight back in her seat. 'Congratulations.'

'*Efcharistó*,' he beams.

Even the word fiancée is still enough to make a shiver travel along my skin, leaving its mark in the way of goosebumps, the way a slug leaves an ugly trail. I glance at this woman who is so confident in her happiness she said yes to wearing a ring. She's attractive with mid-length shaggy hair, blonde at the bottom with darker roots. She could have anyone she wanted, yet she has faith in Yianni.

Part of me envies them. Envies how naive people can be. I could easily feel sorry for myself, that I had to grow up and realise the reality behind it all. The reality behind human nature to lie and cheat. That maybe there isn't one perfect person for everyone. Maybe life is more simple when spent alone.

Like Christos, finding peace and tranquillity instead of searching for something that doesn't really exist.

'That's fine, Yianni. I can cover,' Gaia confirms.

Yianni shoots us all another smile before disappearing back towards the kitchen.

'I'm surprised our paths have not crossed before now. You must have had many family holidays here.' Gaia wrinkles her nose in a playful sort of way.

'Actually, this is our first time here. Mine and Serena's, I mean' – I whip my head from side to side to shake out some sense – 'obviously not Mum's.'

'You've *never* been to Corfu before?' Her mouth stays open, just a small amount, just enough to show the surprise at my answer.

'No,' Serena and I answer in unison.

'But you are from here?' Gaia points a dainty finger at my mother then at the table, as though the table is representative of Corfu. Her eyebrows begin to weigh down her forehead.

'Yes.' Mum picks up some bread and puts it on her side plate. Leaving it there.

'How is this possible? You never wanted to bring your daughters here? What's so bad about the place?'

'Nothing.' Mum picks up her drink and takes a prolonged sip. It's like she's fallen into slow motion.

'There must be a reason not to come back.' Gaia pauses and looks absently to her left. 'You know, normally when people don't come back to their home there are only three reasons. They hate it there, they have no money to return, or there's been a big falling-out and they are afraid.' Gaia tilts her head, studying my mum.

'Well, you know, of course, not everyone is the same.' Mum stutters over picking words as she replaces her glass on the table. Twisting it to be just so.

This girl can't be more than eighteen, yet she's got the confidence of someone older than me. She holds eye contact with barely a blink and makes bold statements with complete abandon.

Gaia makes a small humming noise as she chews and then quickly swallows another olive. 'It's strange though. You don't look like someone who can't afford things, and you don't look like someone who would easily be afraid. You have good posture. Dad always says confidence is being able to hold your shoulders straight. You've got me very interested now.'

'Me too,' I whisper inadvertently. Serena kicks me under the table and I shoot a look, a bulging-eye look, over to her.

'I know, I know. Everyone says the same thing, I ask too many questions. But sometimes the thoughts in my head, they like to come out of my mouth. And why not? My guess, you did something to hurt your parents. Am I right?'

Mum rubs her lips together as though she's trying to smooth her lipstick.

'Something like that. It is hard to come back when you know you've caused others pain.' This is the closest I've come to hearing Mum admitting something openly. 'How did you get to be this straight-talking, Gaia? Your father speaks clearly, but he doesn't say all that much.'

'I think my mum was pretty outspoken. That's what my dad tells me. She passed when I was very young. I had to grow up fast, you know? Life can be so short. We should all ask questions, and never hide from the people who love you. They can be taken away too quickly.' She puts another olive in her mouth, only this time she chews it slowly, thoughtfully.

'Here comes your father.' My mum's voice is laced with relief as Anton fills the entrance, followed by a tall woman bending forward to hold the hand of a little girl in a pretty white dress. I'm pretty sure the buttons on the front are meant to be at the back, just as Gaia said.

Everyone stands to greet them. Gaia has that spring in her step again.

I've never met a girl quite like Gaia before, but she's definitely someone I'd want on my side in life, and someone I wouldn't want to come up against. There's a deep fire in there; the heat of it can be felt within a moment of being in her company.

Something about her wise words and her directness might've shaken something loose in Mum, but I'm not sure Serena liked it much. Out of the corner of my eye, I can see tension rolling over her. Her smile looks forced and tightly squeezed.

I wish Mum could tell us what really happened back then. It might not be that bad, and at least then Serena and I could deal with it and maybe we could all move on.

Chapter Thirty-Seven

People around us laugh in their little bubbles as they stroll along the pavement or stop to read signs on walls or stands outside tavernas and cocktails bars. They step in and out of gift shops, never leaving empty-handed.

We move differently to the current of people around us. We move along cautiously, steadily, Mum and me reacting quietly to Serena's gossiping.

'I'm still not sure of that girl, Gaia. Isn't Gaia the name of a goddess? Her mum seemed nice though. A bit clumsy, I didn't like to say she got some of that mojito on my skirt when she sent it flying. At least it's a clear drink. I liked her though.'

'Stepmum. Melodie is Gaia's stepmum,' I correct.

Serena grabs my arm. 'Oh yeah, stepmum. What did you think?' She cranes her neck to look at Mum. 'Mum? What did you think? Mum? Mum? Thalia!'

'Huh?' Mum blinks at Serena like she's never seen her before.

'I was asking what you thought of Melodie and Gaia. More Gaia, really. She liked to ask a lot of questions, right? And had an opinion on everything.'

'She did. But I thought she asked some very interesting ones about Lorena's new business idea. I think she's someone who is interested in people, that's all.'

'Maybe.' Serena folds her arms over her chest. I think she's disappointed we don't want to fall in the gossip trap.

'She told me she's thinking about being a psychiatrist or something,' I add in.

We fall back into a silence encased in the noise of the world around us. Music and laughter bounce off our bubble, unable to enter.

Gaia's questions have made me want to start up again. I can't help it. The only word rattling around my mind is *why*. Why didn't we have family holidays here when we were little? Why did we have to miss out on having our grandparents in our lives?

'Look who's in Cicala again.' Serena begins to take slower steps.

I glance into the warm glow of the restaurant and catch the shape of Christos at the bar. He's easy to spot, as it all opens out just a step or two above the road.

'Do you want to say hello?' Half of Mum's face lifts into a playful smile.

Serena shrugs. 'Can do.' She steps past us and towards the taverna. This is nothing like her previous desperation to see him. It's much more tame.

Mum and I share in pulling confused faces behind her back as we follow inside.

It's Alec who catches sight of us first. He comes over to kiss our cheeks briefly before moving back to his place behind the bar.

Unlike the last time I saw Christos in here, now he's nursing a beer, not a bottle of vodka.

'Hi, friend.' I kiss his cheek.

A spike of adrenaline runs up inside my chest as I take in the smell of him. My brain is beginning to associate him with things it shouldn't. With activities it shouldn't.

This is going to be harder to kick than I thought.

Christos's face lifts into a soft smile behind his beard.

'How was the meal? Alec tells me you were giving gifts to Anton's daughters tonight, Thalia?'

'Yes, we had stars named after them and gave them vouchers to a jewellery shop in Corfu Town. I know it might seem odd for the little one, but Anton can pick her something she will like for when she's older. I think it was well received. Anton seemed pleased. I'm eternally grateful to him, and to Alec.' She looks across the bar under her eyelashes at him, a gentle smile crossing her lips.

'They are good men.' Christos nods.

Serena begins to order drinks with Alec, three Baileys on ice.

'And so are you. Don't think it's going unnoticed, all the work you are putting in for my daughter. Spending time helping her to build a future here.'

In the warm, golden glow of Cicala's bar, I can't be sure, but I think Christos is blushing.

'No, I don't think I help enough. We will be set up soon. I have been discussing workspace with Spiros. Unless you will be working from home? But I think maybe no. We need to know for the forms, and we have some ideas for you. Not for now. Maybe tomorrow? Spiros said he has some time after the tours tomorrow.'

'Sounds good.' A smile lingers on my lips as I look at him, appreciating all he is doing for me.

After last night, and our moment of declaring friendship, it's easier to be around Christos. I know his secret now. That his sister drowned in the sea. That's why he doesn't like going to the beach or near the water. It's clearly the reason he's so closed off from people.

At this point, I feel as though any follow-up questions aren't mine to ask. He shared something with me, a part of him, a part of his past. A painful part at that. I guess that's what I needed. Something to show me he was real.

'I think I'd like to sit on the comfy seats.' Mum indicates towards the soft cream semicircular chair at the large round table where we sat with Spiros and Eleni, under the stars and the large decorative olive tree. 'Would you like to join us, Christos?'

'That's kind, but I'm here to speak with Alec.'

'You're welcome to come over if you change your mind.' Mum scoops up her drink and moves to the table.

'Message me what time for tomorrow, yeah?' As I reach for my glass, I unintentionally graze my chest over Christos's arm and our eyes meet in such a way that makes my insides feel like jelly.

I back off quickly, my heart in my throat. His eyes stay on me and there's that look in the dark depths. That look I've seen there before and already know too well.

Turning away, Serena and I move towards where Mum is sitting. She glances over her shoulder then leans close to me before I slide in next to Mum.

'I know you said he doesn't date or whatever, but he was obviously checking you out.'

My cheeks flush, I can feel the heat rising over my skin. Thank God for my tan and the golden lighting. Hopeful it'll cover it.

'My skirt isn't tucked in my knickers or something, is it? It's more likely to be that.'

Serena sputters laughter and we both check my skirt and my back.

'No, you're good.'

'Phew.' I slide around the sofa and closer to Mum. 'Do you remember that time when Serena had her skirt tucked in her knickers and that old lady actually came and pulled it out for her?'

'Please don't remind me!' Serena buries her face in her hands as Mum throws her head back in laughter.

'Shopping in Cambridge?' Mum presses her hand on her flat stomach as it bounces with laughter.

'Yeah!' I can feel tears rising up, squeezed out with breathless laughter.

I remember it so vividly. We were in M&S and Serena decided she wanted to try on a maxi dress. She didn't buy it in the end, but when she came out, her skirt was all tucked up. We were in the queue for Mum to buy some bits, I think maybe some jewellery, and that's when the elderly lady noticed.

'What did she say again?' I manage to ask before more laughter drowns my words.

'Excuse me, love' – Mum wipes her eyes – 'just as she tugged her skirt out for her.'

'I was mortified.' Serena sinks into her chair as we continue to laugh. 'Christos? Oi, Christos, come and save me.' Serena tuts when he doesn't respond right away. 'It's those bloody small ears of his, he can't hear me. Christos!'

'Small ears?' Mum and I say at the same time, then we look at each other and manage to laugh harder than before.

'Yeah, haven't you noticed? Christos has tiny ears.'

Christos saunters over with his beer in his hand.

'Can I help you?'

Mum wipes her eyes again, then leans in across the table so she can get a closer look at him, squinting. 'Oh my God, he really *does* have tiny ears.'

'They're dainty. I think they're cute.' Serena smiles up at him, laughing.

I don't join in, although I can't help but continue falling about laughing. All I can think is how glad I am that it's only his ears that are so small.

'You bring me here to laugh at me?'

His deadpan tone gives nothing away. Not to anyone but me. I'm beginning to read him. The small movement of his teeth over his lower lip. He's entertained by our laughter – or at least, he isn't bothered by his small ears.

He takes a deep inhale, puffing out his chest, exaggerating his muscular frame. He shakes his head as he exhales, turns on his heel and heads back towards the safety of the bar.

'I assume he says more to you when you're working together?' Mum angles herself to me, diverting her words away from the bar.

'When they're not having sex,' Serena mumbles.

My head whips round so fast I think it might fall off as I catch sight of Serena disappearing into her drink. All the hilarity gone.

I stutter over words but only manage sounds like 'Wha?' and 'Bu?'

'Excuse me?' Mum looks from me to Serena.

'I'm joking, I'm joking. We all know that after Jonah and Dad, Lorena has lost faith in the whole relationship thing anyway, right?'

'Right.' I pick up my own drink and let the ice hit my teeth as I take deep gulps of the creamy Baileys.

Mum has never said explicitly that she knew what happened between Christos and me. Although, from the very start, there was an air of disbelief that all I did was help him out that first night . . .

I hate that I've put myself in a position to hide things. Up until now, Serena has at least been acting like she thinks nothing is going on between me and Christos.

My pulse skips along at an alarming rate.

'I spoke to Dad again earlier.' Serena puts her glass down and flicks a perfect lock of caramel hair over her shoulder. 'He keeps saying about how sorry he is, you know? How much he misses us all.' Serena looks up at Mum from under her fake eyelashes. It's that same coy look she gets when she's asking a question she knows

Mum probably won't say yes to. Like staying out late when she was younger after saying how sensible a group of friends were, when we all knew they weren't *that* sensible.

Mum doesn't say anything. Her lips lock together as though a zip has formed between them and it's tightly closed.

'When are you going to go and visit him?' I do my best to keep my eyes on Serena and not Mum.

'I don't know. Soon, probably.' Her shoulders clench and release.

'Please don't stop seeing him for me. I don't want that. I want you both to be happy. He will always be your father, and I will always be your mother. There is no need to pick sides or loyalty. Seeing him doesn't mean you don't love me, and nothing could stop me loving you two girls.' The light that shines in Mum's eyes when she says that is enough to make a flame ignite inside me. A comfort and warmth that can only be found in the arms of a loving parent to their child.

'Thanks, Mum.' Serena slides her hand across the table towards my mum and they squeeze them together.

I don't know what I'd do without these strong women. I'd probably still be a mess on the floor of my place back in England, wondering what it's all about.

My eyes wander to Christos. He's looking in our direction, along with Alec behind the bar. I shoot them a friendly smile and they both return it.

Mum's right, they're both kind men. I just wish I had the capability to trust someone the way I used to, without wondering what they're *really* doing behind my back.

Christos shakes Alec's hand over the bar and they exchange nods. He then makes his way towards us.

'*Kalinichta*, ladies. Lorena, I will see you tomorrow at seven, yes? Spiros has a late tour. They begged, he can never say no.'

'Oh OK, that's fine. Mum, can I borrow the car?'

'Don't worry. I can come and pick you up if you like?' Christos pulls the keys to his van out of his pocket.

'Would you? Thank you *so* much.'

'Six thirty then.' Christos nods and we all chime *kalinichta* and he heads towards the entrance and to the car park at the side of the taverna.

'I'm quite enjoying this. Who would like another?' Mum beams.

'I'll get them,' I volunteer and slide out, awkwardly manoeuvring around Serena.

I gather up our glasses and return them to the bar.

'Three more, please, Alec.'

As Alec begins to pour out our drinks, he looks past me under his eyebrows through the restaurant. I turn to follow his gaze, out across the bar and the taverna. The open side makes it easy to see down into the car park, where Christos has parked at the far end.

He's leaning against his van, smoking a cigarette.

I turn back to Alec. 'I've never seen him smoke before.'

'Mmm.' Alec barely acknowledges me; a deep frown wrinkles his forehead.

Ice clinks from his scoop into the glasses like a wind chime.

I hop on to the bar stool and try to catch his eye. Keeping my voice low, I say, 'He told me about his sister.'

It's enough to grab Alec's attention from pouring our drinks. He looks at me as though I've said something unimaginable. Like I've just told him that I found a scientific equation to cure all disease and I'm holding up the proof.

'He told you?'

I nod.

'About Nephele?'

'Yes.'

'I haven't known him say it since before she dies.' Alec places the Baileys bottle down on the smooth wooden surface. His hand lingers on it. He's only poured two of the three drinks, but it's like he's forgotten what he was doing. Perhaps even where he is.

'I know he says it is his fault, but he is wrong. Don't listen to him, yes? I hope, in his future, he knows this.'

As Alec begins to come alive again, in the same way a clockwork toy does when it's been wound, I stop still. As though he's stolen my energy to reignite himself.

He said she drowned. How could that be his fault?

I glance over my shoulder to catch Christos stubbing out his cigarette before opening his door and slumping into his van.

There's way more to him than he told me.

This is exactly why it's pointless making a commitment to trust anyone. You can never truly know someone, because how can you know what they're hiding?

Chapter
Thirty-Eight

'Now we have the address agreed, you can file your papers tomorrow.' Spiros thumps his hands down on the thick wooden table and it's enough to give me another flashback to Christos and I challenging its strength.

'I'd really like to start playing with some product ideas as soon as possible. Could I have some oil from the grove? Part wild olives, part Lianolia olives if possible, please. I've got some ideas I'd like to start thinking about and working on. Obviously, long term, I want to do something a bit more complex, but I really need to get started.'

'We have some, not much. We use what we keep, we sell the rest. Christos, could you find some before we leave?'

As he stands to leave and find me some oil, Christos presses his hands into the table, making it creak.

I swear I've had palpitations throughout this meeting, with recurring images of me and Christos more wrapped up than the swirling trunks of some of the olive trees.

'Are you looking forward to tomorrow night? The big farewell party and big engagement party?' Spiros opens his hands and arms to show just how *big* it's going to be. 'Eleni is so excited for it. I haven't seen her in two days, all she does is planning, planning, planning! It's going to be good.'

'I'm looking forward to it.'

Spiros looks at the heavy gold watch on his wrist. 'I have to be back, Eleni left me a long list.' He kisses my cheeks. 'Christos will bring you the oil. See you tomorrow.'

Spiros plods back over the meandering land. His land. The land Mum grew up running around.

As the grey-haired man walks away from me, I think of the little boy from my imagination, climbing olive trees barefoot and chasing butterflies.

I don't really want to have the blunt sledgehammer nature of Gaia, but I do want to know how it all went from having this wonderful time with his sister to not seeing her for thirty years.

'Spiros, wait!' I begin to jog along the rough terrain, skipping over the uneven dried grass and stones, roots and plants. 'Wait!'

He turns, eyes narrowed in concern at my squawking.

'Spiros . . .' By the time I get to him, I need to catch my breath. The heat has snatched it from me and made my skin cry.

'Lorena, what on earth is the matter?' He places a heavy hand on my shoulder and grips hard.

'I was thinking, do you have any photos? Of Mum and you?' I puff and do my best to stand tall again. 'From when you were kids . . . and maybe up to when she left?'

His hand drops and finds his thick waist, shifting his weight.

'Yes, yes, somewhere. My parent, they had many. Eleni will know where. I will ask her. It will be after the party. Is that OK?'

'Of course, of course. Thank you.' I switch my weight from one foot to the other. 'Spiros, I know Mum doesn't want me to ask, and I know she's probably asked you not to talk about it, but what happened back then? What was so bad that I couldn't meet my grandparents?'

His hand finds my shoulder again, this time softly with a gentle squeeze.

'It is not my story to tell. You know this, Lorena. I can show you photos, though. That, I can do.'

'Thanks, Spiros.'

He nods and begins his departure towards the hedge once more.

For a moment he pauses, slowly twisting to face me but not meeting my eyeline.

'But, in my opinion, nothing. Nothing was so bad. But maybe I say that because I missed her.' He turns and walks away, disappearing behind the hedge.

I suck in a deep breath to stop my chest working overtime after my short jog and Spiros's words. My knees are weak and my head's spinning.

I'll get to see some photos at last, at least. I can replace the image in my head with something real. A true glimpse into the past. My mum's past.

I know it's not my past, but it feels like it is. Like it's a part of me that I've missed out on. Anton's daughter's face, Gaia, when she realised we hadn't had a single family holiday here, hadn't known our grandparents . . . that we have no idea about our Greek heritage, don't speak Greek.

The pain in my chest shoots into my spine, like part of my heart was removed at birth and now I can feel my chest caving in where I should've had grandparents and family filling it up. They were all surgically removed, and I'm not even allowed to know why.

Anger overtakes the pain.

Spiros said it was nothing in his eyes. That there was no reason good enough for Mum to do this to me, to Serena.

I've done my best to be considerate of my mum while trying to find out why my childhood only included my father's parents, up until they passed away.

'Lorena?'

Air rushes into my lungs at the sound of Christos's voice behind me and my hand slaps to my chest as I twist to see him clutching three cans of olive oil.

'Christ, you made me jump.'

'It is pronounced *Christos*, not *Christ*.' I know he must be joking, but there's no tone to give it away. 'How did you not hear me? I was walk like I always walk.'

'I don't know. I was in my own head.'

'Is there something wrong? You look pale.'

'I was getting angry at my mum in my head, for hiding things from me for all these years. I don't know. I don't want to go home now. I might drive around for a bit.' I shrug then put my hands out. 'Thanks for the oil. Now all I need is lab supplies. And a lab . . . or even my own kitchen.'

'Come, I will take them to the car. But remember, I drove you, so it's my van.'

'Thanks for the reminder. I guess I won't be driving around then. I need to hire my own car or something. I can't keep asking Mum if I can borrow hers. It's like being seventeen again. Poor and desperate. Do you think Spiros could find me a job here so I can make some money to keep hiring a quad bike or a car?'

'You can pick olives in October. It's a shit job, but it's money.'

I went from earning a steady wage to nothing so quickly it still doesn't seem real. I was never going to be a millionaire, but I was doing well. Tears threaten and my throat suddenly feels thick. 'Are you hungry? I can make some food. Make you feel better.'

Christos is always nearby to prop me up when I'm a wreck. It shouldn't be his job, but I'm glad of his company.

'As a friend.'

'Only as a friend.'

Chapter
Thirty-Nine

When I arrived here before, I'd been drinking and it was dark, then when I left, I was hiding from the light hoping not to be seen, squinting and shying away from the sun.

It's different now.

Now, Christos's little house is showing its true appeal. It has a flat roof with chairs and a table just waiting for the sun to set over the sea. His place is on the perfect slope overlooking . . . everything. Corfu at its finest. The world falls away towards the blue expanse with cypress trees and olive trees in a delightful embrace before it.

The sky is ablaze with deep reds and burnt orange. It won't be long until sunset now. The sun is already well on its way down.

As I get out of his van, I pull down my sunglasses and look across the water from the side of the road, between his place and the next one along. I bet if I could look at it from the roof, I'd see how beautifully the sea is glittering.

'Are you coming in, or looking for boats?'

'I hadn't noticed your view when I was here before. You must spend a lot of time up on your roof.'

Christos stops and turns to face me. 'We can sit there, if you like? I have some stifado. Eleni always tells me she makes too much food and gives me some. But the stifado is the best, she knows it's my favourite. There is plenty, if you like?'

'I'd love that, thanks.'

'Beer?'

'Sounds good.'

'I'll bring it up.'

Christos indicates towards the concrete stairs creeping up the side of his house.

He turns away and moves to his front door. The door isn't locked. It's probably never locked.

The cicadas are louder here than by the sea. Although it's not as loud here as in the olive grove. The odd car passes by, but there isn't the summer foot traffic you get near the beach and in the tourist spots. This is a real village with real people who live here day after day, not just for the summer months.

I climb the steps and as soon as I'm at the top, I know I'll never want to leave. This is a view that's worth being inland for. It's worth not having the same sea breeze cutting across the humid air biting my skin, it's worth driving out for, worth more than money can buy. From here, the sun seems further away than it does when I'm at the beach. Everything does. Suddenly, I've been given the gift of space and distance.

Pulling out a white plastic chair, I slide down into it to watch the setting sun as it bruises dark mauve streaks across the sky.

Christos's heavy feet pound on the stairs. As he gets to me, he places a bottle of beer down on the table.

'Cheers,' I chime, even though I don't pick it up.

Christos begins to sip as droplets slip down my bottle to the table.

'You've changed,' I say as I look him over.

He lowers one eyebrow, then the other joins it.

'Your clothes. I meant your clothes.'

253

He looks down at the cotton short-sleeve shirt with half the buttons undone, and the dark shorts. His whole face lifts in comprehension.

He looks perfect.

He's just the right amount of casual and comfy but still clean and smart. His work polo shirt always looks smart and crisp, but it's better to see him as him.

Neither of us tries to fill the space between us. We let the warm air connect us, and nothing more.

There's an itch at the back of my mind where questions about Christos's sister are resting, but after a lot of thinking last night, I realised it must've been a big step for him to tell me about her at all, based on what Alec said at least. That he never talks about her.

All I could think about last night was Serena, and if she died and if I felt like it was my fault. It explains why he lives alone, doesn't want to make connections. I can't imagine the pain he must always be in. When I do try to imagine it, I feel physically sick.

'Dinner will be thirty minutes.'

'Thanks. And thanks for letting me hang out here.'

He doesn't reply, he lets us fall back into silence, both facing out towards the distant sea and the shadows being cast by the enormous cypress trees. The sun looks as though it might be deciding to leave us for good as it flares purple and red in a passionate goodbye.

'How long have you lived here?'

'Since I was eighteen.'

'So, what's that? Maybe ten years?'

'A little more.' His lips turn up under his beard and his eyes flick away from the sky and briefly towards me.

'Noted.' I pick up my bottle and take a sip. I don't usually drink beer. It's too bitter for me. But any cool drink is good in this heat.

Placing it back down, I wipe my hand over my leg to get rid of the condensation.

'Do you rent? If I had a view like this, I don't think I'd ever want to leave.'

'I did. A few years ago, Eleni let me buy it from her and Spiros.'

'Eleni? Eleni and Spiros owned this place?'

Christos presses the bottle to his lips and tilts it to take a deep swig.

'Yeah.' He slides lower in his plastic chair.

'I guess that's part of all the help they've given you.'

'Yep.'

All the help, feeling sorry for him, has to be linked to Nephele. It all makes sense as to why Eleni would give so much extra support to her cousin's son. If she really felt bad for him. I wonder whether his parents blamed him too, if he blames himself. Whether they're alive.

The more my mind races, the more I realise I don't know very much about this man. I only know how he has treated me. Or at least, how he has acted around me and in front of me.

Thoughts of Jonah slip in between the cracks, in between the folds of grey matter, to dig deep into my thoughts and lodge there. How you can live with someone and blind yourself to thoughts of who you think they are rather than who they actually are. But all you can really go on is how someone acts in front of you. The rest is just hearsay.

At the same time, knowledge is power, and power is how to protect yourself from pain.

'The other night, when you were drunk?' I shift in my chair to face him a little more. 'Was it to do with . . .' My voice trails as the question slips out. Suddenly, I'm aware I'm pushing again, and not everything is about me and my pain and my inability to trust. I don't want to ruin his peace, the only thing he asks for.

'Nephele.' As her name passes my lips, it instantly evaporates in the last piercing heat the sun has to offer for the day.

'It was her birthday. Or . . . it would have been.' He exhales. 'She would be twenty-four.'

My throat swells and each time I swallow it's like choking back grit. She would've been the same age as Serena.

'You know,' he continues, 'I never talk about her. In eleven years, I never talk about her. Not to anyone. Meeting you at the beach is the first time I'm there in eleven years.'

From wishing I had information, I'm suddenly overwhelmed by it. Incapacitated by it. A deer in headlights has nothing on how I feel as the sun throws one last splinter of light right on me, as though pointing out that I asked to know this pain. I pushed, and now I'm going to have to deal with the spotlight on me.

I lick my lips and try to find words. 'So, why now? Why come to the beach to see me?'

'I . . . I had this feeling like you need me. Like you need help. I can't leave anyone who needs help.'

'I didn't really realise that all this time you've been taking pity on me.'

'I never said *pity*, I do not *pity* you. This is different. Not like you needed something or someone to feel sorry for you. Like you needed . . . *me*.' He pauses, and under his breath he says, 'Maybe I needed you.'

The alarm on his phone bursts into life, making some nearby birds take flight.

'The stifado is ready.' Christos slides out from his plastic chair and leaves me feeling more bewildered than ever.

How can finding out more about a situation lead to more confusion? I thought information was king. A way to figure things out, not be left more puzzled than ever.

Maybe I needed you. Did he say that, or did I imagine it? He said it so low, I can't be sure.

The sun vanishes completely into the Aegean, and I'm left with a bruised sky and a confused soul.

Chapter Forty

'That stifado was perfect. The tomato sauce was beautifully rich and the beef was so tender. It fell apart. Wow.'

I've never had a meal with another person before and said so little. Not unless we were watching TV or something like that. Actually, I had one really bad date years ago that was pretty much me blabbering then full-on silence. But that was just before I started university.

The difference is, this wasn't awkward. This is because I've spent the whole time inside my own head wondering whether I should ask about the fact he thought I needed him, and if he actually said he needed me. And if he does need me, how can I help him? He's done so much for me, I want him to feel he can ask for help too.

'You can thank Eleni for the food when you see her. She is the only one to make a stifado almost as good as my mother.' His mouth moves under his beard, maybe a brief smile, maybe not. 'Eleni will be happy you are here. They are happy I have a friend.' Christos rolls his dark eyes and doesn't sound at all happy about this fact, but he doesn't seem annoyed about it either. Even the eye-roll lacks conviction.

'I think we both need friends at the moment.' It's the perfect bridge after our quiet eating. The perfect lead to pull him back around and find out what he meant.

I pull a little more, harder this time. 'What did you mean before? About me needing you?'

'Was I wrong?'

He looks me straight in the eye. Unflinching.

Normally, he only looks at me for this long when he wants it to go somewhere else, but that's not the impression I'm getting from him now.

He's still. Calm.

I let the question mull in my mind as I think back to going down to the beach. Sending that text, even using the dreaded thoughts of fate, pushing for him to see me.

'No, you're not wrong. I guess I needed some sort of proof you were a good person . . . or something. All the shit with Jonah has left me with more trust issues than I know what to do with.' A childish giggle falls out of me and I instantly wish I could put it back where it came from.

That awkward girl trying to be a strong woman who has so easily had her life shattered by a man. Which is exactly why I can never let it happen again.

'You can trust me. I won't lie to you. I have no need to lie to you. What would I have to gain?'

'Maybe, but you won't tell the whole truth either.'

'What makes you say that?'

I hesitate, considering my words and thinking back to Alec's surprise and his accidental revelation.

'Alec said something.'

'Oh?'

'He said you feel guilty about your sister's death. You didn't tell me that part. All you said was she drowned. Is that maybe why you needed me?'

'I need another drink. Do you want one?'

'Yeah, sure. I'll have what you're having.'

He moves to the edge of the roof and marches down the steps. I'm not even sure how he can see where he's going, it's getting so dark. There's nothing to stop anyone from coming up here and stepping right off the edge too. It's just a step and splat. There's no rail, no safety measures. Nothing.

A few houses nearby have their lights on, and beyond the sprawling green olive trees there are pinpoints of light. As though the sky has let the stars come on holiday here too. They glitter across the land more densely as they get closer to the shore.

It's only a moment before the sound of Christos's feet scraping back up the concrete stairs gets louder and louder. He places down two beers and a candle, which he promptly lights.

He sits back in his chair and goes on to light a cigarette too.

'I didn't know you smoked.'

'I don't. Do you want one?'

I shake my head before tucking a loose strand of hair behind my ear. 'No thanks. If you don't smoke, why are you smoking?'

'I have one or two when things are too hard. I don't like the taste, or the way it makes me feel sick if I have too many, but,' he shrugs, 'it takes the edge off my thoughts.'

'I guess, not talking about Nephele for eleven years, and then here you are talking to me about her. That must be a lot. If I lost Serena . . . I have no idea what I would do.'

The end of the cigarette lights up the night, burning and glittering as Christos takes a deep drag on the little poison stick before sharply exhaling smoke into the dark.

'You know how you said I can trust you and you won't lie because you have nothing to gain?'

Christos clears his throat then hums an acknowledgement as he watches me over the flickering yellow candle.

'Well, same goes. You can talk to me about Nephele, or anything really. I'm completely objective. I'm a friend, but a friend with enough distance that I won't have my own thoughts and enough emotional baggage that I'm not intimidating. If that makes sense?'

He flicks ash on to the roof and smiles as he sinks lower in his chair again.

'She had been, I can't think of the word in English, falling to the ground a lot. Like sleeping but not.'

'Fainting, collapsing?'

'Yes, this. She was collapsing and always thirsty but it was a hot summer and she was thirteen and Mama was sure she was not drinking enough. They took her to the hospital, but no one was very worried. They took some blood to test just in case, but we didn't think too much about it.' Christos takes another drag on the cigarette. 'Then there's a call, late on a Friday. They said they think she has diabetes. I know nothing about it, they give her an appointment to come in and speak with someone, do more tests on Monday. They said make sure she eats often and drinks plenty of water. The specialist will see her and give all the information. We were all more worried, but happy that we know they can help.'

He stops and looks out towards the navy sheet that is the distant sea. Between his finger and his thumb, he slowly rolls the cigarette back and forth.

I don't speak, I give him the space to find his own words again. I know this story ends badly. That's all I do know. Knowing the ending is making me feel sick and there's nothing I can do that will make Christos feel better at the end of it, which hurts more than I could've anticipated.

'Every Saturday in the summer Nephele wants her big brother to take her out on the boat. It was a little old fishing boat, nothing great, but she loved to swim. She was a very strong swimmer and my dad would joke and call her a dolphin. Before we went, Mama says to take her to the shop, get her some food and take lots of water. I gave her ten euro and she goes in the shop and buys one of the big tourist bags of those sweets, you know with all the fruits on the packets? The really big bags only holidaymakers buy to take home and, I don't know why, to give out at school or work, I guess? In the car she eats them, on the boat she eats them. Loads of them.'

I already know what happened, enough of an educated guess anyway. I want to tell him I don't need to hear the rest, I don't want to hear the rest. But now he's telling it, and I can't stop him. I've made him get this far, telling me, of all people, after eleven years of silence.

'She said she needed to swim because she was tired. It would wake her up.' He begins to shake his head before taking a last drag on the stub that's left in his hand, dropping it to the ground and grinding it out with his foot.

'She was good at swimming under the water. She could go over a minute, easy. She would do it every week. So I waited without thinking.' Christos pauses, frozen in time and his thoughts. In the flickering candlelight, I can see the tension in his face as he relives it. 'They think it was maybe that she got too tired, or a coma. I didn't know all the sugar was bad.' His voice stays low and dark. 'It was food. That's all I thought. It was my fault for letting a child pick the food, letting her eat all that shit, not jumping in sooner to find her. She died because her older brother is a fucking idiot. I don't deserve to live. So I don't. I exist to help others to honour her. She was very caring, always helping people.'

'It's not your fault, and if she were still alive—'

'I've heard it before, she would not blame me. No, she wouldn't, but—'

'If it were the other way around, and you died, would you blame her?'

'No, bu—'

'Would you want her to live her life?'

'Yeah, bu—'

'Then there are no buts. You should *live* in her honour. *Live* because she can't. Not punish yourself because no one ever taught you about diabetes. This is why you haven't had friends for eleven years? Or a girlfriend?'

'All this coming from the woman who will *never marry* or *live* because one man stole some money? Did he treat you well?'

'Yes, but—'

'Did he have a genuine addiction problem? Gambling, you said?'

'Yes, bu—'

'Do you think he loved you and would never have done these things if he didn't have this problem?'

I stumble over the messages he sent. The ones begging for forgiveness even though he disappeared forever into God-knows-what and God-knows-where.

'Yeah, I do think he loved me. As much as he could.'

'And you are still willing to give up happiness for this. I murdered my sister, they should have put me in prison.'

I scrape my chair towards him and pull one of his hands from where it's clasping the other one.

'You are a wonderful, kind person who is trying to honour his sister by making the world a better place. If you didn't do it on purpose, it's not murder. You clearly loved her.'

His hand grips harder on to mine and his chin drops so I can't see his face.

'I don't need to know her to know Nephele adored you. It's hard *not* to adore you. She wanted to spend her Saturdays with you and probably looked up to you. It would hurt her to know the pain you still put yourself through.'

'Why do I have this problem?'

'Because you loved her and you were responsible—'

'No, not that problem. I know why I have *that* problem. That was my fault and no words can change it. Why do I have this problem of you.' He pulls his hands from mine and tugs his fingers through his beard as he sits upright in his chair.

'Why is it so hard to keep myself away from you? I tell you things. I can't keep my hands off you.' He sniffs in that way people do when they're trying not to cry, but instead he quietly laughs. 'I asked for torture, penance, I never would imagine this is it. You are it.'

'I don't want a relationship. Ever.'

'And I don't want that. I don't want *happy*. I want peace. Then I see you and . . .' He turns away from me, shaking his head. Tension ripples over his muscles, I can see them in the golden shimmer of the candlelight licking his skin.

'You know there have been women in the past who try to change me, who try to find out *why* I am alone, *why* I am this way. Ones who want me to love them.'

'Well, maybe that's it. You know I don't want to love you or be in a relationship with you. I'm the exact opposite to everyone else. Maybe that's why you're able to open up to me. There's no fear of me trying to trap you into a relationship.'

He looks back at me with an intensity like nothing I've seen before. As though something inside of him is being torn up and he desperately needs help but there's no way he'll ever ask for it.

My phone screen lights up the night and begins to ring. Serena's face is there on the screen.

'I best answer that.' I pick up it. 'Hello?'

'You need to get back home, now.' Serena spits the words under her breath.

'What?'

'Now,' she growls.

The line goes dead.

Without knowing whether or not this is one of Serena's exaggerated dramas or a true problem, it's hard to know what to do.

'Serena just said I have to go home now, but I can stay if you need me to?'

'No. I will take you. I think I've had enough torture for one night.'

Christos blows out the candle, and we both get up to leave.

Chapter
Forty-One

My hand rhythmically taps on my knees.

Tap, tap, tap. Tap, tap, tap. Tap, tap, tap. Tap, tap, tap.

'It's going to be all right.' Christos doesn't sound convinced.

After our conversation about Nephele, we're both on edge. Particularly where sisters are concerned.

It's not a long journey back to Agios Stefanos from Christos's place on the outskirts of Agios Athanasios. Twenty-five minutes, perhaps.

He doesn't speed or break any laws, but there's something about the way he accelerates and his hands grip the wheel in the light from the dash that tells me he's as anxious as me.

'I hope you don't feel like I *made* you tell me things about Nephele.'

'No one has ever made me do anything I didn't want to do. I've told you before. I'm a donkey.'

'Me neither. Not really.'

Christos dips the beams as a bus passes us full of people heading back to the airport, finished with this year's annual visit to paradise.

'I really wish Serena had said more.'

'Do you want to call her again?'

'There's no point. She didn't answer the first five times, she won't answer now. She's probably being dramatic.' I'm not sure if I'm reassuring myself or him. 'When life is a little boring around the edges, she's *really* good at making a mountain of entertainment out of a dead molehill. You should've seen her the day Mum told us about Dad going off to Mexico with some woman from work. You'd have thought it was *her* husband off with someone else.'

'I can imagine it.'

'What was Nephele like? I know you said she was kind . . .'

'She was. She used to raise money for charity by painting stones and selling them in the summer. She could have the money for anything, but each year she wanted to give it away to someone who needed it more than her. We have a little brother too, Panayotis, he was only two when Nephele disappeared in the sea. She was always teaching him and playing with him. She had him counting all the numbers.'

'You have a brother? You've never mentioned him before.'

'I only mentioned my sister because I didn't want to lose you. I mean, I know you need my help, and I didn't want you to feel like I was not honest with you. You know? What the hell . . .' He stumbles over his words before trailing off completely, squinting at what he's seeing in his headlights.

I take in the same scene that's snatched his words from his head. The same scene that's made my stomach lurch and my palms sweat. The scene that's actually able to push out Christos saying he didn't want to lose me.

In the orange glow of the streetlight, our front garden has a man sitting on one of our old plastic chairs with what looks like fresh blood over half his pale-grey T-shirt, a towel wrapped around his head and Serena standing over him, her arms working overtime as she seems to be telling him off. Our front door is wide open and there's no sign of Mum.

Before Christos's van has fully stopped, my seat belt is undone and I'm opening the door.

I jog over towards Serena, blurting out words before I can reach her. 'What the hell is going on? Who the hell is this?'

'Hey, Sunshine. Who's the big fella?'

It's only now he's facing me and I hear his voice that I recognise him. Him and his faded Bon Jovi T-shirt. My dad.

'What the hell happened?'

'Are you all right? Do you need me to remove this man?' Christos growls over my shoulder.

'No, I don't think so. Christos, this is my dad, Matt. Dad, this is my . . .' I look up at Christos and try to put a label on him. '. . . friend and sort-of business partner, Christos. Now, can someone please explain what's going on and why you're covered in blood? Where's Mum?'

'Inside,' Serena begins, stepping forward and into the limelight being cast by a situation she can shine in. One that seems to have her favourite thing in it: drama. 'Dad showed up grovelling and Mum hit him over the head with a glass and now I'm telling him to go to hospital.'

'Why didn't you tell me this on the phone?'

I lift the towel on my dad's head to see a split eyebrow and a lump on his forehead that resembles a small red horn.

'Because when I called you, he had just arrived, and I knew something was going to happen but I had no idea *this* was going to happen, did I? I didn't want them to hear me chatting away on the phone.'

'You need to see a doctor. I will take you.' Christos takes my dad's arm and stands him up.

'I'm fine,' he insists.

'No,' I interject, 'you're not. Do as you're told and I'll deal with you later.'

'I'll go with them.' Serena takes Dad's other arm and leads him towards Christos's van.

'I'm not a child,' Dad grumbles.

'Just go, Dad.'

'Fine, but tell your mum I forgive her.' I grab Christos's other arm, forcing him to release my father into Serena's care and turn to face me.

'Thank you for doing this.' I reach my hand to his cheek, half my palm resting on his soft beard. 'I want you to be happy.'

He leans down towards me and whispers, 'That is what I was afraid of.'

Without thinking, I kiss his cheek before he turns to leave.

The van speeds away and I'm left standing on the dusty verge. People have been eyeing the scene as they pass, looking and whispering.

I turn to our open front door to find my mum and get some answers.

The living room is clean and empty. The way it always is. Scanning the room reminds me of all those weeks ago when I first walked in here, searching for something and not knowing what it was. Only finding dirt and unfinished business. Now it's a beautiful clean open space with a classic black wood burner, just waiting to be furnished.

'Mum?' I grab the banister of the stairs and tiptoe on the first step as though it'll help to project my voice. 'Mum?' I close my eyes and focus, to give my ears the best chance of hearing her call back to me.

Nothing.

I hop off the step and move towards the kitchen and dining area. Through the window I can see her slumped in a chair outside, her head resting heavily on her right hand.

'Mum?'

'Before you say anything, I know I shouldn't have thrown the glass at him, but he pissed me off and the glass was already in my hand.'

'What the hell happened? I've just sent Dad off with Christos and Serena to get stitches or something. Why was he here?'

Mum begins shaking her head before tilting it to the navy sky as I pull a chair over to sit next to her.

'That prick – sorry, I know he's your father. I shouldn't say that.' Mum rubs her hand over her forehead and pushes her wild mass of curls off her face. 'He shows up here saying he has made a mistake. He should never have gone to Mexico and all the other cliché lines you can think up.'

'That doesn't sound like a reason to make him bleed.'

'No, at that point I only told him it was all too late and he should bugger off back to England.'

'So why the hell did you hit him?'

In the light pouring into the garden from the kitchen, I can see the muscles in her jaw harden.

'Mum?'

'Because he told me I *knew* I couldn't do any better than *us*, than *him*.' Her eyes narrow as though she can see him there in front of her, before she adds under her breath, 'Arrogant shit.' She bursts into life, facing me and looking more Greek than ever before with her arms telling half the story for her. 'And do you know the worst thing?'

'No?'

'He meant it, like it was somehow a good thing. He could throw me away and sleep around but he learnt something, he learnt that he missed me. But I don't believe that for a moment. That girl probably got bored of him without the excitement of going behind my back. I'm sure she thought she was the first and that they would never get caught. He thought I would put up with him until the day I die. But that's it. I've had enough. No more.' She crosses her arms and slumps back in her chair.

I open my mouth to question half a dozen things she just said but she doesn't give me a chance.

'And another thing' – her arms are alive again – 'who shows up without a word? Did he mention this to you?'

I shake my head, but she isn't waiting for a verbal response.

'Serena looked surprised, she thinks she can lie, but she can't. I don't think he told her beforehand.' There's a pause in her thoughts. 'She knows you've slept with Christos.' Mum gives me a side glance.

'Wha— what?'

'You are not subtle, and we've played your game, but we all know you too well.'

'I mean, I admitted it to her, but she acted like she didn't hear me, or didn't understand. And how long have you known?'

'Day one. I'm your mother. Don't think anything goes unnoticed.'

'I mean, I thought maybe, but then . . . you all went along with it so . . . Great. Noted. More lying, more hiding things.' I roll my eyes in frustration. 'So, she doesn't hate me?'

'I think she wants to, but she can't. She might also be denying it. Or asking him about it right now in front of your father. Now she has Christos to herself without you there for the first time.'

I slap my hands to my face to cover my eyes. It's not enough. My mind's eye takes over and plays out an embarrassing and ugly scene with them all talking about me. My hands fall away.

'How did this become about me? Are you doing this to hide from the fact you threw a glass at Dad?'

She purses her lips. 'Maybe.'

'Very mature, Mum.'

'You know, Lorena, you don't always grow up. Sometimes you just get wrinkles and people look at you like you're old, but on the inside you still feel like that same stupid girl who jumped into mistakes like they were adventures and would run around barefoot climbing trees. It's only my body that's changed, not my soul.' She exhales and, linking her fingers together, she leans forward and looks at the shadows dancing on the ground. 'That is not completely true. We do change and learn, but in so many ways, most of us *old* people don't feel the age we look.'

'You're not old and you don't look old either.'

'Thank you, Lorena. You're too kind. Now, I think I will continue to let my maturity slip and I'll go to bed and ignore the events of the evening. Before you or Serena ask, no, your father cannot stay here, and I have no desire to know where he is until he is back in England. *Kalinichta*, my love.'

I glance over my shoulder as Mum heads for the back door.

'Dad said he forgives you.'

Mum briefly falters and her hands clench before she continues on without a word.

For the second time this evening, I'm left in complete shock sitting on a cheap white plastic chair in the dark.

Chapter Forty-Two

It's past midnight when Christos's van pulls up with Dad in the front. As the engine cuts out and the overhead light comes on, I can see Dad has a square gauze stuck to his head.

The door swings open and he shoots me a winning smile, as though I'm nine years old again and he's told me we're off to Disneyland. The only difference is, he looks like he's got hold of Serena's dentist and had his teeth bleached a shade of white that, at his age, makes them look a little like cheap dentures. They do in the streetlight, anyway.

'Hey, Sunshine. We're back. How's your mum?' Dad envelops me in an embrace.

I quietly slip my hands around his waist and let my head fall heavy on his shoulder before anger tugs at me and pulls me away from him.

'She's pissed off. Why did you come here?'

'Didn't she tell you?'

'Yeah, she did.'

Serena cuts in, 'They said he needs to be monitored all night, in case of concussion, and' – she folds her arms, scowling at Dad – 'he has nowhere booked to stay.'

'I thought I would be staying here.'

Serena and I chime with *really?* and *seriously?* at the same time.

Dad shrugs and all of a sudden he looks like a greying teen.

Since when did my parents decide not to be grown-ups anymore? Were they always like this and now I'm getting older I'm paying more attention? Or maybe they're just letting us see more of the reality of who they are behind the curtain of being our parents.

I'm still reeling in my head about Mum accusing Dad of multiple affairs, but I know this isn't the right time of day to pull on that string.

'You can stay on my couch. I will wait up with you.' Christos looks down at my dad, like he's the adult talking to a foolish kid.

'That's very kind, mate. But you really don't have to. I'm sure one of the places in the village can put me up.'

'I'll come with you.' I look up into Christos's kind face and squeeze his arm in thanks. 'It's not fair for you to stay up and watch our idiot father—'

'Oi!' Dad protests.

'I'll come and sleep on the chair,' I continue. 'Let me just grab some things, OK?'

Christos nods and I begin to jog back towards the house.

Feet tap along behind me.

'Lorena, wait up,' Serena hisses into the dark of the house.

'What's up?'

We both try to jog on tiptoe up the stairs, darting into my room. Only switching the light on once we're inside so we don't draw attention to ourselves with Mum.

'I didn't know, I promise. If I'd known he was coming, I would've said something. I thought things weren't great with that Megan. Little things in the background of the calls made me think it wasn't all champagne and candles anymore. But I didn't expect this, not in a million years.'

'Serena, calm down. I believe you.'

I dart about the room, grabbing knickers and shorts and make-up to put in my backpack.

'Can you grab my toothbrush for me?' I glance up at her as I tuck a towel in the bag.

'Sure.' She slides out of the door, only opening it as much as is necessary for her to slip through.

Apparently, we've all reverted tonight. The way she slithered out reminds me of our late-night chats in my room. When they were done, she would barely open the door to slip out into the dark and down the landing to her room.

She slides back in and passes me the brush and a small tube of toothpaste. It must be one of her travel ones. It's not mine.

'Thanks.' I grab the toothbrush and words bubble up before either of us let go. 'Mum told me you know I slept with Christos. I thought maybe you didn't hear when I said or . . . I'm sorry. It just happened. I'm really sorry—'

'It's OK. I don't care.'

'I should've told you.'

'You did. I chose to block it out when I should've been asking girly questions and supporting you back on the horse.'

'Please never word it like that again.'

She lets go of the toothbrush and we both let out a trapped laugh as I finish packing my bag.

'You didn't speak to him about it, did you?'

'In front of Dad? Yeah, of course.' She nods overly enthusiastically. 'We both know how Dad just *loves* to know all about our sex lives, and I thought *Hey, do you know what will make tonight so much better? Telling Dad Lorena has slept with the guy taking us to get his cut fixed up.*' She lowers her chin and raises both her eyebrows, waiting for me to say something.

'OK, OK, I get it. Thank you. I'm still sorry, I know you liked him, and I accidently slept with him.'

Her eyes narrow. '*Accidently*,' she hums before continuing. 'It doesn't matter. Now it's all out in the open, I want all the details when you're back. How long you've been seeing each other, where it's all going.'

I freeze. 'We aren't seeing each other. I've told you. I don't want a relationship ever, ever again. I wasn't joking.'

'For God's sake, not this again.'

'And Christos is perfect, because he doesn't want one either.'

Her eyes roll. 'The reason you think he's perfect is because he's an idiot like you? Who hurt him so bad then? I guess you can both be miserable forever.' Her eyes bulge on the word *forever*.

'Is that what put you off him? I really thought you would hate me for this. I was terrified.' I swing my bag on to my back.

'Actually . . .' Serena pulls at the seams of her shorts, the legs down, the waist up. 'I have something I need to tell you, but not now, OK? There's enough going on right now. Tomorrow? OK?'

I search her face. Her perfect polish has slipped. She's beautiful with or without make-up, but right now her mascara has rubbed black marks under her eyebrows and a touch under her eyes.

It's been a long day for all of us.

'Fine. But I'll hold you to that, you've got me intrigued now.'

'You know that's all I want in life.' She grins, tilting her head in a perfect selfie pose.

We embrace and I pull her in a little tighter than normal.

'I can't believe Dad is here,' she whispers close to my ear.

I close my eyes again to stop myself thinking about what the hell is going to come next. I used to have everything planned out. Every detail of my life.

This year changed all of that.

Chapter Forty-Three

'It seems like days since we were here, not hours.' I shake my head at all the thoughts rattling around in there. 'So much has happened today, it feels more like a week.'

Christos doesn't reply. He puts the water bottle back in the fridge before passing me a full glass.

'Thanks.'

Even way past midnight, and after a full day's work and making dinner for me, Christos still looks good. His deep tan looks like rust in the kitchen strip light.

'Serena knows about us.'

'*Us?*' Christos leans against the same counter as me.

'Not *us*. But what happened. She seemed fine about it. She's never fine about things that could be made into fun and drama. It was like a calm alien had taken over. That or Mum and Dad's drama has actually overloaded her. She's reached her maximum limit.'

'I'm not that much drama, am I?' Dad appears in the doorway of the kitchen.

'Yes, you are.' I point to the water Christos has left on the kitchen table for him. 'That's yours.'

'Thanks.' He picks it up and stands opposite us before leaning on the table.

'I wouldn't do that.' Christos takes his weight off the counter and points towards Dad. 'Matt, the table, it is not that stable. One of the legs has come loose.'

'Really?' I tilt my head, thinking how well it held our weight.

Christos shoots me a look over his shoulder and says slowly, 'Yes. It happened very recently.'

'Not to worry. I think we should all be getting some sleep, don't you?' Dad steps away from the table. 'Thanks again for letting me stay, Christos.'

'It is no bother.' Christos looks right at me, not at Dad in the slightest, and says, 'If you need anything, I'm only upstairs.' As though my dad is someone I need to be worried around.

We all move towards the living room and while Christos makes his way up to bed, I settle on the armchair and Dad plumps the cushions on the sofa. In the lamplight, he faffs about before plonking himself down to face me.

'Do you think she'll forgive me? I was just being an old fool, easily persuaded by a pretty face. I've seen her pissed off before, but . . . blimey, you should've seen her. She's never gone for me like that before.'

'No, Dad, I don't think she'll forgive you, and quite frankly, if she did, I would lose all respect for her.'

'Don't be like that.' His face falls as easily as a house of cards.

'Like what? You treat her like shit on your shoe and expect to be able to scrape her off, dust her down and everything to be normal again. Only now you've got the bonus of a beach house in Corfu. No, Dad. I love you, but, come on! If someone treated me like that, would you want me to stay with them?'

'It's different, it's us. Anyway, if it was a genuine mistake . . .'

'Seriously?'

He pushes his fingers through his thick grey hair and lies back on the sofa, crossing his ankles.

'This is a funny old place for a young bloke. Looks more like an old lady's gaff without the ornaments.'

I pull a hairband off my wrist and tug my hair back into a low ponytail as I contemplate what the hell I'm going to do with this man. The one who told me men should always treat me with respect and is now saying it's OK to lie if it was somehow a genuine mistake.

'I'm going to get some air. You get some sleep. I'll check on you later. Night, Dad.'

I head towards the kitchen and out of the back door, then I march up the concrete stairs, using my phone as a torch, and place myself back where the evening started.

This is the time of night reserved for wildlife. The bats and the owls and the millions of cicadas singing. Most of the distant lights have been extinguished and peace crawls up from the sea and settles on people's houses and hotels for the night.

Sadly, the peace hasn't reached me.

I wonder whether Mum and Serena are awake, if Mum came out of her room and whether they're talking out a plan without me. All I want is for them to be OK. I had wanted for the next time I saw Dad to be as far from this as it gets. I wanted it to be simple, to find a new solid base of a relationship for us to work on.

He's taken a sledgehammer to everything.

I yawn and stretch, tired but still wide awake.

I have half a mind to go back down there now and scream and cry. But that's not me. That's never been me. I'm the one who gets things done and Serena is the one allowed to be emotional. I'm the one who keeps it together and holds her hand.

'Do you need company?'

I whip my head round. The shadow of Christos lingers at where I guess the top of the stairs is.

'Didn't you need a torch to get up here? You must have the eyes of a cat.'

'The stairs go past my window. I saw you come up. I'm no cat, but I am used to sitting here in the dark.'

'You can't have had your light on.'

Christos moves towards me. A flash from a lighter illuminates the night and makes him look like he's about to tell me a horror story. That or set light to his beard.

The only difference to earlier is, he hasn't got a shirt on and the burning lighter isn't the only fire he lit. I wriggle in my seat, wishing his beautiful distraction wasn't another thing to contend with today.

He leans forward and lights the candle we abandoned earlier in the evening. I guess I can count that as yesterday now.

'No, my light was off but there are no shutters or curtains and I could see you stamping your feet. How is your father?'

An involuntary growl rumbles in my throat and my chest. 'Infuriating? Arrogant? A bloody great night-ruining nuisance? I'm exhausted but the thought of being in a room with him is enough to keep me awake with sheer anger at his stupidity.'

'You can stay in my room with me. If you like?'

My eyes meet his. In the flickering candlelight he must've read all my thoughts from that one simple motion.

'It doesn't *have* to mean that.'

'I should check on my dad.'

'There were no signs of concussion. But I agree with you, maybe you set an alarm? Check on him every hour?'

'Mmm . . . maybe every three?'

'I need to be up in four.'

'Every four it is then.'

Christos chuckles before he blows out the candle and we follow my phone light part-way down the stairs, then climb in his window.

◆ ◆ ◆

Moonlight streams in through the window and settles on the tips of Christos's eyelashes. He looks so peaceful with his eyes closed, resting on the pillow next to me.

No matter how silver the moon, nothing could make his rich, ruddy skin look pale or insipid. Instead, he looks like he's been carefully sprinkled with a silver highlight.

I hadn't realised there were no shutters or curtains. I guess alcohol and a naked Christos were enough to stop me noticing anything much about the world around me.

'You know, if you want to sleep, you close your eyes.'

'How do you know they're not closed?'

'I can feel you looking at me.'

He opens one eye and squints at me with a small smile on his lips.

'Thank you for today. For talking to me, for helping with my dad. You might just be the best friend I've ever had. If I did want to fall in love, which I don't, then you really would be perfect.'

I regret the words as soon as they pass my lips. His eyes are darker than any I've ever seen in my life and I stole the smile from them, leaving a hollow sadness to weave its way in.

'I can't be happy.'

'One day, hopefully you will find peace.'

'I would make you miserable. Every year I get so drunk I pass out, I never go to the sea or leave the island, I have nothing to give anyone.'

'And yet you've given me everything. You give everyone everything, all the time. You put others first, you spread love

281

and kindness . . . Also, this year you didn't pass out. You stayed awake with me.'

I place my hand on his cheek and let my thumb gently smooth along his cheek bone.

His words from earlier dance around me, that he didn't want to lose me, that being near me is torture, because he doesn't want to be happy. It's a strange compliment, but oddly one I understand.

His face moves towards mine and our mouths come together in a soft and tender kiss. Our tongues meet briefly before we both pull away and say our goodnights.

I roll over and close my eyes with Christos's kiss still lingering on my lips and in my head, leaving me tingling all over.

Chapter
Forty-Four

'We can still turn around and go home and it wouldn't matter, Mum.'

'Lorena, I am perfectly fine. Let's enjoy the party.'

Serena and I pass a look between us behind her back, but we don't say anything as Mum presses the doorbell.

I'd be surprised if anyone could hear the doorbell over the music and chatter that's audible from out here. It's not like the door will be locked. Mum knows that. She takes this moment to drag in a heavy breath through her nose. She's probably taking her last opportunity to collect herself. I can understand it. This party is likely to be filled with people from her past. My hope is that someone will let slip why she left in the first place.

Mum has refused to even acknowledge Dad's existence today. Other than to explicitly tell us we *are not to tell Spiros* that Dad is here. She said it would be too upsetting and she doesn't want to ruin their relationship all over again before they've even had a chance to truly heal it. Which makes me wonder if Dad was why she left, or if he was somehow involved in it all. Maybe my grandparents didn't like him much. Spiros did say he thought it was nothing much, after all.

Christos has said Dad can stay at his for as long as he needs to. He's always there, doing helpful deeds and pretending he's the bad guy when all he does is good.

When I woke up this morning, Christos was watching me sleep. I had to throw his earlier comment back in his face, the one about sleeping with your eyes open. There was a softness about him. Like something had shifted. He didn't instantly shut off, and neither did I.

Maybe I imagined it. Maybe he was feeling a bit lighter after talking about Nephele for the first time in eleven years, or maybe it was seeing my ugly life sprawled out on his sofa that made him feel better about his.

The front door opens to reveal Spiros and Eleni, arms around each other and champagne glasses in hand, welcoming us into the party.

Cheeks are kissed and we're sucked right into the action, being introduced to people who we're distantly related to, or who know all about us, but we have no idea about them. I do my best to stick close to Mum and Serena, knowing they must be feeling fragile.

I am.

I get caught by a woman whose name I've already forgotten, and her son, who I think she's pushing on me. He seems uninterested. Polite and chatty, but not in the way she perhaps hopes by the way she's talking him up to me and asking about my current relationship status.

A Greek voice sounds in my ear, greeting the woman and the man I'm talking to. I can feel his voice in my chest, then his familiar fingers wrap around my upper arm.

'And Lorena.' Christos kisses my cheeks as though it's been weeks or months, not a matter of hours since we last spoke.

'You made it.' I beam up at him before turning back to the people I've been talking to.

'Please excuse us,' he says in Greek.

Christos's hand finds my lower back and we slide past them and move towards the veranda. Unlike the intimate gathering of family from almost a month ago, the house is bursting with people and life. They spew out in all directions with glasses of champagne or olive-oil cocktails. Canapés are everywhere. They're all dainty and elegant. There are lots of fresh prawns, mini pastries and, of course, olives.

'Thanks for saving me from the set-up.' I nudge into Christos and shoot him a smile.

'You know he is gay. She wants to marry him off to someone who doesn't already know.'

'She wants me as his beard?'

We find the only available spot to stand next to the Perspex railing to look out across the party and the hectares of olive groves beyond.

'*Beard?*' Christos leans his forearms on the Perspex and strokes his chin.

'A beard covers your face.' I reach up and gently tug on his. 'I'd be used to cover his true identity. It's not a bad set-up, actually. If I married him, we could both live separate lives and no one would go on at us to settle down with someone or fall in love. Although . . .' – removing my hand from his face, I hold a finger up – 'in this day and age, I'm surprised his mother's on the hunt for a beard.'

Christos stands up straight, and instead leans the side of his thigh against the clear plastic.

'His father is very old and very religious. His mother knows, she looks to find a way to keep them both happy.'

As I nurse my cocktail, I can feel his eyes on me.

'Lorena?' There's a dark richness in his voice. That tone that makes me feel like liquid.

When I don't answer, he hooks my chin and makes me look at him.

'You say I *deserve* to be happy, I *deserve* to let myself have these things. You should not let one man taking your money stop you having what you deserve. He should not make you think marrying a *beard* is the right thing.'

A smile penetrates my face and rises like the sun in the morning.

'*I* would be the beard. Not him.'

He rolls his eyes and catches the eye of a waiter, who brings over a tray of cocktails. I pick up a fresh one and he takes his first.

'You look handsome tonight.'

'Do I not normally look handsome?'

I tilt my head and don't give him an answer.

He does, though.

Despite his attempts to hide and lean into the messy, rugged look, it looks like a stylish choice: to have bed head, a bushy beard, the grandad collar shirt and smart linen trousers. It's a look that on some people would look too hippy-dippy or too messy. On him, it looks like a well-thought-out style. One that suits him.

I don't know what it is. But on him, it works. His handsome face, piercing black eyes and well-built frame could probably make anything look good.

When I don't respond, instead taking a moment to study him, a blush touches his bronzed cheek bones.

'You look good too. This is normal for you, of course.' I look down at the skimming olive-green fabric; it seems like the perfect choice. 'Your dress is beautiful.' He leans close to my ear and in his low caramel voice says, 'But it would look better on the floor.'

'We should take a photo.' I have to change the subject away from *that*.

'Don't they have a man for that?'

'Yes, but come on.'

I dig my elbow into his ribs, pull my phone from the bag on my shoulder and stretch out my arm to take a picture of us together. The very first one of just us.

'Hello, lovebirds. Am I interrupting?'

We separate to find Serena, arms folded and head tilted, watching us.

'*Lovebirds?*' I screw up my face. 'We're friends.'

'Uh-huh. In my whole entire life, Lorena, I've never known you to sleep with one of your *friends*.'

'Serena.' I narrow my eyes on her.

'Am I wrong?' There's a tone in her voice that makes my stomach feel like someone's run it over.

'Can I borrow your *friend*, please, Christos?' Serena links her arm in mine.

'See you around.' He smiles and walks back towards the house.

He doesn't rise to the sarcastic tone of the word 'friend' when it falls from Serena's lips, nor does he seem at all bothered by it.

We begin to take steps down to the swimming pool and the gardens. We stay linked together, more to keep ourselves steady on our heels than anything else.

'I wish you'd told me how much you like Christos, Lorena. Seeing you two together like that . . . I'm hurt you didn't feel you could trust me. I know I liked him for all of five minutes, but come on, we're sisters.'

'I didn't want to hurt you or make you mad, then I sort of did tell you—'

'OK, that one's on me, but if I'm honest, it's the lie about your feelings that hurts more. You two are so clearly more than a hookup. It was different when I thought it was a hookup to get over Jonah . . . this is way more than that.'

'It's really not.'

287

Serena stops. With her cypress-green eyes, she stares deeply into mine.

'You're not just lying to me, then, you're lying to yourself.' She shakes her head and exhales.

'Seriously—'

'I don't want to argue about it. In fact, there's something I've been keeping from you too.'

'I thought we told each other everything?'

'Like you've been telling me all about your feelings for Christos?'

'To be fair, I *did* tell you about him and there are no feelings.'

'Agree to disagree on that one. And you were happy to let me carry on pretending I had misunderstood for weeks. You moan about Mum hiding things and telling half a story, or Dad keeping secrets, but we all do it. We all think we know best and, because we love each other, we all think we're doing the right thing. All of us, but we can't all be right – however much Mum says she's always right, she's not. None of us are.'

Serena's words rattle against my bones and absorb deep into them. She's right. This whole time I've been lying, thinking somehow my deception is more valid because my reasons are more valid, but I guess everyone thinks that.

'I'm really sorry.'

'It's OK. How boring would it be if every night we relayed every single detail of each other's lives? I'm OK not knowing everything, babe.' She playfully tugs on my dress. 'I hope this makes you see things a little differently about Dad. Before you say anything' – she holds up her hands – 'I'm not saying what he did was OK, but sometimes we think we can hide things and get away with things and we don't start out wanting to hurt anyone.'

My head sways from side to side. 'Fine. I guess I'll think about it. Now tell me what *you've* been hiding from me.'

She takes both of my hands in hers. They seem so soft and small.

'I know you don't want to hear this, but, I'm in love.'

I stumble to find words and eventually settle on, 'Who?'

'Petros.'

'Giórgos's business partner?'

'The one and only. He asked if I would show him round. Blind leading the blind of course, because I'm as new to the area as him, but we got on so well. He quickly made me forget all about Christos. It's why I wasn't *really* bothered when you slept together. I'm only hurt you couldn't talk to me about it. I was already doing some *sleeping* of my own. I just wasn't ready to tell you, and have you look all confused because you've decided to take against happiness because of that shit Jonah. I'll never forgive him if he's stolen that from you for good. I can forgive the stealing and the desperation and all that crap. It's money. It's stuff. The man had issues and it's not right, but you can learn from it, you can earn more money. But to steal your belief in love and family . . . I'll never forgive that.'

'Dad didn't help.'

'I take it he decided to do as he was told and stay at Christos's tonight instead of going exploring or whatever it was he was talking about earlier.'

'Yeah. Forget him, though, I *am* happy for you. I want to know everything. Just because I don't want to do the whole relationship bit anymore doesn't mean you have to hide yours from me.'

A pang of guilt hits me. It's my fault she hasn't told me. I've been closed off from her, the way Mum has been with me, the way Jonah hid problems from me, and because I'm closed off, she has been too. I've been closed off with Mum too, not wanting any judgement and using the excuse of trying not to hurt anyone. Without knowing it, I've been hurting myself by keeping part of me from them.

'I hate Jonah so fucking much,' Serena puffs.

'Don't.'

'I do.'

'What's going to happen with Petros? He goes back to Athens tomorrow.'

'I know . . .' She swings her body slightly from side to side, like a little girl might. Her neat waves swing around her shoulders and her cream dress follows suit.

'I'm going to visit him in ten days. Or that was the plan, anyway. As long as we can get Dad back to England and Mum settled again, then I'll be off to stay in Athens for a few weeks. Maybe a month.' She leans in close to me, gripping my arm with her spare hand. 'With the wedding and Petros and me, there's talk of moving their office to Corfu. If things carry on like they are, Eleni might get her dream of Giórgos moving back here.'

'That's so exciting!'

'I know.' She grips my arm even tighter than before. 'I'll go find him now. Don't be hurt, but you're the last to know. Now we're well and truly official.'

She turns and looks about on tiptoes to see over people and round them, before almost skipping away to find him.

I shouldn't be, but I am hurt. It's not like I wouldn't celebrate her happiness. There's nothing I want more than to see her smile. We've all got tangled lives and trying to keep the mess contained just seems to make it more messy.

Nephele crosses my mind. Twenty-four. The same age as Serena. She should be here, falling in love and enjoying being with her family.

I wonder what happened to Christos's parents and his little brother. I've wanted to ask him, but there's been no time since last night.

Today has been a blur of babysitting Dad and Mum in separate turns. I'd be with one while Serena was with the other, then we'd switch. I remember being so happy on New Year's Eve about starting this year. How it was going to be the best and most exciting year. Funny how the best-laid plans can be easily snatched away.

I catch sight of Christos, chatting to an attractive woman with big wild curly hair. In fact, he's not chatting. She is. She's talking to him intently, and he looks as though he's sinking into himself while her drink begins to slop from one side to the other.

There's no sign of Mum or Serena now, so I head in their direction to save him from this lovely-looking woman, who I'm sure is getting on his nerves.

She's talking in Greek but I can understand some. It's fast, about his mother and how dreadful it still is for her, how he should talk? Maybe talk to her?

'Hello, I'm Lorena, Christos's friend. I don't think we've met yet.'

I hold out my hand but she doesn't take it.

'Of course, it makes much sense for you to have each other for friends.' She cackles slightly. Now I'm closer to her, I can see the scowl lines in her forehead and deep set around her mouth. 'I see your mother, she has returned. I could never believe when I hear it. I had to see for myself. Not *Matt* with her. After what she did to Kaitlyn. Her and your dreadful father.'

'Lorena, come away, she's had too much to drink.' Christos takes my hand but I snatch it away.

'Who are you?' I point at the woman.

'I am an old friend of Eleni and Spiros. I introduced them, you know.' She carries on with her heavy Greek accent. 'I am a good friend of Vaso, *his* mother.' Her finger digs the air towards Christos. 'Maybe he had not mention his mother? Your father, he is sick, you know this? *Sick.*' She repeats it in Greek – I'm pretty sure it was a repeat, even with the fast pace of her words.

'Don't talk to him like that.' I wish I could spit Greek words out of my mouth instead of having them all stuck in my head.

'Lorena, what's going on?' Serena's hand is on my other shoulder and in the corner of my eye I can see Petros on the other side of her, puffing his chest out. It's the opposite to Christos. I've never seen him look so deflated.

'This is the other sister. Yes, you look like him. In the eye, they are the same. Do not trust her.' The woman waves her drink at Petros. 'She will be a nasty cheat like her father.'

She's taken it too far and I know my sister too well.

I thrust my arm out across Serena and begin to drag her away as she starts to raise her voice. I'm surprised at how much she can swear in Greek. I'm sort of impressed. We stumble back as the woman says things back in Greek before someone else steps in front of her, stopping the onslaught.

I can only hope Mum didn't hear any of that.

'I need a moment alone with my sister.' I barely look at Christos or Petros and link arms with Serena while she rants about *that stupid bitch* and *how dare she it's none of her business.*

We stop around the fairy lights in the firepit.

I begin to pace, overtaking from Serena's ranting. 'That woman knows something, more than what happened with Megan. She looks like Mum's age. Dad cheated? Back then? On Mum? It doesn't make sense. Maybe she was making it up to be horrid. I'm so confused. Dad cheated back then?'

'I already know.' Serena stops pacing, smooths her hands over her arms, then places her hands on her hips.

There's something about her tone. It's not like she's agreeing, like, *yeah, I know.* It's more than that.

'You already know what?' I do my best to stay blank. I have no idea what she's talking about, but I can't show her that. I have to hold it together now.

'Before you say anything, I was trying to protect you and him and I know that's ridiculous, but you've had such a down on him, anyone would think he'd cheated on you. I mean, like earlier, you're part blaming him for not wanting a relationship ever again.' She points back towards the party before letting her hand drop to her side.

My brain scrambles about.

'I mean' – her hands find her hips again and she grips so hard she wrinkles the fabric of her fitted dress – 'it's in the past. We all make mistakes. That bitch had no right trying to drag it up. If Mum doesn't want us to know—'

'Serena, stop. I think I know what happened.' It's not exactly a lie, more a giant exaggeration based on what I've just heard the woman say. 'But you tell me what you think you know and—'

'I *do* know. It's not what I *think* I know. I spoke to Eleni before confirming it all with Dad. I've been here a lot, with Petros. After a few drinks, I needled some of it out of Eleni and got the rest from Dad.'

'What's true?' I stamp my foot and screw my hands up into little balls at my sides.

Mum's voice cuts through the air between us like a hacksaw. 'That your father was here to marry someone else.'

Chapter Forty-Five

I stumble back like Mum's voice has its own mass and it's knocked me over.

'I wanted to protect you both, and him . . . and maybe myself. Maybe I've been selfish with the information. I never wanted you to see me like that. As the other woman. That woman back there never liked me, by the way. It didn't help that the woman your father was here to marry was a good friend of hers.'

'He wasn't here on holiday with his friends?' I whisper.

'No.'

'He was here to get married?'

'Yes.'

'You knew all this and didn't bother to tell me?' I turn to point at Serena.

It's not her fault she didn't tell me. She's been trying to protect me in the same way I was trying to protect her. I know that now, but it doesn't stop me craving answers.

'I was worried about you. Mum didn't know I knew.'

'Lorena, this was never your sister's story to tell.'

'You're right. It was yours and Dad's. I expect him to not bother to tell me anything, but I used to think we were close. I'm not a bloody child. I don't need your protection anymore, Mum.' I stab my finger to my chest. 'After Jonah, I got up and got dressed and put a smile on my fucking face and carried on living, carving something new. Doing my best, but even that wasn't enough for you to see how I can handle the shit life throws at me—'

'Lorena, stop it,' Mum demands, gritting her teeth. 'I never said you were a child, but this was never about you—' She steps towards me and I take one step back.

'I can't believe you were the cheat all along. No wonder you've wanted to hide it all from us. You're just as bad as Dad.'

Mum's eyes reflect the fairy lights as they fill with tears. She doesn't let them fall. She holds it in, even with her jaw jutting out like she wants to fight. We both know if she tries to open her mouth to call me out, all she'll do is weep.

'I've got to go.' I move past the two women in my life who mean the most.

I thought we were a triangle, holding each other up. Even triangles can crumble under the weight of hiding the truth.

Mum tries to catch my arm, call my name, but I can feel my own eyes beginning to show my pain. There're people everywhere. Keeping my head down, I do my best to avoid them all.

This is Giórgos's and Aliki's last night to celebrate with everyone they know before they organise the big day. It's a celebration. There's no way I want to ruin that.

I'd like to say a last goodbye, but I can't. I have to find a way out of here. The walls are pulling closer in and the skirt of my dress catches around my legs, making me feel claustrophobic and more tangled than ever.

Weaving in and out of people without getting stopped is tricky. Each time someone tries to chat to me, I tell them I really need to use the bathroom and move away as fast as I can without looking like I'm running. My heels catching every now and then as I skip and glide between happy faces.

I make it out of the front door without adding to the insanity, only to realise I don't know how to get home. I don't even want to go home. There's nowhere I want to go.

That's when I see him, sitting on a low wall before the sloping driveway with all the cars parked along it. It's as though he's there waiting for me.

'Why are you this side of the party?'

Christos looks up at me and I slowly take steps towards him.

'I was going to leave, but then . . .' He looks me over as I stop only a few feet from where he's sitting. 'I·did not want to leave you here if you need me.'

I can't look at him. Instead, I tilt my chin to the stars and do my best not to let the tears fall and ruin my make-up. I put real time into it today. It was the perfect distraction for everything that has been going on. It kept me away in my room, alone with my thoughts for an hour, which was what I really needed.

I'm not ready to ruin all that hard work. I've had enough of my hard work ruined this year.

'How is life this fucked-up?' I'm not sure whether I'm asking the stars or Christos.

He stands up, but I still don't look at him. I'm aware of him hovering over me in my peripheral vision.

'Come here.' He pulls me into an embrace. One I wasn't expecting. One I didn't know I needed until his arms are there, around me, and my face is pressed gently against his shirt and I'm inhaling his scent.

His masculine smell is a comfort to me now. Something that calms me against myself.

'Let's get out of here.' I look up at him, and he nods.

He takes my hand. It's the first time he's held my hand like this. Like we're a couple walking back together after a night out. It's big and rough in mine as our fingers knit together.

I'm not sure who needs who more. That woman, that witch, went for both of us, and as far as I know, she was completely unprovoked.

'Are you OK to drive?' I study him under the dim light of the stars.

'I had one drink. It's all I was going to have. Someone has to keep an eye on your dad.' I can hear the laughter in his voice with the music and chatter filtering out from the party.

'Don't. For a moment I thought we were going to the peace of your house, and we would be alone to hide from all the arseholes in the world. I'd forgotten he was going to be there.'

'We can hide on my roof. He will not be checking there. If we are quiet.'

'I love you.'

As soon as the three little words slip out of my mouth, vomit feels like it's close behind. My heart doesn't stop beating. That would be preferable. Instead, it punches my ribcage in a desperate attempt to escape.

I begin to stutter, 'I, I meant I love the idea. Not I love you.' I screw up my face and remove my hand from his to hide in it. 'Could this night get any worse?'

'Did anyone die?'

'No.'

'Then it could always get worse. I knew what you meant. You're happy we can hide. Don't worry about it.'

We slip into his van and leave behind the disaster of family and the heartache of the past.

As if it's actually possible to run away from that.

Christos has tried. Tried to run away from the past, but it's always there. A shadow that's always attached, no matter how far we run.

Although, he still lives on the same island he grew up on, and I've moved over a thousand miles to escape my shadow. I thought mine was haunting me. But after only a few months I've loosened the ties to Jonah at the very least. With Christos, it's way more complicated.

'How old were you when Nephele died?'

'Eighteen. Old enough to know better.'

'I'm sorry about what that woman was saying to you. You don't deserve that.'

'Nothing she said was lies. Not about me. To you, she was wrong. You are nothing like your father. I don't think this of Serena either. Not that side of him anyway. He isn't all bad, you know.'

'Thanks. Well, I got to find out why Mum and Dad never came back to Corfu and what the big shame on the family is. Apparently, Dad was here to get married to some other woman and went off with Mum. *She* was the original affair.' I begin to shake my head at the incredibility of it all.

It's impossible to know anyone or trust anyone. Male, female, it doesn't matter. We're all as hard to read as our own DNA. An impossible web of information that forms a person but with no clue what information is wrapped around the next double helix.

I exhale through my teeth, knowing that I'm as big a fraud as anyone. No one can be honest *all* the time. Serena showed me that at least. Forced me to see I'm not better.

'I do love you, actually. But as a friend. OK?' I look over at him in the driver's seat and rest my chin on my left shoulder. 'Thank you for looking after me from the moment we met.'

'Me? Look after you? Is that possible? I had to force help on you when I know you need it. You are the most independent woman I know.' His eyes briefly flick over me, his face only just lit by the dash. 'I love you too,' he adds, 'as a friend.'

His hand reaches for mine, and we hold hands comfortably for the rest of the journey back through the winding roads of Corfu.

Chapter Forty-Six

'This is going to hurt in the morning.' My voice is strained under the sea of stars.

'Don't pretend you don't love it.'

He's right.

There's something magical and primitive about sleeping under stars. Even if it's on a concrete roof with only two duvets as a mattress and a few sheets to cover us. I'm already well aware my hips are going to hate me tomorrow.

'I'll be impressed if we aren't bitten to death while we're out here too, you know,' I add.

'Still worth it?'

'Totally.'

It's been a hot summer, hotter than I've ever lived through for this length of time. Sleeping outside is the perfect remedy to cool the skin. I didn't have anything with me, only the clothes I was wearing to the party. Christos offered me some of his clothes, but my dress is actually pretty comfortable.

Without thinking, I snuggle into Christos, finding the nook in the curve of his solid arms and chest.

'Do you know any of the constellations? I only know about three.' I look up at the vastness of the sky. Night is the only time when the curve of the world is tangible as the stars stream all the way around.

'Not many. That was for Nephele. She was going to study the stars. That was her dream.'

'And what was your dream? Back then?'

'I didn't have one yet. We were not a rich family. I worked all summers, and with my father we got the little boat. My mother would clean in some of the hotels and my father would fix things. I was OK at school, but Nephele was very smart. Every day I wish it was me at the bottom of the sea, not her.'

'You can't think like that.'

'That woman tonight, Andrea, that's her name, she was right. It was my fault. I was a bad brother and son. My parents lost their daughter and they didn't even have a body to bury, to mourn her the way she deserves. They must be like me, always wondering what happened to her . . . Now my father is sick, and I'm not there to help. They do not want me there and I don't blame them.'

'What happened with your parents? After Nephele?'

'They never *said* they blame me. But after a week of searching and crying we were told there was no hope, she would never be found, and I left. Nothing would ever be the same. I broke our family and we all knew they would be better without me.'

'I hate hearing you talk like this. You're the most generous and caring person I've ever met. You're completely selfless—'

'No. I'm not.'

'You are.'

'No. If I was, I would never let myself be around you this much. Like you this much when I can never be what you deserve.'

He looks down at me, nestled into his nook, and his beard tickles my face. I tilt my chin up towards him.

Softly, our lips find each other, and my hand slides along his chest, over the bristles of his beard and behind his head as his hand wraps around me, bringing me in.

This feels different to before. I should get up and run, but I can't.

His rough hand runs up my back as our mouths combine, deeply, tenderly. One finger, then the next, slips under my spaghetti strap and edges it down over my shoulder.

The sound of my zip cuts through the air as he takes his weight on one arm, lingering close to me, just about over me, and begins to inch down my dress.

I fumble to undo his shirt buttons with one hand. I could do this so easily before, when I had more to drink or was pretending to be angry. Suddenly, my mind has been cast adrift and even simple tasks seem like they're for geniuses.

Enlisting my other hand, I get his buttons undone and tug off his shirt, stopping him from removing my dress. For a brief moment our mouths stop kissing, but like magnets we're soon back together.

His hands work down my dress to my waist, until our bare skin is pressed together. I lift my hips and let him completely undress me before doing the same for him.

When we were together before, it was like we were both starved of attention and affection, greedily taking it from the other, no matter the cost. We didn't care whether we pulled or pinched or ripped off clothes, anything to reach a goal and see who could get there the quickest.

Here, under a sheet on his concrete roof, exposed to the world and the elements, we take our time. His hands travel my skin like a nomad moving from place to place. There isn't a part of me that doesn't get the delicious sensation of his fingers trailing across it.

For a while, my hands cling to the back of his neck for safety. Holding on and wondering what could possibly happen next. Even though I know all too well.

I know exactly what it feels like to have his weight on me and the pressure of him inside me.

It's something I could never erase from my mind, however much I wish I could.

I hate to admit he's the best I've had. I thought, being in love with Jonah, that he was the best. That together, of course it *must* be. We were going to be married, after all. I let myself believe we were special when we weren't.

It wasn't. He wasn't.

All thoughts of Jonah disintegrate as Christos's fingers move down between my legs. My eyes lock shut and an involuntary sigh falls from my lips.

My focus narrows completely, unable to comprehend anything or make sense of the world around me. Instead, my conscious mind circles around with Christos's fingers until I'm holding my breath and arching my back like I'm a puppet and he's my master.

Before I can recover from the haze, a new focus has me in rapture, pinpointing on the sensation of him sinking into me as my feet wrap around his calves to pull his weigh down on to me.

This is nothing like before. Nothing like our crazy animalistic trysts.

In the cool of the night, under the blazing stars, our pace is slow. My hands still cling to the back of his neck, and our foreheads press together and our eyes stay locked.

I should look away.

I can't look away.

My back arches and my hips rise against him, both willing him to go faster while wishing this could last forever.

The stars around him blur into a halo before his lips find mine again and we can't hold in whatever this is anymore.

We press together until the stars fade to black and my broken heart feels like it's shattering instead.

Chapter Forty-Seven

As the sun flickers into view over the deep-green curve of Corfu, we're still awake.

Instead of spending the night dwelling on it all, going over his pain, my pain, the hundred messages on my phone from Mum and Serena, or the ones he has from Spiros and Eleni, we've laughed.

We've shared stories that didn't dwell on pain. We laughed at the silly woman who stuck her nose in at the party, who we've agreed looked more of an idiot than we did.

'When do you think we should look at all our messages?' I rest my head on his shoulder. 'I'm dreading reading them. I think I have voicemails too.'

'Never.' The weight of his head rests on top of mine. 'You will see them all today. It will be fine.'

'And what about you? I'll see my family today and sort everything out. Do you think you can sort things out with your family?'

'No. My brother doesn't know me. I think they have let him forget me. Forget Nephele.'

'Surely they couldn't do that?'

'I hear things, from time to time. About how well he is doing . . . different things. I like to avoid these big family events that Eleni and Spiros host. Not that my parents would go, they know they helped me and look after me. They know I don't want to see them, and they don't want to remember the past. They only have Panayotis now. It's better this way. It hurts less. Not to be reminded.'

'If they can lose a child and move on, why can't you? What happened was not your fault. If anything, it was their fault, your parents' fault. They're the adults, not you. They said you could both go out on the boat and do what you like. They could've said no. You have your whole life ahead of you, I know Nephele wouldn't want this for you.'

'Don't try to blame them. I was eighteen, a man. I should have gone in the sea with her and not let her have all the sweets. I was lying in the boat, getting a tan and dreaming. Everything I did was wrong. They could never know how stupid I would be.'

'But—'

'Stop,' he groans with a quiet softness.

'But—'

'Stop.'

My skin prickles and bumps rise and ripple over my skin at the sharp tone of his voice.

'I should check on your dad.' Christos pulls away from me, like the separating of Velcro.

Even as the warmth of the sun spreads across Corfu one ray at a time, I'm left feeling cold. Hollow. Missing the feeling of his warmth and comfort next to me.

I know this feeling. I've felt something similar before and I know what it means.

It means I have to separate myself from Christos. No more nights on the roof, no more resting my head on his shoulder, no more holding his hand.

Last night was an extreme circumstance for us both. Neither of us could've seen the turn last night would take.

We were vulnerable. *I* was vulnerable.

Not in love.

I begin to put myself together and jump up to follow him while my chest feels as though it's being hollowed out. Carved and scooped, like a Halloween pumpkin.

'Wait for me. I'll come with you.'

Christos trots down the steps before swinging the unlocked door open to the kitchen. I gallop in behind him to find Dad's already up with the lark and sitting at the table. I'm hit with the smell of coffee as soon as I get close to the door.

'There you both are!' Dad almost throws his chair back to stand. 'I've been worried sick. Your mum called me—'

'She called *you*? *Mum?*' I stumble into the room with my shoes between my fingers.

Dad almost pushes past Christos to grip my arms like he's checking I'm real. Dark rings circle his conifer-green eyes and the lines on his face look like they've been carved deeper than ever.

'Yeah, she did. No matter what happens, we are always your parents and always bloody will be. Doesn't matter how old you are. She said something happened at the party and you disappeared. That's all she'd say. That, and if I saw you, I had to ring right away.'

Dad lets go of me and turns towards the table to pick up his phone.

'Your head's looking better, Dad.'

He briefly nods as he taps the screen of his phone before pressing it to his ear.

Guilt hits me hard.

Here's Dad smothering me in love and Christos's parents aren't here for him. What happened was an accident, and he's been unfairly blamed and deprived of love through his entire adult life, and here's me, with parents who will both stay up all night with worry even though I'm a grown adult.

Christos puts his head in the fridge like he's looking for something, standing hunched over it, unmoving, before closing it again and staring at the door instead.

'Thalia? She's here, she's safe . . . I don't know, I haven't asked. She walked in the door, and I called you like you asked.'

I move around the table and to Christos, placing my hand on the soft cotton of his shirt. The tension and heat in his shoulder blade radiates out into my fingertips.

'Christos, I'm really sorry.'

'It is fine. Please, don't even mention it.' He stays facing away from me and there's a darkness in his tone that screams for me to never speak of anything like this again.

My hand slips away like dust in the wind, vanishing.

'Your mum wants to know when you'll be home. She wants to talk to you.'

My eyes linger on Christos and all the pain he holds deep in his chest. True, raw, heartbreaking pain that I can't fix. Pain that maybe his parents could've fixed had they reassured him.

I need to give my mum the opportunity to reassure me. To give me the full picture before Dad or strangers at parties.

'Tell her I'll be there as soon as I can get a taxi.'

'I'll come with you,' Dad blurts out. He then falls into staggered words to Mum. My guess is she's instantly told him no, he isn't welcome in our house. Something like that. He's disgruntled but agrees. There's no way he can get back in Mum's good graces unless he does as he's told.

Not that he ever will. Not the way things were.

'I will take you.' Christos finally turns to face me, only now there's a wall that's been rebuilt. Last night, all barriers had been pulled down and away and there was nothing between us. Nothing.

Now there's a wall, and I'm glad he's put it up. It'll be easier this way. I'm glad he's strong enough to protect us both from us. I'm not sure I am anymore.

Chapter
Forty-Eight

I don't know how to say goodbye to Christos.

My seat belt clicks undone and I know I should be getting out of his van, but there's part of me that knows as soon as I leave, everything's over. Our perfect night is done and I have to carry on, back into my solitude.

It's silly. Dad is still staying with him for another few days before his flight home. I'll probably see him again later today. We'll still be working together too, but as soon as I get out of this van our one perfect time is officially gone. I know it is already. I pushed him too far and burst our bubble. But saying goodbye . . .

I don't know why this is so hard.

'Thank you, for letting me stay with you last night,' I begin.

I want to say more but my words slip away like driftwood back into the sea.

'No, I am grateful to you. You could have stayed with your family last night, they love you and care for you. I know that you will fix things. You saved me.'

For the first time since we were on the roof, he brings his dark eyes to meet mine. My heart pounds harder in my chest, making me light-headed as every atom feels like it's splitting in two.

He leans across and presses a soft kiss into my cheek, his beard gently scratching my face.

'Good luck.' His voice vibrates in my chest, like it's mine and not his at all. 'I am always here. If you need me.'

Tears sting the back of my eyes and a burning sensation rises up in my nose.

I briefly kiss his cheek in return, but I can't bring myself to say goodbye. Instead, I turn and slip out without a word.

Mum's already waiting at the door. I have no idea how long she's been standing there watching me and waiting for me to get out of the van. She's already dressed in wide-leg cotton trousers and a simple white T-shirt, but she doesn't look ready for the day. Her hair looks limp and her skin looks sallow.

She doesn't say a word. Instead, she pulls me into an embrace. My mum isn't usually stuck for words; normally, she overflows with them, finding them where others can't.

Her silence burns a hole in my chest.

The faint smell of perfume catches in my lungs. It's her favourite one. The one she saves for Christmas and Easter and parties. The one she says we shouldn't buy her because it's too expensive, but as soon as it's low, one of us will make sure she's got some for her birthday.

The deep floral notes linger from the night before. The image of her and Serena in among the fairy lights flashes through my mind and I pull from her embrace.

'You were the other woman first,' slips softly past my lips. The ugly truth, not shouted at a party, but laid out for us to see and acknowledge. A wedge holding open the door to a past no one wanted to talk about.

'And he was a cheat from the start,' she says blankly. 'Come. We need to talk.'

I follow her past the living room and take a seat at our new dining table. It still smells faintly like fresh varnish, and it leaves me a little dizzy. She sits opposite me.

'Where's Serena?'

'With Petros, before he leaves for Athens.'

'Oh . . . this early?'

'She didn't sleep well, he was here until late, but I told them to leave and get some sleep.'

'Oh.'

Mum stands up again and moves towards the kitchen. 'Would you like a drink? Have you eaten?' She's stalling. I can feel it.

'I'm fine, I had some water before I left Christos's.'

Mum comes back to her seat, smoothing her trousers as she sits back down.

'Mum, I've been thinking about it, and you don't have to tell me anything you don't want to. Clearly you don't want to, or you would have by now. That woman, whoever she was, was out of line and drunk. She had no right talking to me or Christos like that.'

'That's true, but I've been awake all night, thinking.' She tilts her head to the ceiling before slapping her hands down on the table and looking straight back at me. 'Get changed, let's go for a walk on the beach. I can't bear it in here. The heat is oppressive already.'

'OK . . .'

Mum's up and marching up the stairs with me in tow before I can even think.

It's still early. Really early. There won't be many people about. I'm exhausted and the idea of walking feels like a chore, but I can't resist the idea of sand between my toes, however tired I am.

Slipping into my room, I see there's a note on my pillow. It's a ripped piece of paper with Serena's oversized handwriting scrawled on it: *I love you xxx*

I press it to my chest.

There's no way she should've hidden everything from me. But I understand why she did it. She was as afraid of my reaction as I was about hers with Christos. She doesn't deserve to be my whipping boy. I don't deserve her.

We've both been withholding things from each other lately. Maybe we always do. Maybe she's right, I've been kidding myself thinking we tell each other everything. It's a childish notion and in the bright light of a new day, I wonder why I've held on to it for so long.

Pulling off last night's dress and underwear is a relief, one that makes my body ache for my bed. I push the desire to the back of my mind and slip on swimwear and a simple short white sundress.

Mum's feet pad past my door. I don't know what to say to her. I'm tired to my bones and my head feels like a cloud floating away to somewhere my thoughts can't follow.

I do want the truth, but I also want to hide from it because it sounds dreadful.

I could've confronted Dad before I left, I suppose, but I have a strong feeling he would get irritated or try to put a glossy veneer over whatever happened back then. And besides, I wasn't in the mood to care about the past. All that was on my mind before I left was Christos and his pain and how I could help him in the way he always tries to help me.

Slipping on some comfy old flip-flops, I head down towards Mum, who's already waiting at the open door.

We leave the house at speed, as though we might be able to stamp out our problems, or perhaps run away from them. It's a matter of moments before I'm slipping my flip-flops back off my feet and letting my toes sink into the soft golden sand. It's still a little damp from the early mist that's been carried in by the sea and is already evaporating in the morning rays.

I'm too tired to start a conversation. All my energy is being used to keep me upright and I'm already regretting not accepting some sort of breakfast. I patiently wait for Mum to begin as we get closer to the sea. It's choppy today. The sea breeze blows my hair over my shoulders and whips it around when I least expect it.

We charge onwards, as though we might not stop when we get to the sea. As though we might keep going until our feet don't touch the ground.

As soon as we reach the edge of the water, Mum makes a sharp right and carries on walking.

'I didn't know. Not that anyone would believe me, but I didn't,' she begins. It's almost like she's talking to herself more than me.

She continues, 'It's stupid, but I thought he was a guest. I didn't know he was the groom. Most of my summers were spent with my friends at different beaches, only sometimes here, on this beach. We had the little bit of land with the house that was falling down, but I didn't care for it much. This is where I met him. On this beach, right about . . . here.' Mum stops walking for a moment and stares at the sand.

There's not one grain of sand anywhere near where she's pointing that could possibly be the same as back then, thirty or so years ago. But she's pointing at it like they were there and the whole situation is possibly their fault.

She begins to walk again, slower now.

'He was throwing stones in the sea. Not that we have many stones here, but he was finding them, and he was throwing them. I knew there was a wedding in the coming days. The resort was much smaller then. A simple fishing village that had caught the heart of many and was growing with each season, little by little. The woman he was marrying, *Kaitlyn* . . .' Mum pauses as though saying that name actually hurt her throat and her mouth. 'She had been coming here with her family since the late eighties. Every year. I didn't really know her, but some of the families who live in the village or had tavernas or hotels, they knew the family. They had a lot of money. Holidays were more expensive back then, and coming to Greece, even from England, was considered quite exotic. Not everyone could afford to come here once, let alone each year.'

'They still can't, Mum.'

'True. But people are more well travelled nowadays than back then. Anyway, a friend of mine said she would meet me at the beach after I delivered some oil to a taverna, but she didn't show up, and we didn't have mobile phones the way we all do now. I was here and she wasn't. There was only this handsome man throwing stones at the sea, all alone. He spoke to me, asked me questions and we got on well. He asked to see me again . . .'

The sea growls and foams next to us, as though it's also recalling the story, and the memory of having stones thrown at it and being party to this ugly beginning.

'You know your father. He can be so charming. I had to say yes. The wedding was five days from then. In that time, he managed to live a double life. The girl he was marrying, the parents were a little strict, so they weren't staying in the same room until after the wedding, when their honeymoon was going to start. Looking back, I was the fling your father got stuck with.'

'He didn't have to marry you or stay with you.'

'I had nowhere else to go and neither did he. We got caught together by her parents. Her father followed your dad one night. He had never really trusted him – for good reason, as it turns out. And when he found us together, your father proclaimed his love for me openly to everyone. My parents were so upset, I'd broken up a wedding, *publicly*, and hurt so many people. They were afraid it would damage the reputation of the village, of the island. Tourism was already taking over as a strong source of income. So many people had already left the olive groves to be by the sea and earning money here instead. People were afraid I alone could hurt their income. Not everyone, but some.'

'I still don't understand why your parents didn't want you to come back.'

'Maybe they did.' She shakes her head. 'They probably did. The problem is, the last time I saw my mama, she said if I left with a cheat and a liar, I was a fool and I should never come back. I don't think she meant it. I think she thought I would pick her, but I was young and foolish and pig-headed. I swore to myself it was love and fate and it was different for us. Deep down, I was stubborn. So stubborn. So foolish. I know now, and I probably knew it then, but I would never admit it.'

Mum stops and looks out across the rolling waves, foaming and white.

'You know . . .' She pauses again, her forehead wrinkled in thought. 'If we hadn't got caught, he would've still married her. I really thought he loved me. He had even told me he was a part of the wedding, that's why I couldn't see him until it was late. That he had to help and be present. Everything he said was a lie, but I told myself it was because he wanted me *that* badly.'

'It's not your fault.'

'I hurt so many people, I brought shame on my family and there are still people and places here I've been avoiding, just in case. Alec told me early on that the family never came back. I still don't know what happened to her. When we got to England, we had to live with your father's parents in Suffolk, and I think she was from the north-west. I'm not sure. I've never wanted to know.'

'I need to sit down.' My legs feel as though they're about to give way under the weight of my frame, as though I've gained one hundred kilos.

I drop into the sand and tuck my knees up under my chin.

I'm not the product of love.

Maybe I am; love can grow and develop over time. But the romanticised relationship between my parents is just that. A romantic and childish notion as real as a sandcastle and just as easily destroyed.

Mum wraps her arm around me and we silently watch the power of the water crash down on the sand.

'I'm sorry,' I whisper.

'Please, don't be. We had some good times – as a family, we had brilliant times. He loves you girls, and so do I. Nothing will change that. I think it's time for me to stop clinging on to a relationship that really should never have happened in the first place, but I'm so happy it did. I wouldn't change anything.'

'Even all the pain?'

'It was worth all the pain. Life will always have pain, Lorena. It's part of what makes us grow. I don't want to change who I am now to make my past a little easier.'

I rest my head against her shoulder and close my eyes, hoping that the answers I've found are enough to help clear my mind at last, to remove the burden of questions.

Mum's right about one thing, pain does make us change and grow. I just think it's important not to let it make us grow in the wrong direction, like it has with Christos . . . like it might have with me.

Chapter
Forty-Nine

Images swirl around my head like a baby's mobile above their cot.

The waves swallowing me up in a boiling hot sea as I desperately try to swim out to save Christos. But Jonah is there, dragging him away and pulling him under. No matter how hard I kick, I can never quite get to them.

Voices begin to swirl above me, *you have to leave*, my mum's voice echoes in my head, *now*.

My eyes flicker open to the blur of the late-afternoon sun streaming in through my window. The bed is drenched in sweat. A damp towel from my earlier shower, and the sheets are tangled around my legs.

The voices that were penetrating my dream are real, and loud, and echoing through the floor.

Jumping out of bed, I quickly throw on some clothes before sprinting out of my door and clattering down the stairs.

My mother's holding back Spiros as he barks in Greek at my dad, who's being held back by my sister.

I jar to a stop three steps from the bottom. 'What the hell is going on?'

No one listens to me, they're all too busy yelling in a confused mixture of Greek-lish.

I'm not usually one to yell or scream. I've always relied on Serena to be the one to stamp her foot and make all the noise, but now it's my turn.

I fill my lungs and scream as loud as I can, 'Quiet!' It's enough to get their attention, enough for Mum to pull Spiros back a few steps. His face looks the colour of a plum, and Dad's doesn't look much better.

I trot down the last few steps. 'What's happening?' I look from Serena to Mum, hoping they will enlighten me.

It's Dad who speaks first. 'I was here to see if you were OK, to find out what happened last night.'

His voice is enough to make Spiros roll his eyes and growl.

'I'm fine, I was asleep. Dad, you know you shouldn't be here.'

'I have every right to see *my* wife and *my* girls.' Dad shoots a look at Spiros and barks, 'Every right.'

'No, we're not kids, and you lost that right when you went to Mexico,' Serena chimes in. 'Outside, now.'

A pinch of surprise hits me with her tone and her words. She's usually such sweetness and light with Dad, getting away with anything and everything. I've never seen her talk to him like that. I've seen her butt heads with Mum loads of times, but this is new.

I put my hand on Dad's chest and, together, Serena and I walk him backwards towards the door. Mum coos in Greek to Spiros, making him head to the kitchen.

'It's not my fault,' Dad grumbles. 'You don't reply to my messages or talk to me anymore. What was I meant to do? What happened is between me and your mum, you can't keep shutting me out.'

'I was asleep,' I repeat, squinting in the glaring sun.

319

As my eyes come into focus, I notice Christos's van parked on the dry verge at the edge of our front garden. There's no sign of him.

I fight the urge to ask where he is and whether he's OK, and refocus on this situation instead.

Serena looks like she's fighting an internal battle against tears. Her lips are pressed tightly together, and her nostrils keep flaring.

'Why did you have to do this?' she begins as a tear slips down her face. 'I love you so much and you fuck up and you fuck up. You can't keep turning up here, Dad. You broke us. You broke this family, and you can't pick up a needle and thread and fix it, you can't show up at Mum's house when you like. She moved countries to get away from you. She came back to a place where you laid shame at her doorstep and ruined her reputation. She stuck by you when she didn't have to, and this is what you do.'

Her tears flow wildly now, she can't wipe them away quick enough. Mascara flakes and smears along with them.

'Serena, please.' Dad's voice breaks and his eyes begin to fill to the brim. 'Don't hate me. Leaving was never about you two, you know that. But coming here and leaving Megan was a big part to do with you.'

My fingers weave into Serena's and I tug gently on her arm. 'Go back inside.'

'Don't.' It's like she doesn't hear me, and my hands don't exist. She snatches hers away and points an immaculately manicured nail in Dad's direction. 'Don't say you *left her* like you suddenly realised you'd made a mistake. I *live* on the internet.' She steps closer to him, her eyes narrow and her shoulders taut. 'I have a *million* fake fucking profiles so I can stalk who the hell I like, and your little tart dropped you like a sack of spuds when it wasn't fun anymore. That bitch just wanted you to show off and take her places and buy her crap, not live with you and share the electricity bill. You came here because there was no one to clean up your shit anymore.'

It's like she's sucked all the air right out of Dad's lungs and the blood hasn't just drained from his face to his feet, but somehow she's managed to cut him open and let it drain into the dust without even making an incision.

His eyes drop to her feet and his shoulders round.

'I've missed you girls. If I could have found a way not to drag you into it, not to hurt you . . .'

A family walks past, back from the beach, holding rubber rings and ice-cream cones. Two little girls stare in at us, in at our broken family. We were like them once. Innocently eating ice cream and believing our family was immune to trauma. We were different. We were perfect.

'We all need to stop this. I need this to stop. I've had enough of the pain and the bullshit. How is my fiancé stealing all my stuff and leaving me heartbroken not the most dramatic thing to happen this year?' I turn, rolling my eyes, not really talking to them anymore. 'This all just needs to stop. It *has* to stop.' I turn back to them and the pain written on their faces. 'Serena, please go in and check on Mum and Spiros. Dad, we need to talk.'

Chapter Fifty

'Mum said this is where you met.' I point to roughly the same sand Mum pointed to earlier.

The sea is louder now, even more aggressive, chopping and changing with the wind. I have to raise my voice over the roar.

I stop and look up at my dad, wanting to find a reminiscing softness on his face, but instead it's drawn with lines of guilt.

'I'm sorry, Sunshine, I don't remember. I know it was on the beach. We always used to meet on the beach. I guess she told you then? About why I was here all those years ago?'

'Some drunk woman at last night's party forced her hand. You two should've told us years ago.'

'That's why you did the vanishing act. You were pissed off at me.'

'I was pissed off at Mum.'

'Your mum?'

I think about how I thought she was willingly the other woman to Dad's almost-marriage. I'm still pissed off they both let me find out from a stranger instead of letting me into their world, but I can also understand why this would've been a complicated origin story for a kid. Better to keep it simple for us and just tell us the where, not the how. The thing is, we haven't been kids for years.

'Did you love her?'

His eyes narrow on mine and he snatches up my hand.

'Of course I loved her. I still do, always will. I'm not the best man in the world. I'm not even a great one. I know that, and your mum's known that from the start—'

'Not the *very* start,' I correct.

'No. Maybe not the *very* start. But she heard enough insults being hurled at me early on to know I wasn't adored by *that* many people. Even my own parents didn't defend me or my actions. Or even looked that shocked. In fact' – he looks up in thought – 'they looked more shocked when I told them I was marrying Kaitlyn than when I cheated on her.'

Dad pauses and looks out at the deep blue-grey of the sea and the wild white foam skimming on top of it.

'I didn't really think love was for me. But the day you were born . . . your mum was so brave, so strong. It wasn't easy getting you out. Your mum had made a right nice home for you and you weren't looking to move anytime soon. But she kept strong, and when you arrived and she held you in her arms, I knew then I loved you both. Always will. Even if I'll never be worthy of either of you. Or your sister.'

Words fold in over each other in my throat, forming a hard lump. Dad keeps his eyes on the undulating sea and I do the same. 'I think my parents felt sorry for your mum,' he continues. 'That's why they agreed we could live with them. In the end, I think they loved her more than they loved me. Not that they always showed it, mind. Can't blame them. She's loyal to a fault, stubborn to the end, and loves with her whole heart. A heart I never deserved.'

'So why the hell did you treat her like this?'

He shrugs and shuffles his hairy toes into the sand.

'Because I'm a bloke?'

'That's it? That's your reason? You're a bloke and all blokes think with their dicks?'

'Maybe not *all* blokes. In fact, your grandad was a good bloke, no idea why I find it hard to stay on the straight and narrow, because he always did. He was a perfect example of how to behave. I think Spiros is probably a good bloke too, when he's not trying to throttle me.'

'You need to let Mum be free. You know that, right?'

'Yeah. And you know that not all blokes are like me and Jonah, right? There're other blokes like your grandad and Spiros . . . That Christos seems pretty sound. Likes you enough to put up with me and everything.'

I want to point out he doesn't date and neither do I, that there can't be a future between us. The words stick in my throat, making me feel hollow and numb. I swallow them back because I don't want to hear them right now.

'Where is Christos?'

'Said he would go for a drink. I'm meant to meet him back at the van soon. We should probably head back.' Dad indicates with his head back the way we came.

'And you should head back with Christos and wait for us to come to you. And hire a bloody quad bike or something so you're not relying on poor Christos. He has a job, you know.'

'He said he wasn't working today.'

I roll my eyes and link my arm with my dad's.

I'm only just realising what a stunted child my dad can be.

'I mean it about Christos, you know. Jonah was never good enough for you, but your mum would never let me tell you. She's too nice. You're both pretty good at picking up broken people and trying to fix them.' He clears his throat. 'But that twat thought money was too important.'

'Like you, then?'

'I guess it takes one to know one.'

We move around a sandcastle and a little boy determined to finish it while his parents patiently wait with bags full of towels and toys.

We edge around the sea, doing our best not to get caught by the tumbling water, while others embrace it, laughing when they're knocked in and jumping towards each heavy wave.

'Would you like to be judged by the actions of another person? Some people murder people, some people cheat. Doesn't mean we're all the same.'

'I know, I don't need a lecture.'

'Your sister told me you don't want to date or get married now.'

'That wasn't her information to share. My *sister* shouldn't talk about me behind my back,' I say through slightly gritted teeth.

'Probably, but you know what she's like. She cares.'

'I can't have my heart broken again. I don't want to line myself up for pain.'

I can feel Dad looking down at me, but as we stroll back, I don't meet his gaze. Instead, I stay silent, letting the sea do the talking.

'I'm sorry that I contributed to it. You need to find someone who loves you more than they love themselves. Not someone like Jonah, who would sleep half the morning and be out half the night pretending to be at work. Someone good. Someone who selflessly looks after people and—'

'Please stop.'

'All right, all right.'

We slip our shoes back on to walk along the road. Christos is there, leaning against his van, selflessly waiting for Dad.

'Dad?' I stop before we get to him, turning to face my dad.

'Yes, Sunshine?' His face lifts as he looks at me.

'I know we haven't always been that close. At times it's felt like me and Mum and you and Serena . . . I just . . . I want to find our own space to find some common ground. I think I'd like to find us

325

some peace. OK? I know you weren't trying to hurt me or shatter my belief in marriage, blah, blah, blah, but you did hurt me. We've never been good at communicating, and I know we will never be perfect, but I need you to . . . I don't know . . .'

'I get it. I've got to try harder.'

'I mean . . . I think we both do. Maybe we all do.'

'Peace . . . I like that.' He nods his head and rubs the slate stubble on his chin. 'Yeah, I think me and you can find a little bit of peace.'

His arms wrap around me, and for the first time in a long time – maybe ever – I feel like I have a connection to my dad that's just for us. I'm going to miss us all hanging out as a family, but I know now it wasn't perfect and at least this might be a little more real.

Chapter Fifty-One

Barely a word passes between Christos and me before he takes Dad back to his house.

The breeze means the heat of the day is deceptive and my nose and cheeks are tingling like I've caught the sun.

Stepping into the house, everyone's there, waiting. Or maybe they're not waiting. Maybe they're just talking, debating, living.

'I've spoken to Dad, he won't be coming here again without asking in advance. I also think he'll leave you alone now, Mum. He will always love you, but even he knows he isn't good enough for you. He said it himself.'

Serena begins to sniff quietly behind a tissue. Everyone else stays silent. My mum looks down at her knees and Spiros, who's leaning on the kitchen counter with the palm of his hand, snatches it back to cross his arms with an agreeable nod.

'I'm sorry about last night, Spiros,' I begin, but he quickly interrupts.

'No, no. We are sorry. Eleni and me. I never thought she would be this way, we would never have invited her. We will never invite her again. She was rude to you and to Christos.' Spiros's tone softens. 'We were all saying, we need to all talk more. Your mother, she should have told you the truth about why she left Corfu years ago, and I should know your father is back here now. That man—' Spiros's jaw locks as he shakes out his fingers. 'He is your father, I will bite my tongue. I see he leaves with Christos. Does Christos know what happened here? Thalia? Why you left?'

Mum shakes her head. 'I haven't told him.'

I step forward to explain. 'He only knows what the woman said to us at the party. He agreed to have my dad stay there before we knew what really happened. He would never do anything to hurt you or Eleni.'

'I know, I know. He is a good boy. Always very loyal.' Spiros looks at his heavy gold watch. 'I have to go, Eleni is expecting me home to help with the cleaning.' Mum stands and he takes her face in his hands. 'The house looks good, little sister. We look forward to Sunday.'

Spiros kisses her cheeks and then does the same to me and Serena. As he closes the door behind him, it dawns on me how much I have to say to him. It's all spilling over and I need to get to him.

Serena begins to say she's sorry for one thing or another. I've already forgiven her. I'd forgive her more and many times over, but I'm not listening. I have to leave.

'I forgive you, we all do, but . . . hold on, OK? Stay here, I'll be back.' I sprint out of the door and along the dusty path. 'Spiros, hold on.'

I catch him before he steps on to the road.

'I know about Christos. I mean, he told me what happened with Nephele.'

Spiros's mouth falls open and his eyes bulge. He looks one way then the other and steps a little closer to me. 'What did he say to you?'

328

'He said about how she drowned in the sea and how he thinks it's all his fault.'

'Stop, stop, what? All his fault?' Spiros's eyebrows shoot up and his head begins to shake.

'Yeah, how he wished he hadn't let her get in the sea without him or let her buy her own food. I know it's not his fault, he wasn't much more than a kid himself.'

Spiros's voice becomes slow and as gravelly as the ground. 'He has never spoken about her. Not to me, not to Eleni. Not to anyone. Not anyone who has told me anyway.' His eyes lose focus in thought before abruptly locking on to mine. 'Thank you. You must be helpful for him. You are a good friend. We are so grateful to you.'

Spiros's hands find mine and grip so hard I think my bones might bend.

'I know his parents disowned him and blame him for what happened but—'

'What?' His hands squeeze a little tighter and I can't help but wince.

'His parents, they blame him for what happened,' I repeat.

His hands fall slack, letting the blood rush back to my fingers.

'That is wrong. Very wrong.'

'It's what Christos told me.'

Spiros covers his mouth with his stubby fingers and paces in a slow circle, shaking his head.

'No, no,' he repeats. 'His parents think he blames them. *They* blame them. Never, never are they blaming Christos. Never, never. It was Vaso, Eleni's cousin, who calls us begging and begging for us to take him in and give him work. We were happy to, he is a good boy and we were sorry for their loss.'

'Oh my God, I can't believe this. How is that even possible?' My hand gravitates to my mouth, much like Spiros.

'Vaso told us he gave all the details to police and everyone looking for her but he would not say anything else, he would not let them even hold him. They think he blames them—'

'And he thought they blamed him . . .' My words slip quietly away on the breeze as we stand staring at each other, slack jaws hidden behind hands.

This is exactly why it's important to communicate, to have openness and honesty in a family. For eleven years, assumptions have prevented a family from healing and grieving together. It's stopped Christos even being able to form meaningful relationships because he truly believes he doesn't deserve them. His self-enforced punishment.

I know exactly what I have to do. It's more important now than before. Secrets have been pulling at the seams of my family and we're just starting to sew ourselves back together. Christos has done everything in his power to help build me up, showing only care and kindness. I'm going to try to do what I said Dad couldn't: I'm going to pick up the needle and thread and see if I can start putting his family back together. This is different, though. Very different. I need to try to fix this . . . if I can.

'Can I have their address? I need to fix this. I was going to ask for it because, well, I thought maybe I could speak to them and see if they would forgive him . . . but this changes everything. If they spoke to him—'

'It's been so long now. His brother doesn't even know about him or Nephele . . .'

'How can he not know?'

'Over time he has forgotten them. They thought it would hurt him less this way. They live far in the south now, to keep away from Christos and what happened.'

'I have to try. What's the worst that can happen? They keep not speaking? I have to try.'

330

Since all the secrets have unravelled from my family, everything has felt a little lighter. I hadn't realised how much it was corroding all our relationships. I can't believe how much a lack of communication, an accidental secret, has damaged Christos. I have to help him.

Passing Spiros my phone, he puts their address in my notes before thanking me more times than I can count.

We agree this should be kept between us.

Another slice of deception, even after promising only a moment ago to all talk more. Neither of us wants to hold in this secret, not after we all agreed to be more open.

But this isn't our secret to tell.

Chapter Fifty-Two

It looks like a happy house. Bright red bougainvillea dances along a trellis up the side of the building and over the door. Butterflies dance around a pure white buddleia in such numbers they've almost formed a blanket of wings, transforming the blank canvas into technicolour.

The whole front garden looks like a magical place, with the right balance of wild and tidy.

For days I've prepared myself for this. I wanted to say goodbye to Dad and make sure everything was a little more settled before making my trip to the other end of the island. I haven't had a chance to see Christos, Spiros has been keeping him busy with tours and tasks, knowing what I was going to do. Knowing I'd rather avoid him right now. Hiding this trip from him would be impossible if I was faced with him. I don't want to hide it, but I do want to protect him. I rub my temples at the thought of it all, more deception and secrets. Exactly what I don't want.

I just hope this goes well and he'll understand why I couldn't tell him, and that he forgives me for the secrets.

I've thought about telling him about the eleven-year misunderstanding. Spiros and I even debated whether it should come from him and Eleni, but if this goes wrong, I don't want them to have played a big part. He needs them. If his parents don't want to see him, or they do blame him, it's better Christos never has the pain of knowing.

Spiros agreed and he agreed not to say anything to Eleni yet either. He wasn't happy about it, but he understood. The fewer people who know about this, the better.

I've managed to hold back from telling Mum and Serena too. It wouldn't be fair on Christos for everyone to know all about his life except him. It's bad enough that *I* seem to know more than he does.

I press the doorbell and hear barking erupt from somewhere in the depths of the house.

'*Kalimera.*' A thirteen-year-old version of Christos opens the door. It's how I imagine Christos would look if he shaved his beard off and shrunk to the size of someone yet to be fully formed.

Although Spiros hasn't seen Panayotis since Nephele's memorial, back when he was about two years old, he was confident he would have good English and assured me that both Vaso and Giannis have English equal to his.

'*Kalimera*, are your parents home?'

'*Nai*, yes.' He cocks his head over his shoulder and yells, 'Mama, Baba,' then turns back to me. 'Do they know you mutz?' As is common for native Greek speakers, he pronounces an English 'ch' as a 'tz'. Other than that, his English is clear and he speaks slowly, carefully, making sure each word has been understood.

'No, not at all, actually.' I find myself rocking on my heels, wondering what to say.

He nods and openly takes me in, his eyes scanning over me. He has the same serious face as Christos too.

A woman, Vaso, comes to the door. Her hair is just past her ears, with big round slate-grey curls. She has the same deep dark eyes as Christos.

333

'*Kalimera.*' She looks me over in just the same way her son did.

'*Kalimera.* My name is Lorena and I was hoping to speak with you and your husband about . . .' My eyes flick from Panayotis to Vaso. He's already much taller than her and well on his way to being the height of Christos. 'Something private.'

She speaks in Greek to Panayotis, but I'm pretty sure she's told him to fetch his father. As soon as I'm sure he's out of earshot, I lean closer and whisper, 'It's about Christos.'

Her eyes flare open and she ushers me in. She begins calling her son back with urgency, her voice mildly shrill, striking a painful chord so close to my ear.

Vaso moves me towards the living room. It's full of floral patterns and wicker everything.

As soon as Panayotis enters the room again, she demands he get her purse. He quickly returns with it and she pulls out twenty euros, thrusting it into his hands, wrapping his fingers around the note before ushering him out of the door to buy some sort of food or drink. I think. I wasn't really sure of the last part, it all happened too quickly.

As soon as the front door is closed, I can hear her rushing back to me.

'What is it, what is wrong with my boy? Is he unwell?' Deep lines of concern gather in folds on her forehead. 'Why is Eleni not here herself, she promises me, if there is problems she will tell me.'

'No, there's no problem, honestly. I just need to talk to you.'

She drops down on to a wicker seat and leans in, her elbows on her knees and her hands clasped together. She really does have Christos's eyes, they're the same almond shape as his, only hers are hidden behind small circular glasses.

'I'm his friend. We met this year actually, and, well, we're very close. He told me about Nephele. Apparently, he hasn't told anyone else about her before, he's never mentioned her name since she died, from what I gather. Anyway, he told me he blamed himself for her death and that's why he left home . . .'

I carry on explaining about the party and how it all came out. She lets me talk without interruption. The quieter she is, the more my mouth carries on going, to fill the room with his emotions and his pain, until eventually I can't think of a word more to say on the subject and I fall silent too.

'He blames himself.' Her voice is shaky and quiet. 'Eleven years I have thought he leaves because he is angry at us. We should never let them go on the boat. It was us at fault, never him. Never my Christos. He would not talk to us, he loved his sister, he would never hurt her. He left a note saying he feels shame and he must leave. We thought it was shame for us, that he could not look at us.' Her bottom lip begins to tremble and she removes her glasses to pinch the bridge of her nose.

'He's decided he doesn't deserve happiness, because to him, he took Nephele's life away when he couldn't save her, so he thinks he shouldn't have a full life. A life for a life. I'm hoping, if you could tell him it isn't his fault, and that you never blamed him, then he might be able to take steps to a healthier outlook. He might be able to find the peace he has been looking for all these years.'

She presses her face into her hands. Her body rounds and she looks so small, so fragile.

With a sniff, she removes her face from the palms of her hands, instead continuously wiping her thumbs over her eyes to stop the tears rolling further down her face.

'We have sheltered Panayotis from it all. He doesn't remember his brother or sister. How can I explain this to him now? I can't lose another son or break my husband if Christos hates us. I want to see him, but . . . I could hurt more people for my selfishness. My husband is very sick, I do not want to make him worse . . .'

'So that's it? You're going to give up on Christos?'

'No, I never give up.' She looks stunned at my accusation. 'We paid Eleni good money towards his house when he thinks they're giving him a very good price to buy. It was a good price, but not as good as he thought. They send us letters and we never go to family parties so we don't hurt him. She sends me photos of him at Easter and I make him food for her to give him when she visits. I love my sons, but I need to protect my youngest . . .'

A burning feeling swells inside my chest like I've swallowed the sun and I need to get out but I don't know how to convince her. I've told her everything I can. The burning in my chest can't be extinguished.

'I understand,' I choke out, because in some very small way I guess I can. I don't have children, and I have no idea how it must feel to lose two in such a short space of time. Everything must've been placed on Panayotis. All the pain was probably channelled into giving him love and security. Everything must've been about protecting the one child they could protect.

I stand and put my hand out to shake hers in some strange attempt to form distance.

She takes it and places her left hand on top. 'Thank you for coming here. It is good for me to know he has such kind friends.'

I want to tell her I'm one of about two who've stuck by him, but I resist the urge. Christos and I have only known each other a matter of weeks, that's nothing . . . even if it feels like everything. Even if it feels like I was meant to have Jonah take everything from me so I could hit rock bottom and find someone when I wasn't looking. To find someone so selfless, so loving – even when they don't want to be – that it's as though only they could prove to me love is possible after being so broken.

All I want to do is run away, because now I can't imagine how Christos can heal from his past. How can I make him believe that we could be good together and that he deserves to be happy? It won't matter to him that, against my better judgement, I could be in love with him, because he won't allow us to be together.

I know that it won't matter, because he doesn't believe he should be allowed happiness or a meaningful life and I have no new way to convince him otherwise.

'Thank you for your time. I wish your husband well.'

'Thank you, he is having treatments, we cross our fingers.'

'How bad is he?'

She looks to the ground and her shoulders rise and fall. 'We will have some results again soon.'

Anger tickles in the back of my throat. I have to find words to fight for Christos because he's not here to fight for himself. He knows his dad is sick, that stirring cow at the party told him, but he doesn't know the extent. The fact he hasn't come down to find out what's going on makes me worry that things might not be so good.

'Don't you think Christos deserves to know how ill his father is? Deserves to see his father if he's so unwell? What if—' I don't want to say it, I know she knows how it could all end.

'I know' – her voice is as feeble as a lost child's – 'none of this is Christos's fault. But it is not the fault of Panayotis either.'

She's made up her mind, there's nothing I can say to change it. Even if the idea of this bullshit makes me want to scream at the top of my lungs, I can't. I have to hold it in. Maybe one day Panayotis will learn the truth and feel just as upset as me when I discovered all the lies I'd grown up with. Maybe it'll be worse for him. He's had his brother taken away. I don't know who I feel more sorry for, him or Christos. They're both being denied a chance to know each other and to have another family member to love in their lives.

'I'll cross my fingers for him.'

Vaso gifts me with a brief smile. She leads me to the door but hovers before opening it.

'Do you have photos? Of Christos? I love seeing his face.'

'Oh, yeah, of course.'

I scramble to pull my phone from my handbag.

I flick back to the selfie we took at the party. He looks happy. We both do. I've never seen such a beaming smile on my face. We're so close together my hair is wrapped over his shoulder.

I'd do anything to go back to that moment, to our strange and perfect night.

I pass her the phone, and a smile spreads on her face. Tears reflect the image in her eyes before she puts her glasses back on to see it clearer.

Her fingers gently touch her lips. 'Are you only friends? You look like a very beautiful couple.'

'No. He doesn't think he deserves love. He's never had a real relationship.'

She looks back at the image. The smile that lifted her face back to a younger version of herself has been snatched away and misery pulls at her eyes and her mouth all over again.

I take back my phone, knowing there's nothing else I can do, and that next time I see Christos I'll have this secret that will create a brand-new ugly barrier between us.

Before I leave, I turn back to ask her a question passing through my mind. 'What food do you send him?'

'Mostly stifado, it was his favourite.'

Despite myself, I smile at her, wishing things could be different.

Chapter Fifty-Three

'Are you still avoiding Christos, and if so, are you ready to explain yourself to me?' Serena perches on the end of the bed. 'We're not meant to be hiding things from each other. We agreed.'

A storm has been rattling around all day, with rain hammering on the windows. I've spent the afternoon shuffling cards and playing solitaire on my bed.

It still doesn't feel cold, but it's definitely cooler than the height of summer. There are fewer people about now and I'm beginning to realise just how few people actually live here in Agios Stefanos versus how many are here over the summer months.

'I'm not avoiding him. If anything, he's avoiding me.'

'And you're avoiding half of what I just said.'

I still haven't seen Christos properly since the night of the party. That was more than a week ago now. Since seeing his mum yesterday, I still haven't worked out how I can be around him without feeling like I'm lying to him.

Because that's exactly what I would be doing.

Hiding the fact that I've been talking about him behind his back. However much I was doing it out of love, I can't see him thinking my meddling was a positive, particularly as his mum didn't decide to undo all the problems and miscommunications of the past. She didn't rush to Christos and make everything better. She's left him to be broken for the rest of his life.

'It's probably because you're both in love and you're both too afraid,' Serena announces.

'I'm not afraid.' I stop shuffling the cards and actually look at her.

She's not caked in make-up or wearing designer earrings or sunglasses. She looks like a tanned version of the twelve-year-old that used to follow me about and steal all my clothes.

'You look pretty,' I say as I go back to shuffling.

'Don't lie, I'm not even wearing make-up. How can I ever trust your opinion if you tell me I look pretty when I'm not even wearing make-up?' Serena sounds genuinely offended by the compliment.

'I'm being honest.'

'If you're being honest, admit you're afraid.'

I slam the cards down on my bed.

'Fine. I am afraid. I'm afraid we can never be together because he has more issues than you've had hot dinners and I don't want to hide things from you but this isn't my secret to tell. Happy?'

A knock rattles the front door like the thunder overhead.

We both fall silent to see if we can hear who it is. Serena cocks her head to get a better idea, squinting her eyes, too, for good measure.

'Who is it?' she hisses. 'Sounds like it might be a bloke? Is Christos meant to be coming round? Maybe you can sort some of these issues?'

'No, he messaged about the business, but I delayed him to tomorrow.'

'I'm here if you do want to talk about it.'

'I know.' I stop shuffling the cards but don't meet her eye. 'I'm just not really ready yet, if that's OK?'

Serena presses her lips together in a gentle smile. 'Of course it is.'

The front door closes again, and Serena jumps up to investigate.

Putting the cards down, I decide I might as well join her and stretch my legs.

'Who was that?' she demands of Mum before she's even halfway down the stairs.

'Alec.' Mum doesn't look up at us; instead, she flops down on the brand-new sofa that arrived while I was off badgering Christos's mother.

'Is he not coming in?' I call over Serena's shoulder as we make our way down the creaking stairs.

'No.'

'What did he want?' Serena picks up a magazine off the sofa and flops down to join Mum.

'To ask me out on a date.'

Serena yanks the magazine back down from her face and hits Mum on the knee with it.

'Ouch.' Mum nudges back into Serena, her face screwed up in an annoyed frown.

'What did you say?' Serena's mouth stays open with excitement as she looks from me to Mum.

'He's taking me to Corfu Town tomorrow evening. It's the end of the season, he has no work tomorrow.' She's so casual about it, it might as well be Serena talking about an upcoming date.

'But what about Dad?' The words come out of me with very little thought.

'What about him?' Mum pushes her hair off her face.

'He begged forgiveness, you didn't believe him—'

'So?'

'What if you trust Alec the way you trusted Dad, and he breaks your heart just like Dad did?' I carefully sit down on our new soft

341

leather armchair, desperately searching Mum's confused expression for answers.

She leans in like she's about to reveal something I could never have known.

'The only way to avoid all risk is to die. I'm not ready for that, Lorena. I want to live. Part of life is breaking things and putting them back together. If you don't know pain, you don't know love.'

'Aww, Mum,' Serena coos, 'I'm so happy for you.' She leans her head on Mum's shoulder and I feel a pang of envy at it all. I wish I could've gained that perspective sooner and I wish Christos could open his heart up and be able to believe and take risks.

Panayotis is being denied the love of his brother, and he doesn't even know it. Christos is doing it on purpose, denying all love, cutting it out with a scalpel. The way I wanted to. The way I tried to, but I can't.

A loud bang pummels the door again.

'Maybe Alec's changed his mind,' Serena giggles as Mum stands to find out who it is.

Popping her head round the door, she takes hold of a large parcel and brings it into the room.

'Serena, it's for you. What have you been ordering now?'

Slapping her hands down on the sofa, almost throwing the magazine in doing so, Serena jumps up and virtually snatches the large thin box from my mum.

'Oh my God! It's here! That was so fast!' She lets out a high-pitched squealing sound, making Mum press one finger to her ear.

With complete abandon, Serena begins ripping into the box, tearing off the tape and carefully pulling out something covered in bubble wrap.

'I was in here the other night, right? Just chilling on the floor, before the sofas arrived, you know, and I thought, something's missing. Even with the fresh paint and the sofas on the way. I knew it would need something, and it came to me, I knew exactly what it was.'

Her hands un-weave the final wrapping to reveal a photo of the three of us from Aliki and Giórgos's party. It's a candid shot of us laughing.

Stepping forward, I want to touch it, but falter. It's already in a sleek black frame and it's big, but not garish.

'It's beautiful. We actually all look good in this.' I smile in appreciation.

'I remembered there was that photographer doing the rounds. With everything that happened, I'd forgotten. Anyway, I called Eleni and had this made. I thought it would look amazing on the chimney breast or something. What do you think? Mum? You haven't said anything. Do you hate it? I really thought you'd like it.'

Mum steps forward and I catch sight of the tears glittering in her eyes.

'I love it,' she whispers. 'Thank you, my darling, it's perfect.'

Serena beams and takes it over to the mantelpiece, carefully resting it there. She steps back and Mum puts her arms around us both as we all admire our smiling faces. It doesn't look cheesy: Serena's head is thrown back in real laughter, I'm lifting my glass and looking to one side and Mum is glowing, with her arm around Serena and her head on my shoulder.

With the new sofas and this wonderful photo taking pride of place, it really does feel like home. I can't believe how little time has passed since we stepped through the front door like three pieces of flotsam, not knowing who we really were, and now we've made a home. A real home. Something we can be proud of. It took help and hard work, but I wouldn't change a thing. Back when this was concrete floors and thick layers of dirt, I had doubts I'd ever think of it as home.

I love it here.

'I know this year has been hard,' Mum begins, 'but moving here with you girls has been the best adventure of my life. It's like I've been gifted a second chance. Having the two most wonderful daughters is a blessing. Thank you both.'

It has been a hard year, but one we all needed to happen. We didn't know we needed it, but I wouldn't change it either. Mum is like a new woman, and I've never seen Serena more content.

'I love you two,' I whisper.

'Love you too,' they both chime.

A triangle really is the strongest shape; together, we've made each other stronger. With these two by my side, maybe I'll be able to get past Christos, eventually.

My heart sinks at the thought of him and the knowledge that our one perfect night is all we'll ever really have.

'That reminds me, I have something too. To mark this occasion. Wait here.'

I jog up the stairs, leaving Mum and Serena shooting each other confused looks.

Back when Jonah took everything, there was one random item I couldn't bring myself to sell or leave behind. It was an engagement gift from Mum and Dad, but really, it was from Dad.

Dragging out one of my suitcases from under my bed, I dig under some clothes and pull out the heavy orange rectangle. Vintage Veuve Clicquot, still in its box.

Carefully, I pick it out. It'll have to go in the freezer for a bit. I shouldn't really have left it like this, but it's too late now.

This is the perfect moment for it, we've really achieved something here and helped each other to heal and find a new life. We deserve a glass of bubbles to mark the occasion.

Opening the box reveals something I've been trying hard to forget. A piece of lined paper rests on top of the bottle.

The letter from Jonah. The one I've been avoiding and hid here to forget about it, because I never thought I'd be able to read it again. I never thought I would be strong enough and I never thought I would want to celebrate anything again, so hiding it with the champagne seemed, at the time, to be the perfect place.

Carefully, I open it out and look at his scrawling writing wriggling around the lines.

Lorena,

I have to write this letter quickly, and I'm sorry about that. I wish I could tell you more, but there's no time, not now.

I'm sorry about a lot of the crap things I've done in my life but leaving you like this is a big one. I've got myself in trouble. I never wanted to share any of this with you, or disappoint you. I'm in debt with some people and I'm afraid they might come for you if I stay. I have to keep you safe. I know I've got a problem. I can't exactly deny it anymore, can I? It's gone too far.

I like to gamble and sometimes I don't know when to walk away, I guess that means now I have to walk away from you, which is the shittest thing I've had to do in my life. I really thought I had it under control but, yeah, I didn't.

I'm so sorry. I've had to clear out the account as well as the house. I know you'll be able to make more money and you'll be better off without me. You'll find someone better than me, I just wish I was good enough for you, but now you know the truth . . . I'm not good enough.

I will always love you, and believe me when I say, I really do love you and I'm doing this to keep you safe.

Jonah x

I fold it up and tuck it back in the box as I remove the bottle of champagne.

If I saw him on a bus or walking down the street, I know now I could tell him I feel sorry for him. That I forgive him. Yes, I'd like my money back, but if he hadn't done what he did, I would never have lived here, I would never have met Christos and I would never have had this time with Mum and Serena, and found this new life that's made me find a new light. A brighter light.

I still don't believe in fate, but I know that without a very specific set of circumstances, I wouldn't be where I am right now, toasting the two women who mean the most to me instead of raising a glass to a marriage that was doomed.

It's like the splitting of the atom, it had to be pulled apart to find out what was really inside it, and we've found out what's really at the core of us. Under the secrets and the pointless lies, there's always been love.

I might not like the lies and the deception that has gone on over the past year, or even my whole life, but I have learnt that we don't always owe people an explanation for things we do and decisions we make, and there's sometimes a fine line between that and actively withholding the truth. It's not easy to see the difference when you're desperately trying to do the right thing. I know that now, from hiding my feelings for Christos.

The only hard part is waiting to decide how to move forward with Christos now I can admit I have feelings for him, while withholding a truth from him. Knowing that there's a high chance he'll never let me in again, that the sweet torture is too sweet and he won't allow me to touch him or hold him ever again.

Holding the weight of the bottle in my hand, I know it's over between us. Tomorrow, when we meet to discuss what we need to do next with the business, nothing will be the way it was. Even if he could let himself fall in love with me, I would then have to tell him what I did yesterday, and I can't see him forgiving me. Finding out that it was all one big misunderstanding but his mother didn't want to amend it would break his heart, I know it would, and I'm at the centre of that pain. If he finds out, it's me who's caused the extra heartache.

Tears bite at the corners of my eyes and my ribs feel tight.

I can't let this pour out, not right now. I want to celebrate with my mum and sister. I want this to be about us, and what we've achieved together.

I'll let myself feel the pain of losing something I never really had tonight, when I'm alone.

Since Jonah, I've become accustomed to pushing down tears and swallowing them back. I've almost got it down to an art form.

I trot down the stairs with lively footsteps.

'Vintage champagne, anyone?' I wave the bottle as I reach the bottom step.

They both ooh and cheer when they see it.

'I'll put it in the freezer for half an hour, get some nibbles out and we can have a girly evening. Is the takeaway pizza place still open? We could have some glasses of this, get some pizza?'

My ideas are greeted with more cheers of delight as I make my way to the kitchen.

Tonight is about us. Tomorrow, I'll deal with Christos.

Chapter
Fifty-Four

My body has felt like a delicate leaf shuddering in a breeze all day long. The sun coming back out hasn't changed that.

Christos set our meeting for 6 p.m. at the olive grove and I haven't been able to think of anything else. I've barely eaten too, which hasn't helped with my shaking body. It's as though I've been chilled to the bone but I'm perfectly warm. In fact, it's been a delightful bright and sunny day. It's like Corfu has remembered how to bring back summer after a storm.

I stop the car in the lay-by, tugging up the handbrake and cutting the engine. I close my eyes as my fingers hover over the seat-belt buckle.

He should be here already. I'm ten minutes late because I was helping Mum and Serena pick what Mum should wear for her date with Alec. She went with a wide-leg jumpsuit paired with big earrings and a kimono blouse over the top. She looked relaxed and gorgeous. It felt good to see her excited for a date; it helped to suppress some of my anxiety for today.

I run it over and over in my mind, trying to figure out how I can be near him without laying out the truth that I went behind his back, or telling him that I've accidently caught feelings for him and it doesn't feel like a cold I'll be able to shake in a week. These feeling have gone straight for the jugular and round my entire circulatory system.

My only choice is to stick to a business agenda from now on. That's all I have now.

I click my belt off and slide out of Mum's rental car before marching up the incline to the entrance to the olive grove.

With only a handful of nuts to sustain me all day, palpitations soon kick in with a dizzying effect, blotches shooting in front of my eyes.

By the time I get to the opening in the hedge, I'm out of breath.

Pausing to recover, I look out towards the little stone shop and across to the table, but there's no obvious sign of him.

I make my way to the bench not far from the shop to wait for him there. If I wait at the table, the memories of us knotted together will be overwhelming.

Sitting on the bench, I close my eyes and let the first of the autumn sunsets warm my face. I fill my lungs with the scent of trees and the earth, letting the hum of nature soothe me, because this day has already been hard.

I wish I could let it go. I can't fix Christos, I can't fix his past and all I've done is make life harder for both of us because now I can't even be a true friend. I was the one who pushed him to tell me what he was hiding, and he was right to be wary of trusting me with his secrets. I broke his trust and told Spiros and went running to Christos's mother.

Last time we spoke, back on his roof, he shut me out because I dared to say his parents shouldn't have blamed him for what happened. Since then, he has barely said a word to me. Even his message about this meeting seemed pretty matter-of-fact. There's no way in any imaginable universe he's going to be happy that I went behind his back. I was stupid to think it was a good idea.

Now, I can barely imagine what came over me to do something like that. Desperation to fix something unfixable, I guess.

Maybe I should get it out of the way tonight and tell him. If there's one thing I've learnt this year, it's that, eventually, secrets become uncovered. He will find out, it's just a matter of when and how.

My fingers tap on the solid wood bench and my knees begin to bounce up and down. I should tell him now, tell him what I've done, give him the truth and he can decide what to do with it. He deserves the truth. If he hates me, at least I did my best. If I tell him the truth, I can hold my head up and know that, even though I might have got it wrong, everything I've done was done because I care about him, and I genuinely want what's best for him.

I open my eyes to the dying flares of the sun. Deep oranges and crimson fight for attention, streaking over the silvery olive trees. Soon, all the olives will be gone. Removed.

Maybe I should remove myself too. He might not want to work with me after this. I don't want to make things hard for him here. He's already had a tough enough life.

Footsteps split the air at speed behind me, cracking twigs and kicking up dust.

I twist to find Christos looking right at me, his face glowing bronze in the sunset and still not giving away even an inch of his thoughts. I'll miss his almond eyes and dry quips. I'll miss him.

Standing, I turn to face him head-on. Already my knees feel weak, but I know I have to find the strength he deserves.

'Christos, I need to talk to you.'

'No,' he puts both of his hands up, 'me first.'

My mouth hangs open in complete confusion.

'Was it you?' he begins.

My eyes flick from the ancient olive tree I touched when we first met and back towards him.

'Sorry, I'm not sure I know what you're talking about.'

My teeth dig into my lip. Terror races in my heart. He looks so angry, like he might hate me forever if I say it *was* me.

He puffs out a laugh through his nose.

'I know it was you, who else could it be?'

He leans in closer to me. His eyes are glittering as though they're filled with stars and the delicate skin around them is tinged pink, like he's scrubbed at them for a day.

I swallow hard.

It's too late. Somehow, he's already found out what I've done and he already hates me. Sadness and fury are enough to drive the dagger of hate right through me from one broken look. All I can hope for now is the swift delivery of venomous words to inflict a final blow.

I lick my lips to prepare myself for an explanation, it's all I have left to shield myself, only I'm overcome with fear that I'll lose my new best friend, and no words come out.

He's the one I secretly know I'm very much in love with.

'Lorena?'

I can't hide it from him. He deserves the truth from me.

'Yeah. It was me.'

The look in his eyes is wild. 'I knew it was you. You made her come to see me?'

'I went to talk to your mum, but I only did it because—'

I don't get to finish my thought, let alone my words, before Christos's mouth meets mine. He pulls me in and I melt.

I'm not shaking anymore. Not even a little. It's as though my lips have taken strength from him and I have all the energy in the world again. As though his lips are the sun and I needed them to photosynthesise.

Reluctantly, I pull away.

'Thank you,' he whispers in my hair, and I can feel his chest begin to vibrate with tears or laughter or both. 'Thank you.'

351

'What the hell happened?'

Christos rests his forehead against mine and he smiles under his beard.

'My mother came to see me. It's why I am so late. She said a beautiful woman came to her house and told her that I blamed myself for what happened to Nephele, and that I was not allowed to do that anymore, because it was never my fault. The problem was, she couldn't remember your name, only your beautiful face.'

Christos's hand cups my cheek as his thumb skims along it.

'Thank you for what you have done for me, Lorena. I will never be able to repay you in a thousand lives, but I will do anything if you will let me try.'

I look up at him with a smile. 'We could always check how sturdy that table is again.'

He breaks into laughter before pressing his lips briefly to mine.

'Happily,' he says with a brief raise of his eyebrows.

As he takes my hand, it feels like I'm in a dream.

'I was ready to give up on us. I thought you would hate me for meddling.'

He stops and looks down at me, his face turning more serious.

'I understand what you did, that you want to help me. For a moment I was hurt, but' – he shakes his head – 'I feel grateful to have someone care about me the way you do.'

He pulls me in, holding my face in his hands again, looking me over.

'I love you, Lorena.'

I can't believe it's real as he takes deep breaths so close to mine.

I close my eyes, taking in the smell of him and the sweet smell of summer on his skin, and for a moment, maybe I could believe in fate.

'I love you too, Christos.'

Epilogue

'I don't want any more bloody secrets, Christos. It *has* to be today.' I tug on the bottom of his shirt like an irritated toddler.

'Neither do I. Now take this, and these.' He passes me a bottle of champagne and a bowl of nuts.

A groaning noise releases from my throat before I trudge through our house towards the back garden.

'Pick your feet up,' he nudges me. 'We do not want questions, not yet.'

He gives me a sly wink. He's not really one to wink. He's bouncier than I've ever seen him. It suits him. He doesn't hide behind his beard anymore; even though it's still there, he sits proudly inside it. I love who he has become. A happy version of who he always was.

As we step out on to the patio, I beam again, because ultimately I'm happy too, even if keeping just one secret from my mum and sister is enough to eat away at me from the inside out.

This is the first time in a long time everyone has been together in the same place. I like it when both Mum and Dad are at a party, and everyone can get along. Sometimes I catch Dad looking at her in a certain way, like he's lost his favourite toy and nothing else will quite fill the void. Mum never notices; her eyes are always set on Alec.

Christos pops open the first bottle of champagne and passes it to Alec to begin filling everyone's glasses. The next bottle goes with a bang and we all bubble with laughter.

As Alec reaches Serena, she begins to tell him in Greek to stop, almost pulling the glass away before it's even half full. I've never seen her refuse a full glass of champagne before. Petros's arm slides over her shoulder as Alec fills his glass instead.

Christos joins in with pouring wine into glasses and as he fills the last one, he turns to my empty glass and hovers. Before he lets even a drop into the glass, he opens up to the curve of people in our garden, all with beaming faces in the spring sunshine of Corfu. Their glasses raised, waiting for a pre-Easter toast.

'I would like to raise a toast to my beautiful wife—'

Before he can continue, it hits me. Blood rushes from my heart to my feet and right back up again with a dizzying force.

My arm outstretches and I point directly at Serena, who's frowning at me.

'You're pregnant!' I announce.

Our garden echoes with gasps as people look to Serena and back to me, waiting for confirmation of my proclamation.

She begins to shake her head, golden-blonde highlights dancing over her shoulders.

'So are you,' she pouts.

For a moment, nothing is said as people's eyes bulge and mouths go dry from holding them open.

We both erupt in squeals as she jumps to her feet and we hug each other.

'Well, that ruins my speech, *nai*.'

I look over my shoulder to see Christos shrugging with a grin under his beard, as Panayotis comes over to slap his older brother's shoulder and embrace him. They've been so close, maybe more so since their dad passed away. It's been wonderful to watch their relationship grow.

Mum's warm arms wrap around us both and she whispers, 'I knew you were both pregnant before you even said.' She giggles, then her voice lowers. 'But here is something you don't know.'

We both pull away, exchanging worried glances.

'Alec proposed, we're engaged.'

After all that happened back when we first came to Corfu, I really thought the truth was the only way forward, but I've realised we can't tell everyone everything all the time. It's impossible. And anyway, without secrets, there wouldn't be any wonderful surprises.

ACKNOWLEDGEMENTS

I would like to thank everyone who has had a hand in making this book what it is.

Firstly, I'd like to share my gratitude to my editors, Victoria and Lindsey, for their encouragement in the early stages of this book. It's like having two cheerleaders behind keyboards and I love it! I couldn't ask for more. I feel encouraged while being inspired with each and every edit.

Thank you to Jenni for making sure my ideas are clear on the page, and for understanding what I mean more often than I do!

I'm so grateful for all the editors and proofreaders for their hard work. My books wouldn't be the same without your insight. I'm very privileged to have the talented Lake Union team working on my books.

I would like to thank Nicola and her whole wonderful family at Cicala for letting me place a fictional character in their beautiful taverna. I've always avoided having named fictional characters working in real places, but they were more than happy to have Alec working for them and I'm so grateful for that.

I would also like to thank Dimitris at Natur Aura for always being so supportive and helping me to fill my home with traditional Greek wine cups, just like the ones purchased by the wonderful women in this book.

Thank you to everyone at San Stefano Travel for always helping me to discover new places to dream about. Noula and the whole team are so helpful and knowledgeable, your trips always help to enrich my books.

I would also like to acknowledge Paige from Millmead Business. We've been friends for so long, and being able to throw things at you with complete trust gave me the head space to dream when I needed to.

Lastly, and most importantly, I would like to thank my family for being so understanding of the problems associated with living with a creative and dramatic human like myself. Thank you all for everything you do. I'm the luckiest mum, daughter, wife, sister and auntie to have you all put up with my strange mind. I love you all. xxx

ABOUT THE AUTHOR

Photo © 2023 by Samuel Thomas

Francesca Catlow writes bestselling fiction filled with passionate love stories that feature flawed, and sometimes broken, characters as they face a crossroads in their life. She often explores heartbreaking themes while also whisking readers off to beautiful locations.

Francesca loves to travel. Born and raised in the heart of Suffolk, England, she has travelled extensively in Europe with her French husband and, more recently, their two children. In 2024 she relocated to France where she spends her days dreaming up stories and her evenings sitting in her garden relaxing with her family.

In 2023 Francesca was a finalist for the prestigious Kindle Storyteller Award, and was nominated for an Innovation Award for her work with libraries in Suffolk.

Francesca loves to hear from her readers – if you would like to contact her, you can do so on her social pages, or subscribe to her newsletter.

To stay up to date, and for free content, please visit

https://francescacatlow.co.uk/subscribe

Facebook: @francescacatlowofficial

Instagram: @francescacatlowofficial

X: @francescacatlow

TikTok: @francescacatlow

For trigger warnings visit: francescacatlow.co.uk/trigger-warnings/

Follow the Author on Amazon

If you enjoyed this book, follow Francesca Catlow on Amazon to be notified when the author releases a new book!
To do this, please follow these instructions:

Desktop:

1) Search for the author's name on Amazon or in the Amazon App.
2) Click on the author's name to arrive on their Amazon page.
3) Click the 'Follow' button.

Mobile and Tablet:

1) Search for the author's name on Amazon or in the Amazon App.
2) Click on one of the author's books.
3) Click on the author's name to arrive on their Amazon page.
4) Click the 'Follow' button.

Kindle eReader and Kindle App:

If you enjoyed this book on a Kindle eReader or in the Kindle App, you will find the author 'Follow' button after the last page.

Printed in Dunstable, United Kingdom